# The Prison of Angels

by David Dalglish

## BOOKS BY DAVID DALGLISH

### THE HALF-ORC SERIES
*The Weight of Blood*
*The Cost of Betrayal*
*The Death of Promises*
*The Shadows of Grace*
*A Sliver of Redemption*
*The Prison of Angels*

### THE SHADOWDANCE TRILOGY
*A Dance of Cloaks*
*A Dance of Blades*
*A Dance of Death*

### WATCHER'S BLADE TRILOGY
*Blood of the Underworld*

### THE PALADINS
*Night of Wolves*
*Clash of Faiths*
*The Old Ways*
*The Broken Pieces*

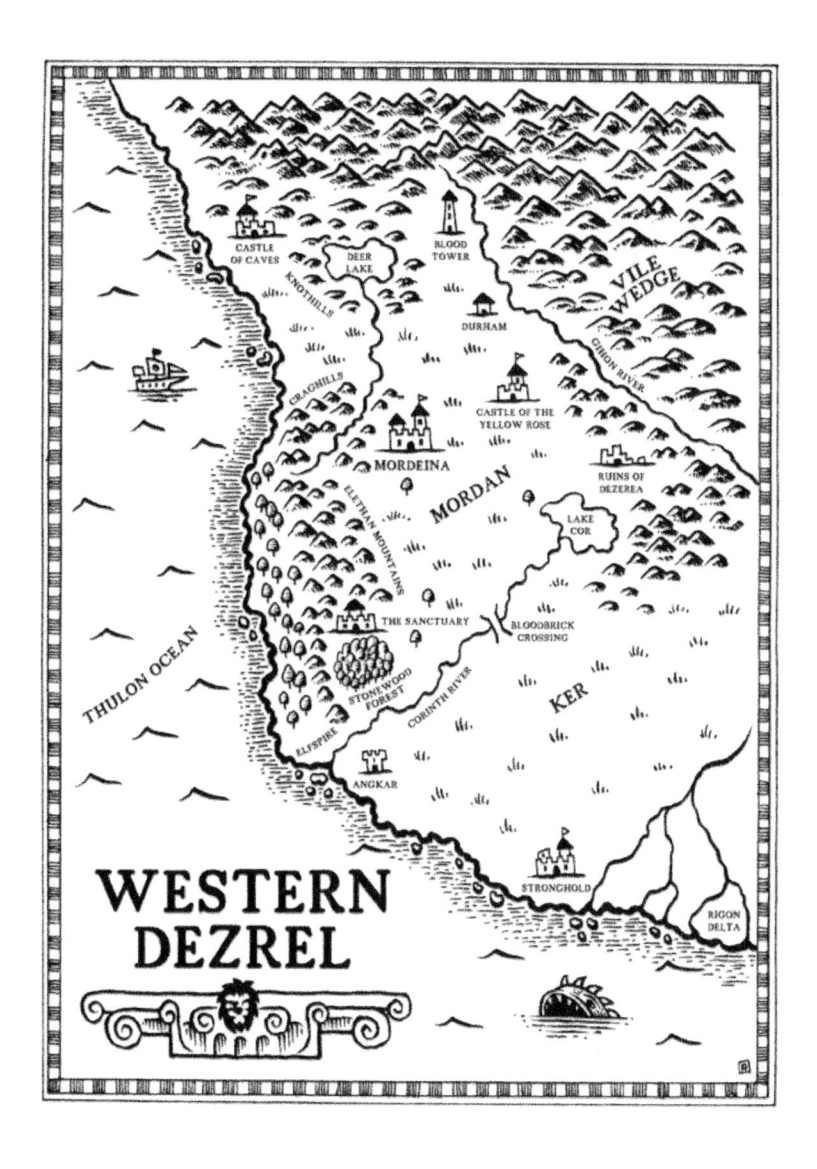

David Dalglish

The Prison of Angels

## Prologue

The entire town of Norstrom gathered around the rapist, yet they could do nothing. Three of the elders shouted in vain to keep the crowd calm. A fourth stood beside Colton, doing his best to console him.

"They know what's right," the old man said, rubbing his crooked nose. "Locke's too far gone. They'll kill him, quick and painless."

Colton glared at the bound fiend. The man had been forced to his knees, his arms tied behind his back and a rope strung around his neck. Colton tied the rope himself, hoping no one would notice how tightly he'd been looping it until it was too late. They did notice, and Locke continued breathing, awaiting the mockery to come.

"What's right, sure," Colton said. "But what about what's best?"

"Are they not the same?"

Colton shook his head.

"Right now they're as far apart as the Abyss from the Golden Eternity."

The signal had been given from the golden scepter, so it would not be long now. Together, townsfolk and rapist waited for the angel to arrive.

"I'm sorry," Locke kept crying, his words shouted down by the hundred others in attendance, all so Colton would not hear. But he heard anyway, and the words put a knife in his gut. His poor Krista. Two years old. Two fucking years old.

The angel and his executioner's blade couldn't arrive fast enough.

"Colton!"

He turned, saw his wife Lily pushing through the crowd to join him. She held Krista in her arms, the child's face pressed against her bosom. Krista's eyes were shut, and she shook as if nightmare hounds howled for her blood. Reaching him, Lily leaned in close so she might be heard without shouting.

"Come with me," she said. "Please, Colton, you don't need to be here. You don't need to watch."

But he did need to watch. He had to make sure justice, *true* justice, was served.

"I'm sorry," he said. He reached out for Krista, stopping when she flinched. Her innocence was gone, her trust brutalized out of her. Nothing could describe Colton's rage, nothing, and he turned once more to where the man lay tied.

In Colton's pocket was a slender knife, and he clutched it tightly.

"Here, at last," said the elder, tugging on Colton's sleeve while pointing to the sky.

Flying through the blue came the angel, his white wings the same color as the clouds he soared beneath. His golden armor shone, and when he dove for the town, Colton felt his breath catch in his throat. Despite his fury, despite the sickening nature of what was to transpire, he still felt himself swept with awe. Even though they had become increasingly commonplace, it did not diminish the awesome presence of an angel of Ashhur. The angel landed just outside the town center, and the people quickly gave way so he might approach. His hair was a deep white, his eyes a sparkling bronze. From his hip swung a long blade with a golden hilt.

"I am Ezekai, and I bring the blessings of Ashhur," the angel said. His voice was deep, authoritative, the tone of a soldier. "I saw the signal in the sky and have come. What matter requires my aid?"

It was tradition, newly begun, that elders would describe the crimes, but Colton would have none of that. He pushed to the front, determined to hide how much he feared the celestial being before him.

"We have no need of your aid, just your sword," he said. "I found this man in my barn atop my daughter, still attempting to remove his trousers. Cut his head off his shoulders, and let this be done with."

Ezekai's bronze eyes glanced to the bound Locke, then over Colton's shoulders to where his wife and daughter stood.

"Your family?" Ezekai asked. Colton nodded. The angel approached, and his delicate features softened.

"You have felt a darkness no woman should ever feel," he told Krista, reaching out his hand. She flinched, but it seemed not to bother Ezekai. "Especially so young. So very young." His hand brushed against her face. Colton felt a lump grow in his throat as he watched Krista immediately relax. Her grip on Lily's neck loosened, and then unbelievably, she smiled.

"No nightmares will follow you," Ezekai said softly. "You will be happy, and you will know joy."

"Praise be to Ashhur," said a man beside Lily, and many others echoed the call. Colton felt his hands shake, and he fought to keep his rage strong. He told himself it didn't matter if she'd been purged of the awful memories. What happened next did. Ezekai dipped his head in respect to Lily, then turned his attention to Locke. The rapist groveled, on his knees, his face pushed into the ground. Snot dripped from his nose, mixing with the dirt.

"Is it true what they say of you?" the angel asked. "Know that by your words, I will judge you, and that with my god's blessing I will detect any lie."

"Yes," Locke said. "Ashhur forgive me, yes. It is."

Colton's jaw trembled. Ezekai knelt before Locke and lifted his chin so they might stare eye to eye. Locke was an older man, rail thin with a hawkish look to him. He'd never fit in well with the townsfolk, and now they all knew why.

"Do you understand the sin you've committed?" Ezekai asked.

"I do. I'm sorry, please, I'm sorry. I can't help it. I've tried, I've tried, please…"

The angel stood.

"Locke, do you repent of your crime?"

"Yes, yes, I do!"

"Do you seek the grace and mercy of Ashhur, your god?"

"Yes," Locke said, sobbing now.

Ezekai looked to the town. All eyes were upon him. Lily's hand slipped into Colton's, and he squeezed it.

"He speaks with truth and sincerity," the angel said at last, and it was like a wind blew through the town. "Locke, I forgive you of your crimes. Go and live your life without sin."

"No," Colton said, pulling away from his wife and forcing his way to the front of the crowd. "That won't work, not this time. He's sick. He's a danger to us, to our children! She's only two, gods damn it, and still he tried to take her."

"This is the law we live under, the law of Ashhur," Ezekai said. Colton hated the way the angel looked down at him, like he was an ant or a child. "Locke's repentance is real, his sorrow genuine."

"Of course it is! A man would say anything, do anything, to save his life. He doesn't mean it. That sorry sack of shit cries only for himself!"

"I would know if that were true," the angel said, shaking his head.

Colton spun, addressing the crowd, almost daring them to look him in the eye.

"Do all of you accept that?" he asked them. "Do you feel we've seen what's right? Do you think we've had justice?"

With the decree given, the men holding Locke released him for fear of the angel's wrath. The man staggered to his feet, still tugging at the ropes around his wrists.

"Please, Colton, I beg of you," Locke said, reaching out his hands for Colton's shirt. "Forg—"

Before any could stop him, before any could even think of what he meant to do, Colton pulled the knife from his pocket and thrust it through Locke's right eye. It had to be quick, he knew. Had to be fast, lest the angel heal him. Deeper and deeper he shoved the blade, and all around he heard screaming. Men tackled him, but he let out a laugh, for it was far too late. Locke's body lay in the dirt, arms and legs convulsing.

"You damn fool," someone whispered into Colton's ear, but he didn't know who. There was too much commotion, too much fear. Strong men lifted him to his feet, men he worked with in the fields and shared stories with at the tavern as they guzzled down Ugly Bett's ale. When Colton looked up he saw the angel towering over him. His bronze eyes stared at the blood on Colton's hand. He showed no sign of anger or frustration, only sorrow.

"I will not ask of your guilt, for the blood on you is free for all to see," Ezekai said. "Before I execute you, tell me, Colton, do you repent your crime? Will you kneel and ask for Ashhur's mercy and grace?"

A bitter smile tugged at Colton's lips as he struggled against the men holding him.

"Repent?" he asked. "No. Not now, not ever."

He heard Lily cry out, but his heart was pumping too fast, his mind lost in a whirl of exhilaration and terror too deep to feel regret. Locke deserved to die. It was the one thing he knew, the one thing he firmly believed with every shred of his soul. Looking upon the angel, he would not lie, would not disgrace himself with such pathetic sniveling.

"You speak your truth," Ezekai said as he drew his sword. "And it saddens me greatly. You were a good man, Colton. Let there be no doubt."

The gathered crowd, which had fallen deathly silent, let out a sudden roar. Colton's smile grew as he heard it. In his mind he heard the chant multiplying, felt the anger spreading across Mordan like a wave. Righteous men and women, fists to the air, crying out against their prison of angels. He would be the spark, he thought, the flame that set the land ablaze.

"Stand away!" Ezekai cried, and his golden blade circled over his head. Colton saw the people step back, obeying despite their anger. Just a dream of change, thought Colton, but he clung to it anyway. He couldn't think of Lily, couldn't think of Krista growing up without him. What he'd done was right, was best…

Up came the blade.

"You're killing the wrong man," Colton said, his voice rising. "The wrong man, you hear me? The wrong man! The—"

Down came the blade, and though it ended his cry, it still echoed on and on through villages miles beyond.

# 1

"Are you sure we have to do this?" Harruq asked as Aurelia looked over his armor for what felt like the hundredth time. Her fingers brushed away dust noticeable only by the sharpest of elven eyes.

"It'd look bad," his wife said, frowning as she adjusted the long red cloak that had been tailored just for the occasion.

"I don't mind looking bad. I think I prefer it."

"For Antonil."

Harruq grabbed Aurelia's hands, and when she glared up at him he smiled. Slowly she relaxed, leaning her head against his dark leather armor.

"You mean something to them," she said as he held her close. "To *all* of them, and right now Antonil needs every bit of love from the crowds he can get."

Harruq let out a defeated sigh.

"I know," he said. "So do I pass inspection?"

"Close enough for human eyes. What of me?"

She twirled in her beautiful, elven-styled dress laced with gold. Her hair was looped into an intricate design, the braids across her forehead looking like a circlet. Seven emeralds hung from silver thread curled into the braids on either side of her face, and each time she twirled they sparkled with magic.

"Why'd you marry me again?" he asked.

"Stupidity. Now let's go. We can't keep them waiting forever."

He extended his arm, she took it, and together they stepped out from behind the curtain, then hooked left down the crimson carpet. Standing about were dozens of guards in glimmering armor. Between them stood King Antonil Copernus.

"Large smiles," Antonil said, and the amusement in his eyes made Harruq want to smack him, royalty or not.

"You owe me," Harruq muttered. The way Antonil laughed made the half-orc worry greatly.

"That I do," the king said. "You'll find out how much soon enough."

Before Harruq could enquire further, Aurelia pulled him along, across the last of the crimson carpet, over white marble stones, and emerged into the roar of the gathered crowds beyond the doors of the great castle of Mordeina. Thousands of people lined either side of the road that led down to the twin walls of the city. Harruq felt his throat constrict, and he forced himself to breathe. So many people…

"Walk," Aurelia whispered into his ear, hiding the command with a pleased smile. Harruq forced one foot forward, then the other, and at last the spell brought on by the crowd broke. He grinned, feeling like a goof. With his free hand he waved to the people, guessing it the proper thing to do. Aurelia kept both her hands on his arm as they walked, looking as elegant as a princess. Down the steps they traveled, people hailing him a hero, cheering for the mighty Godslayer. The children in particular pushed hardest to the front, crawling if need be to see through the line of soldiers that held back the masses. They gawked at his armor, and he saw several making motions with their hands. Knowing what they wanted, he chuckled, drew Condemnation from its sheath, and held the black blade above his head to even greater cheers.

"I thought you didn't want to do this," Aurelia said, still smiling.

"I don't," Harruq said. "But I might as well enjoy it."

"If you must," Aurelia said. "But control your eyes. Some of the younger girls seem to have problems keeping their blouses on."

To this Harruq sheathed his sword, kissed Aurelia on the mouth, and then hurried on. A second roar began, and he glanced back to see King Antonil exiting the castle, flanked by his handpicked guard. At first he felt pride knowing his cheer had been louder, but worry quickly washed away that feeling. It hadn't been just a little louder…the cheer for Antonil was weak and fading fast.

"You weren't kidding," Harruq muttered. "I didn't think it was this bad."

The Prison of Angels

The farther from the castle they went, the rowdier the crowd became, and the people's shouts weren't always so joyful. Catcalls mixed with the cheers, and as Antonil neared, Harruq heard them grow stronger.

"Traitor!" someone shouted.

"Coward! Murderer!"

"Foreigner!"

The worst, though, the one that echoed throughout the crowd, was the title that had haunted Antonil's reign since his second year.

"All hail the Missing King!"

At the very bottom of the hill, where the road met the first wall, Mordan's army gathered. Thirty thousand men, all enlisted to retake the east from the horde of orcs that had gone unchecked since the end of the Gods' War. The parade was for their departure, the launching of Antonil's second campaign to retake his homeland. Much of the celebration was bittersweet, but still the underlying anger surprised him. Was it because of how terrible Antonil's first attempt at freeing the east from the orcs had gone? Or was there something more?

When Harruq and Aurelia arrived, the soldiers drew their swords and raised them high. He passed below them, a roof of steel above. At Antonil's arrival the blades lifted higher, and they let out their cry.

"Long live the King!"

Echoed by the voices of thirty thousand, the words gave Harruq chills. He felt Aurelia squeeze his arm, showing she felt it too.

In the center of the soldiers, a wooden platform had been hastily constructed. On it were two seats. One was empty, waiting for Antonil to take his place. In the other sat Susan Copernus, his wife of five years. She was young and slender, her milky skin powdered into an almost ghostly white. Her brown hair was looped similarly to Aurelia's, only with less intricacy and more jewels. Up the stairs of the platform they stepped, the two taking their designated spot beside the queen.

"Were you lonely waiting for us?" Harruq asked her as Antonil climbed the steps.

"I daily count the hours until you grace my presence," she said. Her voice was deathly serious, but he could see the laugh shimmering in her eyes.

"It's all right," said Tarlak Eschaton, standing on the other side of the thrones. "I kept her entertained until your arrival."

Harruq grinned at the yellow-robed wizard. His red hair and beard were neatly trimmed, but age lines had started to show across his cheeks and beneath his eyes. Still, his smile was youthful, and his hat pointy as ever.

"You got roped into this as well?" Harruq asked.

"Roped? Nonsense, you brute. I volunteered to spare the queen the indignity of begging for my presence."

"Come now," Susan said. "I love you both equally, though I fear I do not love you as much as the commoners do."

"A shame you had to land the killing blow on the war god," Antonil said to Harruq, having heard them. He reached out his hand, and his wife stood to accept it. "My life would be much easier had it been me."

"You slew a dragon," Harruq said.

"What's a dragon compared to a god?"

"Enough," Susan said, kissing Antonil's cheek. "Do not belittle your accomplishments."

"I'm not the one belittling them," Antonil said, and the king's words were tinged with frustration. Despite it, he turned to the crowd, lifted his arms, and smiled his best smile. The crowd cheered, but not long. The procession was not quite complete. Directly above the wooden platform, high amid the clouds, floated the golden city of Avlimar. From its tall arches, its silver buildings, and its thin, lengthy bridges descended hundreds of angels, their white wings filling the sky. They flung petals of flowers as they crisscrossed about, which fell upon the crowds like rain. As the pinks and violets landed atop his hair and shoulders, Harruq held out a hand.

"Little much, isn't it?" he asked as petals gathered in his palm.

Aurelia leaned close.

"Antonil's not the only one trying to win people over," she whispered.

The Prison of Angels

All along the walls of the city the angels landed, keeping their wings stretched to their fullest extent. Their skin was of all colors, their hair shining, the whiteness of their robes matched only by the feathers of their wings. A low moan came from their throats, a deep chant that reverberated throughout the city. Louder and louder it grew, and as one they drew their swords and shouted the name of their god.

"*Ashhur!*"

The force it nearly knocked Harruq off his feet. He shook his head as many others hurried back to standing.

"That's one way to make an entrance," he muttered.

The leader of the angels landed before them, just beyond the platform. He did not need its height to stare at them eye to eye, for he was a giant of an angel, his golden armor gleaming. His name was Ahaesarus, and it was at his side that Harruq and Aurelia had fought to slay the war god Thulos, preventing him from conquering the world of Dezrel. Beside Ahaesarus landed his war general, Judarius, and his high priest, Azariah. The two were eerily similar, with green eyes tinged with gold and their brown hair cut short around their necks. But where Judarius wore armor and carried an enormous mace upon his back, Azariah had only his robes and his soft hands, skilled at clerical magic. Together the three bowed to Antonil, who stood and bowed in return. Harruq dipped his head in respect.

"Heroes of mankind, King and Queen of Mordan, I greet you," said Ahaesarus. His voice was deep, befitting one so giant. "This day you march against blasphemous beings. Know that Ashhur gives you his blessing, and with loving eyes he will watch over your homeland in your absence. You will always have a safe home to return to, King Antonil Copernus, and the arms of friends ready to embrace you."

Ahaesarus drew his sword, a masterful construction of steel, gold, and diamond that was as tall as Harruq. He held it with both hands above his head, and he cried out, his words repeated by the rest of the angels.

"Ashhur bless the King!" they cried. "Ashhur bless the King!"

That was it, the last of the ceremony so far as Harruq knew. He let out a sigh, glad he hadn't screwed anything up. But Antonil stood, and he looked far from relaxed. Ahaesarus bowed to him, then stepped away so the crowd might see their king. Harruq shot Aurelia a glance, but his wife only shrugged.

"Tomorrow we march," Antonil said. At first it was hard to hear him, but a quick twitch of Tarlak's fingers and his voice strengthened, magically carrying throughout the city. "With me march your sons, your husbands, your lovers and protectors. I swear to protect them, honor them, and let not a single life lost be in vain. In my absence my beautiful wife rules…at least, she would if circumstances were different."

Susan smiled, and that smile filled Harruq with terror. He knew that smile, that glow. *Not good,* he thought. *Antonil you bastard, you better not be doing what I think you're about to…*

"My wife carries my second child," Antonil told the crowd. Scattered applause accompanied his words. "And I would not burden her further during such a time. So now, before you all, I appoint my steward. He is a man well known to you, whose bravery is unquestioned and whose strength none would dare challenge. He will guard my throne in my absence, administering the king's justice."

Harruq felt ready to explode.

"The Godslayer, Harruq Tun," Antonil announced over the roar of the crowd. "Harruq, come stand before me."

He felt Aurelia squeeze his hand, and he fought to remain calm. The eyes of the kingdom were upon him. The thought of messing up terrified him, as did ruling as a steward, but to reject Antonil publicly would be an insult the king's fragile reputation could not endure. So he stepped before Antonil, doing his best to hide his glare from hundreds of onlookers.

"Kneel," Antonil said, and Harruq did. "Harruq Tun, I declare you Steward of Mordan and protector of the realm. Rise, and rule in my absence."

Harruq stood, and he leaned forward so he could speak just to the king.

"I'm going to murder you," he said.

"You have no need to repay me," Antonil responded, "for there is no debt to repay. Just rule well, as I know you will."

## The Prison of Angels

At first Harruq was confused by his words, but the spell was still on Antonil, and the king's voice carried throughout the city. The half-orc shook his head. Sly devil. He'd murder Antonil twice now for this.

"A fine choice," Azariah said, putting a hand on Harruq's shoulder. "If there is anything you need, any question, my knowledge is open to you."

"Thanks," Harruq said, glancing around with wide eyes. He felt like a trapped deer with a crown placed upon his head by a pack of wolves. Unsure what else to do, he waved to the crowd. They cheered back, and he prayed he might live up to their jubilation. Did they really think he'd do any better than Antonil?

That was it, then, the last of the procession. The soldiers were dismissed to spend the night with their loved ones or get drunk one last time with friends. They scattered among the people, who hurried to one of dozens of carnivals set up as part of the celebration. The angels took wing, with only the ruling three remaining behind.

"I hope authority doesn't make you grow fat and lazy," Judarius said, smiling at him. "You still owe me a sparring match or three."

"I have bigger fears than that," Harruq said, spinning on Antonil. "Have you lost your damn mind? Me, steward? Why not place a donkey in charge for all the good I'll do?"

"He makes a good point," Tarlak said. "Either way we'd have an ass sitting on the throne."

"Don't panic," Susan said, leaving her seat so she might kiss Harruq on the cheek. "I'll be here the whole time. You won't be left to hang."

Harruq rubbed his neck. A hanging sounded more preferable than sitting on Antonil's throne and listening to hours and hours of complaints, pleadings, and accusations.

"Antonil, a word with you if I may?" Ahaesarus asked, and Antonil nodded.

"Harruq, come with us," the king said. "Ahaesarus, up to that wall if you'd please."

The angel grabbed each by an arm and with a flutter of his wings they soared into the air. Moments later they landed atop the inner wall of the city, which was now completely empty. Suddenly free of the crowd, Harruq felt his stomach unclench for the first time in an hour.

"Much better," Harruq said, turning on Antonil. "Now care to tell me what just happened down there?"

"I'm sorry, Harruq. I thought you'd say no if I asked you any other way."

"Antonil, you know my place is with you and your army. I kill things with swords. That's what I do. Just because your wife is pregnant doesn't mean I should…"

"But she's not pregnant," Ahaesarus said, crossing his arms and frowning at Antonil. "Is she?"

Harruq's jaw dropped. Antonil shook his head.

"No," he said. "It's just a ruse to justify Harruq's appointment as steward."

Two deaths wasn't enough, Harruq decided. Now it was up to three.

"You tread dangerous ground," the angel said. "You made us complicit in your lie, and neither I nor my angels appreciate this in the slightest."

"What he said," Harruq grumbled.

"I have my reasons," Antonil insisted. "Harruq, please listen to me, not as your king but as your friend."

The half-orc sighed, nodding at Antonil.

"Fine," he said. "I'm all ears."

Antonil turned, and from the wall he gestured to the grand city of Mordeina and its castle upon the hill.

"This isn't my home," he said. "I hoped otherwise, but nothing has changed over the past five years. My home, my heart, and my kingdom are all in the east, ruled by tribes of orcs. The people know this, and because of that they resent me. You're not a fool. You're not deaf. Surely you hear their rumblings better than I?"

Harruq crossed his arms and refused to look him in the eye.

"Of course you hear it," Antonil said, and he let out a groan. "Too many resent my power, as do they resent the angels. This is the chance my enemies have been waiting for. I cannot leave Susan alone. I won't risk her life, not now. So be the figurehead I need you to be. Susan will run all the important matters, and truth be told, that's not much different than how it has been. But I won't let her be intimidated. I won't let others think she can be bullied or usurped. The people love you, respect you, even fear you."

"You want me to take the danger while your wife rules in secret," Harruq said. "Is that what you're asking?"

"Will you deny it, Harruq? Who has less to fear from an assassin's dagger, you or my wife? Who in my kingdom has the presence to intimidate you?"

"And what of my family?" Harruq asked. "What of my daughter?"

"Only a madman would dare harm the child of Harruq and Aurelia Tun," Antonil said, and he smiled to hide his discomfort at the notion. "But your daughter will be with my son. They'll be guarded together, protected together. I'm putting everything in your hands, Harruq—my family, my son, my entire kingdom. Can I trust you?"

"We'll be here watching," Ahaesarus said, trying to comfort the half-orc. "Avlimar is close, and if you are in need we will always be at your side. You have nothing to fear."

Harruq glanced back and forth between them, then hung his head in surrender.

"If I'm a steward," he asked, "does that mean I have to wear a stupid crown?"

"Nonsense," Antonil said, smiling. "You're in charge now. You'll wear what you like. Or at least, what Aurelia will let you."

Harruq laughed.

"A crown it is," he said. "Now fly me down. I'm not ruling just yet, and until I am, I plan on finding out how much of your alcohol I can drink before passing out."

## 2

The ax came down with a thunk, easily splitting the log in half. Qurrah Tun wiped a bit of sweat from his brow. He prespired not from exertion, but from the heat. Controlling the undead being with the ax required little effort on his part. With a slow but steady motion his undead servant pushed the split wood to the side, bent down for another log, and set it before him on the heavy stump.

"Qurrah?"

The half-orc looked up from where he sat leaning against a tree with a book in his lap.

"Yes, Tess?"

Tessanna came around the side of their cabin as the ax fell, splitting another log. Her long black hair ran all the way down to her waist. A single braid looped around her forehead, pulling her bangs away from her face. Despite her plain brown dress she looked like a goddess to Qurrah, with her pale skin, slender body, and eyes so black only a hint of white showed at the edges. The only mar upon her perfection were her arms, laced with dozens of scars, most of them self-inflicted.

"Someone's coming," she said.

"Well then, let's meet him at the road," he said, putting his book away.

"He's not using the road."

Qurrah let out a sigh. The arrival of an angel may not always bring bad news, but it did mean complications. They were stretched too thin across Mordan to dally with trivial things.

"Then let him come to us," he said, taking her hand. "You aren't nervous, are you?"

Tessanna smirked at him.

"With the two of us together? It would take many, many more angels to make me nervous...and only if I had a reason. Do we have a reason to be nervous?"

"It could be sad news, perhaps a death in the family."

"I'd know before they."

## The Prison of Angels

Qurrah took her hand and together they walked to the front of their cabin. He believed her. She'd always had a strange connection to his family, especially since the tragedy with Aullienna. The thought stung him, and he forced his mind to think of other things. If something bad had happened to Harruq, Aurelia, or especially his daughter Aubrienna, he'd have heard of it long before an angel could make the flight from Mordeina.

Mind distracted, he almost missed the landing of the angel, who softly curled about in the air so his feet touched ground with nary a sound. His hair was short, brown, and his green eyes sparkled with gold.

"Welcome to our meager home, Azariah," Qurrah said. "You risk much coming to me. Your kind isn't welcome within Ker's borders."

"I come as an ambassador, not an enforcer," Azariah said. "Besides, when I am in the sky, who in Dezrel might harm me?"

"I could if I still had my wings," Tessanna said, picking at the hem of her dress. "But I don't need them anymore. At least I hope not."

"No angel would dare pretend to know the goddess's intentions," Azariah said, turning to her. "But your power may have waned for a reason, and it might return with equal reason. Celestia would not leave you helpless should a need arise."

She smiled at him so beautifully, but Qurrah sensed the daggers hiding behind it.

"Helpless?" she said, and a brief flicker of flame passed from her palm, across her knuckles, and back into her fingers, where she snuffed it. "I have forfeited my wings, and the power of a goddess is no longer mine, but do not think me helpless, angel. It would be poor sport watching you try to fly with your wings ablaze."

Qurrah put a hand on her shoulder and squeezed as Azariah dipped his head low to show he meant no disrespect.

"It is wrong of me to be so careless with my words," the angel said. "Especially since you and I are in such similar situations."

Qurrah heard the thunk of an ax, and he turned around to see his pet flailing at the log, which he'd failed to fully split. Frowning, he waved a hand at it, ceasing all functions until he could deal with it later. When he turned back he caught Azariah frowning at him.

"Your power still wanes?" Qurrah asked, trying to prevent a conversation he had no patience for.

"It does," Azariah said, walking toward their cabin. "It is strange, for I cannot decipher the reason. Not all of our kind suffer like I. The warriors and enforcers still retain their abilities, limited as they are. We can still calm troubled minds and sense truth from lie, but more and more our priests struggle to have our prayers answered. It is a humbling thing, Qurrah, to go from the mightiest priest of our lord to a mere winged man who even the lowliest scoundrel could pierce with his sword."

"Humility in an angel?" Qurrah said, smiling at Azariah. "And to think you act like the age of miracles has passed."

"It is with humility I can accept the coming changes and prepare for them. My priestly spells vanish. Perhaps it is our descent to this world, our proximity to its sin and corruption. Perhaps Ashhur slumbers, or Celestia's control over him has increased in response to the war that sundered her land. None of these things can I change."

He opened the door to their cabin, holding it so the two might enter first. Tessanna took Qurrah's arm, hovering close beside him as if she were afraid. Normally Qurrah would think it an act, but there was never any knowing with Tessanna. Her mind, while worlds better than when he first met her, was still a fragile thing, and rarely predictable.

Inside the cabin was their bed, a small table, and a dormant fireplace. It wasn't much, especially compared to the splendor his brother now lived in, but it was theirs. Given how he and Tessanna had nearly destroyed all of Dezrel, it felt like luxury enough.

"How fares my brother?" he asked as he thought of Harruq. He sat in a chair beside the table, and Tessanna sat next to him, her head leaning against his shoulder.

"I will speak of him soon enough," Azariah said, flashing an indecipherable smile. "He is the reason I came, but I would first make a request before I lose my courage. I cannot change the loss of my power, but I can adapt. I can embrace this new world we are to rule. Qurrah…can you share with me your knowledge of the arcane arts?"

It took a moment before Qurrah could compose his thoughts.

"You want me…to teach you?"

"Is it so strange?" Azariah asked. "My hands were not meant to hold a blade. Tell me, could you take up your brother's swords with any degree of skill?"

"Well, no."

"Then why should others expect the same of me? I once wielded great power. I would do so again."

"He would be the perfect pupil," Tessanna whispered into his ear. "He is an angel, after all."

Her giggle showed her true opinion on the matter, however.

"There must be better teachers than I," Qurrah said. "What about Tarlak? He even lives in Mordeina."

"He travels with King Antonil on their campaign to retake the east, and I cannot afford to be away for such a lengthy time."

Qurrah's brain scrambled for other alternatives.

"The Council of Mages," he said. "What of them?"

Azariah shook his head.

"If you think Ker carries a distrust of my kind, you should hear the opinions of the Council. No, they will not teach me. Neither will the elves, for those who still bear the gift of magic in their blood are closely guarded, and are not prone to sharing."

"Not all of them," Qurrah insisted. "I'm sure Aurelia would be willing to—"

"You must understand something," Azariah interrupted. "I hold a position of great respect. Should mortals hear of my training, I would be mocked, or doubted. There are many of my own kind who distrust the learning of magical spellcasting, even a few who would declare it blasphemous. That you are here, acting the recluse, helps put my mind at ease concerning this matter."

"I could teach you," Tessanna said.

"Wait a moment," Qurrah said. "Wait…"

"From what I know of you, I fear I would not be an appropriate student," Azariah said. "Magic comes to you easily, and its very nature is unpredictable. But I will accept…should your husband have no objections."

Their eyes turned on Qurrah, and he felt like a caged animal. Tessanna's fingers played with the neckline of his shirt, and the tension in her shoulders told him she feared his rejection. Letting out a sigh, he kissed the top of her head.

"We will both teach you as best we can," he said. "Though I fear you will have a lengthy flight between every lesson."

"Perhaps not," Azariah said. "But speaking of lengthy flights, do you have something I might drink?"

Tessanna retrieved a wood-carved cup from a cupboard, filled it with water from a pitcher, and then dipped her finger inside.

"Wine," she said, handing it over. "Don't worry, it is very weak."

"Many thanks," Azariah said. Putting the cup to his lips, he drank until it was gone. "Much better," he said, setting it down. "Now, about your brother, and our training. I've come to ask you to return to Mordeina. You don't need to live next to him if you would prefer some separation, but I think it would be helpful to have you two nearby in case something goes wrong."

"Is Aubrienna in danger?" Tessanna asked. A bit of life leapt into her wide gaze.

"I do not know," Azariah said. "And it pains me greatly to admit even that. The shadow of Avlimar should be a safe place, but Mordeina still bears many sinful hearts."

"But why?" Qurrah asked. "What has he done to earn himself enemies?"

The feathers in Azariah's wings ruffled.

"Antonil appointed Harruq steward over the kingdom in his absence," the angel said with a sigh. "The king is not beloved, and those scheming against him will turn those schemes upon your brother. I fear his life will soon be in danger."

Before Qurrah knew it, Tessanna's hand had slipped into his. He squeezed it tight, then met Azariah's green eyes with his own.

"We will need time to decide," he said.

"And time you will have," Azariah said, pushing back open the door to their cabin. "I'll be flying northeast to meet with the paladins, though I won't be staying long. When my business with them concludes, I will return here for your answer."

Qurrah nodded, but he did not stand for the angel's exit. Another dip of his head in respect, and then Azariah left the cabin. With a heavy gust of air the angel soared skyward, leaving them once more alone in their cabin. The tranquility they'd had before, though, was shattered. Qurrah said nothing, only sat at the table frowning as he tried to make sense of his jumbled thoughts. Knowing his brother might be in danger brought out the strong instinct in him to go to his aid, but things were just not that simple.

When the great betrayer of Veldaren traveled somewhere, he did not go unnoticed.

"You want to go, don't you?" Tessanna asked him as she stood from the table. "But you're also afraid."

"I am."

Tessanna stood before their bed and crossed her arms over her chest. She glanced over her shoulder, let her hair fall over her face.

"Would you like to have me?" she asked. "Help clear your mind?"

He rubbed his eyes, then blinked as she tossed off her dress.

"Sure," he said. "Why not."

It did indeed help clear his mind. Afterward they lay naked together, the light of the cabin dwindling as the sun descended below the tree line. Tessanna's hands traced unseen runes across his chest, her eyes staring into nowhere.

"If you want to go, we should go," she said.

"If that oaf's a steward, then all of Mordan balances on a precarious peace," he said. "Our arrival might do more harm than good."

"You don't know that," Tessanna said, her fingers pinching the skin of his chest. "The angels forgave you. Everyone knows you slew Karak's prophet, and what of your stand at the Bridges? You gave your life for them, for all of them."

"No one survived to tell the tale."

"You and I survived."

"All the more reason not to tell stories. They won't believe it, and they won't care. I'm the man who helped burn Veldaren to the ground. I helped open the portal to let the demons in. To come to Mordeina and insist on aiding Harruq would be disastrous. My very presence will contaminate him."

"I'm the one who let in the war god," Tessanna said. "I'm the one who pushed you to Velixar. Do I contaminate you, Qurrah? Would you go alone, leave me here to protect the cabin from the forest's encroach?"

He fell silent, trying to decide the right words to say.

"You are my everything," he told her. "If we go, we go together. But the angels' forgiveness means nothing, not to the people. I know they hate me, and they have every reason to. That's why we came here, Tess."

"Is that why? To hide?"

"To make a new life. To start over."

She sat up, the blanket falling away to expose her thin body, her spine faintly visible in the dying light. Her arms crossed, holding herself as if she were cold.

"If that is why we're here, then it's not a new life," she said, her head dipping low, her eyes downcast. "It's a prison. I ask you again…do you want to help Harruq?"

"Yes," he said. "I do."

"Then we're going, old sins and angry peasants be damned. We're not the enemy, not anymore."

He took her in his arms and pulled her back down to the bed.

"If we're not, then who is?" he asked her as he held her close.

"What if there isn't one?"

"The people must always have a villain."

She curled around so they lay face to face.

"If they must, then they'll find another. And another. The orcs, the elves, the people of Ker…"

"The angels."

Her dark eyes stared into his.

"Then Harruq needs our help all the more. I have watched him suffer enough. He won't again, and not for that. Not for Aubrienna. Even if all the realm crumbles, she must live. She must."

## The Prison of Angels

She slipped free of their bed, and naked she left the cabin. Qurrah lay there for a moment, almost giving her the privacy she wanted. But what if that wasn't what she wanted? He didn't know. He never knew. Tossing aside the blanket, he went to the door and peered out. The sight stole away his breath, and he was fearful of revealing his presence. Sorrow tugged at his heart, and he felt painfully helpless.

Tessanna stood in the glimmer of the rising moon. Her arms were raised heavenward, her head tilted back as if she might drink in the light of the stars. A soft wind encircled her, coming from nowhere and everywhere. Words of magic flowed from her lips, gathering shadows. For the briefest moment she lifted up, the grass touching just the tips of her toes. And then she fell, so softly, so gently, back down to the ground. No tears ran from her eyes, but the sorrow was there, as easy to see as her stark black hair. Qurrah turned away, feeling like an intruder. Into the cabin he went, shutting the door behind him. His lower lip trembled. In his head he kept seeing it, the image of her rising. Rising, as if she were still the goddess.

Rising, as if she still had her wings.

## 3

Lathaar was in his study when someone knocked twice on the door before pushing it open.

"Is he here?" he asked as Jerico, platemail armor finely polished and shield slung over his back, stepped inside.

"Well, it's a flying visitor," Jerico said. "But not Dieredon. Hurry. I'd hate to keep an angel waiting."

Lathaar let out a sigh. Grabbing his swords, he followed Jerico down a single flight of stairs, into the main foyer, and then out the large wooden double doors of the rebuilt Citadel. In the building's shadow the two paladins stood and looked to the western sky. Far away, looking barely bigger than a bird, Lathaar saw the angel.

"Where are the students?" he asked.

"I've got them around back, sparring. Figured the distraction would do them good in case any noticed the angel's arrival. I'd like to hold a conversation without fifteen hundred questions interrupting it."

"Discipline, Jerico, we need to teach them discipline. That you fear them acting unruly is a poor sign."

Jerico laughed.

"It's because they *are* an unruly bunch. Take heart, though. I don't think we were so much better back when *we* were in the Citadel."

Lathaar grinned.

"Speak for yourself. I was a model pupil."

"No wonder you're so bland."

The angel neared, and now those white wings were greater than any bird that had ever lived. He wore no armor, just a robe tightly cinched due to the constant force of the wind. After a quick loop above the Citadel he banked downward, coming to a gentle stop before the two paladins. They both bowed low, humbled by a visit from the high priest of the angels.

"It has been too long, Azariah," Lathaar said. "You haven't graced us with your presence since the day the last brick was put into the Citadel."

Azariah smiled at him.

"Indeed, and I was hardly needed then. You two had the energy of children, you were so excited."

"Good thing, too," Jerico said. "Because the children we took in had far more energy than us."

Lathaar ran a hand through his brown hair, trying to hide his nervousness. Something about Azariah felt unsettling, as if the angel were terribly uncomfortable. But why?

"Do you come bearing news?" he asked, hoping to pry out the reason. "The best we receive here are rumors from traders, and they're as consistent as the direction of the wind."

"No news that would concern you," Azariah said as he began walking toward the back of the Citadel, where the young paladins-to-be sparred. The two followed, and a glance showed Lathaar that his friend also felt similarly confused by the visit. "Just the usual politics in the capitol. Antonil has launched another campaign to retake the east, but I'm sure you already know of that."

"Just that it was being planned," Jerico said. "I was hoping he'd delay for a few more years. I'd love some of our students to be old enough to accompany the campaign."

"Paladins would do well to lead the troops on the battlefield, but it seems Antonil could not be persuaded otherwise. Hrm, are these your students?"

Before them were thirty children, all fairly close in age. The youngest were twelve, the oldest sixteen. Jerico had grouped them by age, and they sparred with a variety of wooden swords and daggers. A few also held thin sheets of tin to use as shields. At sight of the angel many stopped and turned, several wise enough to also bow. Jerico clapped his hands at them, ushering them back to their practice.

"I should get to instructing," Jerico said, tipping his head to Azariah. "If there is nothing else?"

"No, go. The infants in Ashhur are most precious to our future, as is their need for discipline."

Jerico shot Lathaar a look, then went to the circle with the youngest children, pointing out the flaws in their stance as they ran their drills. Lathaar watched him for a moment, then noticed Azariah surveying the students.

"Have you come to inspect our recruits?" Lathaar asked him.

"More out of curiosity than anything," Azariah said. "You drill them strongly in marshal matters, though I wonder if their faith is given the same testing of mettle."

Lathaar let out a sigh. It'd been something he'd discussed repeatedly with Jerico, and over the years they'd not come to any sort of satisfactory answer.

"We try," he said, figuring if there was anyone who might help them in this, it was Azariah. "We teach them the prayers, the lessons, beat into their heads the ferocious need for prayer. But this world we live in…it's not the same, is it? How do I teach them matters of faith when Ashhur's angels soar through the clouds? How do I teach them to remain on guard against enemies when Karak has been defeated and his followers scattered to the wind? How do I convince them they are beacons of light amid the darkness when there is no darkness?"

"But there *is* darkness," Azariah assured him. "The world has not ended. It still moves on, filled with sickness, death, and despair."

"I tell them," Lathaar said, shaking his head. "I tell them, and I don't think they believe me. Their faith is hollow, Azariah. I know it. I feel it in my gut. So few of them carry any true love for Ashhur. When they hold their weapons, only the slightest hint of blue shines. And if they were to be tested, truly tested? Ashhur save us if someone like Velixar should get their hands on them. When Jerico and I were in the Citadel, we were outnumbered. We were seen as a dying order, soon to be overwhelmed by Karak's forces. In every prayer, every day of training, we knew deep down in our hearts that we were the last hope for a troubled world, the last stand against an encroaching evil. But we aren't anymore."

He looked to Azariah.

"You are."

This took the angel back, and he paused.

# The Prison of Angels

"You give us a role we cannot have," Azariah said after a moment of watching the students train. "Your paladins are what men must aspire to be. They are to be the light of our god manifested in mortal men, to show humanity's full potential by embracing Ashhur's commands. We angels cannot be that. We are not men, and mankind will never believe us, never understand us, until they themselves enter the Golden Eternity. A sickness runs through this land, and it must be cured. Convince them, Lathaar. Convince them their need is not yet over."

Lathaar nodded, and he felt a little better hearing those words. Perhaps he'd been looking at things the wrong way. Rebuilding the Citadel had been a mark of honor for him and Jerico. They'd begged for every scrap of coin. With their close relationship to Harruq, the king's advisor Tarlak, and the angels, it should have been easy getting aid. But all of Mordan had been devastated, and the first year in particular had been one of frantic rebuilding and political upheaval. Through it all they'd fought, determined to have their home rebuilt in defiance to Karak's past evil.

But they'd rebuilt the Citadel simply to rebuild it, and now pressed with the functions, the responsibility, he and Jerico were struggling. Had their own aimlessness poisoned their students?

"You've given me much to think over," he said. "Thank you."

"I am glad I could be of some help. And do not be too difficult on yourself. I sense the faith of those here, and there are many who are stronger than you believe. To help ease your mind, I will show you."

Azariah stepped into the training arena and lifted his hands. Immediately all eyes were upon him. Lathaar watched, arms crossed, curious as to what the angel planned. His robe shimmered white, and from his mouth issued words of a prayer too soft for Lathaar to hear.

"Come to me, children," Azariah said afterward. "Come to me, faithful. I would see your hearts naked before the eyes of your god."

From the tips of his fingers flared a sudden brightness, coalescing into a shining ball of white, like a miniature sun hovering above his palms. It pulsed, and with each pulse a wave of light washed over the paladins and students. The force of it knocked them to their knees. Even Jerico fell to one knee, and Lathaar did the same. In his mind he felt a sudden closeness to Ashhur, a presence he'd not known since the last days of the Gods' War. Before it he felt naked and afraid. The light grew brighter, and he opened his mouth to speak, to cry out. All around the world had vanished, so that he saw only darkness where the grass and the rivers should have been. Piercing that darkness was Azariah, a being so unearthly that it filled Lathaar with awe.

Before a cry escaped his lips he saw a light burning from within his chest, where his heart should be. The bluish-white glow was strong, and as he knelt it continued to grow so that it nearly enveloped him. A thought struck him. He reached for his sword, and as he drew it the glow from his chest swirled down his arm and into the blade, manifesting itself again. Looking around, he saw his students, all kneeling, and from their chests emerged similar glows. Just as Azariah said, many were strong, bright, filled with life and devotion. Jerico in particular was nearly blinding to look upon. But also he saw dimness in many, emptiness. It hurt him seeing it, and he could not help but feel responsible.

The darkness broke, and the light vanished. It happened so suddenly Lathaar let out a gasp. How long had it been? He didn't know. What had felt like minutes may have only been seconds, so strangely that vision had distorted time. Colors rushed back into his eyes, the green of the surrounding hills, the gentle blue of the Rigon River rolling beside the Citadel. The students rose to their feet one by one, some muttering to themselves, others praying. Jerico shot him a look, but what it meant he couldn't decipher. And then he saw Azariah.

The angel knelt on his hands and knees, gasping for air. His wings shivered, and feathers fell like leaves in an autumn wind. Lathaar reached down for him, but his offered hand went ignored. With a loud groan Azariah pushed himself to stand. His bearing was unsteady, but with each passing moment the color returned to his face and the firmness returned to his voice.

"I hope you gained what you needed," Azariah said, turning to go.

The Prison of Angels

"Wait," Lathaar said, hurrying after him. "Is something wrong? You look—"

"I am fine," Azariah said, interrupting him. "I...no, Lathaar, you do not deserve such harshness. Ashhur's power is fading from me, fading from all of us. When did you last talk to one of your priests?"

Lathaar frowned.

"High Priest Keziel stayed here a few months before returning to the Sanctuary, but that was not long after we first rebuilt the Citadel. A few have traveled here from time to time, but not recently, no."

"They suffer, same as I. The world of Dezrel is fading, paladin, and the celestial magic I once possessed fades with it. Forgive me, but I came here to see if your kind felt it as well, but it appears the glow of your blades remains strong."

"Praise Ashhur for that," Lathaar said.

The angel fell silent, deep in thought. Lathaar stood there, giving him time. Shifting his weight side to side, he glanced up at the sky, then chuckled.

"It seems you're not our only winged visitor today," he said.

They both looked upward, to where an elf in dark green camouflage rode atop the back of a beautiful winged horse, her white wings the only thing that could match the splendor of the angels. The elf circled twice, then dove low, landing just before the two. With inhuman grace he leapt from the horse's back, and in unison the creature and master bowed. The elf's hair was long and brown, carefully tied so it would not interfere with his vision or movements. From his back hung a wicked looking bow, attached to leather straps that wrapped about his chest and shoulders.

"Greetings," said Dieredon, Scoutmaster of the Quellan elves. "I come as requested, though forgive me for the delay. The Vile Wedge has gotten far wilder in the past few years."

"I'm just glad you're safe," Lathaar said, bowing in return. He glanced at Azariah, noticed a hardness in the angel's eyes that worried him.

"I must be leaving," said Azariah. "I still have much to do. Trust your students, Lathaar, and have faith in them. Should Ashhur be kind, they will repay that faith tenfold."

With a curt nod to Dieredon, Azariah spread his wings and then leapt into the air. Lathaar watched him go, careful to reveal nothing to his elven guest.

"Have I done something to offend?" Dieredon asked.

Lathaar shook his head.

"No, it just seems that even angels can have a long day. But let's not think on that. I'm glad you're here, Dieredon. I'm in need, and you're the best person imaginable to help me."

"Ask, and I will do what I can, my friend."

Lathaar led him back around the Citadel, to where the students had resumed training. They passed through the various age groups, gathered together in small circles. Most wielded swords and shields, trading blows as they searched for openings in their sparring partner's defenses. Further back they passed a few who wielded swords in each hand, and many others wielding maces like their trainer, Jerico. But at the very far end sat a young lady, her chestnut hair cut at the shoulders and then pulled into a ponytail. Unlike the others, she wore soft leather gloves, and in her lap was a bow.

"Jessilynn," Lathaar said, drawing her attention upward. She smiled until she saw the elf, and then the smile fled her face. Immediately she leapt to her feet, fumbling through a bow. At sixteen she was one of the oldest students at the Citadel, but to Dieredon she was but a child, nothing compared to his centuries of life.

"You must be Dieredon," Jessilynn said, her eyes staring at the dirt. "Jerico and Lathaar have told me so much about you. Consider me honored to be in your presence."

"Well-spoken," Dieredon said, crossing his arms. "Though I fear your teachers' stories. Paladins may not lie, but I still believe they are prone to exaggeration."

"Nothing of the sort," Lathaar said, grinning. "Jessilynn, fire a few arrows at a target. Don't be nervous, either."

Jessilynn nodded, and without looking at either of them she grabbed her bow and turned around. Thirty yards away was a bale of hay, and leaning in front of it were several planks of wood that served as targets. For a moment Jessilynn dipped her head, closed her eyes, and began to pray.

"She was part of our inaugural class," Lathaar whispered to Dieredon. "It was a big stink, too, our very first female paladin. Plenty of the priests were furious, but Azariah declared it good, and that ended the grumblings. Our younger classes have more now, and it isn't the trouble or difficult matter we thought it'd be. As for Jessilynn, to be honest her skills with a sword aren't very impressive, and neither can she wield a shield with any sort of grace. But the bow…"

Lying at her feet were a pile of arrows, and with her prayer finished Jessilynn leaned down to grab one. Pressing it against the string, she pulled it taut, then hesitated. As she did, a soft blue began to glow from the arrowhead. Then she let it fly. It arced through the air, leaving behind it a blue-white trail. The arrow missed the wooden targets, instead vanishing into the hay with a brief flicker of light.

Dieredon looked at Lathaar, an eyebrow raised. In response, Lathaar just shook his head.

"It gets crazier," he said. "Jessilynn, another."

She grabbed a second arrow, and this time she looked far less tight as she nocked it for flight. After another moment of hesitation she let it fly. Its aim was true, striking a thin board in the center of the hay bale. Upon contact the wood shattered as if blasted by an enormous hammer. Onward the arrow continued, vanishing into the hay. Seeing the explosion, Jessilynn hopped once in the air, her ponytail bouncing.

Now both of Dieredon's eyebrows were raised, and his mouth dropped open a little.

Jessilynn spun around to bow, and she was unable to hold back her pleased smile. But at least she tried.

"I hope my demonstration was sufficient," she said.

"Jerico's shield gives us some precedence in dealing with this," Lathaar said. "The problem is, neither of us knows what we're doing with longbows. I've only shown her the most rudimentary basics, and even those might have been wrong. Basically, she's self-taught."

"Of that, there is little doubt," said Dieredon. "Her stance is too narrow. She sights down the arrow while gripping it too tightly. Her follow-through is incorrect, and I cannot believe I must say this, but she even nocks the arrow incorrectly."

Each critique made Jessilynn wince as if she were being stabbed with a dagger, but she remained quiet, her attention undivided.

"That's great and all, but can you train her?" Lathaar asked, stepping away from Jessilynn and dropping his voice. "We can't help her, and you've seen what she's already capable of untrained. We can't let such a unique talent go wasted. She could take down a bull with a single shot. What she needs more than anything is a teacher. That's why I sent for you, Dieredon. Who else is better with a bow than you?"

"Flattery won't help you here," Dieredon insisted. "I can't train her. The amount of time it would take to make her even proficient would be too much of a sacrifice. The Vile Wedge stirs, Lathaar, and orc armies surround our forests at all times."

"Take her with you, then."

Dieredon rubbed his eyes with his fingertips.

"What of her lessons here?" he asked.

Lathaar thought of what Azariah had said, as well as his own beliefs on the matter. His students had been coddled. They were out of the darkness of the world, living in safety and comfort.

"She knows the prayers, the lessons, the verses," he said. "Everything else she'll learn on her own, or from you. Please, Dieredon, she's quiet, focused, and will take to your lessons well, I promise. I've talked with Jerico, and we've both prayed about this for months. This is the right thing to do, I'm sure of it."

The elf let out a sigh.

"Six months," he said. "That's all I guarantee. And she'll learn everything I teach her, not just about the bow. She'll wear the armor I tell her to, move silently as needed, learn to forage, to craft her own arrows, anything and everything to survive out there with me. She won't be a paladin when she returns, not in discipline or tactics. She'll be a ranger. Can you accept that?"

Lathaar turned to Jessilynn, knowing without a doubt she'd been listening in.

"Can you?" he asked her.

Jessilynn's green eyes sparkled, and she clutched her bow tight.

"Will I learn to shoot like you?" she asked.

# The Prison of Angels

"In six months?" Dieredon laughed. "Good gods, you humans. By the end of six months, my hope is you'll know how to hold your bow without hurting yourself. Now do you accept? Know that we will soar to many places on my horse, Sonowin, so if you fear heights you should remain here and accept a more appropriate teacher. A human teacher."

Lathaar watched as Jessilynn's grin spread ear to ear.

"I get to ride Sonowin?" she asked. "I accept, of course I accept!"

And then she was off, calling out to her friends while rushing around the Citadel, to where Sonowin waited patiently. Lathaar watched her go, and when he caught Dieredon glaring at him, he smiled.

"I did say she was focused," he said, and laughed at Dieredon's exasperation.

# 4

The crowd was twice the size it had been a week before, and ten times larger than the week before that. Kevin Maryll did well to hide his satisfaction. By leaving, Antonil had done more to undermine his own rule than anyone else over his five year reign. Any other human, at least.

"But what do we say to these angels?" he cried, his hands shaking to convey the sheer depth of rage boiling within him. "What do we say when they declare us liars, thieves, adulterers? Do they give us proof?"

*No!* the crowd shouted.

"Do they give us witnesses?"

*No!* they cried again.

"That's right! Nothing, they give us nothing but their word. They give us nothing, then take from us everything, our land, our possessions, our very lives. And what do we say? What *can* we say, when their word is the only law that matters?"

A chorus of denials washed over him, varied in wording but similar in tone. Kevin drank it all in, at last letting himself relax. These were the fruits of his labor, hard-fought and long won. For years he had spoken out against the rule of angels. When the Gods' War first ended his cries had fallen on deaf ears. No one would listen, for surely he was mad to say they should not trust the saviors of Dezrel. But patience and time had proven him right. Now over a hundred men and women surrounded him in the streets of Mordeina, blocking off a large portion of trade just so they might hear his truth.

"The gods started this war. The gods and their followers tore this land asunder, filling its rivers with blood and its fields with corpses. Yet now the puppets of the victor, these enforcers, these so-called angels, would lord over us. Who will protect us from them? Who will stand tall when they execute an accused thief yet let a confessed murderer go free? Who will represent us, who will be our voice to the heavens to shout in a loud and clear voice that *we* will rule mankind, not them?"

"The king will!" a man shouted from somewhere in the back, perfectly on cue. Easily worth the three copper he'd paid him.

"The king?" Kevin asked. "The king will protect us? The king will speak for us? Aye, a good king that is, my friend, so bring him to me. Show me. Tell me his name. Where is our king? All of you, I ask, I beg, tell me where is our king?"

*Missing*, the crowd shouted, and the chant soon was on the lips of all hundred. *The Missing King! All hail the Missing King!*

"To him I go!" Kevin shouted to them. "Let the castle hear my words, let the throne be painted with the truth. I will not walk to my death across a bed of angel feathers, nor bare my neck to gilded blades whose gold hides metal long stained red with blood. My fellow man, we will have a voice, one that will be heard!"

Their cheers urged him on, and as he walked down the street dozens flanked either side of him. Just before the hill he looked up to the floating city of Avlimar. Several angels circled the clouds, watching, waiting. Protecting, they claimed.

"Do you see me?" Kevin whispered to the sky. "Do you still think you can stand in my way?"

Up the hill to the castle gates he went, knowing they would not, could not, stop him any longer.

※

Harruq slammed the door shut, flung his back against it, and let out the most heartfelt groan his tired body was capable of.

"How?" he said. "How does Antonil not go mad?"

Aurelia looked up from where she sat on the floor. They were in a small room adjacent to the throne room. The furnishings were few, the windows slender and tall. The floor was carpeted, though, and Harruq flung his boots off so he could feel its softness on his toes. Before he could complain further he heard his daughter call out to him, using the name he was most proud of.

"Daddy!"

She raced barefoot across the room, instinctively weaving through the mess of wood-carved toys. Without slowing she slammed into his leg, hugging his thigh.

"Hey Aubby," Harruq said, rubbing the top of her head and making a mess of her long brown hair. "Give daddy a chance to breathe."

She squeezed tighter, then returned to her toys. Without bothering to find a seat, Harruq slumped to the carpet, still leaning against the door. He didn't want to say anything, do anything, just sit there.

"Things haven't gotten easier?" Aurelia asked him as she absently made one of the toys, a cat painted blue, spin and dance through the air as if on invisible strings. Aubrienna watched, delighted. Telling her mother to wait, she grabbed another toy, that of a dog, and began having it chase after.

"Easier?" Harruq said, rubbing his temples. "Dealing with Velixar was easier. These people are insane. Six hours I listened to them grumble. They want land, they want food, they want soldiers. Bandits are here, demons are there, and each person acts as if our entire army didn't just leave for the other side of the continent. And they were the reasonable ones! I'm beginning to think the castle guards hate me, because they didn't turn *anyone* away. For Karak's sake, I had one woman ask if I'd touch her hands to cure her arthritis. Who do they think I am?"

Aubrienna looked his way, and he could see the vague worry in her beautiful brown eyes.

"Daddy...daddy's upset because he had to listen to people," she said to Aurelia, who kissed her on the nose.

"That's right," Aurelia said. "And people can be silly sometimes." She turned her attention back to Harruq. "How many requests did you turn down?"

Harruq rolled his eyes.

"Five...maybe six if I count the hand lady."

His wife laughed.

"You'll have the kingdom bankrupt within a week."

"I'm not made for this," Harruq insisted, not seeing the humor in the situation that his wife did. "Some old woman comes up saying she needs money to feed her grandbabies, but the money lenders won't help. Now what do I say to that? I'm not a big enough bastard for this job, Aurry. They should have picked Qurrah instead. He'd know a clever way to tell these people to go home and leave him be. Not me, oh no. I just...I just couldn't sit out there anymore. I couldn't listen to another word."

"Are any still waiting?"

Harruq felt his neck flush.

"I may have left a few standing out there," he muttered.

Aurelia shook her head.

"Get over here," she said.

He got up with a groan, then sat down beside his wife. As she cuddled against him she lifted her free hand, sending more of the toys dancing. Aubrienna frowned, for they were moving too fast for her to catch.

"Mommy, slow down," she said, holding up her toy. "My puppy can't reach them."

The whirlwind of cats, trees, horses and soldiers settled, and one by one Aubrienna began knocking them from the air with her toy.

"Ruling isn't easy," Aurelia said, watching their daughter play. "You need to stay calm, and know when you're reaching your limits. When it comes to your decisions, remember, everything is a balancing act. Help those who need it, and encourage those who would falter, but not so much that they depend on you when they should instead depend on themselves."

"Figures an elf would mention something about balance," Harruq said.

"Are you saying I'm wrong?"

He turned and kissed her.

"I'm saying I'm tired and can't think straight. Just ignore me."

The door cracked open. Harruq felt a surge of panic. They wouldn't follow him in there, would they? A paranoid delusion of beggars, petitioners, and politicians trailing around his bed day and night filled him, and if it had been anyone else than Queen Susan who stepped through the doorway he'd have screamed.

"Am I interrupting?" she asked.

When he shook his head she opened the door wider, and in rushed little Gregory Copernus, heir to the throne of Mordan. He was six months younger than Aubrienna and a good three inches shorter. His hair was short and blonde, neatly trimmed like the little lord he was. Every time Harruq saw Gregory and Aubby together he kept thinking how tall his little girl would grow up to be. Orcish blood, he thought. At least it had *some* benefits.

"I thought the two might play for a time," Susan said.

Gregory was immediately at Aubrienna's side.

"Here," she said, handing over the blue dog after an intense period of mental debate. "You can have this. I'll play with the kitty."

She grabbed a purple kitten from the floor, meowing with it. Gregory began barking, and in no time they had chased each other into a corner. Harruq watched with a smile on his face, but the smile couldn't last. Susan remained standing, and he sensed she'd not come just so their children could play.

"How are things out there?" he asked, glancing up at her.

Susan carefully shut the door, then crossed her arms. Her skin wasn't nearly so pale as during the parade, and with her straight hair falling free about her face she looked far more pleasant than when dolled up with jewels and dresses. Antonil was a lucky man, he thought. Shame he didn't have the brains to stay home instead of constantly fighting wars against orcs.

"I listened to a few more, then sent the rest away," she said. "As you can do at any time. Harruq, if you feel overwhelmed please call for me, or send the petitioners home. You're the steward. They will wait for you. Even coming into your presence is a gift they have no right to demand."

"I know," he said. "But I should be able to handle this. I'm sitting on a stuffed chair, half-drunk, making arbitrary decisions. This isn't hard. I can do it."

"You're wrong, Harruq," Susan said, her voice firm. "It *is* hard. And the more you convince yourself otherwise the more frustrated you'll become. You didn't grow up with this, didn't train for this. You're more at home with a sword than a scepter."

"There were several I did want to hit with a sword," he admitted. "Safe assumption that's not an acceptable diplomatic response?"

Susan laughed.

"When it is, I will let you know," she promised.

A knocking came from the other side of the door. Susan cracked it back open and leaned out. Harruq heard muffled talking, then saw the queen's shoulders visibly sink.

"Harruq," she said, pulling back inside. "There's one more guest that refuses to leave."

His left eyebrow lifted.

"Hit him with a sword?"

Susan's smile didn't reach her eyes.

"It's my brother," she said.

Harruq held back his groan.

"All right," he said, pushing himself to his feet. "I guess we can't be rude. Aurry?"

"I'll be fine," Aurelia said, standing as well. "But I'm not staying cooped up in here. Aubby, Greg, let's go to the gardens."

With a quick motion of her hands she ripped open a swirling blue portal, kissed Harruq on the cheek, and then pushed the children through. After she stepped inside the portal vanished, leaving Harruq and Susan alone.

"Lead on," he said, and the queen did. Back into the throne room they went, Harruq plopping into a seat he had already grown to hate. The long hall before the throne was empty but for a single man, who entered through the double doors without waiting for approval. Harruq reminded himself to yell at the guards.

"Welcome," Harruq said, his voice anything but.

"Yes, welcome," Susan said, having waited to speak as a sign of respect. She opened her arms and smiled.

Kevin Maryll accepted the embrace, then kissed his sister on the cheek. He had the same soft face as his sister, but his eyes were hard. His hair was dark, cut short, as was his beard.

"My dear Susan," he said, "my sympathies for what you must yet again endure."

"The castle is not so empty that I will suffer," she said, then stepped back so she might gesture to Harruq. "Besides, I have a steward to train, and he does much to keep me entertained."

Harruq opened his mouth, then closed it. For once, he really didn't know what to say.

"Ah yes, the Godslayer," Kevin said. He walked to the foot of the throne and then bowed to one knee. "Consider me honored to be in your presence."

Harruq bit his tongue. He'd met Kevin several times, and each meeting had been painful, filled with awkward moments due to Kevin's inability to discuss anything other than what was most pressing to him. And since the Gods' War, that had been one thing and one thing only.

"I hear the city has taken a restless turn," said Susan, trying to draw his attention back to her. "I pray your travel here was uneventful."

"Oh, far from," Kevin said, his eyes never leaving Harruq's. "But for my safety, I trust my sword, not prayers. Men surrounded me from the moment I stepped into these streets. Everywhere I went I heard their shouts. Unrest, fury, distrust and betrayal all about me as I made my way to the castle."

"What did they want?" Harruq asked.

Kevin gave him a look, a combination of condescension and inflated self-worth that nearly ignited his temper.

"Why, for me to continue talking, of course," Kevin said. "For at last I was telling them the truth they've been aching to hear."

And that was it, of course. Harruq tried, and failed, to hide his annoyance. Of all the opponents to the angels' new role in society, none were more vocal, and more popular, than Kevin Maryll. The fact that he was the queen's brother gave him a freedom to speak and act that many others could not, or dare not, use so blatantly.

"The angels are here to help," Harruq said. "And it's only because of them we're not bowing to Karak."

"And so instead we bow to Ashhur and give thanks for being spared such a horrific fate. We bow, even as they raise their executioner's blade."

"Enough, please," Susan interrupted. "I will have no bickering. Kevin, let me fetch you a servant. There are dozens of rooms here in the castle, and they are all available to you during your stay."

Kevin took his sister's hand and kissed it.

"I have places to be, and goals to accomplish," he said. "And sadly, I cannot do either cooped up in the castle. I merely wished to ensure my little baby sister was doing well in her husband's unnecessary absence."

Harruq swallowed hard. Every sentence had a jab to it, hidden or otherwise. As with the angels, none were more outspoken against King Antonil's rule than Kevin. With the army marching east for another war, it took little for Kevin to draw an audience for his grumblings. But how many listened? Harruq didn't know. That type of politics was beyond him. He had a sword, and he smacked things with it really good. Now if only he could do the same to Kevin...

"My lord and husband's absence is for the good of Mordan, and for all Dezrel," Susan said, a bit of fire leaking into her voice.

"Of course it is," Kevin said, all smiles. He bowed low, winked at Harruq, and then turned to leave. Harruq watched until he was gone, the guards shutting the doors behind him with a heavy thud, and then smacked the arm of his chair with his fist. The outburst seemed unusually loud, and he immediately felt childish when he saw Susan watching him.

"Do you remember when I said I'd let you know when striking someone with a sword was an appropriate diplomatic response?" she asked. Harruq lifted an eyebrow. "Sometimes I wish we didn't have to act so appropriately."

Harruq laughed. It felt good to do so.

"Come on," he said, standing. "I don't want to sit here fuming about your idiot brother. Let's find where Aurry's taken our kids."

"I have other duties I must attend," Susan said, offering him a curtsey. "Go be with your family."

"Is it anything I should know about?" he asked, not liking the worry she hid behind her eyes.

"If Kevin is rallying people, giving speeches...I despise the need, but he must be watched. Let me handle this matter, Harruq. He is still family, despite how much he might hate my husband."

"Whoever you have watch him, make sure it's not an angel."

Harruq grinned, but the humor fell flat. There was too much worry, too much truth to the joke to laugh. On impulse he took her hand and kissed it, much like Kevin had.

"You'll do fine," he said. "We'll all be fine. No matter how many speeches your brother gives, there's only so much he can accomplish. We're guarded by angels, Susan. It's not like he can start a war. And if he does, well, you'll have the nastiest bodyguard around. I've killed a god before, did you know that?"

"I've heard rumors." She pulled free her hand, rubbed it with her other. "Take care, Harruq, and pray the time passes swiftly.

Antonil will be gone for so long, and in my nightmares I see him returning to a kingdom of ash."

"No," Harruq said, shaking his head as he headed for the door. "I gave everything to save this city, this land. It won't be ash, Susan, no matter how hard anyone might try."

"And if someone *does* try?" he heard her ask.

He looked over his shoulder, flashed his best smile.

"Then I'll act inappropriately."

## 5

As Tessanna prepared the last of her things, Qurrah went out behind their cabin to where his undead servant patiently waited. The body was that of a stout man, no doubt a hardy fellow when he'd still drawn breath. Qurrah ran a hand down the side of his face, feeling the necrotic energy still flowing through it. King Bram had given them the land, in honor of their desire to be free of both angels and men in the wake of the Gods' War. It had been abandoned for many years, left for the forest to slowly reclaim it. They'd chased away the weeds, cleared away the animals, and in doing so discovered the old family grave.

He'd been dead for at least ten years, but that hardly mattered to Qurrah. From the ground he'd summoned the skeleton and, with Tessanna's help, slowly applied a false flesh to hide the bones and rot. No soul remained in it, for Qurrah would not subject anyone to that punishment, not ever again. The thing was a useful tool, nothing more. They'd not bothered to name him, just like Qurrah had never named his robes or the burning whip he still kept coiled around his arms when he felt afraid.

"You have been good to us," Qurrah said, hand still touching the thing's face. "Rest now, and return to the dust. We have need of you no more."

He pulled in his strength through the contact, the powerful magic returning to him. The servant collapsed, the false flesh becoming a gray powder that hovered in the air like a fog. The bones thudded dully, covered by worn clothes and a bit of hair. Qurrah looked at it, feeling a bit sad. It was definitely good he had not named the mindless thing. He'd grown attached to it as it was.

From the ground he looked up, forcing his attention to the forest around them. In the past few years he'd developed a greater appreciation for the wilderness, for the song of the birds and the rustle of the leaves as the wind blew through them. In it he sensed a peace that would forever elude him. But at least it was a peace he could be close to. At least he could try to steal its comfort like the leech he often was in life.

"Qurrah?" Tessanna called, stepping out from the cabin. The half-orc glanced her way.

"Here," he said.

She placed a small bag beside the door of the cabin and then joined his side, looping her arms around his elbow. Leaning against him, she looked to the pile of bones and clothes.

"He was a good servant," she said.

"True. Always quiet, never intruded when he wasn't wanted."

Tessanna laughed.

"We should have brought him with us to Mordeina. He could have carried our things."

Qurrah tried to match Tessanna's mirth but could not.

"I'd prefer we travel unknown," he said. "Having a dead man attending our needs would not help in that regard."

She kissed his cheek.

"You worry too much. What does it matter if we draw attention? They can do nothing to us."

Qurrah went to the cabin and picked up his own satchel, stuffed full of books, spare clothes, and, coiled at the very bottom, his whip. Slinging it over his shoulder, he rejoined Tessanna, who waited patiently on the edge of the road leading out of the forest. Azariah had said he would return for their answer, but Qurrah had no intention of waiting. Better they leave now, before any sort of preparations might be made for their arrival. When the angel returned to the cabin and found it empty, he trusted Azariah to know what their choice had been.

"How far?" she asked him as he looked one last time at their home.

"Just shy of the border," he told her. "Azariah said that the people of Mordan are threatening to turn on Antonil. I would hear their whispers for myself. Perhaps outside the city walls I may help my brother more than at his side."

Tessanna nodded, then closed her eyes. Lifting her arms, she whispered words of magic, her slender fingers clenched. The fabric of reality tore, a swirling black portal ripping open before them with a sudden gust of air. Its substance was shadow, and in its depths was the faint swirling of stars. Without hesitation Qurrah stepped inside, felt the familiar sense of vertigo, and then stepped out many miles away. Tessanna followed. From the corner of his eye he saw her stumble, and dropping his satchel he turned to catch her as she heaved. Bloody vomit spilled from her mouth, splattering on the grass below, and her arms clutched him with terrified strength.

"It's nothing," she said when she was able to breathe. "Nothing."

But it wasn't, Qurrah knew. The old Tess could have sent them halfway around the world without batting an eye. She sensed his unease, though, and pushed him away.

"We're here," she said, wiping her mouth. "So lead on, dear husband."

He retrieved his satchel, biting his tongue to prevent a fight. To force his mind off her, he looked about to see where, exactly, she'd taken them. They were in the shadows of a forest, the tree trunks slender, the bark a pale brown. The area around them was flat and covered with knee-high grass, so that despite the distance they could still see the river flowing a quarter-mile ahead.

"That way," Tessanna said, gesturing northeast. "The bridge shouldn't be far."

Her voice was already growing stronger, and it helped put Qurrah's mind at ease. Taking her hand in his, they began walking. The tall grass annoyed him, and he thought of the ticks and chiggers that might be crawling up his robes. With a thought he made his feet trail a dark cloud. Wherever he stepped the grass wilted, any insects unable to flee in time falling to their backs and dying.

"I thought we weren't to attract attention," Tessanna said.

"We're not in civilization yet."

The immediate area around the river was rocky, left barren and muddy from the spring rains. The two followed alongside it, and as the day crawled along they saw their first sign of the bridge in the distance.

"The Bloodbrick, correct?" Qurrah asked.

"You said you wanted to be at the border, so here we are."

The Corinth River formed the barrier between the two nations of Ker and Mordan, with the Bloodbrick as the only significant crossing. In times past it had been left unguarded, with Ker nothing more than a puppet of the other kingdom. But then the Gods' War had come, and in return for Bram overthrowing his demon rulers, Antonil had severed all ties between the two nations. More importantly, he'd vowed to keep Ker fully independent of Avlimar and her angels.

So when Qurrah saw the army massed at the southern side of the Bloodbrick, he was far from surprised.

"Such paranoia," Qurrah said as they walked through the thin mud.

"Is it?" Tessanna asked. "Azariah implied the people were ready to rebel. And he did not say it, but what if they seek to rebel against the angels as well? Bram may have good reason to fear."

Qurrah shrugged. Bram had always come across as a man ready to believe the worst in anything, though that hardly made him a defeatist. No, it just made him that much more prepared for when trouble *did* arrive. Of the four nations, Neldar and Omn had been thoroughly destroyed and overtaken by orcs. Mordan's capital had been ravaged by battle and her countryside left in shambles from rebellion. But Ker, however…Ker had thrived, left nearly untouched by the devastation. And so her power had grown, as had the arrogance of her king.

"Should we disguise ourselves?" he asked as the bridge neared.

"No," Tessanna said, and her tone left no room for argument. "I tire of hiding. If we are recognized, we are recognized. I walked at the side of gods and prophets. I will fear no lowly border guard."

"That's more than a border guard," Qurrah said, frowning. By his best guess, at least ten thousand men gathered in various camps. The idea that Bram might be planning an invasion was preposterous, but then why such a strong show of force? He didn't like it. And with that many eyes, there were bound to be a few who'd recognize them. Neither were particularly inconspicuous looking, him with his gray skin, orcish face, and curved ears, and Tessanna with the body of a goddess, long black hair, and those solid black eyes. He longed to use a disguise, but Tessanna had made her opinion clear, and he would not challenge her, not on this. At least the scars beneath his eyes were gone, having fallen away when Azariah returned life to his dead flesh after the demon god's death.

"I need no magic to sense your fear," she said, holding his hand as they approached the army. "We've come to help your brother, yes? Then perhaps we may do some good here, for I doubt an army gathering at his southern doorstep is there without reason."

They veered farther from the river, so they might travel along the road before they reached the army protecting the bridge. The nearer they came, the stranger the sight. They weren't even checking those who traveled into the nation, only out. Qurrah squeezed Tessanna's hand tight as they approached the first dozen tents.

"They don't even look for spies," he said quietly to her.

"Perhaps they only fear the spies that fly through the air?"

He shrugged.

"Then why did Azariah not mention it to us?"

"Perhaps he didn't know it to mention?"

The soldiers milled about, some gambling, some singing and playing simple instruments, while a good many drank. Only a few kept their attention on the road, and they had the bored look of someone forced into duty.

"Stay on the path," one said as they passed. "No gawking, no begging, no selling wares."

"Not even these wares?" Tessanna said, tilting her head back a little to better show her breasts. Qurrah pulled her along before the soldier could respond.

"Are you out of your mind?" he hissed.

"Do you know of a better way to learn information than from a man's bed? Whores learn secrets spies cannot."

She returned his look with a dull gaze, then giggled as if she were a little girl.

"You're cute when you're jealous," she said, letting the matter drop. The concentration of soldiers thickened the closer they moved to the bridge. Ahead of them rode a large group, an apparent family traveling north with all their possessions. Their single wagon was loaded with belongings, and at the first stone of the Bloodbrick they were stopped and lazily searched over by two men holding halberds. A third guard stepped in front of Qurrah and Tessanna and lifted his hand.

"Hold up," he said, offering no other words than that. He glanced back, watching the others search the wagon. Qurrah bit his tongue, and in the very center of the encampment he waited, trying not to look nervous. He felt stupid for being nervous in the first place, but it'd been five years since he'd been around people in general, let alone a large army. Tessanna was right—he really had been hiding from society in their cabin. Of course, standing in the middle of ten thousand men felt like a horrible time to realize it.

"Is there something they search for?" Qurrah asked, thinking he might try to learn something instead of standing there shuffling his weight from foot to foot.

"Keep your tongue behind your teeth," the soldier said, barely giving him a glance. "I'm not here for questions. Just wait your turn."

"You made the man mad," Tessanna said, still seeming terribly amused by everything.

"Mad?" the soldier asked, actually turning to face them. "Girl, you haven't…"

He stopped and stood perfectly still, his jaw hanging open the tiniest bit. There was no mistaking his gaze, which focused on her strange eyes.

"Your name," the soldier said.

"I thought you weren't here for questions," Qurrah said, feeling his heart speed up. Ignoring him, the soldier drew the sword at his hip.

"Your name," he said again. So far he kept the blade tip pointed downward, but he seemed about to jump at any second. Tessanna smiled at him, long hair flowing down the sides of her face.

"Tessanna," she said at last.

The soldier looked ready to shit himself—whether from fear or surprise, Qurrah couldn't say. He took a fresh look at Qurrah, and his face paled, showing he knew exactly who stood before him.

"James!" he shouted. "Get the fuck over here, right now!"

The two guards at the wagon turned around. Others around the camp heard the shouting, and seeing the drawn blade they rushed over. Qurrah held his arms out at his sides, hoping to show he posed no danger. Tessanna remained perfectly still, her sly smile receding inward, becoming a calm look of apathy. Qurrah envied her.

"I only travel to meet my brother," Qurrah said, hoping someone in charge might hear and listen. "We are no threat, no—"

"Quiet," said an older man who pushed to the front of the gathering crowd. "You, are you the Betrayer?"

Qurrah glared at him even as a wall of swords encased him and Tess. As if they could stop him, he thought.

"I doubt I am the first, nor the last, to have ever committed that particular sin," he said in answer. Apparently that was enough for the soldier, though, for he turned his attention to Tessanna.

"You said your name was Tessanna," he said. "The prophet's bride?"

"I was," she said, her voice nearly toneless. "But that fiend lives no longer, as will you if you touch a hair on my head."

"She was never his bride," Qurrah said, unable to help himself. He hated the title given to her, formed by the twisted story most commonly told around hearths at night. Only once had Qurrah worked up the nerve to ask his brother what the tales said. In them, Qurrah had betrayed Veldaren, his glorious brother, and then the whole world by helping the prophet Velixar summon the war god Thulos. From then on, Qurrah was seen as the hapless puppet and Velixar the true evil. Tessanna was Velixar's bride, his dark angel, and if the age of the audience permitted, many storytellers liked to embellish the sick, perverted love that had supposedly gone on between them.

"So she wasn't, was she?" the soldier asked, his glare showing he was an inch away from striking the half-orc. "Let's see what Bram has to say about that."

Qurrah sighed. Would it matter telling them Bram knew where they lived, had known for the past five years since he himself had overseen the deeding of the land to them?

"Yes," he said. "Let us see, but put away your swords for all our sakes. You never know when one might cut a piece of hair by accident."

Escorted by over thirty men, they walked into the center of the camp. Neither were restrained in any way, and Qurrah sensed the men were too afraid to try such a thing. In many corners of the world Qurrah and Tessanna had become the boogeyman of campfire stories. He could only guess what some of them thought he might do if they laid a rough hand upon him. The way they held their naked blades, it seemed more like they escorted wild bears than a frail half-orc and a short, slender woman. If not for the inherent risk in it, Qurrah felt tempted to growl at them. His brother would have, he thought, and it put a wry smile on his face. He'd growl and wave his arms about like an idiot, just to show he was unafraid of their numbers.

Sometimes he wished he was more like his brother.

At one of many fires they stopped, and the men encircling them gave way. Lord Bram Henley stood waiting, arms crossed over his chest. His hair was long and black, falling down to his broad shoulders. From his right eye down to his chin was a thin straight scar, self-inflicted in the tradition of his family line. If he was surprised to see Qurrah and Tessanna, he did not show it.

"Well now," Bram asked. "What have you two been doing to stir my camp in such a way?"

"Existing," Tessanna said, her voice flat.

The rest of the soldiers tensed, but Bram only shook his head and chuckled.

"Of course," he said, turning to his solders. "Leave us. They are not enemies of Ker."

None appeared foolhardy enough to argue with their king, so away they went, leaving Qurrah and Tessanna standing before a man they hadn't seen in several years. To Qurrah's eyes he looked older, far older than he should have given the relatively short amount of time that had passed. Perhaps being a king aged a man faster, or maybe it was just the stress of always checking the skies for white feathers.

"I'm glad you're here," Bram said, sitting back down before the fire in a wooden chair. "Hardly three days ago, I sent riders to your cabin, though I didn't expect them to return with you in time. That you come to me, well, I'd say it was fate if I believed in that sort of thing."

"If not fate, then coincidence," Qurrah agreed. "But what have we come in time for?"

The half-orc looked about but saw no other chairs. Shrugging, he sat on his knees before the fire. Tessanna sat next to him, leaning her head on his shoulder. So far she appeared bored, withdrawn. It was a mood she'd fallen into less often over the past few years, but coming back into civilization seemed to have reawakened it.

"I assume you receive little news in your isolated cabin?" Bram asked.

"Little if any," Qurrah said, neglecting to mention Azariah's arrival.

"Then I'll keep details at a minimum as to not overwhelm you. King Antonil marches this way with an army, intent on another foolish crusade to drive the orcs from his native kingdom. Within the hour he should arrive to ask permission to travel through my lands."

"How does this involve us?" Qurrah dared ask.

"I'd have you at my side when I tell him no," Bram said. "At least for now. In a few days, perhaps even a few hours, I will let him pass. I only desire to see how he reacts. Trust me, I do not desire war."

"Forgive me," Qurrah said, "but I fear my question was not answered."

"You must realize you mean something," Bram insisted. "Even with your own brother as Ashhur's avatar, even with your body made new by the hands of angels, you still will not live under their rule. You came to me for help, for freedom. I need your defiance. I need the people to see we still have a choice."

"You give us reasons we never had," Tessanna said before Qurrah could speak. "You tell us our value is in refusing to be puppets, then seek to use us as puppets for your own cause. If you'd stand against Mordan, stand on your own strength."

Her voice remained eerily calm, but Qurrah could feel the anger growing beneath it.

"I do not wish to use you at all," Bram said. "I only thought you would agree with my efforts to hold back the angels' encroachment."

"Angels?" Tessanna said, the last of her apathy vanishing into a wide-eyed look of fury. "Karak took away my lover, then gave me back a monster. Ashhur took that monster and gave me back my lover. I do not hide from the angels. I do not fear their eyes. It's men like you I hoped to avoid. Men who would use me, put me on a pedestal and ask others to bow. I'll take my knife and bleed you all if I must to prevent the prayers."

At last Bram was taken aback, and he lifted his hands to show he meant no insult.

"You'll be put on no pedestal," he said. "And I assure you, no one will bow. But Antonil's army nears, and you will accompany me as my guests."

"And if we refuse?" Qurrah asked.

"If you would deny me such generosity, then I will deny my generosity to you. I will revoke your land and declare you unwelcome in the nation of Ker. Only if I must, of course. Surely I do not ask for much in having you stand silent at my side?"

Qurrah looked to Tessanna, to see how she would react. Did it truly matter if they were there or not? Bram wanted them used as figureheads, and nothing more. They could do this one thing, then continue on their way. His wife, though, still appeared furious, and she gave no attempt to conceal it.

"I will have no part in this," she said, standing. "And neither will Qurrah. I watched him be Velixar's puppet. He won't now be yours."

Hearing this, Qurrah expected Bram to be furious, or to carry out his threat. Instead he sighed and shook his head.

"You're returning to Mordeina for the first time since the war, aren't you?" he asked. "Then you don't understand what it is like. Go then, and see. You won't understand until you are there. If you flee to my borders, I promise to protect you, so long as you admit your error."

"What do you mean by that?" Qurrah asked as Bram started to leave.

Instead of explaining, the king gave him a bitter smile.

# The Prison of Angels

"Pleasant travels," he said.

Tessanna stared as he left, as if driving nails into his back with her eyes. Qurrah took her hand, and she whirled on him, her look that of a crazed animal.

"He won't use us," she said.

"I know."

"I won't let him. I won't let *anyone.*"

He kissed her forehead.

"I know. So what do we do now?"

Before she could answer a trumpet blew from beyond the bridge. The soldiers shot into motion, grabbing helmets and readying weapons. Tessanna's cold hands wrapped around Qurrah's.

"I want to see," she said, pulling him along.

Many glared at them, but none were brave enough to stop them as they headed for the road. All along either side gathered Bram's army, banners carried high, armor polished to a shine. Lost amid the chaos, the two lovers peered down the road, to where King Antonil's army came riding.

# 6

Calm as King Antonil seemed, Tarlak thought he surely must have ice in his blood. How else did he remain so composed when staring at the army, ten thousand strong, that guarded the Bloodbrick Bridge?

"Well Tarlak, I can see you fidgeting over there," Antonil said as the two rode at the forefront of their army. "You're my advisor. Care to advise me?"

"I'm not sure there's any other way to explain it," Tarlak said. "He doesn't plan on letting us cross."

"I outnumber him three to one. Trying to stop us is madness."

"Bram hasn't always struck me as the most rational of men."

"Nonsense," Antonil said. "He's the most rational man I know. That's why he's so frustrating to the rest of us."

Tarlak shrugged.

"However you want to explain it, it still worries me. Is he playing with us, or does he really think a war is best for anyone? Games or madness, neither one I'd want to be involved with."

"Could you form a crossing for us if he refuses, perhaps farther north?"

Tarlak rubbed his chin as he stared at the river.

"Damming it wouldn't do much," he said. "River's too large, too deep. Levitating thirty thousand men over the water isn't going to happen, either. Best I could do is try to freeze the top, forming a bridge while letting the river continue to pass beneath. It'd take a lot of concentration, though, and I'd prefer we just walk across the stone bridge the idiot king is guarding."

"Duly noted. Bring me my generals. Until we see reason otherwise, we'll pretend Bram has every intention of letting us cross. I don't want to show up brimming for a fight."

"There's thirty thousand of us wearing armor and carrying swords, not counting the angels accompanying us," Tarlak said. "Unless we approach naked, we'll look prepared for a fight. But yes, keeping everyone calm is probably best."

The Prison of Angels

Tarlak turned his horse about, found the nearest general, and relayed Antonil's request for a meeting. That done, he returned to the front, putting himself at the far corner of the vanguard so he could not see or hear the discussion. So far the generals had shown significant mistrust of him and his yellow robes. Given the absolute destruction various spellcasters had rent upon the land during the Gods' War, he didn't blame them. Much.

As Antonil talked, Tarlak scanned King Bram's army. Ten thousand approximately, all appearing well-armed and well-trained. They ran about like ants upon seeing their approach, but Tarlak sensed they weren't there for war. The bridge had no defenses placed upon it, no barricades or spear walls. The same went for the men on the far side. They had built no ballista or catapults, weapons that could have devastated Antonil's army while they struggled to cross the bridge. No, either they planned an ambush, or a show of force. If it was a show of force, it was a hollow one. Antonil hadn't the slightest desire to invade Ker, not with his homeland still occupied by orcs. If it was an ambush…

He snapped his fingers, and fire sparked from his fingertips. If it was an ambush, they'd get to see just how much destruction a spellcaster could wreak.

"The king requests your presence," one of the fatter generals said, disturbing Tarlak and his thoughts.

"Very well," Tarlak said, nodding his head and then tugging on the reins of his horse. The Bloodbrick was less than a quarter mile away, and despite Antonil's assurances, Tarlak felt unease spreading through the men. He felt unease as well, but for a different reason. Something about the distant army felt vaguely…familiar, like a thorn in his mind.

"I want you at my side when we request passage," Antonil said as Tarlak rejoined him.

"I was thinking I presented greater tactical value elsewhere."

"And where's that?"

Tarlak gestured behind him.

"All the way in the back. If there's to be a fight, I'd prefer thirty thousand men be between me and it."

The laughter helped ease their tensions. Closer and closer loomed the bridge, until at last Tarlak and Antonil rode together toward Bram's army, a token guard on either side of them. Riding out to meet them was Lord Bram and his own personal squad of knights. Banners for either side flying high, Tarlak held his breath as his liege spoke.

"Greetings, King Bram," Antonil said. "My friend. My ally. Once again I march to my homeland, to retake what the orcs have desecrated with their presence. Have you raised an army to join me in this quest?"

Bram shook his head, laughing.

"After how your last crusade went? No, Antonil, I prefer my soldiers alive, not dead."

Tarlak noticed neither made mention of crossing the bridge. No doubt Antonil wanted Bram to offer it freely, and Bram wanted Antonil to ask no matter the answer he planned to give. The wizard let out a sigh. Politics. He hated it.

"Forgive me for my abruptness, but my time is short, and I have need of your bridge," Antonil said. "Would you grant my men and I permission to cross?"

"No. I will not."

Bram answered so smoothly, so quickly, that Tarlak could hardly believe it. He grabbed the side of Antonil's cloak and tugged as the simple answer echoed throughout the camps.

"He's lying," Tarlak said softly, so no one else would hear.

"How do you know?"

Behind them, Antonil's army was stirring, all of them expecting war, or at least some sort of skirmish for such blatant disrespect. Tarlak's mind whirled.

"He's too pleased with himself," Tarlak insisted. "He's testing you. He wants to know how you'll respond."

"How I'll respond? So be it." Antonil drew his sword, and he called out to Bram. "We are crossing, Bram. You have no stake in this, no right to deny me passage. I ride with thirty thousand, and if I must I can call forth a legion of angels. Do you still refuse?"

"I have the right of a sovereign lord to protect my borders," shouted Bram. "But I see even after all this time you will never consider me as such. Move quickly through my lands, Antonil. Do not consider me friend or ally. You war against the orcs on your own."

## The Prison of Angels

Bram turned about and barked a command. His army shifted so that the road between was clear. Without another word, the king rode over the bridge and vanished into the thick crowd of soldiers.

"Not very diplomatic of you," Tarlak muttered as the generals readied their army to march.

"I'm sick of this," Antonil said. "Here, back home, everywhere posturing and politics and betrayal. If he would refuse me, then fight me. If not, then don't waste my time. I will not play his game."

*Man after my own heart*, thought Tarlak.

As they rode across the Bloodbrick, Tarlak didn't bother to tell his king that he *had* played along, whether he'd wanted to or not. Bram had his answer, knew exactly how Antonil viewed his army and his borders. And of course, he just *had* to mention the angels.

Stepping off the bridge and into Ker, Tarlak felt the tingling in his mind grow stronger. He glanced about, unsure of what exactly he was searching for but convinced he'd know it if he saw it. And then, to his left, he spotted the large dark eyes that belonged to only one woman in all of Dezrel. He stiffened atop his horse, their eyes met, and Tarlak felt a shiver run through him as Tessanna offered him the slightest of smiles. A distant part of his mind realized Qurrah stood behind her, face downcast, unwilling to meet his gaze.

*Why are they here?* Tarlak wondered. *Have they turned against the angels after all?*

Sadly he knew he would get no answer. So onward he rode, the hour passing as Antonil's army slowly crossed into the land of Ker.

◈

Bram returned to his tent, furious at the series of events, though his pride dictated he hide it. Antonil had done his best to humiliate him, prove him the weaker. The only way to save face was to pretend the challenge beneath him, and showing frustration would only reveal it for the lie it was. Stepping inside his tent, he let out a sigh, set down his sword.

"I swear, Loreina, things were simpler when we fought armies of demons," he said. "And men were smarter, too."

Rising from the cot, her brown hair braided down to her waist, was his wife. She put her hands around his neck, kissed his lips, then smiled. It dimpled her face, making her look as young as she was when he first married her. The intelligence in her eyes, the fiery ambition, was there now as it had always been. With the encroachment of the angels it had only gotten brighter, so much she demanded to come with him instead of remaining behind in Angkar where it was safer.

"I heard Antonil's words with my own ears," she said. "He would deny your basic right to control your borders. He would deny your sovereignty. Do you believe me now?"

Bram swore, flung off his pauldrons so they fell in a clattering display. Loreina stepped back, gave him his space to brood.

"They won't invade," he said, shaking his head. "Stubborn and foolish as Antonil is, his eyes are only for his former kingdom. He is no threat, not if we stay out of the way of his hopeless crusades."

"It's not Antonil I fear," Loreina said. "It's his replacement."

It was true, of course. The whispering winds of politics blew south, and they whispered with greater certainty Antonil's fate. His grip on Mordan was slipping away with each passing month. Whether through death in battle, betrayal in court, or a full blown uprising of nobles, his time as king approached its end.

"What more can we do?" Bram asked. "His army is the greater, doubly so if you include his angels. Open warfare against Mordan would destroy us all, and that cannot happen. If we fall, then the last hope of there being a free nation in all of Dezrel, at least one not ruled by monsters, falls with us."

Loreina slipped closer, put her hands around his waist.

"Patience," she said. "It is not the same as doing nothing. We keep our eyes open. There will come a time when Antonil is weak, when the angels no longer fly above him. It is in that moment we will refuse to bow our knee. It is in that moment we will show the world we will not be mocked or ignored. We are a sovereign nation, not a footstool."

She was on her knees now, her hands drifting down to his belt.

"And remember," she said to him. "You must remain calm around your men. Don't worry. I'll help you with that."

Bram swallowed, close his eyes, and then mentally swore a hundred times when he heard someone call his name from outside the tent. He recognized the voice, too. It was Sir Ian Millar, his most trusted knight and commander of his armies. The man's service had been invaluable during the Gods' War.

"Yes?" Bram asked through the fabric of the tent.

"Milord, I would seek your advice."

"Can it wait?"

"I fear it cannot."

Bram let out a sigh, pushed back his wife.

"Later," he told her.

"I have duties I must attend," she said, rising from her knees.

"Then much later."

His mood now even worse, Bram stormed out of his tent, still tightening his belt.

"What is it?" he asked Ian. The knight saluted, and the worry in his eyes dispelled Bram's immature mood.

"If you would, please follow me while I explain," the knight said, spinning on his heels and marching toward the bridge.

"Has there been trouble with Antonil's men during the crossing?" Bram asked.

"Nothing beyond the ordinary. It isn't Antonil's men I'm unsure of how to deal with. Watch your step, and then look to the sky."

Bram's stomach tightened, and he knew what he'd see before he ever looked skyward. Flying in v-formations were several dozen angels. Golden-hued armor glinted in the sunlight, and in their hands were the unmistakable shapes of swords, shields, and spears.

"Do they accompany Antonil's men, or are they merely seeing them off?" Bram asked, lifting a hand to shade his eyes as he looked.

"So far they have not crossed the border," Ian said. "They're merely circling their current position. I've ordered our archers ready just in case."

"In case what? You would spark war while Antonil's army marches through the very center of our camp?"

Beside him, Ian stiffened.

"Their kind has been banned from Ker," he said. "Forgive me if I erred in preparing to enforce your laws."

"We gave Antonil's army freedom to pass," Bram said. "One might consider the angels part of that army."

"Then they should have stated as much. I do not care what any one person might say. What do *you* say, milord?"

Bram stared at the angels, his stomach continuing to twist. It felt like there were stones grinding within him. Just the sight of the creatures was enough to make him feel a flutter of fear. Their size, their speed, their ability to circumvent any standard defensive formation or benefit of terrain…they were so clearly not of Dezrel. The hairs on his neck lifted.

"If they try to fly over, let loose our arrows," Bram said.

"If they remain as high as they are, we won't hit them."

"I'm counting on it. Send them a message, and make it as clear as the message Antonil sent me."

Together they watched as the remainder of Antonil's army slowly crossed over the bridge, through the camp, and into the heart of Ker, a great train of wagons marking the last of their passing. It took the greater part of an hour, and all the while the angels circled.

"Do they ever get tired?" Ian asked, still on edge.

"Apparently not."

So far the angels showed no inclination of following Antonil into Ker. As much as Bram wanted a chance to save face, he felt himself beginning to relax.

"Even if they don't pass now, they might wait until dark, or perhaps fly farther north beforehand," Ian suggested while rubbing his neck, which was no doubt sore from spending so much time staring up at the sky. "Bridges mean nothing to their kind."

"No," Bram said. "I know them too well. To cross in secret would mean admitting they know what they do is wrong, or should be hidden. If they're to spit in the face of my laws, they'll do it here, now."

Bram's words caught in his throat. As if they could hear him, one of the angel formations suddenly dipped lower, curling

# The Prison of Angels

around to fly directly over the bridge. Ian saw it, immediately began running about shouting orders. Bram watched their approach, did his best to calculate the angle. Despite his fury for their insolence, he felt a sudden spike of panic. They were coming in far too low, and would fly within the reach of his archers.

"Belay that order!" Bram shouted, but it was too late. The angels were streaking in at inhuman speeds, and for the past hour the archers had been given a single, specific command: if the angels flew over, let loose with all they had.

Up into the air sailed hundreds of arrows, rising together like an inverse rain. The group of angels, seven in all, flared their wings and tried to rise. It didn't matter. Bram saw the arrows climb, saw war ready to spill forth before him. News of a dead angel, let alone seven, would be all it'd take for those watching his nation with hungry eyes to put their plans in motion.

And then a shadow tore open in the air, spreading wide like a shield. Within it were a legion of six-fingered hands, their skin shining a translucent purple. They batted at the arrows, snapping them with a mere touch, as above the seven angels beat their wings and lifted higher into the air. The other formations circled close, and Bram could almost taste the tension spreading. When the last of the arrows was a cloud of splinters falling back to Dezrel, the dark collection of hands vanished as if they had never been.

"What in Karak's name was that?" Ian asked, rejoining his king's side.

"An undeserved gift," Bram said. He nodded to the angels. "What do they wait for?"

"They're discussing," Ian said, having watched them closely.

"Prepare the archers just in case. I was a fool, but not this time. If they swoop in again, they'll be coming for blood. If we're lucky we'll have them dead before Antonil's men find out and try to return the favor."

Before Ian could carry out the order, the angels gathered together into one large formation, turned north, and flew away. Bram closed his eyes, let out a sigh of relief. His army's presence at the Bloodbrick was meant as a message, a warning. The last thing he truly wanted was war.

"Where are our two guests?" he asked.

"I'll lead you to them."

Deep within their camp, the half-orc and his sorceress had been surrounded by his soldiers. So far none of his men had drawn blades or made any threatening motion. Bram understood their confusion. The spell they'd cast had countered an order given by their king, but Bram had also held private conversations with the two prior to Antonil's arrival. Ian called for them to make way, and realizing their king had arrived, they quickly parted.

"Your archers have terrible aim," Qurrah said before Bram could open his mouth. "I dare say you frightened them far more than you intended."

The half-orc was giving him an out, and Bram gladly took it.

"The fault is mine for not giving proper orders, but your magic will frighten them more than my arrows. Move freely through my lands, half-orc, and know you will always be considered a close ally and friend."

Bram meant it, too. Qurrah had read the circumstances and events correctly and then acted to prevent a war Bram himself had admitted he didn't want. Such a powerful ally, he thought. If only he could somehow convince the half-orc and his strange bride to stay at his side, to use their intelligence and power for something greater than themselves.

"Your kindness is overwhelming," Tessanna said. Her hands were wrapped around Qurrah's arm, hugging him tightly. Bram sensed sarcasm in her words. There was no way for him to know their reasons for protecting the angels, not fully, so he let the matter drop. Instead he tilted his head the tiniest amount to show his respect, then marched away.

"What now?" Ian asked him.

"Now we plan," he said, heading for his tent. "Word of what just happened will spread through Mordan quickly enough, and whatever the aftermath, we must be ready."

He glanced to the sky, where the angels were but distant specks.

"Their brashness grows. War is coming, Ian, whether we want it or not. One god has fallen from this land, and the other hungers to possess the rest. How long until they deem our entire nation full of sinners needing repentance by sword?"

"They won't go that far," Ian quietly insisted. "I spoke with many angels during the war. We fought alongside them, and they were selfless allies. They cherish life. They embrace peace, and seek only to protect the innocent."

"That was when we warred against demons," Bram said, shaking his head. "That was when they knew their purpose. Five years is a long time, Ian. Long enough to forget the past. Long enough to become all too human."

Bram looked once more to the sky, shook his head and turned away.

# 7

It was the happiest day of Jessilynn's life, broken only by momentary terror every time Sonowin banked one way or another, forcing her to hold Dieredon tighter lest she fall. Given how they flew high enough to pierce the clouds, it would be a very, very long fall.

"You'd catch me, right?" she asked Dieredon, needing to shout directly into his ear to be heard over the wind that ripped at their hair and clothes. She sat bareback atop the winged horse, with nothing to hold onto but the elf's waist, which she kept in a deathlock.

"If you fell?" Dieredon asked, glancing back at her.

She nodded.

"Most likely," he said. He stared at her, then gently tugged on the reins. Sonowin's great wings shifted angle, and they dipped lower with a stomach-churning lurch. When they leveled out, the clouds were far above them.

"Is it easier to breathe now?" he asked.

Meekly, Jessilynn nodded.

"I didn't want to complain," she said, and she meant it. Her excitement was great, and she hated to spoil it just because her head felt strangely light, or because her stomach seemed ready to empty the little remnants of her breakfast across miles and miles of faded grass.

The land rolled along as they flew north. Jessilynn spent a moment with her eyes closed, her forehead resting against Dieredon's back. Slowly her stomach calmed, the world seeming to spin a little bit less. Rejuvenated, she looked out over the land and felt her spirit soar. Nothing compared to flying like a bird, seeing the shifting of the rivers and the entire limits of vast forests. Carefully she leaned a little to the right, to better see past Sonowin's bobbing head.

"Is that it?" she shouted, almost pointing before thinking better of it.

# The Prison of Angels

"If you mean the gorge, then yes. We're almost to the Bone Ditch."

It was surreal seeing it from such height, a place that had been nothing more than a story to her while growing up. It was said that when Celestia created the orcs, she split the land, starting at where the Rigon flowed out of the northern mountains. It was a massive chasm now, the rock a faded red, the cliff faces sheer. At the very bottom the Rigon flowed along, steady as ever. The great span and deadly fall had been one of the most significant protections the eastern land of Neldar had against the creatures that had been trapped there. But during the Gods' War the orcs within had been loosed, the prophet using his dark magic to aid their crossing.

"What do we do when we arrive?" Jessilynn asked, thinking of the bridges the orcs had supposedly constructed over the past few years.

Dieredon gave her a strange look.

"Land."

Sonowin banked lower, and the growing proximity to the ground increased her sense of speed. The great chasm wound below them like a giant snake, until what had been a speck in the distance grew and grew, and she realized it was the orc bridge crossing the Bone Ditch. There was only one, constructed of weather-worn wood and thick ropes bound together with crude knots. Just thinking about crossing it made Jessilynn sick to her stomach. Sonowin looped around once, and then a hundred yards out from the western side they landed on the dull yellow grass of the Wedge.

Jessilynn leapt off the winged horse, her knees wobbling. Falling down, she clutched the grass as vomit climbed her throat.

"Focus on breathing," Dieredon said, standing beside her. "Even elves sometimes feel discomfort from the speed and heights we climb."

It made Jessilynn feel a little better as she puked onto the grass. Just a little.

"I'm fine," she said, forcing herself to a stand. She pulled her bow off her back and scanned the bridge, looking for any threats. She saw none, and in her mind she heard no subtle warning of Ashhur alerting her to danger, either.

"Where are they?" she asked.

Dieredon frowned.

"Follow me," he said. "Stay silent, and stay alert. Do not look ahead, but behind and to the sides. Trust my eyes for the front."

"Yes, sir," she said.

Dieredon started to walk, then stopped.

"'Sir' is a human title," he said.

She immediately blushed.

"I'm sorry," she said. "I just wanted to show respect. What should I call you?"

Dieredon cocked his head to the side.

"My name?"

The way he said it made it sound so simple, and she felt her blush growing, much as she hated it. She was not some immature girl. Her monthlies had begun years before, and by all rights she was a woman grown, but something about Dieredon made her feel so stupid, so unsure and unskilled. A simple berating by him shouldn't embarrass her, especially when it wasn't much of a berating at all.

Begging Ashhur to clear her head and nerves, she rapidly nodded.

"Of course," she said. "Lead on."

"Good. Keep your bow at ready, and follow behind me at ten paces."

With a near fanatical obsession she followed his orders, and together they made their way to the ramshackle bridge. Every few moments she glanced behind them, where the yellow grass of the Wedge stretched on and on for miles. No matter how often she looked, she saw no signs of life. Up ahead was just as still, and when they reached the first plank of the bridge, Dieredon beckoned her over.

"Look here," he said, pointing to a faded smear of dirt upon of wood. Jessilynn looked, but whatever he saw, she did not.

"It's been at least three months since anyone crossed this bridge," he explained.

"Isn't that a good thing?" she asked. From what she understood, having orcs escape their prison was about as bad as it got.

Dieredon glanced across the bridge to the east.

"Not if there are no orcs left to cross," he said. "Sonowin, come!"

His sudden worry made Jessilynn nervous as she climbed atop the winged horse. Without any of his usual attempts for steadiness, Dieredon tugged on the reins, sending them flying over the Bone Ditch and into the greener lands beyond.

"Where are we going?" she shouted.

"The Green Castle."

She dared not ask why. She felt intrusive enough as it was. For three days they'd camped north of the Citadel, and he'd spent hours fixing her stance, showing her the proper way to grip her bow and draw an arrow. By the third day she could tell he'd grown restless, and come the fourth they'd begun their flight northeast. Hearing the worry in his voice put a seed of guilt in her stomach. What if they arrived somewhere too late, and it was all because of her training? Could she even stay with him in good conscience if that were the case?

They remained low to the ground, passing over hilly lands that seemed to go on forever. The grass was lush, showing the healthy luster of spring. Slowly the hills evened out, and then in the far distance she saw a faint hint of stone that rapidly took the shape of a circular wall built atop a hill. Jessilynn almost asked Dieredon if that was the Green Castle, then realized the stupidity of the question. Beyond the outer circular walls was a slender tower, every facing covered with what she guessed to be vines. Nearer and nearer they flew. The castle took on a more vivid green, and even from her distance she could see the large clusters of flowers that speckled the castle.

Dieredon circled twice, his eyes scanning the ground. His frown deepened, but still he ordered Sonowin to land. Just inside the inner walls the winged horse touched ground. Dieredon leapt off before the beast was still, and he offered her a hand.

"What's wrong?" she asked as she took it. "It's so quiet here."

"This castle belonged to Lord Sully. He was never a friend of elvenkind, but he did aid us in keeping the orcs at bay. When last I left here, his men were patrolling the Bone Ditch to prevent the construction of any more bridges." He gestured about the empty courtyard. "It shouldn't *be* quiet. There should be servants, soldiers, children..."

He pulled off his bow, then hurried toward the castle. Jessilynn tugged free her own bow and ran after him. Her plodding footsteps seemed so loud compared to the elf's silent passage. They crossed through the courtyard, stopping at the large castle doors. They were shut, with no visible sign of attack. Dieredon's frown deepened. The elf briefly investigated the castle doors, tugged once to confirm they were still locked, then peered up the castle walls.

"Check the outer grounds for any signs of life," he said, hopping atop of Sonowin. "I'll investigate the castle, see if I can discover where they've fled. If you find yourself in trouble, whistle as loud as you can."

"I will," Jessilynn said. She clutched her bow and tried not to let her nervousness show. Being alone in the great courtyard made her uneasy. Something had gone terribly wrong, and they both knew it. Dieredon flew higher and higher until he was even with one of the upper windows of a tower, then leapt off Sonowin's back. He vanished into the stone edifice. Wanting to be useful, Jessilynn started scanning the area, trying to decide what she was even looking for.

Aimlessly, she began walking through the courtyard, slowly making her way around to the western side. The hairs on the back of her neck began to stand as more and more things looked askew. She found overturned barrels, broken shafts of wood that might have been spears, bits of shredded clothing. Against one wall of the tower she saw a stain, and stepping closer, she saw the stone was chipped. The stain was, without a doubt, a great smear of blood.

When her fingers brushed against it she heard a distant sound, one she could hardly believe.

Laughter?

Closing her eyes, she did her best to listen, and sure enough she heard it again. From somewhere in the building, she decided, but where? With how large the tower was, it'd take time for Dieredon to find them if he also heard. Jogging alongside the stone, Jessilynn looked for an alternate entrance beyond the locked gates. Rounding the southwest corner, she found a small jut built out from the wall, just narrow enough for a single man to pass through. It was blocked by a single gate. A way to flank attackers at the front gate if the situation demanded it, she guessed. Beyond the iron gate was a second wooden door. From beyond that, she heard another round of muffled laughter.

"Dieredon?" she called out, but so pathetic was her cry that she doubted anyone could have heard her. She swallowed, told herself to be brave. She was a paladin of Ashhur. She was supposed to be a champion of mankind, not a girl quaking in fear at a stranger's laughter.

She touched the gate. With a grinding squeak it pushed inward. It took a moment for her to overcome her surprise. She'd been convinced it would be locked like the front gates had been. Of course, there was still the wooden doors just beyond. Stepping into the dark passageway, she grabbed the handle and pulled.

It opened with a dull thud, revealing a long, unlit hallway. Offering a prayer to Ashhur for safety, she pulled an arrow out of her quiver and pressed it against the string of her bow. The arrowhead lit up with a soft blue-white glow, and with its light guiding her, she stepped into the hallway. The echoes of her footfalls made her wince, and again she thought of Dieredon's silent passing. Jessilynn wore lighter armor than the other paladins, a special suit requested by Jerico himself from a traveling smith. It was heavy leather, studded, with her chest and shoulders reinforced with a variety of plate and chain. She could move far easier than the others in their platemail, but it was still heavy, and worse, noisy. Each step she took sounded like thunder. Her fear made the light of her arrow falter until she could barely see five feet before her.

Again she heard laughter, this time of two different men. Their voices were deep, boisterous, yet muffled too much for her to make out the words they occasionally spoke.

"Hello?" she called out, traveling deeper into the Green Castle. "Is someone there?"

At the sound of her voice the laughter stopped. Jessilynn's heart caught in her throat as she heard movement and the rattle of weaponry. She took a step back, stumbling as her foot landed atop a heavy stone. She flung her elbow to the side to brace herself against the wall, except the wall wasn't there. She landed on hard dirt. The arrow and bow fell from her hands, clattered to the ground in the darkness.

*Stay calm,* Jessilynn told herself. *Stay calm, and don't panic. Feel along the ground.*

The bow was easy enough to find given its size. For another moment she felt for the arrow, then realized she had a dozen more in the quiver on her back. Drawing another, she notched it on the string. The metal arrowhead brightened, surrounded by the glow of her faith, and finally able to see, she looked about.

She was in a large tunnel that stretched sharply into the earth for a distance far beyond the reach of her light. Spinning around, she found the broken bricks of the castle wall, the gap the size of a large man. The panic she'd fought against assaulted her at double strength. The castle hadn't been taken from outside. It'd been tunneled into and taken from within.

She stepped out, pointed her arrow down the hall. She heard a door open, and yellow eyes glinted a mere fifty feet away. Jessilynn let fly her arrow, and as it streaked down the hall she was finally able to see. Orcs, two of them, each wearing crude armor and carrying swords. The arrow struck the first in the chest, blasting him off his feet. The other let out a yell, screaming in alarm. Jessilynn flung her bow across her back and ran. The exit looked so small, yet so bright. Her heart pounded in her ears as she heard more voices clamoring behind her. It sounded like an entire army awakening.

"Dieredon!" she screamed, fear giving strength to her legs. She blasted through the door and out into the painful daylight. "Dieredon!"

Without slowing she raced into the courtyard, wanting to put as much distance between her and the castle as possible. Her lungs burned, and when she reached where they had first landed she spun in circles, looking for Sonowin's great wings. She didn't see them, or the horse they were attached to, anywhere.

From the side entrance orcs burst out, rounding the corner with weapons drawn. At first there were only a few, and they squinted against the light. Grabbing her bow, Jessilynn let fly an arrow at the closest. It sailed wide, bouncing twice off the dirt.

Her eyes widened as the orc closed the distance, rusty sword lifted high to strike. Before she could nock another, an arrow flew in from the sky, piercing the orc's throat. The shaft remained halfway embedded, and dark blood poured around it.

"Your hand!" she heard Dieredon shout from high above. Flinging her bow back over her shoulder, she turned around and lifted her arms. Sonowin dove toward her, Dieredon on her back releasing arrow after arrow. They sailed over her head, and she heard pained cries from behind each time one found purchase. The elf put aside his bow, reached down, and yanked her onto Sonowin's back as the winged horse momentarily halted in place. Then they were moving skyward, and the feel of the wind was enough to bring Jessilynn to tears.

She clutched the elf tightly, then looked down to the castle. In the courtyard swarmed hundreds of orcs.

"They tunneled in," she shouted, struggling to regain her composure.

"Then all is lost in the Hillock. The orcs have emptied out of the Wedge, every last one of them. Thousands upon thousands, greater than any army of man."

Sonowin's wings steadied, and Jessilynn loosened her grip on Dieredon's waist, chastising herself for being so afraid. What was the point of all those years of training under Lathaar and Jerico if she would panic against the very first enemy she ever faced? Still, she couldn't chase away the image of the orc falling backward, her arrow crushing his chest as if she'd struck him with a maul. The way the blood had splattered against the walls, colored purple by the blue hue of her arrow...

"Where do we go now?" she asked, trying to think about anything else.

"The east is theirs, and so the west we must protect," he said. "Over the past five years I've never received word of any other of the races traveling into Neldar."

"Isn't that a good thing?"

"The door to their cage is open in the east, yet they remain behind," Dieredon shouted, shaking his head. "The question is...why?"

She could not imagine a reason. The wildlands were the elf's expertise, not hers. She glanced behind her, offering a prayer for anyone that might still remain lost or hidden in the great nation of Neldar. Celestia's cursed children had taken them as their own, and from the laughter she heard deep within the castle, the orcs were more than comfortable in their new home.

"I'm sorry," she shouted.

"For what?"

"For panicking."

Dieredon lessened his grip on the reins so he might turn about to look at her.

"Are you alive?" he asked her.

"Yes?"

"And did you act when confronted by your enemy, or did you do nothing?"

"I killed one," she admitted. "And then I ran for you."

"Then you have nothing to apologize for. Even for a human you are young, so do not judge yourself so harshly. Remember, you are with me to learn, not to prove you have no need of learning."

He put his back to her, fell silent.

"However," he said, turning back around. A smile was on his face, but it quickly vanished. "You still missed your mark during my descent. Sonowin, take us down somewhere quiet. I think Jessilynn needs an hour of practice to remind her not to rush her aim."

Sonowin let out a snort, and then down they went.

## 8

Ezekai circled the town of Norstrom, debating whether he should land. Ever since the execution of the farmer, Colton, he'd felt uneasy with his duties. A strong part of him wished to speak with Azariah, but the high priest was always so busy that Ezekai continued to postpone doing so. He knew he had been well within the law: Colton had brutally murdered a man in front of the entire town, in front of his own child. But he'd also been a good man, an honest, hardworking man. What madness could have driven him into an act so vile? Was his desire for torment, for retribution, so much greater than his desire for the salvation of others?

Of course it was, Ezekai thought. That was the failing of man. But he wouldn't let it be *his* failing. They just needed to be shown the way. And as much as Ezekai had been troubled by the events, the town continued on as it always had, as it perhaps always would. He saw the farmers in the fields, the shopkeepers selling their wares, plain men and women wandering the streets, perhaps to work, perhaps to shop, perhaps to play. They had not called for him with their scepter, but he landed anyway, folding his wings behind him as he glanced up and down the road.

Children stared at him in awe, as did many of the adults. A few were wary, and one older woman continued on down the street as if she never saw him. It tugged at Ezekai's heart. Always awe, always fear and doubt. Would they ever look upon his arrival with love? Was their trust so terrible a thing for him to yearn for?

"May I help you?" an older gentlemen asked, having rushed out of his rocking chair at the front of the tavern to greet the angel. He walked with a cane, his limp painful to watch as he approached. Ezekai reached out his hand and touched the man's knee.

"Be well," he said, and he felt the magic flowing out of him. It took more than he'd expected to banish the swelling, but then again, everything seemed to take more effort lately. Every angel knew of the priests' magic fading away. So far Ezekai had thought himself unaffected, but now he wondered if that assumption was erroneous.

"Thank you," the old man said, flexing the leg while smiling. "Truly a blessing to have you come this day. We did not think to use the scepter for just the boy, but perhaps Ashhur's wisdom has decided otherwise."

"Perhaps," said Ezekai. "So there is need of me?"

"Indeed," the man said, beckoning.

Ezekai was taken to a small home, one like thousands of others he had visited before. The smell of sickness was strong the moment the door opened. Ezekai bowed his head to the woman who greeted them. Her face was pale, haggard, with her hair pulled back from her face in a knot.

"May I enter?" Ezekai asked.

"Ashhur bless you, of course," the woman said. "My name's Maria."

"Ashhur's peace be with you, Maria."

Wings folded behind him, Ezekai stepped inside, then dismissed the older man. The angel had to keep his head hunched, his height beyond that of normal humans. Just before him was a fireplace, and lying beside it was a young boy, about four years of age from what he guessed.

"That's my son, Kaisen," Maria said, quickly kneeling at the boy's side. "He's been running a fever for four days now, and each night his cough's gotten worse and worse. I told them to use the scepter, to call for someone, but they wouldn't. They said he'd be fine, that he'd…but that cough, he can't even breathe when it hits him."

She looked near tears. Ezekai smiled at her, wishing to do all he could to comfort her. No doubt she'd been sleeping little, each night worrying more and more for her precious child. Sitting down on his knees beside Kaisen, the angel reached out a hand and touched his forehead. The heat was immediately apparent, the fever burning deep within him.

"I've done what I can to make him drink," Maria said. "Wormroot also worked on the fever for a day or two, but then stopped…"

# The Prison of Angels

"You've done well," Ezekai said, still focused on the child. The sickness radiated out from his lungs, and in Ezekai's mind it shone like a red spot amid a field of white. Frowning, he placed both his hands on Kaisen's chest and closed his eyes.

"Help me, Ashhur," he prayed. "I know this is beyond me, but nothing is beyond you."

The power flowed from him with a strength that took his breath away. His arms shook, his head pounded, and still he wondered if it would be enough. So weak, he felt so weak when it came to matters of healing and faith. Kaisen coughed, first wildly, then less so. Maria watched for a moment, then was unable to keep herself away. She clutched her child, her hair coming loose from its knot and falling across the angel's hands as Ezekai continued to pray. Smaller and smaller shrank the red sickness until it was gone, the fever in the boy's flesh beginning to subside.

Ezekai took in a deep breath, then slowly stood.

"I doubt he would have lasted the night," he said, surprised by how much his voice shook. "Four days, you say? Why was I not summoned sooner?"

Maria was crying as she held her child.

"I told them to," she said, not looking at him. "I told them to, but they wouldn't listen. They said…they said it wasn't necessary. That he'd get better."

Ezekai's mouth dropped open, hardly able to believe it. Maria was lying to him. He sensed it in his gut with the properties Ashhur had bestowed upon all his angels. Lying…but why?

"Maria," he said, trying to keep his tone gentle. "I know you hide something from me. Why was the scepter not used? In your heart you knew Kaisen needed my aid. Someone else denied you. Tell me why."

Maria sniffed, still refusing to look at him.

"They'll be mad at me," she said.

It was no lie.

"Who are *they*?"

She gestured to the door and the village beyond.

"They," she said.

"You are under my protection, as are all of the people here. Please…"

She looked up at him with red eyes.

"They didn't want you to see what they did to Saul."

The words, the meaning, the mystery; it all sent a chill down his spine. He didn't even know he could feel anger and fear simultaneously like that. He'd thought it a lost human emotion. Apparently not.

"Where?" he whispered.

She told him. He knelt down, kissed her forehead, then her son's.

"Stay here," he said.

Exiting the home, he let his wings stretch wide. It felt good, but it was the only pleasurable thing he felt. With several heavy beats he took to the air, then circled around to the northern end of the town. There, hanging from a pole, he found the body of the man who had been Saul Reid. His skin was dry from exposure to the sun, with rips in it showing rot. The crows had been at the corpse as well, further deteriorating it. The worst, though, was where the man's crotch had been. All that remained of his genitals was a brutal collection of gore and pus.

Ezekai landed, his hand reaching for his sword.

"What has been done here?" he roared to the village. "All of you, come to me and answer for this!"

Slowly they gathered, men and women lurking at the edges of homes and beyond, not daring to near the pole. None spoke. Again Ezekai demanded answers, his voice carrying. Some went running out to the fields. With each passing second of silence, Ezekai felt his anger grow.

"You," he said, pointing at a brown-haired woman leaning against a nearby home. "Who has done this?"

"Not my place to say," she said. "Ask the men. They're coming."

Another he asked, this a boy of twelve.

"My pa said not to say, not even to you," the child insisted, and it was the truth.

Ezekai turned about and looked to the fields. A group of thirty men was approaching, instruments of their trade slung over their shoulders. He sensed no anger in them, no danger, just…caution. Next to Ezekai, the rotting body continued to slowly swing.

## The Prison of Angels

When the group arrived, they crossed their arms and kicked their feet into the dirt, as if waiting for something. Ezekai had no patience for any of it.

"I demand an explanation," he said.

"He was just like Locke," said one of the men. He was a thin fellow, and the dirt on his face looked like it belonged there. From the way the others looked to him he appeared to be the one in charge of the most recent events. "They did stuff together, the two of them. He admitted as much when we caught him peeping in through my little girl's window."

"You tortured this knowledge out of him?"

The men glanced to one another.

"We made him talk," another admitted.

Ezekai closed his eyes, meaning to pray for calm, but the stench of the corpse was too near. They had killed the man, mutilated him, and then hung him up for all to see. Because of this they nearly let an innocent child die, all so they might hide their deed. When Ezekai opened his eyes, he felt fury burning in his blood.

"You tortured, mutilated, and then murdered a man," he said to them. "Without law. Without justice. Without proof."

"We heard it from his mouth," someone shouted.

"He confessed!" shouted another.

"Under torture!" Ezekai insisted. "How do you know he spoke truth?"

"What of you?" asked the thin fellow with the dirty face. They were closer now, starting to surround him. "How do we know you spoke truth when you forgave Locke? If he fell on his knees and begged, would you have let that monster remain in our village?"

There was no way for Ezekai to know, and no way to explain. When Locke had cast himself to the dirt, the guilt and sorrow overwhelmed every strand of his soul, his yearning for salvation beyond anything Ezekai could describe. The man hated himself, hated his life. Ezekai had shown him a ray of light, had hoped to cure him of the vile desires, and then in that light Locke had asked for forgiveness from a man he'd wronged. That man, Colton, had murdered him in cold blood. Yet now, when faced with another similar situation, the townspeople chose not to embrace the forgiveness, but instead the murderer? It was more than Ezekai could understand. He didn't *want* to understand it. He didn't want to believe it. He cherished these people. He protected them. He *loved* them, even the poor, sick Saul that hung from a rope.

Ezekai lifted his sword.

"This cannot happen," he told them. "It *will not* happen, not again. Not ever."

He turned to cut free the body only to find a wall blocking him. The men were gathering together, holding their rakes, shovels, and scythes as weapons against him.

"He hangs," said the man in charge. "We called no angel, and we're a hundred miles from Mordeina. What Saul did deserved death by every law known to us, even yours, and we administered that law. Don't you dare cut him down."

"The law called for you to shred his loins? The law said your fear of being caught allows a child to die of sickness? Move aside, now."

They did not. He saw their fear, sensed it, but they wouldn't move. Not on their own. But Ezekai would make them. He flung himself forward, his blade whirling. Most of the men turned to flee, but a few tried to fight. Their instruments shattered against his shining blade, their worn iron nothing compared to steel forged in the smiths of eternity. Ezekai shifted, pushed, doing everything possible to harm not a single man. When he cleared the other side, he flapped his wings, rose into the air, and then sliced through the rope.

Saul's body crumpled to the ground. Ezekai landed before it and met the eyes of those who stood against him.

"Bury him," he commanded.

"Bury him yourself," said the dirty-faced man. "What are you going to do if we don't? Kill us?"

Ezekai's jaw trembled.

"You tread on dangerous ground," he said softly. "You aren't above mercy. You aren't wiser than the heavens."

He grabbed the rope and flew, flew until he found a spot far away from the town. Landing on the soft grass, he jammed his sword into the dirt, twisted it to the side, and then tore into the ground. With his bare hands he dug free the rest. His skin was tough, but so was the ground, and it wasn't long before drops of his scarlet blood mixed with the earth. Deeper and deeper he dug the grave, moving with greater urgency. Without a word he pushed the corpse into the hole, then started filling it. At last it was finished, and with solemn silence he sat on his knees. With his wings he patted down the dirt atop the grave, and with his tears he marked the headstone.

Ezekai looked to his sword, its shining blade now covered with dirt, and remembered the impulse he'd felt as the humans challenged him. The desire to prove them wrong. The desire to end their anger, pride, and hatred. The desire to kill.

"Help us, Ashhur," Ezekai said, curling his body together, crumpling his bleeding hands into the loose earth of the grave beneath his chest. "Heavens help us, what are we becoming?"

Harruq stepped out into the private courtyard, still adjusting the straps of his armor. His swords swung wildly at his hips, the buckle not tightened correctly. Not that it mattered. He didn't march into battle, just a spar, one he desperately, desperately needed.

"I was beginning to think you'd changed your mind," Judarius said. An easy smile was on the angel's face, his enormous mace resting across one shoulder. His eyes, a mixture of green and gold, sparkled.

"I'm killing Antonil the moment he gets back," Harruq said, giving his belt a savage tug to tighten it. "Thought it might be best to confess that now, get it all out of the way."

"Pressures of running a kingdom?"

"Pressures of running it badly. Careful with your swings, by the way. I've been told these flower pots are rather old."

Judarius looked at the flowers, growing in vases of white marble, and then shrugged.

"I will do my best," he said. "But if I must, I will replace them with vases of pearl and gold from Avlimar. Are you ready, half-orc?"

Harruq drew his swords, immediately feeling the tension in his muscles beginning to ease. Standing there with his blades in his hands made him think to his days training with Haern the

Watcher. Back then he'd relied on strength alone, his fighting style the equivalent of a bull running someone over. He liked to think he was better now, and as Judarius raised his mace, Harruq wondered if Haern would be proud of him. It was a strange thought, a bitter remembrance, and it nearly cost him his first hit. Judarius's mace swung in, almost lazy compared to what the mighty warrior was capable of. Harruq crossed his swords and blocked, letting out a grunt as he did.

"What's that?" Judarius asked, stepping back and slamming the hilt of the mace toward Harruq's gut. "Have you gotten fat already?"

Harruq shoved the wood aside, twirled Salvation in his left hand, and then thrust. The angel's mace was already turning, easily shoving the blade high. Two more hits he tried, his swords thudding against the enchanted wood that made up the mace's handle. More and more, as sweat ran down his face and neck, Harruq felt his stress ease. This was what he knew. Parry, dodge, thrust, counter. Weapon colliding against weapon, strength meeting strength. What madness had made Antonil think he could handle constant requests for money he did not have, justice he did not understand, and soldiers he could not give?

"You've slowed," Judarius said, feigning an attack but then assaulting anyway. The mace came slamming in, and it took all of Harruq's strength to stand against it.

"I'm getting old. Happens to the best of us."

"You? Old?" Condemnation swung through the air inches from the angel's chestpiece. "You have elf blood in your veins. I think you have a good fifty years more before you can consider yourself worthy of a few gray hairs."

It was something Aurelia had mentioned long before, and it still struck Harruq as odd. It also made him annoyed. So he was just out of practice, then, too lazy and stressed to perform the exercises Haern had taught him. He thought back to when he'd fought the demon god, Thulos, standing against him even when the angels could not. He was pretty sure that old Harruq would wallop the current one, and the aggravation sent him on the offensive, a constant assault that Judarius still blocked with ease.

"You won last we fought," Judarius said. "What happened?"

He finally leapt into the air, his great wings flapping to launch him several feet backward. He landed beside the wall of the courtyard, his wings knocking over two different flower vases. They hit with dull thuds but did not break. Harruq winced anyway.

"I think they'd make me pay for that," he said.

Judarius gave him an incredulous look.

"We spar, yet all you can think about are flowers? Perhaps you should have stayed on your throne."

Harruq settled into a stance, his swords crossed before him as he struggled to regain his breath.

"You haven't scored a hit yet," he said, trying to keep his temper in check.

"I haven't tried."

"If you won't try, then you're right, I should have stayed on the throne. After all, I'd hate to waste my time."

A bit of disappointment flashed in Judarius's eyes. His chiseled body tensed, and he readied his mace.

"Careful," he said. "It isn't wise to taunt an angel."

Harruq smirked.

"Nor a half-orc."

Judarius used his wings to add to his momentum, hurtling across the courtyard with his mace in full swing. For a brief moment Harruq felt afraid, but his pride pushed it away. Legs tensed, mouth pulled into a snarl, he flung both his blades in the way of the mighty weapon.

The shock of the hit stole his breath away, and he flew several feet back, colliding with a marble pillar built near the outer ring of the garden. Harruq slumped against it, leaning his head back and laughing.

"Lost my edge in fighting, too," he said. "Good to know I'm now worthless everywhere."

Judarius approached, his mace flung over his shoulder. There was no joy in his eyes despite his victory.

"You're more troubled than I thought," he said. "Is it really so terrible?"

Harruq let out a sigh as he closed his eyes.

"I was prepared for it to be tough," he said. "But this is still so much worse than I ever could have believed. Everyone looks to me as if I wield so much power, yet in truth I've never felt more helpless in all my life."

He waved his hands about, gesturing to where servants were watching, ready to come to him at a moment's notice.

"Never alone," he said. "Never in need. Never allowed to go beyond the castle without guards. Our kings are prisoners, Judarius. No wonder so many turn mad and bitter."

The angel set the mace down, then sat opposite Harruq, his wings folding behind his back.

"Do not feel you are alone in this," Judarius said. He frowned, looked away as if embarrassed. "I once led armies, commanding angel legions into battle against the demons of our kind. I even faced the mad god, testing my might against him. Yet now what am I? Who do I command, and what enemies do I fight against? All I know is war. All I have been taught is strategy and conquest. And now, here in this peace, I am lost. I am without purpose."

"You protect mankind."

"From themselves," the angel said, shaking his head. "Our enemies are our friends, our friends our enemies. There are no battle lines. There are no sides. If this is a war, it is one I fear I am losing. I have told Ahaesarus that this cannot go on, but he insists."

Harruq was surprised to hear that the angels shared such similar concerns. For some reason he'd thought their opinions would be unanimous, but that showed a mindset so many others had, that the angels were all one and the same. But Judarius and Azariah, both brothers, were about as far apart as Harruq was to Qurrah. His mind drifted, thinking of what the arguments must be like up in Avlimar when the entire angel host gathered…

"Milord?"

Harruq turned, then pushed himself to his feet as he realized the queen stood at the entrance to the garden. She wore a soft yellow dress, and the sunlight shone off her thin crown.

"I'm not your lord," he told her. "You're the one in charge here, and you of all people should know that."

A smile tugged at her lips, but it vanished far too quickly.

"I..." she stopped, glancing at Judarius. "I fear I bring troubling news."

"What?" Harruq asked.

"It's only a rumor, but I believe there is truth in it. Harruq...some villagers were attacked by an angel."

Harruq's mouth dropped open. He looked to Judarius, dreading the angel's reaction, but so far he remained calm, his eyes locked on Susan.

"Go on," Judarius said.

"I've yet to hear a consensus as to where, but it was a village in the south, near the border to Ker. There was a disagreement over the punishment of a criminal, though I can't say the exact nature of it. The angel drew his blade against them. Most say none were hurt, but a few are claiming otherwise."

Harruq sheathed his swords, keeping his hands on the hilts, wishing he could feel the same release of tension as when he first stepped out into the yard. If an angel attacked innocent villagers, for any reason, then the protests would spread. Susan's brother would leap on it immediately, spreading word of the tyranny from the heavens. And as things spiraled worse and worse, both sides would look to him, expecting him to fix it. Expecting him to have the answers.

He turned to Judarius, but before he could speak the angel interrupted him.

"I will discover what I can," he said. "We must not let the kingdom be divided over rumors and lies. Be patient for the truth, Harruq. When everything is known, we will decide the fates of all involved."

Judarius dipped his head toward the queen, then soared off into the sky, heading straight for the distant glimmer that was Avlimar. Harruq watched him go, feeling panic creep around the corners of his mind.

Susan took his hand, and he flinched as if shocked.

"You'll be fine," she told him, her eyes on Avlimar. "Don't worry. I'll always be here."

She kissed his cheek before retreating back into the castle.

"I can't do this," Harruq whispered. He looked ever higher. "You hear me, Ashhur? I can't do this. You've got to help me out here. Because..."

He swallowed, felt a chill spreading through his veins.
"Because this will all crumble if you don't."

# 9

Small squads of Bram's soldiers had followed them at all times, saying nothing, only ensuring that as the week passed Antonil's army never tarried on their way to the eastern side. Sticking to the roads limited what they could see of Ker, which disappointed Tarlak. Through their rapid travel he saw a healthy land, with not a hint of the wreckage that had waylaid Mordan, brought forth by both demons and rebellion.

The Rigon River formed the eastern border of Ker. Twice as wide as the Corinth, its only crossing was via the two fabled Gods' Bridges that connected the Rigon Delta, Ashhur's Bridge over the western spine, Karak's Bridge over the eastern. But as Tarlak approached Ashhur's Bridge alongside Antonil, it resembled little of what he once remembered. In between the arches, where there'd been worn statues of winged knights, there were now rows of barricades. The stone floor, which had once been rare white marble, was now hidden beneath wooden walls and planks. It seemed spears poked out in all directions, as if the bridge were the back of a porcupine. Killing lanes, walls, trenches, all built with one purpose in mind: protecting Ker from the orcs beyond.

A single soldier rode out to meet them as they approached the bridge.

"Greetings King of Mordan," said the soldier. "My name is Yoric, and I control Ashhur's Bridge. I've been informed that your army will pass through without incident. My men have stood down, and we request you make haste to the other side."

"We will do our best," Antonil said.

"Thank you," said Yoric. "So you know, the orcs haven't touched us in months, but I think that's because they figured out we've no intentions of traveling beyond the river. Be careful in there, your highness. It's a different world, even compared to when you last came."

The reminder of his failed first campaign made Antonil's face twitch.

"Your warning is appreciated," he said dryly.

In tightly packed rows his army marched through the winding pathways built upon the bridge, coming out the other side into lands of the delta. Another few hours and they would cross the second bridge, which would dump them out into an area that had once belonged to the nation of Omn. Now only orcs remained, with the exception of the distant city of Angelport, whose walls had helped protect it from the invaders and whose ships kept its people from starving. Being fairly close to the elven lands didn't hurt much, either.

When the last of the soldiers and wagons were across, Tarlak finally crossed the bridge himself.

"Keep the way back open for us," he said, tossing Yoric a wink. "Just in case we come screaming for our lives, a horde of orcs on our tail."

"No orc will cross this bridge," Yoric said. "I assure you, come your return, victorious or otherwise, we'll be here waiting."

"My heroes," Tarlak said, offering an exaggerated bow before snapping his fingers, summoning a gust of wind to blow him into the air and back toward the front of the army, where Antonil marched.

After crossing into Omn, Tarlak oversaw the setting up of the camp, positioning wagons and yelling at men dumb enough to pitch their tents beyond his preset lines. It gave the wizard a headache, but at least he got to take it out on the rest of the men. When he'd circled the enormous camp twice and yelled himself hoarse, he finally joined Antonil. To his surprise, he found the king sitting alone before his tent, a fire burning not far from his feet.

"Shouldn't you be surrounded by generals, advisors, and various bootlickers?" Tarlak asked.

"I sent them away," Antonil said.

"Proof you're a good king, or a terrible one," Tarlak said, grabbing one of many empty chairs from the tent and propping it opposite Antonil. "Sadly, I'm not sure which."

"We'll know the answer by the time this campaign ends."

Tarlak took off his hat, reached inside, and pulled out a long-necked bottle. Popping the cork with his thumb, he took a drink of the wine within.

"So morose today," he said when finished. "What's eating my glorious king?"

"Nothing. I wished to be alone is all, something a certain wizard appears incapable of understanding."

"Have you ordered me to leave yet?"

"No."

Tarlak lifted the bottle in a toast.

"Then I'm staying, your highness. Have a drink if it'll help loosen your tongue. You're too strong to be eaten by nothing, so how about you share what *is* bothering you?"

Antonil reluctantly accepted the bottle. He took a sip, then frowned at it.

"Is there any alcohol in this?" he asked.

"Somewhere in there. That's the fruitier blend. I'm saving the hard stuff for after our first battle."

Antonil chuckled and shook his head.

"You're something else," he said.

"Well aware. Now talk."

After a deep drink, Antonil handed it over, wiped his face on his sleeve.

"I've been thinking of the first campaign to retake Neldar from the orcs," he said.

"Aaah," Tarlak said. "Dwelling on old losses. That's not the best for morale, your highness. In my professional opinion, stop it."

"Duly noted, and ignored. Did I ever tell you how it happened?"

Tarlak scratched at his goatee, trying to remember. Would have been three years ago, so he'd have been…

"No," he said. "I was helping Jerico and Lathaar rebuild their Citadel. The priesthood helped too, but you'd be surprised how much funding I had to beg, steal, and borrow to get that place up and running. I heard about your return. Was all anyone could talk about for a few months, not that anyone really cared about how it had happened, just that you failed."

"I sometimes wonder if the people *wanted* me to fail," Antonil said, eyes staring off into nowhere. Snapping out of it, he reached over and yanked the bottle from Tarlak's hand.

"Careful with that," Tarlak grumbled. "Drink the whole thing and you might get tipsy."

"Compared to Sergan's special brew this is just water," Antonil said. "I can handle water. What I can't handle is watching men who trust me, who expect me to protect them, die by the thousands."

He fell silent, and Tarlak frowned. When it seemed he wouldn't continue, he forced the story along, figuring it better to get Antonil talking about it instead of just brooding.

"So what *did* happen to your last glorious campaign?" he asked.

"I was too confident," Antonil said. "After all, I was Antonil the Dragonslayer, defeater of demons, friend of angels. For eternity's sake, we'd even retaken a city from a god. What could a couple hundred orcs do against us? I had Harruq with me, too, while his wife was away showing their daughter to her distant family in Quellassar. The two of us together, along with eight thousand men strong. What could defeat me? At least, that's what I thought. Nearly every night was a celebration. That army wasn't like this one. A lot of them were from Neldar, had fought with me since our days of fleeing Veldaren when Karak's forces captured its walls. We were coming home. We were going to take our swords and shove them down those orcs' throats, and piece by piece reclaim what was ours."

He shook his head.

"So foolish. So arrogant. We didn't clear out any outlying villages. We didn't check with Angelport, or send scouts to ask the elves for information when we were near their forests. No, we marched straight toward Veldaren. I don't know why. I guess I felt once we retook that city, then everything else would fall into place. Perhaps I thought it'd wash away all the blood and death that had happened since I fled, abandoning it for Karak's prophet. Like an arrow we shot toward the city, but we never made it. Not even close."

Tarlak thought on what he did know about Antonil's first campaign. It'd been cut drastically short, his return to Mordan coming months earlier than expected. There had been only a single battle, but from what everyone said it had been a crushing defeat.

"Where did the orcs finally attack?" he asked.

"Harruq told me they'd been developing siege weapons," Antonil said, seemingly ignoring his question. "I didn't listen. Of course I didn't. The orcs were brutes, stupid, leaderless, or so I thought. When we were three day's ride out from Kinamn we encountered the first of the raiding parties. They were small, quick, and knew exactly how to hit us. They never let us sleep, and they targeted our supplies whenever they could. Thinking they were based out of Kinamn, I steered us toward the city with hopes of crushing the bastards where they couldn't flee.

"Still the raiders hit us, always at night. They slipped in wherever fires flickered out, cutting the throats of my men while they slept. Reached a point where many refused to sleep, and I had to keep huge portions of my army on constant patrol. When the walls of Kinamn came in sight, they were so welcome. The city appeared in ruins, its walls vacant, but every one of my advisors insisted the orcs hid within. The gates were torn open, so we thought we'd have no issues entering. We should have…"

Tarlak took the bottle of wine from Antonil, then gulped down the rest of it.

"How many orcs were inside the city?" he asked.

"At least five thousand," Antonil said, not looking up. "They had archers hiding along the walls, and all at once they stood and fired. Hundreds of men crammed into the doorway, dying instantly. Worse were the catapults. They'd been aimed at the pathway leading into the city, and before the call to retreat had even left my lips they were let loose. Dozens of boulders landed amid us, rolling, breaking our lines like we were playthings. We expected unprepared cowards, hiding from us as we burned out their nest. I couldn't have been more disastrously wrong.

"We retreated, of course. We outnumbered them, but with the catapults, the archers on the walls…what could we do? Several thousand rushed after, swarming us as we retreated. I tried keeping order, to set up a line of defense, but the only reason any of us lived was because of Harruq. Gods, what a sight he was. While everyone else was busy running away, he was screaming and hollering for the orcs to come get him. Even the catapults didn't scare him. When Harruq met the first wave, those around him stood their ground lest they be overwhelmed as well. Even in the chaos we could see those blood-red swords swinging. By the time I halted our retreat and sent men to aid him he'd taken down at least thirty on his own. It was around him my men rallied, and we sent the orcs running back to their city and the safety of their walls."

Antonil shook his head.

"After that, we limped back to Mordeina. Of my eight thousand men, only three thousand returned. We never even stepped foot on Neldar soil. And when I returned to my castle, to my wife and child, I discovered I had a new name. The Missing King, they called me. The joke is on them, of course. I'd have preferred to be gone far longer than I was. No, I'd have even stayed in the ruins of Veldaren, never to return, if I had my way."

"You can't talk like that," Tarlak insisted. "These are Mordan soldiers. If they hear you wishing you could abandon your throne…"

"They'll what?" Antonil asked. "Turn on me? They already have. The whole kingdom is watching me, waiting for me to fail. I first came with eight thousand, and now I come with thirty. I will free my home, taken by the sword, and in the rubble raise my child, my family."

"And what of Mordan?"

The king waved dismissively.

"The angels can have it for all I care. They already rule it, anyway."

Tarlak stood from his chair and bowed low to his friend.

"This campaign will be different," he said. "You have me, to start with. But you are a king, and you rule lands loyal to you. If you do this to expand your kingdom, to retake what is yours, then I will be here every step of the way. But if you think this is your chance to escape everything that is happening in Mordan, a way to sidestep your responsibilities…then I fear I have far more relaxing ways to waste my time."

Antonil swallowed, rubbed his eyes with his hands.

"Forgive me, Tar," he said. "I don't mean it. I do want to escape, but I could never do it. I've never fled my responsibilities, and I never will. That's why I'm here. I was to protect the people of Neldar. They trusted me, and followed me across Dezrel and back again because of that trust. I will repay it. I will free their homes, their farmland, their cities and forests. I may be the Missing King, but I am still king, and will be until my last breath."

Tarlak reached across the fire and smacked Antonil's shoulder.

"Now that's the man I know," he said, grinning. "Let those orcs try to raid us again. Let them be all sneaky at night. They've got a nasty surprise waiting for them. No one out-tricks a mage. And when we reach Kinamn, we'll see how well those catapults work once I've set them aflame."

"You're a good man, Tarlak," Antonil said. "Perhaps I should have brought you with me instead of Harruq on that first campaign."

Tarlak laughed.

"You kidding? I'd have teleported myself back to Mordeina the second those orc archers popped up on the walls. Good night, Antonil."

He raised his empty bottle, attempted a drink from it anyway, and then left the man to his thoughts.

## 10

Beside her, Qurrah stirred, his mouth opening to let out a soft whimper. Tessanna leaned in close, kissed his lips until they shut. They slept not far off the road north, and in the light of the moon Tessanna let her fingers brush her lover's face. Her lips slowly drifted their way to his forehead, where her fingertips had softly traced an arcane, invisible shape upon his skin. And then she breathed. The nightmares, the fear, the tormented memories: they all came floating out of her lover like a black mist. Deep into her lungs she inhaled them, letting them burn within her, squirming in her belly like fire beetles.

"Sleep well," she whispered as Qurrah's body visibly relaxed.

Every night since the angels had healed his corrupted body, banishing the undead flesh and returning him whole, he had suffered those dreams. Every night Tessanna took them, carried them within herself.

It was the stink of Velixar. The stink of Karak. It floated around him, demanding death. Tessanna's dark eyes saw it, began to water as she bent over Qurrah's body and braced her arms. Her thin, pale form shivered as the whispers flooded into her.

*You are mine,* they hissed. *Mine. The promise remains. Open your arms, Qurrah. Come back and embrace me.*

"Never," Tessanna said through her tears. "Never again."

Sleep was a long time coming, and when it did come, she dreamed of fire.

Qurrah was surprised by the amount of travelers they encountered on the road to Mordeina. Hoping to avoid suspicion, he kept his questions few and instead let his ears do the work. Most were traveling north, hoping to find work now that so many able-bodied men had left on Antonil's war against the orcs.

On their fourth day they came upon an inn. Qurrah's coin was few, but the idea of him and Tess sleeping on an actual bed was too tempting.

"Tonight we spoil ourselves," he said, taking her hand and leading her inside.

"We'll have nothing left when we reach Mordeina," Tessanna pointed out.

"True," Qurrah said. "But my brother is steward of the realm. I dare say we'll be fine."

The inn was crowded, and for a moment Qurrah worried there would be no room.

"There's still a bed or two left," a fat man on the far side of the open kitchen shouted, as if reading his mind. "Ginger, get over there and get their things."

A young lad with bright red hair raced through the many tables, then quickly bowed before the two.

"I would prefer to carry them on my own," Qurrah told him. "Just show us to our room."

The kid nodded, beckoning them to follow.

The room was small, barely able to fit the bed within. At least they wouldn't be sharing a room with any of the other travelers, Qurrah thought. He looked over the sheets and pushed against the straw as the boy watched expectantly.

"How long until dinner will be served?" he asked as Tessanna stood in the corner, looking very tired.

"Another hour," Ginger said.

"Very well. Leave us."

The kid nodded and shut the door. Qurrah sighed as Tessanna moved to his side.

"Lice," the half-orc murmured. "And fleas. Such a charming locale."

With a wave of his hand a soft cloud floated from his palm down to the bed, curling over it like mist upon a lake. The cloud was death, and though weak enough even a child could go unbothered, it was still far more than the parasites could withstand. Their tiny bodies would remain, but at least they wouldn't be crawling all over him, biting his flesh.

"Eat without me," Tessanna said, kissing his cheek. Qurrah glanced at her, frowning.

"Is something wrong?" he asked. "You haven't looked well for much of our trip."

"No. I just want some peace. Bring me a bit of bread when you're done, and I'll eat it later."

Qurrah shrugged.

"As you wish."

He left his room and returned to the commons, finding an unused table with only two chairs. He sat in one, put his feet on the other, and beckoned Ginger over.

"Bread and drink," he said.

"Dad says you need to pay for your room before you eat."

The half-orc sighed, pulled out a handful of coins, and settled the bill. It left him with just enough to cover the cost of his food, and he handed that over as well.

"Bring me enough for two," he said before the kid could leave. "I'll be taking some to my room."

Finally alone, Qurrah leaned back and let his ears soak in the conversations. It was still somewhat quiet in his corner, with the bulk of the men and women gathering near the fire. They were laughing, talking, and their mirth made Qurrah feel strangely bitter. He wished Tessanna had come with him, wished he could have flirted with her awhile. Her mood had slowly soured over the past year, though not consistently. Nothing was ever consistent with Tessanna. He doubted she'd ever tell him why, either. Was it their continuing inability to have a child? Her lack of purpose since the Gods' War? Did she just miss contact with the rest of the world? Every time he thought he knew, something else she said or did contradicted the idea.

His meal came, and Qurrah ate it with speed but without any real appreciation. Sipping at the watery beer Ginger brought him, he once more tried to listen in. One of the louder men at the fire was telling a raunchy tale when the door to the inn burst open, and in walked a bearded man with a heavy ax on his back.

"Gervis!" several men shouted, lifting their glasses in toast.

Gervis grinned at them in return.

"You'll all be buying me a round tonight," the big man nearly roared. "Do I have a tale to tell!"

Qurrah leaned deeper into his seat, narrowed his eyes, and hoped it would be of something useful. The men at the fire shifted

## The Prison of Angels

aside, making way for Gervis to plop down before the flames, his ax still on his back.

"Trader just came in from the borderlands," Gervis began, accepting an offered cup from one of his friends. "About a week back they had a hanging at Norstrom."

"Had hangings before," a particularly drunk man shouted, and he laughed as if it were the funniest thing.

"We have," Gervis said, guzzling down his own drink. "But this one was done to a sick fuck who liked to diddle with little boys and girls. But that ain't the thing that got the traders talking. No, this one was done without the angels' permission. By the Abyss, I dare say it was even done *against* their permission."

He had their attention now, Qurrah's included.

"What happened?" someone asked once it was clear Gervis would wait for some prodding.

"Well, an angel finally took note of it. They'd strung the guy from a pole, used his dick as a rope supposedly. No one would claim responsibility, either. Drove the angel mad is what they're saying. Started hollering, waving his sword around."

The men were laughing now.

"Wish I could have seen that."

"Nothing like watching them holier than shit angels squirm a little."

"Red-faced, I bet he was, red like a tomato!"

Gervis gestured for a refill.

"This is where it stops being funny," he said. "Listen close, now. You know I tell no lies. This angel, Ezekai was his name I believe, he demanded they cut down the pervert and bury him. Well, the people of Norstrom wanted no part of that. And when they refused, the angel drew his sword and *attacked* them."

The laughing dwindled to chuckles, then to silence. All around at other tables, conversation slowed. It was as if a hot wind had blown through the place, and Gervis grinned, knowing all ears were now his.

"No one died," he continued. "But that don't change matters none. He drew his sword and started swinging, knocking people out of his way just so he could cut down and bury the fucker. These were just regular people, people like you or me, and he was ready to kill every last one of them to get his way. And what were these people doing? Standing up for their rights, that's what! The law's supposed to be in our hands, in *man's* hands. But they don't like that none, do they?"

Qurrah waved Ginger over and requested more to drink. The moment it arrived, Qurrah guzzled it down, his mind racing. The topic at every table was now the same, grumblings and complaints about the angels. Two men directly beside Qurrah were obnoxiously loud, and he had little choice in overhearing.

"One told my wife I was cheating on her when he found out," one of the men said. "Can you believe that? What place is that for him, huh? Like it matters I had a quick roll around with Jessie. None of their damn business."

"What'd she do?" the man's friend asked.

"Left me, took our kid with her, too. Dumb bitch. I'm better without her."

Qurrah struggled to bite his tongue. Was this what the people really wanted? The right to cheat on spouses and dole out brutal justice? He thought of Azariah's frustration and shook his head. Other than turning a blind eye to it all, what else was there to do? But the simmering anger he felt confirmed what Tessanna had suggested. The people were nearing rebellion against their winged enforcers. Not there yet, not quite. So far there was too much acceptance mixed with the anger. They were upset by things they felt beyond their control. But once they felt they had a choice, once they believed they had the numbers and the power to make things different…

Tessanna sat in front of him at the table, startling him.

"I thought you were unwell," he said.

Tessanna glanced about the common room, hunched down closer.

"I didn't want to be alone anymore," she said, her voice so soft he could barely hear her. "I did, but then I didn't. Is the food worthwhile?"

Qurrah pushed her portion of the bread her way.

"The butter's fresh at least," he said.

She ate it, nibbling like she was a squirrel. Qurrah leaned closer and kept his voice down.

*The Prison of Angels*

"The people are resentful of the angels," he told her. "Simply put, they're human, and they want to be human, with all that entails. So long as Azariah enforces his higher standard through law, they're going to resent him."

"Perhaps your brother can do something," Tessanna suggested. "He's steward now. Surely the angels will listen to him."

"That's if I can make him agree. He might not. Perhaps he'll only view these complaints as nothing more than growing pains."

"Or labor pains," Tessanna said, glancing about. "Though whether child or monster will be born, I'm not sure even the gods know."

Gervis's overwhelming voice roared again.

"Aye, I heard! Crossed the bridge not too long ago. No one knows why."

"His brother's the steward. Maybe he's hoping to get a cushy job."

"A job wiping his brother's ass, maybe," Gervis laughed, and everyone laughed with him.

Qurrah's fist curled tight as his whip writhed around his right arm.

"Behave," Tessanna said, meeting his eye. "They know nothing of you, nothing of me."

"Any of you ever seen that demon girl of his?" Gervis asked. "Firm tits, an ass you could bounce coins off of? Well, a man was talking to me just this other day, told me something I could hardly believe. He lived in Veldaren, was there when them people were attacked. Now everyone knows she was sleeping with that prophet, but this friend of mine was saying it went way further than that."

He waited until people began pressuring for greater detail.

"How much further?" Gervis continued. "Well, he said she spent the whole damn day and night fucking those demons. Kept shouting it was her calling, like it was some sort of worship. Thousands of demons, I tell you, every single one of them, each hung like horses. If you ever meet Tessanna Delone, you're meeting the absolute biggest whore in the history of Dezrel, and that's something you should tip your hat in respect to."

Qurrah's fists slammed into the table. He lurched from his seat, his weight braced against the wood as if his fury overwhelmed his ability to stand. The commotion earned him several glances his way, and when they saw the fire curling off his hands, blackening the table, many hurried up from their seats toward the door.

"No fighting!" the barkeep shouted. "No magic, no swords!"

Qurrah felt his arms shaking as he stared down Gervis. The big oaf had turned his way, and he looked dumbfounded as to the reason for Qurrah's glare.

"Something the matter, friend?" Gervis asked. His hand had fallen to the handle of his ax, which lay by his feet.

"You're telling tales," Qurrah said, feeling an icy calm come over him. "Telling lies."

"Hey now, I'm only saying what I heard. If you have a problem with—"

He stopped, for Tessanna had stood as well, her face catching the light of the fire. If there was anything more recognizable than Qurrah's orcish features, it was those solid black eyes and that long raven hair.

"But I *do* have a problem," she said, sliding around the table and walking their way. Qurrah watched, his fingers tensed. The second something went wrong, he'd be ready with fire and shadows.

"This…this is a joke, right?" Gervis said, staring at her. "A trick?"

"No tricks," Tessanna said, her voice almost seductive. "It's me, Tessanna Delone, lover of the great traitor, Qurrah. Shouldn't you tip your hat?"

Gervis paused, but he had no hat to tip, and he looked like a cornered, frightened animal. At the mention of Qurrah's name his grip on the handle of his ax tightened, and around him several of the men backed away, their hands also reaching for weaponry. They were all keenly aware of him now, and the tension in the room increased tenfold.

"Do it," Qurrah said, his raspy voice piercing the sudden quiet. "If you have no hat, then bow in respect."

Tessanna stepped closer, closer, her hips swaying, her head tilted to one side, a soft smile on her lips.

"I like the sound of that," she said, her dark eyes sweeping over them. "All of you. Kneel."

From her back shot four long tendrils. They were thin, black, and looked like a sick mockery of butterfly wings. They curled around Gervis and the three men with him, pulling on their arms and sweeping out their feet to force them to the ground. Others in the tavern started, readying for a fight, but Qurrah pointed his fingers at them, his hands consumed by fire. His look was clear. The first to interfere would die horribly.

Tessanna slowly sank to her knees before Gervis, who was struggling against the black tendril hard enough to make his face swell red.

"Such a good storyteller," she whispered, yet in the silence Qurrah could still hear her. "Such a funny man. But what do you know of me? Nothing. In your mind I am what you claim me to be."

She slid closer, putting her lips inches away from his ear.

"So what do you want me to be? Do you want me to be your whore? Is that what you want?"

She lovingly rubbed his face, and her touch immediately ceased his struggling. His eyes were wide, and he looked so frightened he might pass out.

"But I'm not," Tessanna whispered. "I'm not your whore. I'm not your joke. The prophet never touched me, do you understand? Never. Nor the demons, nor anyone else since I met my love. Find your laughs elsewhere, little man. Because if you don't…"

She shifted to the side, then kissed his cheek. Her lips blackened his flesh, making it smoke as if she were branding him with a hot iron. He screamed, but her hand covered his mouth, her fingernails digging into his skin. After only a moment she pulled back, and his screaming ceased.

"If you don't," she said, and her eyes swept the tavern, "then I'll fuck you like the whore you think I am. I'm fire, and we'll see just how many of you burn."

The tendrils released, retreating into her back. The men scattered, Gervis leading the way. Others watched, waiting to see if anything else would happen. Nothing did. Tessanna turned to Qurrah, and he saw the anger in her eyes slowly fading. The fire vanished from his hands and he rushed to her side.

"See we're not disturbed," he told the innkeeper, and based on the fear he saw in everyone's eyes he didn't think it too difficult a request.

Back in their room, Qurrah slammed the door shut, punched it with his fist.

"My brother the hero, the Godslayer, the steward," Qurrah muttered. "And what are we? Traitors. Cowards. The great whores."

He turned to see Tessanna sitting on the bed, her hands in her lap. She looked ashamed.

"I lied down there," she said softly.

Qurrah frowned.

"Lied? About what?"

"About touching only you since I met you."

Qurrah closed his eyes, told himself not do something stupid. She'd told him about Jerico and their single moment of weakness. Or had it been strength? It was something he never wanted to think about, to even remember having happened.

"You know I don't blame you for it," he said, putting his arms around her. "I'd put Velixar's promises of power above you in my heart, and Jerico was there for comfort. I'm better than I was then. Right?"

She looked up at him, smiling despite her tears.

"So much better," she said, kissing him.

He held her close.

"Don't listen to what they say," he said. "They're ignorant fools."

"But they hate us so much, and the stories they tell…they do it to make us less than what we were. Less human. More broken. We hurt them, and now they want to make us into monsters, demon-fucking monsters and heartless, slavering betrayers. But I don't want to be that to them. I just want to be…me. But that will never happen, will it? Nothing I do will ever make them see me any other way."

"That's not true," Qurrah said. "We could show them, we could help rebuild the world, help resolve their ire with the angels. It's my fault for taking us away into hiding, for letting the stories grow unchecked. I'm sorry, Tess. I should have known better."

She kissed his lips, then lay back on the bed.

"Qurrah?"

"Yes, Tess?"

She smiled sheepishly.

"I think I'm all right with using a disguise now, at least until we reach Harruq."

Despite the exhaustion and stress of the day, Qurrah laughed.

# 11

Jessilynn lay before the fire, without the strength to sit up. Her arms and back ached tremendously, the result of another lengthy set of hours training while Sonowin rested from their flight. Her fingers felt raw, and the idea of pulling back her bowstring even one more time made her queasy. Staring up at the stars, she breathed in deeply, then let it out, trying to relax her sore muscles.

"I do not understand why you are so upset," Dieredon said, sitting across from her, the lazy fire burning between them. He picked at the remains of a groundhog he'd shot and cooked sometime during the day. "I was told you were familiar with a bow. A few hours of practice should be nothing."

"It's not the time," Jessilynn said, doing her best to not sound defensive. "Before it was just me. With you, it's different. Every shot has to be...I don't know how to explain. Every single one has to be right with you. Ten arrows with you feel like twenty on my own."

"Patience," she heard Dieredon say. "That is the reason. I'm teaching you patience, giving the bow a greater chance to work on you. Your body will adjust in time."

Jessilynn closed her eyes and laughed despite herself.

"Is this one of those 'pain is good for you' lessons? Because I hated those whenever Jerico gave them."

Dieredon chuckled. Silence came over them, broken occasionally by Sonowin's nearby rustling as she grazed on the pale yellow grass of the Wedge. Slowly Jessilynn shifted so she lay on her back, close enough to feel the heat on her face as she stared into the fire. She caught Dieredon watching her, and she felt her heart quicken. She had slowly gotten used to the elf's presence, but still there were times when she could hardly believe where she was. How long ago was it she'd been sleeping in a cramped bunk within the cold stone walls of the Citadel? Two weeks? Three?

"Why are you here?" Dieredon asked. The abruptness of the question caught Jessilynn off guard, and she looked up at him dumbfounded.

"To learn," she said, believing that the safe answer.

"You know I ask for more than that. There is something burning in you, something driving you beyond others your age. I watched you in practice. That final hour you were clearly in pain, learning little because of your exhaustion. Yet still you continued, not once refusing my demand to loose another arrow."

A bit of anger bubbled up Jessilynn's stomach.

"You were testing me?" she asked.

"Of course. I am your teacher, after all. Now answer the question. What is driving you?"

She looked away, preferring to watch the flame consuming the many twigs, which Dieredon had showed her how to stack as to lengthen the life of the fire. Her neck blushed, and she bit her tongue. The answer wasn't hard, but she felt embarrassed to admit it. Still, Dieredon's eyes were upon her, and he seemed perfectly content to wait until she gave her answer. And if she refused, well, it wasn't that far a flight for him to dump her off at the Citadel…

"I want to be like Jerico," she blurted out when it seemed his patience was finally wearing thin.

The following silence was painful as she waited for his response.

"Your hair isn't red enough," Dieredon said.

She opened her mouth, closed it, then giggled upon realizing the elf had actually made a joke.

"Not just Jerico," she said, feeling herself relax. "Lathaar. Darius. Tyrus the First. People revere them. I hear the stories, and all I desire is to do even better. I feel jealous, even. Jerico stood before a portal, slaughtering waves of war demons, not stopping even when a spear pierced his side. Lathaar defeated the ancient evil, Darakken. Tyrus drove the remnants of Karak's beasts into the Wedge near on his own, surviving even though engulfed by thousands and returning a hero. Darius prevented Cyric's madness from overtaking all of Mordan. Every night I went to bed listening to these stories, and when I look at Jerico's shield, I think…"

She fell silent.

"Speak your mind," Dieredon insisted. "You will receive no judgment from me, and no mockery."

Jessilynn slowly forced herself into a sitting position. Her hand fell to the bow that lay beside her in the grass.

"I see the glow on my arrows and believe there has to be a reason," she said. "Jerico's shield was unlike all others, and look at everything he's accomplished. Now I bear a similar gift, a blessing no one in my order has ever received before. What will I do with it? The demons are gone, the ancient evils defeated. What can I do to have my name belong next to theirs, to allow me to stand beside the heroes of my order and not feel ashamed?"

She bowed her head, felt her voice tremble.

"I have such a gift," she said. "I'm just scared that I'll waste it."

For a long minute she endured Dieredon's silence.

"This world is not safe, Jessilynn," he told her, rising to his feet. "Your angels have done great things, but I fear the illusion of safety they have created has been more damaging than they can possibly understand. The east has gone wild, and within the Wedge the beasts are on the move. Every day my kind patrols the borders of our forests, always in fear of orcish fire. The ancient evils may be gone, but new ones have replaced them."

He scattered the fire with his foot so they might safely sleep in darkness.

"I do not know what you will accomplish with your life," he said, his eyes glowing in the starlight. "If you desire to be a hero, you have the necessary strength inside you. I can see it, clear as the stars in the sky. But your heroes didn't become who they were by accident. They bled for it. They died for it. Not for themselves, but for others. Before you yearn for glory, think of the costs."

And then he left her so she might sleep.

◈

They spent much of the next two days in flight, landing only to let Sonowin rest. During those respites, Dieredon showed her how to light a fire with twigs, to hunt game, and forage for edible roots and berries. He barely let her touch her bow, telling her she should let her body rest and instead learn something new. Moving silently across the grass was the hardest for her, and more and more she saw her teacher growing frustrated with the clumsiness of her armor.

"It's made for battle, not scouting," he muttered one late afternoon.

"My arrows glow a bright blue," she responded. "How stealthy do you expect me to be?"

He only shook his head.

"When the fighting begins, they'll know your presence. It's beforehand that matters. Sometimes you may not want to fight at all. It is a hard skill to learn, knowing when you are outmatched."

"So you want me to learn to be a coward?"

"It's not cowardice to adjust the battle more to your favor," Dieredon said. "There's a difference between them ten leagues wide."

"What about all the times Jerico and Lathaar stood their ground when victory was hopeless, yet still won? Haven't you done the same?"

She thought she had him, but instead he only looked more disappointed with her.

"I dare say they were left with no choice," he said. "That's either bravery, or poor forethought, depending on who you ask. Neither is something you should run foolhardily into."

They took to the air on Sonowin's back, and for the next hour Jessilynn sulked, upset at her inability to answer a simple question correctly. If Dieredon noticed, he didn't mention it. The land passed below them, until at last the elf guided them back to the ground.

"Landing already?" Jessilynn asked, trying to pull herself out of her funk. She was being immature, and she knew it. "There's nothing here."

"That's exactly the point."

The elf crouched low to the ground as he walked, eyes scanning his surroundings. For what, she couldn't begin to guess. The more time she spent with him, the more she realized she would never possess a fraction of his skills. The wilderness spoke to him in a way it never would to her. The arrows in his quiver were as familiar to him as his own fingers. Even the weather couldn't surprise him, and twice when it rained he'd informed her a good twelve hours beforehand, showing her how to build a rudimentary shelter with just sticks and dirt. Jessilynn waited, feeling useless, following after when he strayed farther and farther away.

"Nothing," he said, shaking his head after ten minutes had passed and they'd covered a large swathe of area. "Everywhere we go, nothing."

"What does it mean?" she asked.

"It seems the Vile Wedge is empty," Dieredon said, standing and stretching the muscles in his back. "I can't even find signs of recent passage."

"That's impossible," Jessilynn insisted. "You said only orcs had gone east, and our boats patrol the western river, as does the Wall of Towers. If there'd been such a massive exodus, we'd have heard of it."

"Perhaps," Dieredon said, but he didn't look convinced. "We'll continue west for now. Tens of thousands of monsters don't vanish without leaving a trace. They're somewhere, and I will find them."

Jessilynn's butt and back ached from such long periods of riding, but she said nothing, only gritted her teeth as she climbed atop Sonowin and wrapped her arms around Dieredon's waist yet again. The miles passed below as the horse's wings flapped with a steady rhythm. Occasionally she glanced down, but it was always the same rocky hills and dull grass. Part of her understood why the creatures so strongly desired to escape. Living in such a bland, infertile land must have worn on them as the years passed. Not that she regretted it. Humans living peaceably next to wolf-men and bird-men? Preposterous. She knew well the stories Jerico had told of Darius and him making their stand against the army of wolf-men that had crossed the Gihon and made their way west. She'd often imagined herself sitting atop one of the homes, her bow in hand, releasing glowing arrows into the beasts, thinning the horde and saving dozens of lives.

"There," Dieredon said, breaking her out of her daydream. Several hours had passed at a tedious pace. He pointed, and she followed his gaze. It took a few moments before they closed enough distance for her human eyes to see. From her vantage point it looked like a blob of darkness atop the yellow landscape.

It helped none that the sun was beginning to set, obscuring it further.

"What is it?" she had to ask as Dieredon ordered Sonowin to fly higher.

"A group of hyena-men," the elf said.

"Why aren't we following them?"

Dieredon glanced back at her, gave her a wink.

"Consider it a hunch, as you humans might say."

Once they were past the group Sonowin dipped lower. The land grew closer, and she saw more clearly the red stone jutting out from the grass, the spattered collections of trees that grew short and thin of leaf. Dieredon leaned so far off Sonowin's side she feared he'd fall. They banked lower, lower, until the ground was frighteningly close below them. Jessilynn kept her legs clenched against the horse's sides, begging Ashhur to calm her nerves.

Up ahead the hills grew taller, and above them drifted a lazy column of smoke. Dieredon said something to Sonowin in elvish, and then the horse's wings sharply changed their angle, blowing back against the air current. They soared upward, killing more of their momentum, and then with hardly a bump they landed at the foot of the hills. Jessilynn hopped off Sonowin's back, following Dieredon. Something about the way his body tensed made her uneasy, and the mischievous grin on his face helped none, either. He seemed excited, yet all she felt was fear.

"What's beyond the hills?" she asked, keeping her voice a whisper. She already felt too loud because of the soft rustling of her chainmail against the studded leather backing.

"That's what we're here to find out," Dieredon said as they continued to climb.

"Then why not fly over with Sonowin?"

The elf shook his head, a gesture Jessilynn was becoming all too familiar with seeing.

"The sun's not yet set, and the sky is clear," he said. "I don't want them to know we're here."

He hurried ahead, his excitement growing. Despite his speed, he made not a sound. Jessilynn bumbled after, more and more thinking she needed to make some adjustments to her armor. Why he hadn't forced her to already was baffling. Perhaps he was waiting to see if she did it on her own, just as he waited to see if she would complain when he pushed her too far in her training.

When Dieredon neared the top of the hill he lay on his stomach and crawled to its peak. When he looked beyond, she saw a jolt go through him. He held his palm open toward her, and she dropped to her belly, figuring he wanted her to show equal care. Something in the way he froze there, the way his excited grin had fled...what was beyond the hill? What could scare the Scoutmaster of the Quellan elves? Elbow over elbow she crawled across the yellow grass, until at last she joined the elf's side and overlooked the land below.

"Ashhur help us," she whispered, unable to stop herself.

The hill ended sharply, revealing a wide cleft. It looked like a gash rent into the world, with many surrounding hills also ending just as steep. The space between was wide and flat, much of it covered with dry red clay, the sparse grass there smashed or dead. And in that massive area, spread out below them like colonies of ants, were the creatures of the Vile Wedge.

Nearest to her were the wolf-men, packs of them gathered around the small fires that dotted the ravine. She couldn't even begin to count their number, but they were the most numerous of all the species as far as she could tell. Amid the cacophony of sounds rising up to them, it was their growls that were the loudest. Beside them, in the heart of the gulch, were the bird-men. They sat in circles, their feathery arms wrapped around their bodies. Their colors varied wildly, more so than any of the other beasts. Most were dark black, like a raven, but others were white, blue, red, even a few pinks and purples among their plumage.

Beyond them were the goblins, miniature humans with grotesque heads. They were the only ones gathered that wore clothing, tattered loin cloths sewn from the yellow grass of the Wedge. Their encampment seemed the most industrious, with actual tents scattered about. Their skin varied in color, though not as much as the feathers of the bird-men. Most were an ugly green, with red the second-most common color. Also unlike the rest, they wielded crude weapons made of wood and stone. Nearest to the goblin camp were the hyena-men. They were the most hyper, yipping about and snarling at one another. The hunch in their back looked uncomfortable, almost obscene. Unlike the rest, their fur was unanimously a dirty shade of spotted orange.

On the far end of the ravine, their forms just barely visible to her eyes, were the goat-men. She'd heard of them rarely, their numbers were few. They walked about, bare-chested, their faces long and horned. Their arms and hands were like that of a human, but their legs were covered with fur, their feet ending with hooves as large as a horse's. She saw them talking, but the distance was too great for her to make out any sound.

Between each race were large gaps, with what appeared to be poles or spears jutted into the ground to form the borders. Fire, ordered encampments, alliances between races...all of it was counter to what she'd believed possible. The creatures in the Wedge were mindless, brutal, devouring each other like the monsters they were. They weren't supposed to reason. They weren't supposed to be more intelligent than any other pack of wild animals. From them she heard yips, snarls, random curses, and amid it all were words shouted in the common tongue. That she could understand them, could listen to their words as they shouted and mocked one another...

Most terrifying, though, was their number. It was beyond counting, almost beyond estimating, but between them she knew there had to be twenty thousand, if not more.

"What is going on?" Jessilynn whispered. She almost felt paralyzed as she lay there. If any spotted her, or even smelled her with their animal noses, they'd swarm in an instant. Sonowin wasn't far down the hill, and surely they could reach her before any beasts curled around the sides of the ravine, but still, that was a race she didn't want to take part in.

Directly below her she watched a wolf-man come in from the south entrance of the ravine, carrying what looked like the upper half of a cow. It flung the corpse before one of the fires, and with frightening speed dozens of the beasts tore into the thing, grabbing at innards and ripping flesh free with their claws. Jessilynn watched, a chill spreading through her veins.

"A gathering of the subhuman," Dieredon whispered, and over the sounds below he was barely audible. "Of the like I've never seen, never even dreamed."

"I don't understand. They hate each other, don't they?"

He nodded.

"It's that hatred that has allowed us to keep them in check. But this...this isn't normal. I'd say it impossible if I didn't see it with my own eyes. The entirety of the Wedge has been making its way here for months, abandoning all former territorial lines. We must find out who leads them, who is capable of creating such an army. Perhaps magic is involved, maybe even priests or wizards."

"How?" Jessilynn asked. "How do we find out without them discovering us?"

Dieredon stared, and the longer the silence lingered the greater her fear grew.

"I don't know," he said at last.

It was the most frightening thing he could have possibly told her.

## 12

It wasn't the stress the position put on her husband that upset Aurelia. She knew Harruq could withstand it, no matter how much he might complain otherwise. It wasn't the responsibility, for she knew his decisions would be the right ones, regardless of his doubt. No, the thing that upset Aurelia most about Harruq's role as steward was the sheer loneliness it brought about in her.

"Mommy, look!" Aubrienna called, pulling her from her thoughts. She sat on the edge of a fountain in one of the castle's many gardens. Aubrienna and Gregory played on the far side. They'd been chasing each other with wooden weapons, Gregory wielding a sword, Aubby a wand, but the toys now lay in the grass. It seemed a new game had piqued their interests.

"Careful of thorns," Aurelia told them, seeing they had begun picking flowers. Aubrienna was the one taking charge of things, as she often did. Aurelia watched as her daughter began putting the small daisies into Gregory's hair, the little girl frowning every time they didn't stick. Gregory mostly let her, trusting her implicitly. The sight put a smile on Aurelia's face, and she wished Harruq could watch as Gregory finally grabbed a tulip and yanked it free so he could place it atop of Aubrienna's head. Both giggled as it fell off, landing on the stone walkway.

"I'll get it!" Aubrienna said, reaching down and then handing it to Gregory.

"Thanks," Gregory said, beginning his second attempt to place the flower in her hair. "Now you stay still. Stay!"

Aurelia leaned her chin on her palm. Her husband's long hours left her alone, for being at Harruq's side when he made his judgments risked undermining his authority. It wasn't as if the people of Mordeina mistrusted her, she knew that. If anything, she was beloved, more so than the actual queen. Current fashions in the city had already begun to mimic the dresses she wore, becoming more elven in style. Harruq's popularity hadn't waned either, but things had already grown uneasy. He needed to convince everyone from lords to beggars that he was competent enough to rule as steward. Too many knew of Susan's involvement already. If the general populace realized how much of a puppet ruler Harruq actually was, it'd render everything they'd done pointless. His public dealings with the people were therefore of the utmost importance.

So she stayed with her daughter, letting Aubrienna's light and happiness brighten her own dull existence in the city of humans as they passed the hours together until her husband fled the throne for their embrace.

"That's enough," Aurelia said, glancing up to see over a dozen flowers now uprooted and laying about. They both looked her way, frowns on their faces, and she realized how harshly she'd reprimanded them. She let out a sigh, berating herself for taking out her frustrations on the children. It simply wasn't fair. Aubby missed her father just as much as she did.

"We were...we were just playing with the flowers," Aubrienna said, as if explaining it would clear everything up.

Aurelia stood and wandered their way, smiling to show she wasn't upset.

"It is all right," she said. "But I don't want you playing with the flowers anymore. The gardeners work very hard to make them grow so beautiful."

Aubrienna looked around, as if unsure if she were in trouble or not. Gregory had no such need.

"I'm sorry," he said, eyes to the ground. Whether necessary or not, he'd decided apologizing was a good way to head off a paddling. The castle servants were hesitant to lay a hand on the little kingling, but Aurelia had no such reservations. In her mind, the last thing Mordan needed was a brat for an heir, not that there was any real danger of that. Gregory was such a sweet child. It was Aubby who was the real troublemaker. Aurelia blamed Harruq for that, naturally.

"It's all right," she said, kneeling down before them so she might look them in the eye. "How about we go get something to eat, hrm? I bet Merelda has something nice brewing in the kitchen just for you two."

The promise of sweets sparked their eyes alight, and Aurelia grinned. Perhaps a sweetcake might help her own mood.

## The Prison of Angels

She offered them her hands, then froze. It was as if she had suddenly gone blind, but not in her eyes. The sense of magic within her, the connection with the weave of her goddess that granted her power, vanished. Replacing it was a pulsing emptiness coupled with a vague feeling of unease. Without thinking she grabbed the arms of both children and yanked them to the ground while ducking her own head.

Two darts plinked into the stone beyond her, careened wildly before landing in the grass. Aurelia's eyes widened as she stared at their sharpened points, the tips dripping with some sort of cloudy liquid.

"Stay down," Aurelia whispered, fear and fury overwhelming her initial surprise.

There were two entrances to the garden, one on the east wall, one to the south. Aurelia had the children ducking behind a white marble ledge, its top decorated with dozens of potted flowers. They were on the far side, nearly equidistant from either entrance. She flexed her fingers, thinking to summon a portal to escape, but the magic didn't come to her. It was as if she were underwater trying to gasp for breath.

Gregory began to cry, and Aubby's face was scrunching up and turning red, frightened tears about to release from her as well. Aurelia lunged for the first thing she could use as a weapon: Gregory's wooden sword. In her hands it was more of a dagger, but the wood was solid, and she peered over the ledge to scan for their would-be assassins. There were three of them, one at each door plus a third rushing through the garden, two glinting daggers in hand. All three were dressed in the strangest garb, their clothes a mixture of reds and grays. Their faces were covered with a dark gray cloth, revealing only their eyes and hair.

The one at the door to her right caught her looking and flung another dart. Aurelia ducked, her heart pounding as panic threatened to overwhelm her—not for herself, but for Gregory and Aubrienna. If only she had her magic. She had her training with Harruq from their sparring years ago, instilling moderate ability to defend herself with her staff. But against skilled assassins, wielding only a child's toy, what chance did she have?

Preparing herself for the end, she swept her eyes over the two children, and as she did she caught sight of a strange spherical object not far away from her, lying in the grass. Its surface was made of obsidian, and it was heavily cracked. From those cracks pulsed a rainbow of colors, almost like a heartbeat. Without thinking, without daring to fear for her safety, she lunged out into the open for it. The nearest assassin was almost upon her, and in response to her unexpected motion the man twisted, kicked off the ledge she'd hidden behind, and continued after her. Aurelia spun in air, lashing out with the wooden sword. It clipped the man's thrust, shoving it harmlessly aside.

When she landed she grabbed the sphere, surprised to discover how light it was. With all her strength she hurled it toward the nearest doorway, then rolled. Daggers thudded into the grass. Coming out of her roll, she let out a gasp. With the object's removal she felt her magic returning into her like floodwaters rushing through a broken dam. Feeling more alert, more whole, she bared her teeth and stretched out her hands toward the leaping assassin. Lightning shot from her fingers, crackling with energy. The hit halted him in midair, spinning his upper body backward. When he landed she struck him again, the electricity arcing about his body.

"Close your eyes!" Aurelia screamed at the children. Gregory would see nothing, what with his fists pressed against his face, but Aubrienna had been watching even as she cried. Praying her daughter would listen, Aurelia stood, summoning an invisible energy shield to block any more darts the assassins might throw. But the two men at the doors apparently had new tricks in mind.

A ball of fire burned through the air, aimed straight for Aurelia's chest. It struck her shield and detonated, swirling outward in a thin line, consuming the nearby plants and blackening the vases. Aurelia managed to duck beneath the flames just in time, only to see the other assassin outstretch his hand. Twin glowing orbs arced out, veering over her cover and slamming through her shield with ease. She let out a cry as they struck her chest. The pain was intense, and she fell back to the ground. Writhing, she bit her tongue in an attempt to focus. The two orbs had caused no physical damage. They were just trying to keep her down long enough to finish her.

The Prison of Angels

The bite to her tongue didn't work, but hearing the two children crying did. The fools wanted a sorcerer's duel? Then so be it. She'd faced an enraged Tessanna, stood toe-to-toe against the prophet. These assassins? They had picked the wrong target.

Shoving herself to her feet, she raised her hands and summoned the most powerful protection spells she knew. Fire and ice crashed against her shields, burning more plants and spreading frost along the ground, but nothing could penetrate. Aurelia's fingers danced, and she allowed herself a smile.

"You want fire?" she asked. "Then have it."

A great stream burst from her gathered palms, belching out as if from the belly of a dragon. It filled the doorway, easily overwhelming the man's attempt at a magical shield. When it subsided, his body was but blackened ash. Turning to the other, she saw him fleeing.

"Not so fast," she said through clenched teeth, summoning a swirling blue portal. Its location wasn't far. Stepping through, she reemerged at the end of the hallway the final assassin had attempted to flee down. He skidded to a halt, his eyes widening behind his mask. Aurelia gave him no time to react. Unleashing all her fury, she tore bricks free from each side of the castle walls and then slammed them together. She heard the assassin's bones snap, saw his skull crunch inward. His body dropped to the floor like a rag doll, and it was only then Aurelia felt she could breathe.

She ran back to the garden, pausing only momentarily at the door. Two guards lay slumped outside the entrance, thin darts protruding out from their necks. Aurelia passed them by, holding in a shudder. Checking the other exit, she found two more dead guards. The waste of life infuriated her as much as it frightened her with the implications.

"Mommy!"

Aurelia turned, felt her heart break upon seeing Aubrienna rush out from cover and run toward her. Her cheeks and neck were red, her face a mess of snot and tears. Aurelia scooped her into her arms, then went to Gregory. She set her daughter down, wrapped them both in her arms, and tried to calm them.

"Hold your ears now," she said, pulling them closer to her chest. Turning her head toward one of the doors, she gathered magic into her voice.

"Guards!"

The sound must have echoed throughout half the castle, for within a minute, dozens came rushing in, cursing at the sight of their dead brethren.

"Take them to Harruq, and make sure they don't leave his side," she said to the man in charge. "I don't care how disruptive they are, they don't leave. Is that clear?"

"Understood," the soldier said, scooping Gregory up into his arms. Another pulled off his mailed glove and offered a hand to Aubrienna.

"Mommy, don't go," she begged. She had started to calm down, but was only the slightest push away from breaking again.

"I'm sorry sweetie," Aurelia said, kissing her forehead. "Go to daddy. Mommy has people she needs to see."

She sniffled but managed to keep herself together. Aurelia felt guilt watching them go, but she shoved the feeling away. Now was not the time. As squads of soldiers spread out to scan the castle for any more intrusions, or at least discover how the assassins gained entrance in the first place, Aurelia opened a portal to her and Harruq's room. From there she grabbed her staff, one of her few cherished possessions she still had from their flight from Veldaren. Leaping back through the portal into the garden, she approached the rainbow sphere that had given her so much trouble. The closer she stepped to it the more she felt her magic fading, until when it was at her feet she was powerless once more.

With a satisfying *crack*, she smashed it with the butt of her staff. The sphere broke easily, letting out a great puff of smoke and color as it did. Scooping up the surprisingly cool shards, she closed her eyes to create another portal. The masks the assassins wore were familiar, and that they wielded magic made them doubly rare. But there was one man she knew that matched both qualities, a man that might either be behind the attack, or know who was responsible.

Through the portal she stepped, still holding the shards. When she exited, she was on a distant street in the trade district of Mordeina. The men and women passing by turned to gawk, and for once Aurelia wished she might fit in a little better. No time for a disguise, though, so she hurried to the tavern she'd been told to

## The Prison of Angels

go to if she ever sought to make contact. It wasn't the tavern itself she needed, though, but the dark alley beside it. A child sat there on a crate, looking bored. His hair was disheveled, his face dirty, but there was something of an act to his appearance. The alertness of his eyes, the healthiness of his skin, belied the supposed starvation of a street rat.

"Hello," Aurelia said to the boy.

"Don't feel like talking," was his response.

"I fear I'm not as wise as I thought," she said, as instructed. "Might you help me?"

The boy stared at her, then gave a curt nod.

"Wait here."

Aurelia stepped into the alley, holding her staff in one hand, the shards in the other. Several minutes passed, but at least she was out of clear sight of the traffic.

"Bored of your life in the castle?" asked a woman's voice from above.

Aurelia glanced up to see Veliana peering down from the rooftop of the tavern, a smirk lighting up her lone good eye. She wore the colors of her new guild, dark gray shirt and cloak with black sleeves and pants. In her left hand she twirled a dagger, her fingers dancing.

"I'd prefer the boredom over today," she said. "Where's your guildmaster?"

"Right here," Deathmask said, stepping out of the alley's shadows, his arms crossed behind his back. His long dark hair curled down around his neck. A gray mask covered his mouth and nose, but his eyes were sparkling with humor. "Ah, Aurelia, how good it is to see you again. Your beauty is as stunning as ever. Such a shame you waste it on that oaf of a half-orc you call a husband."

"I'm in no mood," Aurelia said, tossing the shards at his feet. "Someone tried to kill me and my daughter, and Antonil's son as well. I want to know why."

Deathmask lifted an eyebrow.

"Interesting. And you think I have the answer why?"

"All three assassins wore masks similar to yours."

"Hardly unique to cover one's face."

Aurelia crossed her arms, reminding herself not to take her frustration out on the wily rogue, despite how much she wanted to roast him down to ash so he'd match the name of his guild.

"They were also proficient with magic," she said. "Only one guild in Mordeina has members with any magical training that I know of: yours. And if it wasn't you, then you of all men should know who it was. No one has a better finger on the pulse of the underworld than you."

"No one since the days of the Watcher," Veliana said, laying on her back and continuing to twirl her dagger. "By the way, should I mention how stupid it'd be of you to come here if you actually thought we were guilty of the attack? But you're not that stupid, which means you don't think we were responsible. So please, lay off the demands, and keep the shallow reasoning to yourself, hrm?"

Fire swarmed around Aurelia's right hand.

"Easy now," Deathmask said. "I'd rather not have anyone die. No profit in it. Aurelia, when you arrived you oh-so-politely tossed something at my feet. Care to tell me what it was?"

"It was a sphere before I smashed it," Aurelia said, turning her attention back to Deathmask. Her fist clenched, removing the fire. "The assassins threw it at me just before they attacked. Somehow it created a hole in the world's magical weave, preventing me from casting any spells."

Finally she saw a bit of interest spark in Deathmask's eyes.

"Really now?" he asked, kneeling down and picking up one of the shards. "Interesting…"

"So please, what can you tell me? They wore gray and red, and all were light of skin if that helps."

"So they even dress similar to me now? How interesting. Are you sure I'm not the man responsible for the attacks? Enough coin and even I might rethink my allegiances. Angels do tend to make life as a rogue difficult."

"We went through too much together for you to turn on us without a chance to rectify things first," Aurelia said.

Deathmask laughed.

"Sentimentality? I think you confuse me for someone else, elf. No, the proof you need to know I wasn't behind this is much simpler. If it had been my guild making the attempt, you wouldn't be out hunting for the party responsible. You'd be dead."

He tossed the sphere shard back to the ground.

"What he threw at you is known as a voidsphere. Rare, but not impossible to craft if you know what you're doing. As for these assassins...no, I cannot tell you who might have hired them, nor the name of their organization. If any other guild started showing an affinity toward spellcasters, I assure you, I'd know about it. I'm sorry, but if you need answers, you'll have to look elsewhere."

There was no hiding Aurelia's disappointment. She clutched her staff and took a deep breath. The city wasn't big enough for a new guild with such power at their disposal to go unnoticed for long. Someone had to know.

"Please," she said. "If you learn anything, find me or my husband."

"I will," Deathmask said, winking. "If the profit's right."

Aurelia turned, ripped open a portal, and vanished.

※

Veliana watched the elf disappear into the swirling blue, then leapt down from her perch atop the tavern.

"You lied," she said.

Deathmask shrugged.

"I do that from time to time."

Veliana knelt before the shards of the voidsphere, scanning over the intricate detail required to carve the magic into its surface.

"What does it mean?" she asked.

"Games," Deathmask said, leaning against the wall. "People are playing games, and no matter what happens, we will benefit. Nothing can be worse than the way things are now."

"And if they kill Gregory?"

"Do I look like a man who will shed a tear?"

He was grinning, she could tell by the way his cheeks pulled upward at his mask.

"You look like a heartless bastard," she said, standing.

"You're making me blush. But no, Vel, until we know everyone's aims, we keep our mouths shut and our eyes open. Can you do that?"

"I can," she said. "But you still could have told them who was responsible. That alone would have been worth a princely reward."

"And ruin all this fun?" he asked, scattering the shards with his foot as he walked toward the street. "I dare say, Veliana, it's like you don't even know me anymore."

## 13

Entering Mordeina was a far different experience than Qurrah expected.

"Where are the angels?" he asked as they stepped through the second of the enormous gates. When he'd left years ago, they had flown about the city like hummingbirds around a flower. Now, though, it seemed even the floating city of Avlimar was absent of life.

"They hope to guard an entire nation," Tessanna said, pulling on his arm as they jostled through the overcrowded road leading directly up the hill to the castle. "Surely you didn't think they'd all be here?"

"I still expected more of a presence," Qurrah said. He caught sight of words scrawled upon the nearby buildings, written with a dark red paint of some kind. Each one effectively said the same thing: *all hail the Missing King*.

"Azariah was right," Tessanna said, and she pointed to where a man had gathered a crowd about him as he shouted from atop a makeshift pedestal of boxes. "Things are not well here."

The two made their way closer until they could hear his words. The speaker was a man Qurrah did not recognize, dark of hair, clean cut with a soft face. His eyes, however, bespoke madness.

"Now they brandish swords against our fellow men!" the speaker cried. "Now they threaten the blood of the innocent along with the guilty. Will we still let them lord over us? How many years until we are all afraid for our lives? How long until the very words I speak now are considered blasphemy that requires their justice?" He nearly spat out the word. "Their *grace*. Their *protection*. Where is our voice? Where is our king?"

"I've heard enough," Tessanna said, tugging on his arm. Qurrah stared at the man, letting his face burn into his memory. He held such anger, it was beyond rationality by that point. It was beyond convincing. This was a man frighteningly similar to Velixar, and that he had assembled such a massive crowd surprised him none. Such was the draw, and danger, of a man willing to tell others what they wanted to hear, feeding them half-truths and exaggerations so they might be angry instead of afraid.

At the castle doors the two stopped, unsure of how to gain entrance. They still wore the magical disguises they'd cast upon themselves, shifting their features, adding color to Tessanna's eyes and melding Qurrah's ears into something human. Fortunately they had time to think without being noticed, for another crowd had gathered at the gate, harassing the guards.

"The steward is seeing no more petitioners today!" the guards shouted, but the annoyed looks on their faces showed they knew it'd do little to make them disperse.

"What's that orcish bastard going to do about the angels?" the man beside Qurrah yelled.

"Nothing," said another, shouting loud enough to ensure all others heard him. "He's too busy sucking an angel's dick. How else you think he got on that throne?"

Qurrah's fists clenched as the crowd laughed. He'd never considered himself all that protective of his brother, and was surprised to find just how furious these disrespectful comments made him. Pushing to the front, he stepped before one of the guards, who tensed. He didn't lift his weapon just yet, but it was clear he was ready to if needed.

"I must speak with Harruq," he told the guard.

"You deaf? He's not taking petitioners, now get back before I make you."

"I'm not deaf," Qurrah said, banishing his disguise with a thought. "I'm his brother. Tell him Qurrah and Tess have come to visit. I guarantee you he'll grant us access."

The guard froze, and he glanced to the man beside him for any indication of what he should do. The other guard just shook his head.

"Go tell him," he said. "I don't want my head on a spit just because I turned away the steward's brother."

"What about them?"

He gestured to the mob, and Qurrah understood his fear. So far they seemed content to mock, yell, and insult, but at any moment their thirst for blood might rise. Such was the nature of a mob. Qurrah beckoned Tessanna closer. The moment she took her first step her disguise vanished, lengthening her hair, returning the blackness of her eyes and the paleness of her skin. Several beside her let out gasps upon seeing the change. For her part, Tessanna looked simply bored.

"Yes?" she asked Qurrah.

"The guards are afraid things might turn violent."

"They're right to be."

Qurrah chuckled.

"Never mind, then, I will handle them myself."

He stepped into the space between the guards and the mob. He felt their eyes upon him. A couple had overheard his discussion with the guards, and like lightning his name spread. He let them look, let them see the true face of the fairytale monster they'd made him into.

"Did you not hear?" he asked them. "The steward is not seeing any more petitioners."

Qurrah dropped to one knee, slamming his palm to the ground. A thin wall of shadows burst from the dirt, climbing over ten feet into the air. It formed a semicircle, sealing the door and the guards within its translucent protection. From the other side people yelled, and a few hurled stones that bounced off with a high-pitched *twang*.

"That will last an hour," Qurrah said, turning back to the guards. "Long enough for one of you to find my brother."

The first guard nodded, looking frightened but doing a fine job of trying to hide it. Turning, he banged on the giant doors twice. When they opened, he slipped inside just before they reclosed.

"Where are the rest of the guards?" Tessanna asked, eyeing the castle curiously. "It seems odd you would be alone. Is the threat not out here among the angry people?"

The remaining guard opened and closed his mouth, confirming Qurrah's suspicions that something more was amiss.

"I cannot say the reason," the guard said at last. "Forgive me, but until milord gives me permission, I can say nothing."

Qurrah and Tess shared a look.

"Very well," he said. "We'll leave you be."

A few minutes later the great doors reopened. A guard stepped out and beckoned to them.

"Follow me," he said.

They did, and it was only when the doors shut behind them were they finally free of the angry shouts of the people. Down the carpeted hall they walked, until the guard veered to the right, leading them into a small but well-furnished room. It had several chairs, a table already set with food, and a hearth that was currently empty given the warmth of the day. Tessanna grabbed an apple, took a bite.

"Wait here," was all the guard said before exiting. The door slammed shut, and from the outside they heard the lock slide into place.

"Trusting fellow," Qurrah said.

"While he was watching, you changed your appearance and then summoned a wall of darkness," Tessanna said, rolling the apple from hand to hand. "That he left us alone at all seems pretty trusting to me."

Qurrah chuckled.

"Since when did you become so understanding?" he asked.

"How else would I have stayed with you so long?"

She laughed at him, her eyes sparkling with humor, and Qurrah laughed with her. She seemed so happy, so content, so…normal. It wouldn't last long, he knew. It never did. But he'd appreciate it while it was there.

"Are you nervous?" she asked after taking another bite.

"A bit. How long ago did he visit our cottage? Surely a year now, if not longer. Aubrienna will be twice the size she was when we last saw her."

His niece's name was like a trigger, and immediately Tessanna ceased eating her apple. She lowered her head, shoulders curling inward. Nervous, shy, regressing. Qurrah put a hand on her shoulder, kissed the top of her head.

"You've been forgiven," he said to her. "Don't forget that. You're her aunt, that's all she knows you as."

"Her crazy, crazy aunt," Tess said, peering up at him through her long bangs, but despite her obvious discomfort, she smiled.

## The Prison of Angels

Qurrah kissed her again, then held her against him as he tried to ignore his own nervousness. It had been a long while since he'd seen his brother. Perhaps he'd be unwanted. After all, he was a living memory of all the agony his brother had suffered, a specter from a far darker past. Harruq's life had become so grand now. Exotic wife, beautiful daughter, friend of kings and steward of a kingdom. Would he, in his poor existence and plain robe, be just an unwanted reminder of childhood days stealing food and scrambling to find shelter when the weather turned sour...

A heavy fist knocked on the door twice before it barged open. Qurrah lurched to his feet, feeling like he'd somehow been caught. Standing there was his brother, wearing that same old leather armor Velixar had given them ages ago. Their eyes met, and all of Qurrah's fear and nervousness went flying out the castle and into the heavens.

"Qurrah!" Harruq exclaimed, wrapping him in a bear hug. "Why didn't you tell me you were coming?"

"Because then you wouldn't have the chance to tell us not to," Qurrah said, and he smiled at his brother. "I hear you've become a man of importance. What fool did you con to get that stupid crown on your head?"

"The only fool here is the one wearing the crown," Harruq said, his grin spreading.

He let go of Qurrah, returned to the door. Guards stood before it, their weapons at the ready.

"It's all right," Harruq said. "Bring them in."

One of the guards shifted, and in rushed two children. The boy was unfamiliar, but Qurrah easily recognized the little brown-haired girl, with her father's height and her mother's sparkling eyes. Qurrah knelt, opened his arms, and she quickly rushed his way.

"Hi uncle," she said, curling into him, and Qurrah was stunned by the familiarity she seemed to display. It'd been a year, after all, and Harruq had only brought her down to see them a handful of times. She acted like she felt safe in his arms, though, and that made it easy to ignore his own surprise and clumsiness. He closed his eyes, remembering a similar life he had robbed from all of Dezrel. Some day he prayed he might not have that pain and guilt haunt him. Someday, he just wanted to hold Aubrienna and be happy.

"She's quiet today," Qurrah said as Aubrienna continued to snuggle deeper into his robes. Meanwhile, the boy went and sat in one of the chairs, seemingly content to be alone and play with the toy soldier he carried. They both looked sullen, maybe even upset, depending on how he interpreted their silence and averted stares.

Harruq's smile wavered, and he turned to the guards.

"Give us some space," he said before shutting the door. When he turned around, Qurrah was floored by the rage in his brother's eyes. Had he ever seen him angrier? Just once, he thought. Just once.

"What's wrong?" Qurrah asked.

"Assassins," Harruq said. "Aurelia's out looking into it. While I was sitting on that damn throne, three men attacked Aurelia and the kids as they were playing in one of the castle's gardens."

"Who would dare?" Tessanna said, turning both their attentions to her. She'd remained quiet, lurking in the background when the children came inside. "Who would try to kill Aubrienna? Tell me, Harruq. Bring me to him if he lives, and I will make him suffer."

Harruq swallowed.

"They're dead," he said. "Aurelia killed them during the attempt."

Qurrah saw the rage and fear in his lover's eyes, nearly rivaling that in his brother's. She looked at Aubrienna, went to speak, then stopped. Qurrah knew she sought Aubrienna's embrace, but she feared what her very presence might do to the child. That she also loved her beyond words, that she saw her as the child she could never have, seemed a cruel fate for her unstable mind to struggle with.

"Do you want to go to your aunt?" he asked Aubrienna.

"All right," she said, sliding down from Qurrah's lap. Tessanna dropped to her knees, and when Aubrienna came to her, Tess wrapped her tightly in her arms. Eyes closed, she pressed her cheek against the top of Aubrienna's head.

"No one will hurt you," Tessanna whispered as she rocked back and forth. "No one, I promise. I promise."

Qurrah turned to Harruq, and he felt his own anger rising. Someone had struck at his family?

"Do you know why they attacked?" he asked.

Harruq shrugged.

"Popular as I am, I've got plenty of enemies, and Antonil has more. They may not have wanted Aurelia or Aubby. Gregory might have been the real target."

"Gregory?"

Harruq gestured to the quiet child.

"Gregory Copernus, as in Gregory, heir to the throne of Mordan."

From outside the door they heard another set of knocks. Harruq opened the door, and in walked a tired, disheveled Aurelia.

"Deathmask knows nothing," Aurelia said, wrapping her arms around Harruq and leaning her head against his chest. Her eyes flicked in the direction of Qurrah and Tessanna, but if she was surprised by her guests, she didn't show it.

"Then we're already out of ideas," Harruq said. "Shame you couldn't leave one of them alive."

"Sorry, honey, but you're not the only one with a temper when someone threatens our child."

Qurrah coughed to steal their attention.

"Perhaps you've forgotten," he said. "But the dead talk to me just as fine as the living…"

※

Thankfully they'd left the bodies intact, at least the two Aurelia hadn't burned to cinders. The guard in charge said they'd hoped their clothing or faces could be identified. Qurrah doubted either would be useful, but he didn't need such material clues. No, he had access to something far more useful.

"Clear out everything around him," Qurrah ordered. "Leaves, flowers, even bugs."

Harruq began sweeping the area as commanded. Qurrah watched him, feeling a tug of nostalgia. How many times had they worked his magic together, dabbling in arts that were so often beyond him? Not that he missed the experiments themselves. Thinking back to those times, sifting through body parts with his necrotically tuned mind…it'd been like a child cutting animals with a sword thinking himself training to be a knight. The shame of it was enough to make him shiver and push the memories far away.

"Find me small, smooth stones for the runes," he told Aurelia. "You should know the type I need."

Indeed she did, even if she didn't know the exact runes themselves. When the spell enacted, Qurrah's magic would flood into the carved runes. If shaped into something malleable as dirt, they'd be too weak, and the magic would break them, scattering the dirt and banishing the magic. But stone? Stone would hold. When he yanked this assassin's soul back to the world of Dezrel, Qurrah wanted him completely, thoroughly enslaved.

Tessanna lingered behind him, her hands on his shoulders as she quietly watched. When he had the first of the stones, Qurrah took out a dagger and breathed against it. The tip shimmered purple, and then he began to carve. The blade easily sliced through the stone, creating the straight and curved lines he needed. One after another he carved them, never hurrying. When finished with each stone, Tessanna would stand, situate it in its proper place around the body, and then return to where she had been sitting. Harruq and Aurelia watched, holding hands in the garden. It was just the four of them together, and for some strange reason it made Qurrah feel very much at home.

When the ninth stone was finished, he stood and stretched his back.

"Make sure not to interrupt me," he said. "Especially you, Harruq."

"I was there when you brought back the ghost of our father," Harruq said. "So don't act like I've forgotten how to behave during a ritual."

Qurrah chuckled. That, at least, was still a memory he cherished. Their father had been a coward and a racist, loathing the orcish race despite his coupling with their orcish mother. More and more Qurrah understood it for the confused, angry, and violent act it was, and more and more he both pitied and loathed his father.

Of course, they'd killed him prior to summoning his ghost and hadn't known his true relationship to them. The half-orc shook his head. No, even his better memories were tinged with death and guilt. Such was the past, he thought to himself. At least he could move on into the future with his head held high.

"Aurelia, have you ever witnessed something like this?" he asked.

The elf shook her head.

"No," she said. "I'm not sure I want to, either, but I will. This man tried to kill Aubrienna. I want to know why."

"We all do," Qurrah said. "And between me and Tess, I promise you, he will not have a chance to deny us. Everyone, quiet now. Let the ritual begin."

Qurrah knelt outside the circle of stones, putting his hands on one of them. The ancient word carved upon it was the same as the first word of the ritual. He'd chant them all repeatedly, filling them with magic like one would fill a pitcher with water, but this one was the first and most crucial. The words left his tongue, tinged with melancholy, and the magic began to pour out from him. Tessanna was at his side immediately, her hand atop his. They echoed one another, demanding the veil of life be split, using the body as a guide to find the soul it had once belonged to. The stones began to glow, first purple, then a vibrant orange, as if within the stone were a great swell of fire eager for release.

Faster and faster they spoke the words, until with a great tormented shriek the ethereal visage of the man rose from the dead shell of his body.

"Welcome back," Qurrah said, rising to his feet. "I assure you, your stay here will not be pleasant."

The man continued to wail. He still wore the clothes he'd had on when he died, which Qurrah knew was common. Returning to the world of the living, even as a spirit, meant a frantic attempt to become as they were before, almost like a coping mechanism. The wailing was also normal. Qurrah himself had experienced the transition once, when Velixar had ripped him out of eternity and back into his rotting corpse. The sensation was beyond explanation, a combination of confusion, pain, and abandonment. Qurrah's memories of everything beyond had fled him, and he suspected they would always be denied to him until he once more left the mortal coil.

But just because it was normal didn't mean he had to endure it.

"Silence," he ordered. The runes flared, and the spirit obeyed. Qurrah stepped closer, watching the spirit's eyes. When at last he saw a bit of sanity returning, he knew the transition was complete.

"Answer all questions asked of you," he ordered. "And speak no lies."

"As you wish," the assassin said. His voice was thin and whispery, as if he were in a distant room.

"What is your name?"

"We are not given names. We call each other by our colors."

Qurrah glanced to the others, frowned.

"Then what is your color?"

"My designation was Crimson."

"I can already tell this is going to go well," Harruq muttered. Qurrah winced, prayed his brother was wrong.

"Why did you attempt to kill Aurelia and the children?" he asked.

Crimson looked to Aurelia, and it seemed he recognized her.

"Because that was our task," Crimson said, as if it were obvious. "It is my highest disgrace knowing we failed. You should be dead, elf. We do not fail."

"Silence," Qurrah said. "Answer only the questions asked, spirit. You are not beyond feeling pain, let me assure you that."

Crimson glared but obeyed.

Qurrah looked at the others, to see if any had ideas where the line of questioning should go.

"What is the name of your organization?" Harruq asked.

"We have none that we are told."

"Your headquarters," Aurelia said. "Where is it located?"

"I do not know. I shared a room with three brothers. We left through a single door. Sometimes it took us to a new place to train. Sometimes it took us to a place to scout. Most times, it took us to who we were to kill."

The more Qurrah heard, the more he felt his stomach tighten. What he was witnessing, it was unreal.

"What were the names of those who taught you magic?" he asked.

"I do not know. We were only given numbers."

"Who were your trainers in swordplay?"

"I do not know. We were only given letters."

Harruq paced beyond the circle of runes.

"Are you sure they can't lie?" he asked. "This is getting stupid. What life did this guy lead?"

Aurelia reached out and grabbed his hand to stop his pacing.

"Raised in a single room, taught by men he didn't know," she said. "I think Haern might have known something of that life."

"One last question, spirit," Qurrah said, sensing everyone's patience nearing their limit. "Where is this door now? Where is it waiting for you?"

For the first time the spirit gave pause. Qurrah watched, then touched one of the rune stones with his finger. Power surged through it, pulsing into Crimson. The ethereal being let out a wail, its features fading for a brief moment.

"Answer me," Qurrah said, his voice calm.

"I do not know how to answer," Crimson said.

"Try."

"If we had succeeded, I would have known. I did not, therefore I do not know. That is the only way I can explain it."

Qurrah stood, glanced to the others. When none offered anything, Qurrah turned and dismissed Crimson.

"Go back to the Abyss," he told him. "Maybe down there you'll learn some answers."

He scattered one of the rune stones with his foot. Crimson shimmered and vanished, so that only his cold, pale body remained in the center. Harruq pulled free of his wife's hand, walked to the center, and gave a solid kick to the dead man's ribcage.

"Stubborn bastard," he grumbled. "That can't all be true…can it?"

"Most assassins are trained to withstand various forms of torture," Aurelia offered. "Is it possible that he could resist you, Qurrah?"

"No," Tessanna said. "That's not it. I sensed it as well. He spoke the truth, and even spoke it freely."

"You're right about one thing, though," Qurrah said, turning to face Aurelia. "That was a form of preparation against interrogation. These assassins, they've been created with a very real awareness of what someone like me can do. Whoever hired them did so knowing that no matter if they were taken dead, alive, or forced to speak after death, there'd be nothing to learn."

"That's it?" Harruq said. "That's all we get, even with your magic? Unbelievable. It's a shame Tarlak isn't here. Maybe he'd have some ideas."

"I can only help with what I know," Qurrah said. "But we're not completely in the dark. Such assassins take a lifetime to craft, and significant magic and coin. Whoever you have made as enemies, they are powerful and wealthy. I can't say I'm envious, Harruq."

Harruq crossed his arms and frowned.

"I think I'd rather be in the dark," he muttered.

"There is one man that might fit that definition," Aurelia said. "Lord Maryll."

Qurrah tried to match the name up to a face or position but failed.

"Who?" he asked.

"Lord Kevin Maryll," Harruq said, letting out a sigh. "The queen's older brother."

Qurrah's mind rapidly connected to earlier in the day, and he knew the answer to the question before he even asked it. The clothes had been too fine, and he had seemed much too certain that no guards would halt him despite his clogging of the main traffic to the castle.

"Is he fair skinned, dark hair, short beard?"

"You saw him in the streets, didn't you?" Harruq asked.

"I did. He had a crowd gathered, a boisterous one at that. It seems he and the angels don't get along, and neither does he look favorably upon his brother-in-law. I think it might be time you sit down and have a talk with Kevin."

Harruq groaned.

"Yeah," he said. "Gods damn it, I think you're right."

# 14

"This isn't necessary."

The queen paced back and forth before Harruq, who slumped in Antonil's throne.

"It is," he insisted. "You have to know that."

"You're going on assumptions based on learning nothing from a dead man," Susan said. "Forgive me for not being impressed."

"Not trying to impress you, only discover who tried to kill your son. These weren't normal assassins. They weren't even unusual assassins. These were expensive, dangerous, rare men that until today none of us knew existed. So before three more of them try to slice out my wife's throat and cook her with a fireball, I'd like to do whatever I can to find out who hired them. That sound fair to you?"

Harruq knew he was crossing the line, but he didn't care. His family was in danger because of this stupid role he'd accepted, so if he was going to withstand the risks, by the gods he was going to at least take advantage of the power. Those soldiers who remained had been sent out into the city, with orders to apprehend and bring in Lord Maryll for questioning. Harruq waited for him in the throne room, swords lying across his lap. He'd been sheathing and unsheathing them for the past ten minutes, desperately wishing he could plunge one of them into heart of whoever tried to kill his precious Aubby.

And his gut said that person was about to stand before him in the next few minutes.

"Let me talk to him," Susan said. "He listens to me, trusts me. If you start asking him questions, he'll think you're accusing him, and…"

"I *am* accusing him," Harruq said.

"Without proof? Without reason?"

"You know damn well we have reason. He hates your husband with a passion. Not much of a stretch to carry that over to his son."

"He's my brother," Susan said. "He's family, and nothing has ever been as important to Kevin as family."

"Me too," Harruq grumbled. "And that's why he's coming in for a talk."

The queen threw up her hands, stopped her pacing.

"I could override you," she said.

Harruq nodded.

"You could. And if you do, this whole charade is over. I'll step down as steward, grab Aurelia and Aubrienna, and high-tail it to the far ends of Dezrel. And you know what, your highness? I'm really, really hoping you override me right now."

Susan fell silent, and she respectfully dipped her head.

"I'm sorry," she said. "I will not undermine my husband in such a way, nor make him seem a fool. Question my brother, but do not harm him unless you have proof. Will you at least grant me that request?"

"Fair enough."

She stared at him, and he wished he had enough skill at reading people to understand the thoughts racing behind that stare. At last she curtseyed and hurried out of the room, leaving Harruq alone but for a few of his most trusted guards, who lurked behind various pillars and curtains. Kevin was one man, and so long as Harruq held his swords, he wasn't afraid. The others had wanted to be there with him, but Harruq had rightly guessed Susan's response to that. Already they treaded on thin ice. It'd do no good to toss in more weight.

Minutes passed at an interminable pace. When the doors finally cracked open, and Kevin Maryll stepped inside, Harruq almost felt happy. Almost. The desire to draw one of his swords was still the stronger impulse.

"Harruq!" Kevin shouted, hurrying down the carpeted hall. "Where's Susan? Where's Gregory? Are they all right?"

"They're fine," Harruq said, shifting in his seat. The handle of Condemnation was cold in his palm. It took every shred of his self-control to keep the blade sheathed.

"They are?" His relief appeared genuine. Harruq kept telling himself it was an act to keep his rage high. "The guards would only tell me there was an attempt on her life. They wouldn't say anything else. Did you capture the men responsible?"

"I don't know," Harruq said. He shifted again. Kevin was so close, now. Just a few steps and a thrust and he'd be dead. Not that he was imagining doing that repeatedly, of course. "I was thinking bringing you here was a first step to that."

Kevin froze in his tracks.

"Excuse me?" he asked.

"Those assassins were hired by someone wealthy, someone with many connections. Someone who might want King Antonil's son dead. And perhaps it's just me, but haven't you been out firing up crowds and spreading hatred against Antonil? Or should I say, the *Missing King*?"

Aurelia would have told him it was tactless, but Harruq was too amused by the shock in Kevin's eyes at such a blunt accusation to care.

"You bastard," Kevin said, his voice rising. "This is my sister you're talking about, my nephew! You think I'd want them dead because of my frustrations with Antonil and his angels?"

"The thought occurred to me," Harruq said. He stood, wanting to intimidate Kevin with his height and size. Kevin, however, seemed far from intimidated. He looked furious.

"When Antonil reclaimed Mordeina, his rule was tenuous at best. Many lords wanted to break up the nation, with the angels as the sole unifier among the various territories instead of a king. *I'm* the one who prevented that. Regardless of all he accomplished, Antonil was just a lowly soldier, without a hint of noble blood in him. Susan gave him that. She gave him legitimacy, she gave him a son. She became the queen he needed so others would view him as king. And all the while I whispered in the ears of other lords, telling them we needed a king, we needed a ruler."

Harruq shifted uncomfortably, feeling a bit of his righteous fury dwindling down, becoming more petulant and uncertain. Still, he had to continue. He had to know for certain.

"You act as if you gained nothing," he said. "Your sister's rise in power only increased your own. And because of that, you're now safe to rally men around you, spouting out hate and ignorance."

Kevin's eyes widened.

"Do you know why I rally those people in the streets?" he asked Harruq. "I do it to *protect* Susan and her son. My blood will become the blood of kings. My sister a queen, my nephew the first of Mordan's new generation of rulers. But every single bit of that is in danger so long as priests and angels lord over us, bringing us their rules, handing out their law with impunity."

Kevin spat at Harruq's feet.

"You think you know me, you think you understand why I do these things. You're a damn fool, half-orc. Look to the heavens, and for once, open your eyes. In my heart I do not believe my nephew will ever be king. How long until a man with wings sits on that throne? And what will we do then? What will we lowly, simple humans do?"

Harruq was caught off guard by his sincerity, his ferocity. Was it possible he was uninvolved? Looking back at it, it did seem a slight stretch. If Kevin had problems with Antonil and the angels, wouldn't it make more sense that he strike at them instead? Despite all his annoyances, he'd never shown any hostility toward his sister.

Thinking of the angels reminded him of similar matters he'd been delaying bringing up, but with Susan absent, there was really no better time.

"You have to stop these rallies," Harruq said. "The city's already in unrest because of the army's departure, and you're just making it worse."

"Oftentimes things must get worse before getting better," Kevin argued.

"Riots will begin any day now," Harruq said. "People will die. This needs to stop."

"Then stop it!" Kevin gestured wildly. "I only give voice and reason to their unrest. I only allow them to see the reason for their anger. Do you think Mordeina is the only place turning against this oppression? The countryside is worse, so much worse, and yet I'm not there to stir it up. For five years now the angels have dealt death and spared lives, all without a single care for the desires of mortal men."

"Then what do you want me to do about it?" Harruq asked. "How in the fires of the Abyss am I supposed to stop it?"

Kevin calmed down a bit, becoming more earnest, more businesslike.

"At the start of the month I sent riders to all four corners of Mordan," he said. "Every single settlement has already received my request. I'm calling in elders, spokesmen, anyone who can come and speak for the people of their respective towns. It shouldn't be long before the first of them arrives."

"Why? What do you think this will accomplish?"

"We live under the rule of angels who supposedly follow a god," Kevin said. "A god that none of us can hear, a god whose own priests say now slumbers after the war. Yet we are powerless before their rule. Some men live, and others die, and there is no consistency, no justice. Murderers and rapists should be strung up to hang, yet many find themselves forgiven, only to repeat their crimes months later. We need a voice. We need a say in these things. I'm summoning them all to hold a council. I want the angels to hear the concerns of those they rule over. I want them to admit they aren't gods, to open their eyes and realize that we do not serve them. They serve us."

There was some wisdom to the idea, Harruq had to admit that. And over the past several days he'd been hearing of the growing unrest, especially over a supposed attack in a village that no one could identify for certain despite his best efforts. If this council might prevent riots, it'd be worthwhile. And the representatives were already on their way...

"What do you want me to do?" he asked.

"Make the angels attend. Make them promise to listen, and convene a vote on the requests our people give. And if not..." Kevin gestured to the throne. "You are steward of the kingdom, ruler over the men therein. If the angels will not answer to you, then what is the purpose of having a king?"

"I'll talk to Ahaesarus," Harruq said. "I can't promise their cooperation, but if this will help, then I'm willing to try. But in return, you need to calm the people instead of inflaming them. You're getting what you want, so give me what I want, or I'll send troops to arrest you in the street no matter what Susan thinks."

"Your eloquence knows no bounds," Kevin said, bowing. "Tell the angels to convene the council a week from tomorrow.

That should be enough time for everyone to arrive. Now if I might have my leave, I'd like to check on my family."

The lord turned and marched to the side of the throne, into the darker recesses of the pillars.

"Oh, Kevin," Harruq said, unable to help himself. "There is one way to prove to me your innocence. Stand before an angel. Swear to him you had nothing to do with the assassination attempt, and let him judge whether you speak truth or lie."

Kevin looked over his shoulder as he stopped before the door leading deeper into the castle. Instead of the anger he expected, the man only laughed.

"You're such a fool," he said. "A damn, stupid fool in so far over your head you haven't a hope to avoid drowning. The angels aren't your savior, Harruq. They're your executioner. The sooner you realize that, the better."

The door slammed shut behind him, and Harruq had only impotent rage to offer in return.

---

Qurrah was not much for putting off uncomfortable things, so when they'd been assigned their room in the castle, and Tessanna slumbered restlessly from their journey, he left her there and sought out Harruq's room. To his mild surprise, two guards stood before the door, and they tensed at his arrival.

"I only wish to ask my brother a question," he told them.

One of the guards rapped on the door. After hearing it unlock from within, the door popped open, and Harruq's face peered out. Seeing Qurrah, he grunted and opened it the rest of the way, revealing him standing there with only a loose bed robe wrapped around his muscular body.

"Something wrong?" he asked.

"No," Qurrah said. He glanced at the guards, then decided there was nothing too unusual about his request. He'd still be honoring Azariah's desire for privacy.

"How does one get to Avlimar?" he asked.

Harruq raised an eyebrow.

"With wings. Care to explain?"

"I'd rather not."

Harruq shrugged.

## The Prison of Angels

"Wait here."

He shut the door, returning less than a minute later. In his hands was a golden scepter. Its length was about half his arm, and at the very top was a silver stone barely larger than a man's pinkie.

"Get into open space, hold it aloft, and then speak the name Ashhur," Harruq explained as he handed it over. "Someone will come find you, I promise. After that, it's up to you to convince them to give you a lift."

"I'll return this before the night's over," Qurrah promised, holding the scepter against his chest. It was surprisingly warm, and he detected an aura of magic about it. Harruq yawned, waved him away.

"Return it in the morning," he said, shutting the door.

Qurrah chuckled, caught the guards looking at him. He shot one a wink, then hurried away. After two tries, he managed to find his way out of the castle, stepping out into the courtyard surrounding the structure atop the great hill it'd been built upon. The night sky was heavily clouded. Only Avlimar was visible, just a distant gold star. In that darkness, Qurrah held the scepter above his head, noting it much heavier than it should have been. Steadying it with both hands, he whispered the command word.

"Ashhur."

He squinted his eyes, expecting some sort of bright flash or signal. Instead, the silver stone began to glow softly, its golden light soothing to look upon. It pulsed once, twice, and then into the sky shone a great pillar, piercing the clouds so that its light pushed on through the slowly forming gap. Qurrah's mouth dropped open, impressed. Its color was like that of Lathaar's sword, or Jerico's shield, a strong blue-white, vibrant with energy. In the center of the beam, soft smoke curled and rose, vanishing the moment it left the beam. The light spread nowhere beyond the beam, not even brightening his hands as they held the scepter. Given its distinct brightness and color, he had no doubt it could be seen for miles and miles even during the day.

In less than a minute he heard the sound of flapping wings. An angel landed before him, one of their warriors, his body clad in armor and a spear strapped to his back.

"I am Loen, and I bring to you the blessings of Ashhur," the angel said. "I saw the signal in the sky and have come. What matter requires my aid?"

"My name is Qurrah Tun," he said, bowing his head in respect. "I seek permission to travel to Avlimar and speak with Azariah."

A look of curiosity passed over Loen's face and quickly vanished.

"I remember you," Loen said. "You were of much interest after the trial to decide your fate. You look healthier, now. More alive."

Qurrah felt mildly embarrassed thinking of the trial, when he'd been ready to accept death at the angels' hands. Only Harruq had stopped them by demanding whatever fate be given to Qurrah also be given to him. The idea of killing his brother while trying to atone for his own sins…Qurrah couldn't do it. His brother's selflessness had been the only reason he'd lived, and that's what shamed him. At the time, Tessanna had been alone with that monster Velixar and Thulos's legion of demons. Qurrah had been willing to give up even her, had twice tried to make his brother end his life so he might not feel guilt or anguish.

Such weakness. Such childishness.

"I'm a better man now than I was," he told Loen. "Perhaps that is all you see?"

"Perhaps. Azariah is in his study. If you do not mind waiting outside it, I will see if he accepts your company."

"Thank you," Qurrah said, bowing his head again. "How will I arrive?"

The angel took the scepter from Qurrah and then tucked it into the same loops that held his spear.

"Do not fear falling," he said. "But if you are afraid, I suggest closing your eyes and not looking down."

Qurrah smirked as the angel flapped his wings several times, lifting them into the air. He'd stepped into the chaos that was Tessanna's mind and seen the nightmares of her past; heights weren't going to frighten him. Wrapped in the angel's arms, he felt plenty secure. The wind whipped against his face, and he had to squint his eyes to see. The city of Mordeina shrank below him, and

## The Prison of Angels

high above, the shining star that was Avlimar grew closer and closer.

The strangest sight was the floating rock beneath it all, as if the pull of the world meant nothing on the parcel of land broken and hurled free from the Golden Eternity. It looked brown and compacted, like any other earth, but it supported the great weight of the structure built atop it. Every precious metal was crafted into spires, towers, slender homes and broad bridges. Some buildings were gold, others silver. To his surprise, there were many gardens, their vibrant colors easy to see despite the night. Avlimar was always lit, no darkness allowed within. Copious amounts of torches lined the buildings, and it seemed the very gold of the streets hummed with ethereal brightness. In that light, the green of trees somehow complemented the extravagant colors, adding life and color to the otherwise overwhelming metal beauty.

There were many flat segments of street at the edge of the floating city, and they landed on one of them. Qurrah staggered momentarily when released from Loen's grip, then quickly steadied himself. There was something unusual about standing there, almost like being upon a boat despite no discernible rocking or motion.

"Have you been to Avlimar before?" Loen asked him.

Qurrah remembered arriving as an undead monstrosity, pulled along by Velixar's commands as war demons surged through the windows and towers, battling angels by the thousands.

"Only once," Qurrah said.

"Follow me, then," Loen said. He walked down the street, which slowly narrowed the farther from the edge they traveled. Qurrah marveled at the architecture. It seemed everything was ornamented to an absurd extent. Walls were decorated with intricate carvings, paintings, even sculptures cut into their sides. Pausing at one, he looked at a bewildering collection of overlapped concentric circles, making it seem like the doorway of the home were the center of a great vortex of lines and motion. It had to have taken hundreds of hours to carve, Qurrah thought. Of course, in a land of no ruin and death, time for even the most trivial things could be afforded…

"This way," Loen said, breaking his line of thought. "Azariah rarely stays in Avlimar for long, and I would be remiss if tardiness kept you from meeting him."

"Of course," Qurrah said as his fingers traced along the lines. "Perhaps another time I can explore."

It was to the very tallest of towers that Loen took him, located not far from the center of the city. Along the way, Qurrah was surprised by how few angels he spotted. The creatures did not sleep like regular mortals, so he saw no reason for the silence, yet it was there all the same.

"Why is the city so empty?" he asked as they approached the great spire, which rose like a sharp-peaked mountain, except instead of snowy peaks it was decorated with marble and pearl.

"The harvest is great, the workers few," Loen said. "We are scattered throughout the land, and with our aid, many new towns have sprouted in the far north. But soon Avlimar will be filled with angels to vote in the coming council."

"Council?" Qurrah asked.

"Did your brother tell you nothing of it?"

"No, he did not."

"A meeting with human elders," Loen said, pulling open the golden doors to Azariah's spire. "To hear their concerns, and allow them to open their hearts to us so we might learn how to better serve them."

*Interesting*, thought Qurrah. Was that a result of his meeting with Kevin? Seemed a bit opposite of the intended result, that being Kevin hanging from a gibbet.

"Wait here," Loen said.

The angel stepped through the door, which was oversized to accommodate his wings. All of the doors and walkways were large like that, making Qurrah, who had grown up thin and sickly, feel all the smaller. Staring up at the spire, Qurrah admired the craftsmanship it took to build it. For some reason, it had a newness to it the rest of the city did not. Perhaps it was the height, or maybe because it was the lone building he'd seen so far that possessed a pointed rooftop instead of a flat one.

"Qurrah?"

Azariah stepped out of the door, followed by Loen.

"I'd have words with you," the half-orc said, falling to one knee.

"Of course," Azariah said. "All are welcome here. If we might have time alone, my dear Loen. My guest and I will require privacy for him to speak his troubled heart, but do not go far. He will need you to return home."

Qurrah held back a chuckle. So his troubled heart would be the excuse to hide his lessons at magic? Oh well. Whatever worked.

When Loen was gone, Azariah gestured for Qurrah to step inside. As the door shut, Qurrah's eyes needed a moment to adjust. Azariah's spire was bright even by Avlimar's standards. Light shone not from torches but instead various gems, crystals, chandeliers, even candles carved of marble with no visible wick. It all spoke of magic. Amused, Qurrah wondered if Azariah had lost his clerical abilities because he wasted them on something a simple torch and wax candle could accomplish.

"You should have requested my presence," Azariah said, gesturing for Qurrah to take a seat. The chair was large, the cushions overstuffed with feathers. There was an ornate fireplace before it, and in the hearth burned a fire that gave off heat yet appeared to have no effect on the log within. The carpet was thick, a deep crimson that was easy on the eyes, a welcome respite after all the shining metals. Kicking off his sandals, Qurrah slumped in the chair (which was, of course, far too big for him) and let his bare feet sink into the carpet.

"If I'd known teaching you magic would have such comforts, I'd have agreed far more readily," he said, closing his eyes as the heat from the fire washed over him.

"Such tutelage will no longer be necessary," Azariah said.

Qurrah's eyes snapped open, and he peered around the chair. The angel remained standing beside the stairs leading higher up into the spire. All around him were paintings of forests, of which Qurrah had no doubt Azariah had both been to, and painted himself.

"Is that so?" he said, trying to hide his surprise. "You seemed rather insistent when we last met."

"I'm sure I did."

Qurrah frowned, and he pushed himself out of the chair.

"I came to Mordeina at your request," he said. "And maybe it is just me, but it's a bit rude to request someone's help, then turn them down when they arrive to offer it. Now, I wouldn't claim myself as brilliant in the ways of Ashhur as you, so perhaps you can answer the question for me…is rudeness a sin?"

"Your wit and sarcasm are both unnecessary and unappreciated," Azariah said, crossing his arms.

"Then care to tell me why you changed your mind?"

The angel looked to the side, and he seemed confused, almost frustrated.

"My decision should not reflect poorly on you or Tessanna," he said at last. "My coming to you…that was not wise. If my power from Ashhur is waning, then I should accept that as reality, and not try to hide it. Unfortunately I came to you in pride, seeking to remain the most powerful of angels. I'm sorry to waste your time, Qurrah."

It didn't make sense, no matter how many times Qurrah ran the words through his mind.

"You said you came to me in humility," the half-orc insisted. "Now you say it is pride?"

"I wanted secret training to avoid the mockery of mortal men," Azariah said. "That is pride. I wanted power to replace the power I lost. That is pride. I cannot do this for such a reason. I cannot let my pride control my actions. I thank you for coming, Qurrah, but perhaps humility is what I need to learn now."

"So you're accepting the loss of your clerical magic?"

Azariah sighed.

"Accepting it? Yes. I will not lie and say I am pleased. I will not pretend I do not miss it, nor act like I do not wish it returned. But I won't have you as a teacher, Qurrah, nor your lover. This is a decision I made on my flight home, one I cannot fully explain. I hope you understand."

Qurrah didn't, but then again, he was trying to understand an angel. It seemed that, while on the outside they seemed simple and predictable, the truth of them was anything but.

"Very well," he said. "We will remain here for a time longer, at least until I'm certain of my brother's safety. If you change your mind, let me know."

"I assure you, Qurrah," Azariah said. "I won't."

Something about his tone of voice was strikingly cold. Azariah opened the door, and when Qurrah stepped out, he called for Loen. The angel landed moments later, having spent the time hovering above the spire in a lazy circle.

"Return my friend to the castle," Azariah said. "I have much studying to do in preparation for the convening council, and cannot afford the time."

"I would be happy to," Loen said, turning to Qurrah. "Are you ready?"

Qurrah nodded.

"The night is late. Yes, please take me home."

Once more they walked through the city to the very edge before Loen wrapped his arms around him and beat his wings.

"I must warn you," Loen said. "The trip down is far more intense than the trip up."

At first Qurrah thought it an exaggeration, but as they plummeted off the edge in free fall he changed his mind. Perhaps there were a few things left that might frighten him. Several times he glanced at the angel's outstretched wings, having to remind himself that yes, they could indeed support their weight. As the city neared, Loen banked upward, stealing much of their speed so that during a second descent they came in much slower toward the castle. With surprising gentleness Loen pulled up at the last moment, setting Qurrah's feet on the ground without the slightest difficulty.

"Many thanks for being my guide," Qurrah said, turning to face the angel.

"Perhaps when you are not so tired, and the hour not so late, I can better show you the artwork and structures."

"I would very much like the chance."

Loen saluted. Before taking flight, he placed a hand on Qurrah's shoulder.

"I once doubted your worth, even after the trial," he said. "But I heard of your stand on Ashhur's Bridge. And when you killed Karak's prophet, a great evil left this land. It was like a thorn pulled from all our minds. You have done great things, and I would thank you before I leave."

The admiration left him stunned. He'd gotten used to his accomplishments being overlooked, or remaining completely unknown.

"What little good I've done, I did not do alone," Qurrah said, feeling his neck flush. "But I accept your thanks nonetheless."

Loen took to the air, slowly fading away into the clouds as he soared toward Avlimar. His heart troubled, Qurrah stared at the glowing city, like a great star in the night, and wondered.

## 15

Kinamn looked a desolate wreck, but Tarlak knew looks could be deceiving. After all, why else would he prance around in his yellow robes?

"Are you sure you want to attack?" the wizard asked. Beside him, Antonil nodded.

"This city represents my greatest failure," the king said. "We can't ignore it, and we can't leave so many orcs gathered at our flank. We take it back, or we return now to Mordeina. Those are our choices."

Tarlak shrugged.

"I'm all for going home, but roasting orcs is fun, too. Give the word, my king, and I'll begin the bonfire."

Behind them, thirty thousand men prepared for battle. They were far out of range of any catapult, just in case the orcs there still had them functioning. Dozens of smoke trails lifted lazily into the sky, proving the city occupied.

"It's been several years, don't forget," Tarlak said. "There may have only been five thousand last time, but it wouldn't surprise me if thousands more flocked out of the unguarded Wedge and into the place."

"I assure you, Tarlak, treating the situation lightly is the one thing I will absolutely not do this time," Antonil said. "We go in with eyes open, and more importantly, your magic at the ready. The orcs might have ballista and catapults, but we have an Eschaton, who is worth a hundred catapults."

"And costs more, too, I might add."

Antonil laughed.

"No need to mention it," the king said. "You only remind me daily."

"I know. And one sweet day you'll finally listen, and pay me."

Again they laughed, but for Tarlak the jovialness was forced. He didn't like this assault one bit, but he wasn't the one in charge. So what if they hadn't encountered a single orc raid on their travel east? So what if their supplies had gone untouched, their passage completely unimpeded into enemy territory? Antonil's generals assured them that their numbers were so great the pitiably few orcs remaining would only flee.

But Tarlak's gut said differently, and staring at the broken walls of Kinamn, he knew that something was amiss. He just couldn't decide what.

"The men are ready to move out," said Sergan, coming up to join the three. Sergan was an old, battle-hardened veteran from Antonil's days as Guard Captain for the city of Veldaren. His face was scarred, his beard long, but he wielded his ax with a spryness many of the younger men struggled to match after days of marching.

"Remember, I want the archers spread as far apart as possible," Antonil said. "If they do have war engines, I want their effect minimized."

"And the city gates?" Sergan asked. "You sure you want to cram all twenty-five thousand of our fighting men into such a narrow space? One well-placed boulder from a catapult and we'll have hundreds turned to jelly."

The king gestured to Tarlak, who tipped his hat.

"Consider me the anti-boulder guy," he said. "And trust me, the city gates won't be that narrow after I'm done with them."

Sergan shook his head.

"Putting our faith in wizards," he said. "It's going to get us killed one day."

"Love you too, Sergan," Tarlak said, shooting him a wink. "Now go tell the men to move their asses. We're not getting any younger, and we have orcs to kill."

Horns began to sound throughout the massive camp. They left much of their supplies behind, along with the wagons. With the city a mere quarter-mile away, there seemed little point in lugging it all with them. Tarlak watched it all, thinking of them like an incredibly dangerous nest of ants. Toward the city they swarmed, and Tarlak rode beside Antonil and Sergan. The rest of the generals filtered throughout the army, to command their individual forces.

Tarlak saw the smoke trails within the city extinguish, one by one. For some reason, that frightened him more than anything. A

# The Prison of Angels

foe awaited him behind those walls, moving, strategizing. Yes, they were orcs. Yes, they were stupid. But they still had the blood of elves in them. When it came to killing, they seemed a bit more willing to use their brains instead of muscle. But no matter how clever they might be, Antonil commanded thirty thousand men. Even if they'd doubled their number since the previous assault, they were still outnumbered three to one.

Five to one, really, once they counted in Tarlak's advantage.

As they neared the city walls, the first of the orcs finally appeared atop the ramparts. There were several hundred of them, all wielding long spears.

"Take them out!" Antonil shouted, and Sergan quickly relayed the order. The archers lifted their bows, and five thousand men sent a barrage of arrows toward the walls. The fighters on the front lines raised their shields, and those behind kept their heads down and followed after. Spears rained down upon the soldiers, scoring kills. The archers took down many, and even more spears broke against the shields. Tarlak nodded, liking the sight. He remained at Antonil's side, watching the fight, waiting for the right time.

"They're almost to the gates," Antonil said.

"I know."

"They're not carrying even a battering ram."

"I know."

Tarlak cracked his knuckles, mentally counting down. Three…two…one…

He slammed his wrists together, shouting out the words of a spell. From his palms shot a fireball that grew larger and larger the farther through the air it flew. It arced upward, as if shot from a catapult, then slowly began to descend. Tarlak watched, his eyes tracing its downward fall.

"Come on," he said. "Come on, drop, drop, drop…"

With perfect aim the fireball slammed into the gates when Antonil's men were only dozens of feet away, exploding with enough force that the shieldmen in the front had to brace against it. Metal and wood twisted and fragmented. More impressive, the stone walls cracked and rumbled, and leather-armored orcs screamed and as the towers atop the portcullis crumpled and fell. Suddenly the entrance to the city was triple what it'd been only moments before. Antonil's men let out a cheer, and with renewed vigor they rushed ahead, to where the orcish defenders stood at the ready.

"Something's wrong," Tarlak said. "Antonil, what in blazes is going on?"

There were only a mere thousand to stand against them. They shouted and waved their weapons, crude blades and axes, but against the swarm of men they would be buried in minutes. Antonil frowned, and he clearly had the same worry.

"It's been years," he said. "Perhaps the orcs abandoned the place? Or there was infighting among the tribes?"

Tarlak didn't buy it. He readied his magic, his gut still screaming trap.

And then the catapults fired from either side of the far street. The giant rocks sailed into the air, four at a time. They surely couldn't see the combat from behind all the buildings, Tarlak knew, which meant someone coordinating the attack. With no time to think on it, he acted fast, his hands dancing. In his mind he gripped the broken rubble of the gateway he'd just shattered, clutching it with invisible hands stronger than a giant's. Into the air he flung them, slamming them against the incoming boulders. The hits halted their momentum, showering thick sledges of heavy stone all across the city—which was fine with Tarlak, so long as they weren't landing on their own men, crushing them into jelly as Sergan had so eloquently stated.

More catapults fired, and this time Tarlak was better prepared. Instead of relying on crude rocks, he used the force of magic itself, slamming into them with invisible barriers that shoved the projectiles back before they could even complete their upward arc. A third volley lifted, and Tarlak defeated it just as easy.

"Not even breaking a sweat here," Tarlak told the king. "Perhaps I should have been with you last time."

"Perhaps," Antonil said, clearly distracted. The catapults ceased firing, and Tarlak lowered his arms and took a deep breath. When he brought his attention to the fight, he realized there wasn't one at all. The orcs had been slaughtered in a single wave. Tarlak guessed they'd taken maybe a hundred casualties at maximum, the fight had gone so well. And that really, really worried Tarlak.

"It's not supposed to be this easy," he murmured.

Antonil clapped him on the shoulder.

"If there's bad days, then there's allowed to be good days," he said.

"If you insist."

The archers had begun to join the rest of the men still flowing into the city, and Antonil went with them. Tarlak remained on the outside, watching. Something felt wrong in his gut. The orcs wouldn't have abandoned the city, and he doubted their numbers would decrease so dramatically. More troubling, the city showed too many signs of orcish occupation. All along the walls were crude paintings, signifying allegiance to their tribal lord. From various wooden poles hung flags made of tanned hide. Their distance was too great for him to see, but he knew such decorations meant the orcs considered this land to be theirs to keep and defend.

So why such a pitiful defense?

His feelings of being cornered, of being trapped, led him to glance behind him, and it was there he saw it.

"Oh shit," said Tarlak.

Smoke rose in great plumes from the south. Their camp.

Tarlak slammed his hands together, ripping open a portal to take him to the camp's outer edge. Leaping through, he prepared his magic for a fight. But when he stepped out, there was nothing for him to kill. Only wreckage remained. Their tents had been smashed and ripped, the tent poles snapped. The cattle they'd brought for slaughter were in pieces, intestines ripped open and left for the swarms of flies that had already begun their feast. Worst were the wagons, and feeling himself in a dream Tarlak slowly approached. Every one of them was aflame. Corpses lay about them, throats cut, limbs broke and bodies savaged. Perhaps a hundred had remained behind, tending the animals, preparing the food. They hadn't stood a chance against whatever force descended upon them.

The wizard shook his head, the pit in his stomach growing.

"I hate being right," he said to himself. "Damn it, Tarlak, you know you're allowed to be wrong for once. At *least* once."

But not this time.

In the ruins of Kinamn the three gathered to discuss their options while the rest of the soldiers scavenged the city for anything useful.

"We're fucked," Tarlak said. "Righteously, magnificently, pants-rippingly fucked."

"So eloquently stated," Antonil said, sitting opposite him, a small fire between them. The sun had begun to set, but without tents, the army would have to make do with sleeping under open air or bunking in one of the many filthy homes that remained standing within the city walls.

"Truthfully stated as well," Sergan agreed. "Whoever set this trap showed more cunning than I'd ever give an orc credit for. I looked over the bodies of the thousand left behind, and they were all runties, weak by orcish standards. They were just there to provide distraction so the catapults could get their shots in. Brutal, but efficient. Without Tarlak's help, we'd have lost hundreds of men."

The three fell silent, thinking over what they'd seen. Antonil in particular looked ashen in the face, taking the ambush far worse than the others.

"What do we know of their commander?" he asked. "What orc outsmarted us so easily?"

"Far as I know, Trummug still rules the bulk of the orcs, and has since Veldaren fell," Tarlak said. "But our news from the east is pretty sparse. If Dieredon were around I'd ask him, but he's never mentioned any major upheaval, at least not to me."

"I checked all the flags and banners," Sergan said. "Plenty of drawings written in blood, and most carry the same sign. It's not Trummug's, I know that. Instead, they all show this…"

He picked up a rolled piece of leather beside him and unfurled it. It was a flag, half the size of a man. On its dull brown surface was a symbol drawn with blood, though faded by the sun: two triangles adjacent each other, both pointed upward.

"What are they supposed to be?" Antonil asked. "Teeth? Eyes?"

"Normally I'd suggest the standard lack of artistic skill in orcs," Tarlak said. "But I saw that drawn on the walls of the city as well as many of the buildings. Whatever it is, it's the symbol of their new warlord. Sadly, your men were so eager for a fight they didn't leave any orcs alive for us to question. Hopefully next time you might order them to be more careful."

"I'll make sure we get prisoners," Sergan said. "My gut says we'll be encountering raiding parties from here on out. This new commander was biding his time, waiting until the right moment to hit…and with us out of food and supplies, now is definitely the right time."

"Enough of this orc," Antonil said. "We'll find him in time, and when we meet on the battlefield, we'll crush him. For now, we have larger problems to deal with, specifically the fate of our campaign. What are our options?"

"Options?" Tarlak asked. "Just one. We turn back toward Ker and march as fast as our feet can carry us. We don't have the food for a campaign. They slaughtered our livestock, torched our wagons, and then ran for the hills."

"The orcs fled here in a hurry," Sergan said, shaking his head. "It's not quite that bad, but close. We've discovered various stockpiles left behind, and while I doubt anyone here will enjoy the mystery meats, nor want to know what they are, at least it's still food. No one will be starving for a few weeks, not if we tighten our belts."

"A few weeks?" Tarlak rolled his eyes. "Where exactly will we go in a few weeks? If Veldaren is guarded at all, we won't be able to siege it. If we're harassed on our way east, given even a slight delay, we'll start leaving a trail of bodies. We can't do this."

"We can," Antonil said. "We don't go to Veldaren. We go to Angelport instead."

Tarlak rubbed his eyes.

"Really?" he asked.

"Yes," Antonil said, glaring. "Their boats and walls have kept them safe. We can liberate their surrounding fields, barter for food, and given time, restock with supplies from the west until we're ready to march north."

Tarlak could hardly believe what he was hearing.

"Antonil, my king, you have to understand…this campaign is lost. Those orcs hit us exactly where it hurt the most, and if you think a besieged holdout of a city will be able to support thirty thousand additional men…"

"This campaign is not lost!"

Antonil stood, jaw trembling. Immediately he looked away, as if embarrassed for his outburst.

"It's not," he said quietly. "I won't turn us around. I won't retreat back to Mordan as such a colossal failure again. Thirty thousand men, outsmarted by brute thugs, and sent running with a mere thousand dead runties to our names? No, we strip Kinamn of every shred of supplies, then hurry toward the coast."

"And if anyone tries to stop us?" Tarlak dared ask.

"I hope they do," Sergan said, drumming his fingers atop the handle of his ax. "Because anyone trying to stop us will have food on them. We can make it to Angelport, I'm certain of that. Our men haven't given up yet. To many, this was still a victory, and I have no intention of convincing them otherwise. Tarlak, you've summoned food before. That's why we didn't starve when we fled Veldaren ages ago. Can't you do the same now?"

Tarlak sighed, felt in one of his hidden pockets of his robes.

"I don't have enough topaz," he said. "Not for thirty thousand. I can maybe feed our entire army for a day, maybe two."

"That's two days more than we had before," Antonil said. "Don't lose faith on me, Tarlak. Without you, we're lost."

Tarlak chuckled, and despite it all, he put a smile on his face and tipped his tall yellow hat.

"I guess compared to what we've dealt with before, this is only a minor inconvenience," he said. "I mean, it's not like there's going to be flying demons and an angry war god chasing after us."

"Always looking on the bright side," Sergan said, and he laughed.

Tarlak laughed with him, though it was entirely forced.

## 16

Jessilynn waited in the dark, hating that she'd been left behind. It reminded her of her earliest days after entering the Citadel, friendless and alone because of her sex. She'd only been eleven, unable to fully understand why the other boys looked at her like she was a different species. The days had been long, and that first year she'd cried herself to sleep more times than she could count. But through it all, she'd endured. Jerico in particular had done everything he could to make her feel welcome, accepted. In time she'd finally felt like she belonged.

Belonging, though, still didn't mean she was like the others. Getting dressed, keeping herself clean during her monthlies, even taking a piss meant going off on her own. It was like a sore on the roof of her mouth that refused to go away. Most of the time she could easily ignore it, pretend it didn't bother her, but sometimes…

Without a fire to warm her, or even provide mild entertainment, she sat huddled and did her best to pray to Ashhur. She begged for patience, for calm. Most of all, she asked her god for bravery, because no matter what Dieredon decided, she knew it would not involve running away, not from such a massive gathering of forces.

After far too long, she heard the sound of wings, and then Sonowin softly landed in the flat yellow grass nearby. Dieredon hopped off, and though Jessilynn had stood at his arrival, he only sat down beside her. He said nothing, staring up at the stars in thought. It made Jessilynn uncomfortable, and she crossed her arms and shifted her weight from foot to foot.

"I wish you'd bring me with you," she said, breaking the silence.

"Your armor is too loud. It would give us away."

"Weren't you going to teach me to make new armor?"

Dieredon finally looked her way.

"Indeed," he said. "But it seems we won't have time for such lessons, will we?"

She deserved that, she knew, but at least he was talking to her now.

"What did you learn?" she asked, sitting back down and facing him.

Dieredon looked to the west, where the creatures of the Wedge had gathered in the ravine.

"There does appear to be some sort of ruling council," he said. "The various races on the whole do not interact with one another, but I've seen lone members go into the wolf-men side, or at least close to it. There's a large pile of bones nearby, and it isn't just refuse like I first thought. They're meeting there, discussing. Right now, it appears there is a wolf-man strong enough to frighten not only his kind, but the rest of the creatures as well."

"Then our task is simple," Jessilynn said. "We kill that wolf-man, and the alliance collapses in his absence."

Dieredon nodded.

"That is my belief as well, though it will not be simple. Any creature with such a fearsome reputation will have earned it in blood. It seems this council meets once each night. I think whatever they're preparing, it is about to begin. Arrivals have slowed, and the tension among the races is thick. Whoever is in charge will need to act soon, lest this entire army dissolve into chaos."

"How do we kill their leader?" Jessilynn asked.

"I have to discover who it is first," Dieredon said. "And that means getting close enough to overhear one of their meetings."

Jessilynn thought of the ravine, and of how each entrance was heavily populated with the vile creatures.

"There's no way," she said.

To this, Dieredon smiled.

"Even the eyes and ears of wolves are nothing to me, Jessilynn. But if you've been wanting to be involved, don't worry. Tomorrow night, my life will be in your hands."

Jessilynn swallowed, felt a tightening in her chest. Suddenly, remaining behind seemed like a much better idea.

The wolf-men occupied the larger southern end of the ravine, effectively blocking in most of the races, with the hyena-men filling the smaller northern end. Jessilynn and Dieredon lay flat on their bellies at the very top of the cliff above. Below was the pile of bones, where they expected another meeting to take place. Between the two was a long, thin rope, one end securely fastened to the ground with two different hooks.

"Remember, the fires will be my greatest ally," Dieredon whispered to her. "Their eyes are sharp, but not when so close to light. That means only wolf-men arriving from outside the ravine pose any danger of spotting me. That is when you must signal. Are you certain you have them memorized?"

"One to halt, two to retreat, three if spotted," she said, repeating what he'd told her countless times.

"Make sure you are certain, and make sure you keep the signals clear. Give a test signal early on as well, understand?"

Jessilynn nodded. Her breathing had increased, and she felt strangely light-headed. Her ears were full of the howls and roars of the creatures below, and now the only friend she had for hundreds of miles was about to descend into that beastly den.

"If something should happen, run to Sonowin," Dieredon said as he took hold of the rope and secured it to his belt. "She'll fly you back to the Citadel, and from there it'll be up to you to convince Lathaar and Jerico to act accordingly."

She nodded again, too nervous to speak. Her bow was slung over her shoulder, along with her arrows, and she wished she had them in her hands. She obviously couldn't take on thousands of creatures all by herself, but at least she wouldn't feel so helpless. As Dieredon began his descent, she remained on her stomach, clutching the rope with both hands. The rope was intended solely as a safety line should the elf needed to ascend rapidly, as well as a means of communication between him and Jessilynn. The ravine cliff, while steep, was far from sheer, and with amazing strength Dieredon descended, looking like a spider as he shifted between handholds.

Jessilynn looked away from the elf and instead scanned the area below. She trusted Dieredon and his camouflage to keep himself hidden. The fires dotting the wolf-man section of the ravine were at a perfect distance, too far to cast significant light on the ravine wall, yet still close enough to affect the eyes of those at the bone pile and the surrounding area. Even when she tried to locate him, knowing he was there, she needed a moment. It was his cloak, she realized. Something about its subtle splotches of green and brown seemed to perfectly blend in with the stone.

When Dieredon was a quarter of the way down she tugged on the rope, pulling until she felt resistance like she'd been shown. The elf halted, flattening himself against the cliff face and remaining perfectly still. After counting to ten, she tugged once more. Using the same number as the previously given command cancelled the command. Dieredon resumed his descent, and Jessilynn continued scanning the area. So far, it appeared there were no patrols, which was far from surprising. What could the creatures possibly need protection from? The bigger danger to Jessilynn and Dieredon were the hunting parties, which returned both often and irregularly.

When he was halfway down she spotted a group of seven wolf-men coming in from the south. She tugged once, hoping she hadn't noticed too late. Dieredon stopped, flattening himself again. The wolf-men loped past the great pile of bones, three of the seven carrying corpses across their shoulders. Two were of other wolf-men, she saw, while a third was that of a goblin. Runaways, perhaps? Was it punishment, feasting, or both? She received her answer swiftly enough, as the wolf-men plopped the bodies into the center of their camp and let out a howl.

*Grim but efficient,* Jessilynn thought, a way of simultaneously reinforcing discipline while keeping the army fed. She figured Dieredon would be safe due to the distraction, and she used the rope to give her signal. Immediately Dieredon continued moving. She watched him for a moment, stunned that he could maintain his grip without relying on the rope. His body was slender, but it was clear that all of it was muscle. No wonder he was so frightening in combat, not that she'd seen him fight. She only had reputation to rely upon, but that hard-won reputation was impressive, indeed.

When Dieredon was a third of the way from the bottom he paused without need of signal from Jessilynn. At first she felt an impulse of panic, thinking she'd missed something that he himself had spotted. Then she saw the size of the jutted rock he used as footholds, the deepness of the shadows there, and felt soft pressure applied on the rope. He was either resting, or settling in to listen. Whichever it was, she told herself to calm down. Dieredon was hundreds of years old, and had most likely dealt with far more dangerous situations than this. She had to trust him.

The minutes passed, each one feeling like an eternity. Another hunting party arrived, this one full of bird-men. She gave a single tug so he'd know, and she actually felt a tug back in return. For whatever reason, it made her smile, a reminder that he was aware and in control.

As the night wore on, the sounds below grew louder, more boisterous. The stress picked away at her mind, made her feel exhausted despite her training. She knew she could go at least a full day and night without sleep. They'd been forced to do so several times in the Citadel, but being out in the midst of real danger, with the fear of being eaten or seeing a friend mutilated because of her own mistakes chipping away at her, was a different beast altogether.

So great was the noise below that she almost didn't hear the sound of beating wings. A sudden surge of fear assured her something was wrong. The beating increased, loud enough for her to pick it out among the chaos. Looking up, her mouth dropped open as she realized the implication of what she saw.

Sonowin was in flight.

"Come up, come up, come up," Jessilynn said, tugging on the rope. She felt Ashhur scream warning in her ear after the second tug, and close behind her she heard a low growl. Despite her terror, she did not turn, did not try to flee, instead forcing herself to pull the third time, giving Dieredon the order to retreat.

Clawed hands grabbed her, lifting her into the air without the slightest bit of effort.

"What is this?" asked a gray-haired wolf-man. He held her before him like a curiosity, like a strange plaything. Behind him were twenty more wolf-men, sauntering up the hillside. The entire scene was so unreal, Jessilynn felt paralyzed. She smelled the foul breath of her captor, felt the sharp sting of his claws as they tightened around her arms. His eyes were bloodshot, and they glinted yellow from the starlight. That she understood him made it all the more surreal. She'd been taught the creatures knew the human tongue, but knowing and experiencing were two entirely different things. She knew, right then and there, that she was going to die.

"A tasty treat?" asked another of the wolf-men as he climbed up to join the gray-haired one.

"A scraggly female," said gray-hair. "But with at least some fat on her."

The wolf-man looked down, saw the rope. Letting out a snarl, he shifted Jessilynn so that he carried her with one arm. His muscles were like a vice, and though she struggled against him she might as well have been trying to pry open a rock with her bare hands. Gray-hair sniffed the air, then opened his mouth wide and let out a yip.

"A tricksy elf," the beast said, reaching down for the rope. Jessilynn thought he'd cut it, but instead he took hold of the rope and yanked upward as hard as he could. Dangling over the edge in the wolf-man's arm, Jessilynn had all too fine a view of what happened next. Dieredon was frantically climbing, and though he might have been able to support himself had rope gone slack, instead it pulled against him, dislodging him from the cliff face and sending him dangling above the ravine. The gray-hair tugged again, pulling the rope free of the spikes, and then let it drop. Already having slid down the rope, the elf fell the rest of the short way down, rolling to absorb the impact.

Jessilynn screamed as the wolf-man let out an ear-splitting howl. The attention of the camp turned their way, and suddenly alert, it took only moments before Dieredon was spotted. A legion of howls took up the hunt as the elf sprinted toward the exit. The rest of the twenty wolf-men gathered around the cliff edge to watch the excitement. Jessilynn felt completely ignored, and for some reason that made her all the more afraid. They didn't care about her, found her vaguely amusing at best. She was but food to them. What interest would they show, other than when it was time to rip apart her flesh?

Staring down, Jessilynn prayed for Dieredon's safety, even as she saw how hopeless a situation it was. He'd stashed his bow with Sonowin for the duration of the climb, which left him with only two long-bladed daggers. His speed was incredible as he ran, but the wolf-men could still overcome him. The elf was a blur of motion, and anytime a wolf-man neared, the creature fell back, clutching part of its body or falling dead on the spot. Jessilynn stared, wide-eyed, continuing to pray. Maybe he could live. Maybe he wouldn't suffer for her failure. She should have heard them. She should have realized they were sneaking up on her. All her fault. His death, the death of a legend, would be her fault.

"A feisty one, he is," said one of the wolf-men.

"All elves are," gray-hair snarled. "Perhaps the pups are liars if they cannot kill one elf."

"They'll kill him," said another. "Where else will he go? Sad we won't get a taste."

"I've had elf flesh before. It is sweet, like honey. You would not like it."

Dieredon scrambled toward one of the cliff edges as three wolf-men cut him off. They leapt in unison, and beneath them Dieredon tumbled. Fire glinted off his daggers, and only two wolf-men got up to chase after. The third lay motionless.

"Now he is trapped," gray-fur said, pointing a clawed finger. "They've cut him off."

Over a dozen wolf-men had ignored chasing after Dieredon, instead racing past so they might curl around, forming a wall of fur to prevent him from reaching the ravine's exit. Dieredon raced toward them anyway, as if he might challenge them, but at the last moment he slid to a halt, turned, and vaulted to the side. He struck the opposite cliff face, scrambling upward with amazing dexterity. A few wolf-men picked up speed and leapt, slamming gracelessly into the rock and clawing wildly. They shredded the edges of the elf's cloak, but did little else. Still, Jessilynn could see hundreds of the beasts racing out of the ravine and curling back around, scaling the slope to wait for Dieredon should he reach the top. Below him were hundreds more, howling and yipping at him, eager to feast the moment he fell.

Jessilynn saw him slip, and from a single hand he hung above the maw of snapping teeth. She let out a cry, and it earned her the attention of her captor.

"You care for him?" the wolf-man asked. "You amuse me, human. Watch him die. Cry for him. I love seeing humans weak."

Dieredon had regained his balance, climbing halfway up the cliff. Jessilynn felt a lump in her throat, knowing there was nowhere for him to go. He was just delaying the inevitable. He slipped again, and she saw his movements lacking grace when compared to his initial descent. He had to be wounded, she knew, though she could only guess how badly from such a great distance.

*Let him die from the fall,* she prayed. *Spare him the pain of their teeth.*

Dieredon let go of the rock, and crying out, she watched him plummet. He turned in the air, legs downward, and then swooping in from the sky came Sonowin. Dieredon landed atop her, rolled to one side, and then grabbed her mane with a hand to steady himself. Tears were in Jessilynn's eyes as he flew away. At least he lived. At least someone would know her fate.

Gray-hair growled, his teeth so close to her face.

"Stubborn elves," he said, tossing Jessilynn to the ground. The twenty gathered round, flexing their claws, their tongues drooling.

"We should eat her now," said one. "There's not enough for us as is. The rest will try to take her."

"No," the gray-haired one snarled. "We are late, and the kings might be angry. Let her be a gift. They cannot be angry if we give them human-flesh to eat."

"Our presence is a gift!" one of the bigger wolf-men snarled back. He turned his yellow eyes on Jessilynn, licking the sides of his long snout with his tongue. Gray-hair roared, stepping between him and Jessilynn.

"A gift," the wolf-man said. "Or we shall feast on you instead."

The younger wolf-man bowed his head and flattened his ears. "If you say, then so be it."

The gray-haired one turned and wrapped his enormous paw around her neck. His eyes were all she saw as he lowered himself to her height.

"Walk," he ordered.

She did so, flanked by the pack. The thundering of her heart and quickness of her breathing gave the entire world a flat, glassy look. Unreal, she thought, it was all unreal. Like a bad dream. Part of her wished it was, but her senses were overloaded, giving things a clarity no nightmare could ever possess. Down the ravine they walked as high above she saw Sonowin circling. When the winged horse began to lower, she dared hope he'd rescue her. It seemed gray-hair saw as well, and he snarled up at the sky.

"Come for your pet?" he asked. Reaching out, he grabbed Jessilynn by the throat. The paw closed so tightly she could not breathe, and frantically she clutched at his claws as he lifted her into the air, as if offering her to Dieredon. His other paw tightened against her chest, thick claws easily punching through her armor. With blurred vision she looked up to the stars, saw Sonowin lift back up into the air. Her last bit of hope died, and she knew, absolutely knew her time had ended.

"Such cowardice," the wolf-man snarled, and he set her down. Gasping for air, she fell to her knees, only to find herself yanked back to her feet.

"Walk," the gray-hair said. "The kings will prefer the kill to be their own, but I will present your warm dead body if I must."

Jessilynn coughed so hard she vomited, the bile dribbling down her throat, yet still she struggled to her feet. *One foot after the other*, she thought, beginning her descent down the outside of the ravine, following the pack as they curled her around to the entrance. She tried praying to Ashhur, but her mind was white with terror. She couldn't think. She couldn't form words. All around her were yellow eyes, and there was no disguising their hunger. Into the camp she went, and now there were thousands of them, howling and growling. The sound was deafening, and without even realizing it she began to cry.

*I'm sorry*, she pleaded to her god, though she didn't know why. She felt an overwhelming sense of failure, and though it made no sense, she could not help it. *I'm sorry, so sorry. Please, forgive me.*

They stopped at the great pile of bones where Dieredon had hoped to overhear the meeting. Now so close, she saw the age of the bones, many chalk-white and meticulously clean. Others were red with blood, bits of meat still clinging to them. Overpowering was the smell of sweat from the beasts, and their breath was tinged with the scent of blood. She tried not to gag, but her stomach was already weak. To her knees the gray-hair flung her, slamming her atop the bone pile. The bones scattered beneath her, clattering.

*Think,* she told herself. She knew the prayers she was supposed to pray if she thought herself approaching death. All the comforts of the Golden Eternity, the promises of Ashhur and his angels, she tried to think on them, to face death with the stubbornness and comfort that Jerico had when he'd been captured by the enemy. But all she felt was an aching desire to be anywhere other than where she was, to walk backward in time, to when Dieredon was first climbing down the cliff, and make him stay, make him fly her out of there, out of the Wedge and to the safety of the Citadel.

But instead the wolf-men howled, the sound piercing her ears and overwhelming any rational thought. Sobbing on the bones, she curled her head, closed her eyes, and waited for death.

The howling lessened as she heard movement upon the bones.

"A gift, great kings," the gray-hair said from behind her. "She was with the elf when we arrived, aiding him with a rope."

This was it. Her whole body tensed. A massive paw reached down, and she waited for it to rip open her throat. Instead it grabbed hold of her armor and lifted her upward. Determined to show some shred of dignity, she opened her eyes and looked upon her killer.

There was not one wolf-man there, but two. Both were enormous, seemingly towering over the others. They peered at her, and the intelligence in their eyes was all the more frightening. Both were solid black but for their paws, which were a deep red. The only difference she saw was that one had two circles of white in the center of his face, highlighting his yellow eyes.

"Your armor," the one holding her asked, lifting her higher. "What does it mean?"

The question made no sense to her. What did her armor mean? Could the wolves truly recognize the style of her armor, the meaning of the various symbols?

"A paladin," she said, her voice trembling. "I'm a paladin."

The two wolf-men shared a look as the rest of the pack howled for blood.

"Like him," one said to the other. "Like the one who humiliated father."

"And that is why she must live," an elderly female said, stepping to the edge of the bone pile. Her back was bent low, and white hair marked her ears. "There is much she will know. That knowledge will benefit us all."

"Take her, then," said the wolf-man holding her. With ease he flung her to the female's feet. "Her meat is little, and I will not taste the flesh of man until we are free." He turned to the crowd, his voice roaring throughout the entire ravine.

"Until we are all free!"

Others of the beasts nipped at Jessilynn, but the two wolf-men on the pile bared their fangs, ushering them back. The old female knelt down before her and grabbed her arm. Her watery eyes looked her over with a wisdom that seemed far beyond what Jessilynn thought possible. When she spoke, there was no compassion in her voice.

"Follow me, before you become their meal."

With no other choice, Jessilynn obeyed.

## 17

The village elders gathered, though *elder* was a misleading term. Many were young and fiery of temper, though the presence of the angel host did much to still their tongues. Qurrah watched them assemble into the great auditorium at the very rear of the castle, seldom used but recently cleaned to accommodate the meeting. He stayed at the door, not allowed to enter.

"Strange that I would be denied entrance," Qurrah said to Kevin Maryll, who stood beside him, greeting the various men as they came to take their seat. More than sixty attended, each representing the village they came from. The procession had slowed to a trickle, but still Kevin waited in case more might arrive.

"Your reputation is well known," Kevin said, glancing at him. "But tell me, which village do you represent? Oh, that is right, you live in Ker now. The angels have no sway over you."

"Observing is not the same as speaking, or casting a vote," Qurrah said, already disliking the man.

"Not true," Kevin said. "Your very presence would change things. You're a reminder of a different time, and a threat that no longer exists. We can't be lost in the past. Now's the future, and it's that future I must protect."

He fixed his tunic, which was made of some of the finest material Qurrah had ever seen, then adjusted the short cape around his neck.

"What do you hope to accomplish?" Qurrah asked him as he straightened his hair. "Do you think the angels will suddenly change their minds and bow to this rabble you've assembled?"

"You're just like your brother," Kevin said, licking his fingers and making a second attempt at his hair. "You hold these winged men in far too high regard. They're fallible, and more importantly, they must follow laws and customs just like us. They know this. They believe themselves to represent everything good and just. They say they always know the truth when they hear it. And you know what?"

## The Prison of Angels

He flashed Qurrah a smile.

"I think they're right."

Kevin stepped into the auditorium, and from within two angels on guard pushed the iron doors shut. Qurrah shook his head, wishing he could have met Kevin many years ago, when ripping the tongue out of a living man might not have put such a weight on his conscience. Being barred from listening to the complaints of the people was ridiculous. Worse, Kevin had somehow finagled it so that Harruq was banned as well. *Just the people and the angels,*' Kevin had claimed, though Qurrah sensed the weaseling desires behind it.

Still, sneaking into a meeting he'd been banned from was far, far less a burden on Qurrah's conscience than tongue mutilation. Turning about, he hurried to a nearby door, which led to a closet used by servants. Within were various stored tools, plus a great stack of clean linens. More importantly, the closet shared a wall with the auditorium. Sitting down beside that wall, he put his fingers against the stone and began to cast a spell. A thin tendril of shadow stretched out from his palm, then began to twirl. It dug through the stone with an unnatural silence. When it popped through, light poured into the dark closet. A quick check showed he could see the rows of angels, all circled around the far fewer number of representatives come to speak for the common man.

Dismissing the spell, Qurrah lowered his head, pressed his ear to the hole, and listened.

---

Tessanna lay in their bed, waiting for Qurrah's return. She'd tried playing with Aubrienna, but all the while she felt Aurelia watching her. There was no malice in it, no real anger. But the mistrust was there, however faint, and it made Tessanna sick because she knew it was well-deserved. Wishing her lover could be with her, she lay there, eyes closed, feeling hours pass over her in a steady, uninterrupted flow.

When the door opened, she sat up, smiling.

"You're back," she said. The smile on her face immediately vanished. Qurrah looked in a hurry, and he rushed to the chest where their things were stored.

"We must leave," he said, throwing it open. "Gather whatever you wish to bring with you, and if you have any goodbyes, go say them now."

Tessanna's mouth dropped open.

"What do you mean?" she asked. "What's wrong?"

"I said hurry!" Qurrah snapped. He immediately turned back to what he was doing. Tessanna stood up from the bed, walked over to Qurrah, and then wrapped her hands around him to force him to calm down. When he looked up at her, he kissed her lips, then let out a sigh.

"Forgive me," he said. "But time is not our friend right now."

"Tell me first," she said. "I will not flee the castle like a burglar, no matter what has happened. Now answer me."

"It was the meeting," he said. "The people, they spoke their demands to the angels, and it was all the same. They explained it in different ways, disguised their real demands with impractical ideas, but deep down they wanted the same thing."

He looked up at her, and she saw the fear in her lover's eyes.

"They want death," he said. "They want death, and I think the angels are going to give it to them."

"That's nonsense," Tess said as Qurrah resumed packing his things. She stood over him, watching. "The angels aren't murderers. And what do you mean they want death?"

"Sinners punished," Qurrah said. "Not forgiven. Not remedied. Punished. Killed. Hung. Beheaded. Am I making sense now?"

"Stop it," she said. "Stop snapping at me."

"I'm sorry."

He turned around, sitting with his back against the open chest. With his left hand he rubbed his forehead, as if suffering a headache.

"It's not that they made the demands," he said. "I understand their frustration. That wasn't it. That's not why we must leave. It was the angels. They were *agreeing* with them. I saw them listening, nodding. They looked too eager to please, too eager to abandon what Ahaesarus kept trying to defend. It's like there's a sickness here, Tess. I can't find it, but I smell the scent of disease."

## The Prison of Angels

She sat in silence as he finished bundling the last of his things, then stood.

"They mentioned my name," he said, slamming the chest shut. "I won't repeat what they said, but I assure you, it's a sign our time here is over. They angels are flying back to Avlimar. I want us gone long before they return."

"Whatever you say," Tessanna said. She thought of leaving Aubrienna, of not seeing her for several more years, and felt her heart crack. Still, she would not live without her lover. If Qurrah was leaving, then so was she. Either way she'd be miserable, but at least she'd have his company. Qurrah seemed to sense it, and he wrapped his arms around her waist.

"We'll come back," he said. "When things have calmed down. When people are thinking clearly."

"What of Aubrienna," Tessanna whispered. "She's still in danger. Are we to just leave them?"

Qurrah winced. He'd clearly been thinking the same thing, and it seemed he'd wanted to ignore that fact.

"We have to trust Harruq and Aurelia to protect her," he said. "You must believe me, our presence here does not help my brother. It only hurts him."

"Of course it does," Tessanna said. "That's all we ever do."

Tears ran down her face, but she felt her humanity receding, pulled into a deeper part of herself. Whatever emotions she felt, they suffocated, becoming gray things in the corners of her mind that held no sway over her. Qurrah's face showed his hurt at what she'd said, but she felt no guilt for it, no remorse. She was hurting. Why should he not know it?

"Come on," he said. "I'll tell Harruq we're leaving for Ker. Would you like to say goodbye to Aubrienna before we go?"

As if from a distance, she knew doing so would make her happy.

"Yes," she said. "I would like that."

"I'm sorry," Qurrah said, taking her hand. "I really am."

"I know," she said, as if knowing meant anything at all.

※

Harruq sat brooding on Antonil's throne. He still didn't view it as his own, and he felt sick at the idea that one day he might. Qurrah had informed him of their departure several hours ago.

His brother was probably halfway to Ker by now if he was traveling by magic. Their change in attitude was sudden, but strangely not surprising. It was as if, because of their recent arrival, they were better able to smell the danger in the air.

The only thing left to do was sit and wait for the angels' decision. They were meeting in Avlimar, the many thousands come together from every corner of Mordan to vote on their next course of action. Harruq knew he'd agreed to let it happen, but still, that smug look on Kevin's face when he'd swung by the throne room to inform him of the meeting's end had been more than enough to ignite his anger.

Servants came and went, offering him something to eat or drink. Much as he wanted to, he turned it all down. Wine might calm him, but the alcohol might also make it that much harder to control himself should he not like what he was about to hear. Given Qurrah's rapid departure, he highly doubted the results would be pleasing.

"Milord," a guard shouted from the far end of the hall. "The angel priest, Azariah."

The door opened, and Harruq rose from his chair. He was impatient to hear the results, and annoyed at himself for his nervousness. Azariah walked across the carpet, and he dipped his head in respect.

"We have listened to the desires of the people," he said. "And I have done my best to weigh it against Ashhur's wisdom. Their pain is great, and their frustrations legitimate given all we have seen of the world since our return."

"So what is your decision?" Harruq asked. "What's changing?"

Azariah swallowed, thinning his lips. The act seemed strangely human.

"Those committing lesser crimes will still be judged in the same manner," he said. "Though men given to repeat offenses will be brought to the castle prison. In solitude, it will be easier to enforce the lessons they must learn."

Harruq nodded. That was acceptable enough. He could oversee the prisons to ensure their humane treatment, and besides, prior to the angels most of the petty criminals would have been thrown into the cells anyway. At least now the stay would hopefully be far shorter.

"What of the major crimes?" he asked. The look on Azariah's face only increased his apprehension.

"The greater crimes are what trouble the people. The nature of grace is too heavy for this world, at least in its truest form. The chance for redemption will be offered to offenders as always, but after that, punishment of the physical body will also be given as per the laws of your nation, only with us as the executioners. These sins trouble too many minds, and there are those who feel the physical punishment will serve as a deterrent against those who might seek to abuse Ashhur's forgiving nature."

Harruq frowned, trying to work through the consequences of the decision.

"So from now on, you'll execute them, no matter what they say?" he asked.

"Not just from now on," Azariah said. "Every man who has ever committed murder under our watch will suffer the same brought down upon him. We know every name, every place. If this world would prefer its justice to ours, then we will give it to them. If we have passed judgment upon a man or woman, it will be made again, with no exceptions."

Harruq felt dizzy, and he took a faltering step back. Everyone the angels had passed judgment upon?

"When?" he asked.

"Tonight. We'll announce the decree in each village we land in, just before carrying out the new justice."

Justice. It would have made Harruq laugh if he were not so sick. He kept repeating it to himself. Everyone the angels had passed judgment upon. Everyone…

"Qurrah," he said. "Your very first trial was for Qurrah."

It clearly pained Azariah, but he nodded in agreement.

"It was," he said softly.

Harruq felt his rage growing, long suppressed, but not now. He couldn't control it, *wouldn't* control it. His hands were on the hilts of his swords, and his mind flashed red with blood.

"You can't do this," he said. "He's not the same man he was."

"As we have told the people every day for the past five years. They don't want to hear it."

"I don't care about the people!" Harruq screamed. "You won't send your angels after him. You can't. He's my brother, damn it! You think I'm any better? I killed children, children no different than my little Aubby. Send for your angels, Azariah. Bring Ahaesarus here himself if you must. Serve my head on a platter, straight from Avlimar to the people, and see how much they love you for it. Or am I just lucky to have gotten my act together before your kind came?"

"It was your answered prayer that brought us," Azariah said. The angel looked like his patience was starting to wear thin.

"Then be an answer to prayers! Not this. You're protectors, not executioners. This is what you think will win the people over? Flying through the night, blasting open doors and knocking in walls? Dragging the guilty out into the streets and slitting their throats? Don't do this. Don't. Whatever love the people have for you, whatever trust, you end it right here, right now, if you continue with this plan."

Azariah tried to put his hand on Harruq's shoulder but he batted it away.

"We voted, every angel given equal voice," Azariah said. "I'm sorry, but this is the decision we have reached."

"I act as king," Harruq said. "What of *my* voice, or do our choices mean nothing? Are we given no chance to rule ourselves?"

As much as it obviously bothered Azariah, he appeared unwilling to have his mind changed. Harruq almost drew his swords, but it would accomplish nothing. Even if he cut off Azariah's head the law would be enforced, only with his own life added to the list.

"Qurrah's returned to Ker," Harruq said. It was the last card he had left to play. "King Bram won't hand him over to any angel, especially not for an execution. If you try for him you'll be starting a war. How many lives wasted then, Azariah? How much blood will be on your conscience before you realize it's madness?"

"No exceptions," Azariah said, his soft voice taking on a hard edge. "There can be no exceptions. I'm sorry."

"We won't fight for you," Harruq said as the angel walked for the door. "I'll tell Bram it was done against my wishes, that you don't represent Mordan."

"He will not believe you," Azariah said. "Nor would it be true. We fulfill the wishes of your people, remember? This was the demand made of us, the one requested above all others. A life for a life, they said. No murderer made free, no matter how regretful the heart. And so they shall have it. They never trusted us, never wanted to accept our ways. This world is not ready for the grace we offer. *Kill the killers*, the masses scream. Forgiveness is for the soul, but punishment is for the body. You truly think they'll hate us, Harruq? Come the light of the dawn, let us hear just how many weep for the loss. Despite their penance, their regret, their sincerity, your world will never see them as innocent."

"None of us are innocent," said Harruq. "Would you kill us all?"

Azariah's stare met his own.

"Karak tried," he said at last. "I pray your brother is wise enough to surrender. I do not seek war, but if we fight, I hope your people are willing to bear the bloody fruits of their mistrust. You begged us to listen to them, did you not? You begged that we open our ears to their cries. And so we did. This blood is on *their* hands, not ours. We forgave them. It's this world that wants them condemned anew."

Harruq drew a sword and slammed it into the stone floor. It flared with magical strength, spreading thin cracks in all directions.

"You're supposed to be better!" he screamed, feeling so helpless, so lost.

"We're not," Azariah called without turning about. "If only the people had believed us when we said it."

## 18

Reen stood in the doorway to his home, staring up at the golden star that was Avlimar.

"Close the door," Tracy, his wife, said from her seat by their small fire pit. "You're letting in a chill."

"Feels good," he lied. His eyes scanned the sky. The moon was waning, but the stars were full, and across that somber tapestry he watched the shadows of angels flying in all directions, numbering in the thousands. The whole city was abuzz with news of the meeting, though Reen did not know what to make of the rumors. Too many contradicted each other. Too many were so outlandish as to be horrifying.

"Don't feel good to me," Tracy said, lifting a thin blanket off the floor beside her and draping it over her arms. "Go out for a walk if you need some air."

Reen grunted.

"Not safe," he said, closing the door.

His wife said nothing, only accepted the excuse. He could tell she knew something was wrong, but if he wasn't going to explain, she wasn't going to press him. She was good like that, better than Reen deserved. There'd been many nights he'd freely walked the streets, a long dagger hidden in his pants. When the alcohol had really been in his blood, he'd hoped men would accost him, just so he could take their coin after they lay bleeding in the street.

But that was another time, another man.

"What did you hear from the other women?" Reen asked, deciding he might as well bring his worries out into the open. Tracy frowned at him. She worked with the servants in the castle, one of the few that didn't sleep there due to Reen owning his own property. The quartermasters ran her ragged, but even amid the hectic pace her work required, Reen knew she talked with the other servants. If there was ever a place where rumors of the angels would spread, it'd be the castle.

"Nothing I'd believe," Tracy said.

Reen leaned his back against the door and crossed his arms.

"Humor me."

"The angels had a big meeting with farmers and old men from the outer lands. Most are saying it was just so people could let off steam. Nothing's going to change."

"That's not what I heard," Reen said.

Tracy gave him an exasperated look.

"If you heard more, then why are you asking about my rumors instead of telling me what's bothering you?"

Reen grunted.

"Was hoping you knew more than me, that's all. The men at the tavern are saying the angels are thinking of executing all murderers and rapists, regardless of their confessions."

Tracy's face darkened. The subtle fear he saw was like a dull knife stabbing into Reen's belly.

"I thought you weren't going to taverns anymore."

"I didn't drink anything," Reen said, raising his hands. "Honest."

Tracy settled back into her chair, but the fear still lingered. Reen thought of how he'd been when he came home those many nights. He never laid a hand on her, hardly even yelled at her, but no matter how hard she pretended not to, he knew she saw the blood on his clothes. How else would the stains be gone the next morning? How late did she stay up trying to hide the proof of his sins? The guilt was heavy, unrelenting ever since he started his two years of sobriety. Ever since he killed his friend, Charles.

Ever since the angels.

He hadn't meant to, of course. It's not like he was ever fully in control during those nights. Charles had said something to him, and no matter how hard he tried, no matter how many times he dreamed of that moment, Reen never remembered what it was his friend had said. A bawdy joke, perhaps? A jovial insult? It didn't matter. Something about it had set off Reen's temper, and he'd struck his friend in the stomach with all of his drunken might. They'd both come home bruised and bloody on multiple occasions, but something about the location of his fist, the way Charles's body had been unprepared, came together just perfectly. Charles had lost his balance, and within moments he'd begun to vomit blood.

It didn't take long for the angel to come. In his stupor, Reen never even learned the angel's name, but he knew the reason he was there. The sword on the angel's back had been more than enough. There'd been dozens of witnesses, no need for Reen to confess, no real mystery to the trial. Charles had lain before him, for Reen had not left his side, not even when his friend's body had begun to turn cold. Something about the angel, the understanding in his voice, the compassion in his eyes, left him feeling naked. He confessed to it all, and not just Charles. His drunkenness, his greed, his willingness to kill and maim. Feeling so lost, so afraid, he'd bowed his head and waited for the blade to hit.

But it hadn't.

"I think your old friends at the tavern are too drunk to think straight," Tracy said, pulling him from his memories. "Ashhur wouldn't let his angels do that. It goes against everything he teaches."

"Perhaps," Reen said, joining his wife before the fire pit. "But I don't see Ashhur around to stop them."

Tracy reached out and grabbed his hand, kissed his rough fingers.

"Go to bed," she said. "You'll be up far earlier than I."

Before Reen could answer he heard a sound he immediately recognized. It'd haunted his dreams for months, encapsulating everything about that horrible, broken moment when Charles had breathed his last breath, gagging on his own blood. It was the heavy sound of angel wings. And just like then, he felt his blood freeze.

"Reen Sanderson, come forth," called a voice from beyond the door.

Tracy leapt out of her chair, clutching her blanket to her chest as if it might protect her.

"It's not what you think," she said. "You aren't right. Reen, you can't be…"

He kissed her, then went to the door. When he opened it he found three angels waiting for him. For the moment their weapons were sheathed, and he prayed that was a sign.

"Yes?" he asked them.

# The Prison of Angels

"Our council has convened," the middle one said. Reen noticed the angel refused to meet his eyes, instead looking slightly upward. "We have capitulated to man's law, recognizing mankind's authority to rule themselves as Ashhur has granted."

"Don't give me that," Reen said. "Tell me why you're at my door this late an hour. Let me hear it in plain speech."

"Plain speech?" said the first angel. "So be it. Your sentence of murder is no longer stayed. Please step forward, and let us carry out justice."

From behind him he heard Tracy make the faintest of cries. In truth, he wasn't taking it much better. His legs felt weak, and it was only because he held the door that his hands were not shaking.

"Why?" he finally asked.

"That's not why we're here," the middle angel said. "Step outside, Reen."

"You forgave him!" Tracy shouted, her stupor broken. She rushed to Reen's side, clutching his arm as if to never let him go. "You can't do this, you can't. This is what I prayed for all those years. Don't you see, he's not the same. He's not the same!"

Reen saw the determination in the angels' eyes and knew there would be no salvation for him, not this time. With a firm hand he pushed his wife away, holding her wrists to keep her from striking him. As she cried, he kissed her forehead, then stepped out of his home and into the street.

The commotion had woken many of his neighbors, assuming they'd even been sleeping in the first place. Doors opened, and eyes peered out from windows. None dared ask what was going on. Reen walked forward, into the middle of the three angels. His legs felt like they belonged to someone else. His heart pounded, and he almost laughed as he felt an insane desire for a drink.

"On your knees," said one of the angels, drawing the sword off his back. Reen obeyed.

"Know that this punishment is for your body alone. Your confession was true, and your forgiveness remains. If your heart has remained pure, you will be welcomed into Ashhur's arms, and all the heavens will sing in joy at your arrival."

Reen nearly laughed at the absurdity as he felt the sharp edge of the sword touch his neck.

"Reen!" Tracy screamed behind him.

He shifted so he could look at her one last time. He remembered when he came home two years ago, suddenly given new life by the angels and left with only a single command: to go and live a life without sin. At his wife's feet he'd collapsed and told her everything. Before he felt it leave him, before he felt his old habits return with a vengeance, he'd told her his desire to change. He'd told her he couldn't live with that guilt anymore, couldn't stand her pained looks, her forced silence, and the quiet prayers she offered up in his name when she thought him asleep. Despite his tears, despite how miserable a being he felt, when Reen had looked up at his wife he'd never seen her gaze back at him with such joy, such love.

Now he saw terror. Now he saw betrayal.

Reen glanced up at his executioners, and he spoke with a voice stronger than he thought himself capable of. Not only the angels would hear, but his wife and his neighbors gathering to watch in subdued silence as well.

"Ashhur will welcome me," he said. "My soul's been bought. But will he welcome you?"

There was fear in the angel's eyes as he lifted the blade, and there was anger.

These weren't the eyes he'd seen when he'd hunched over Charles's body. They were something else. He lowered his head, clenched his fists.

"Do it," he said. "Do it, you damn cowards, do it!"

The last thing he heard was the whistling of the blade slicing through the air.

※

Harruq stood atop the highest balcony of the castle, watching the shadows of angels fly over the city. To the people sleeping below, he was their ruler, their king in Antonil's absence. But to the men with wings flying above? Nothing. He was nothing, and never before had he felt so powerless. An hour ago he'd used a scepter, the only one that had shone the entire night. He wondered how freely that blue-white light would glow anymore. That his request had gone unanswered failed to surprise him. It only deepened his sadness.

The sound of wings reached his ears, and he glanced upward. It seemed his request hadn't been ignored after all. Harruq said nothing as Ahaesarus landed beside him on the balcony. The leader of the angels kept quiet, joining the half-orc in leaning against the railing that overlooked the city. For a long moment the silence stretched between them as Harruq tried to think of what to say.

"How many?" he asked at last. "How many in Mordeina alone?"

Ahaesarus's face remained still as a stone, and his eyes refused to look Harruq's way.

"Just shy of two hundred."

Two hundred. Two hundred men executed in the dark of night. Harruq felt his lower jaw tremble.

"Why didn't you stop this?" he asked. "You're their leader. If you gave the order, they'd have listened."

"Not all," Ahaesarus said quietly. "The matter was put to a council, and two-thirds voted in agreement. The priests assure me there is no sin in what we do. Mankind was meant to follow the law, and the death of murderers has long been acceptable justice."

"Acceptable?" Harruq shook his head. "You're kidding me, right? You want to call this...this...*acceptable?*"

He pointed to the city, jamming his finger into the air.

"You think *they* will call this acceptable?" he asked. "You're supposed to be our protectors. You're supposed to be our guides. Now you're nothing but terrors in the night! Now you're just the men swinging the swords."

"Do you think I don't know that?" Ahaesarus snapped. He smashed a fist against the railing, leaving a massive crack in the stone. "But what am I to do, Harruq? We are men, different yes, but as fallible as you. We've been left to govern ourselves. We must find a way to live among mankind, to co-exist so that Ashhur's love may be known to all. Your people wanted this. My angels wanted this. The scribes wrote the letters of law, the priests confirmed their righteousness, and all I'm left with is a hole in my stomach as I watch good men die."

Harruq was stunned by the outburst. He fell silent, trying to think over his words. He'd always viewed Ahaesarus as the unquestioned ruler of the angels, but now he wasn't so sure. In times of war, he'd been their leader, the one to decide all final tactics. Was he like so many others, left to find a new purpose now that the enemies were gone? If Ahaesarus was struggling, then surely every other angel struggled just the same.

"It wasn't supposed to be this way," Ahaesarus said, his voice growing soft, wistful. "Many of us watched over mankind when their race was first molded by the gods' hands. We protected them, healed them so they might flourish. We were their wardens, trusted, respected. The land was so peaceful then, so free of strife. That was before the brother gods warred. Before that innocence was lost forever."

The angel looked to Avlimar.

"The finest memory I have now is of us returning here. When you knelt on that battlefield, the entire heavens watched, Harruq. Even in eternity, the land rumbled from the impact of your faith. Celestia saw it, too, saw a chance to save this world from the desolation the war god would leave it in. The sky split before us, and suddenly I found myself with a chance to be a warden for mankind once more. We slew the demons, cast them down with so righteous a fury I can still feel the power coursing through me. What better way could we protect mankind? How clearer might we fight the darkness than by giving our newly granted lives to save those we loved? And when Thulos was defeated, when the war ended and peace took its place, I thought things might return to that long lost paradise. We would be wardens again, and we would bring Ashhur's love to a land that had been aching without it for centuries."

"You want to return us to paradise?" Harruq asked. "Tell me, how many men did you kill in paradise?"

Ahaesarus shook his head.

"It's not that easy, Harruq. Do you know how many men committed murder during those ninety years? Not a one. It seems paradise is lost to both of us, and I don't know what it is we create in its place."

The shadowed angels scattered, and Harruq saw more and more flying out from the city, including a large group traveling south.

"My brother," Harruq began.

"I know," Ahaesarus said. "Trust me. I know."

"I'm glad you know," Harruq said, forcing his temper down. For once, he had to think. For once, he had to be the one with wisdom. "But knowing isn't enough. What will you do about it, other than standing beside me and wishing for times that won't return? The law doesn't make this right. You know that, deep down you know that. So do something. Anything."

He let out a deep breath.

"Because if you don't," he said. "I will. There's so much you angels can do for us, but trust me, we're quite capable of killing ourselves on our own."

Harruq left the leader of the angels there, exiting the balcony through the single wooden door. Just within the entrance he paused, listening until he heard the sound of wings taking flight. With Ahaesarus gone, Harruq let out a sigh and prayed he'd said the right thing. His stomach felt like a rock when he thought of what the next day would bring. There'd be petitioners, of course, people demanding an explanation. What would he tell them? Was his heart calloused enough to sit there on the throne and tell them they only received what they asked for?

Turning the corner, he startled to find Kevin Maryll leaning against the wall, arms crossed. Harruq saw the smile on his face, the smugness, and knew the man had heard every word.

"What do you want?" Harruq asked.

Kevin shrugged.

"It seems unfair to say. I've already had so many wishes granted today."

It was too much. Harruq snapped, grabbed the lord by the front of his shirt and slammed him against the stone wall.

"Is this what you wanted?" he asked, his face inches away from Kevin's. "Is this what you've worked so hard for? I hope you're happy, you madman."

"I'm ecstatic," Kevin said through clenched teeth.

"People are dying, and you're ecstatic?" Harruq felt an intense desire to draw his sword. To stop himself, he instead struck Kevin's cheek with his fist. Kevin didn't even let out a cry despite the blood that dripped from his lips.

"Hit me again," Kevin said, his voice like ice. "Act like the thug I know you are. You were born scum, Harruq, a homeless thief with a whore for a mother and a dead elf for a father. Everyone knows the story. It's sadly a rare few of us who actually listen."

"You have no idea what I've suffered through," Harruq said.

"And I don't care! You rule, not me, so it's time you looked out that balcony and accepted the truth."

Kevin grabbed Harruq's armor, yanked him closer. His eyes filled his vision, wide with fury, hard with certainty.

"Those angels don't care about us. They can preach mercy and love until their wings fall off, but that's not how they see us. We're just cattle to them! Look how easily they turned. Look how easily they butcher us, so long as they feel their priests can justify it. We wanted a greater stake in our fates, and in answer they slaughter hundreds."

Harruq shoved him against the wall a second time, then stepped away.

"You're wrong," he said.

"Am I?" Kevin spat blood onto the carpet. "Angels fly to Ker for your brother, did you know that? I suspect you do. His name came up in the council during its final minutes. Do you know what they called him, your precious, reformed brother? *'An acceptable loss.'* This is a hard lesson, Harruq, perhaps the hardest lesson of all. The nation you rule is headed for war. It's one we'll win, of course, but thousands will die. So accept the silver lining. The people of Dezrel will finally see the angels for what they truly are: superior savages that would lord over us all. A hard lesson, learned in blood."

"You're enjoying this," Harruq said, feeling sick. "How?"

"Because I want a king, not a god. You told Ahaesarus if he didn't stop this, you'd stop it yourself. It's the smartest thing I've heard you say since taking over Antonil's role. For all our sakes, I hope you meant it."

Kevin fixed his shirt, then gave him a low, exaggerated bow. As he walked off, the image of plunging Condemnation through the lord's back flashed through Harruq's mind. He forced it away. The man's words haunted him, and he retreated back to the balcony, wanting one more breath of fresh air. As he leaned against the railing, his hand touched the broken section Ahaesarus had struck. He stared at the stone, then looked to the slumbering city. Throughout he saw the angels flying, the faint white of their robes seemingly a lie.

"What are you to us?" Harruq whispered. "And what are we to you?"

To that, he had no answer. Not anymore.

## 19

In such a crowded ravine, solitude should have been a near impossibility, or at least that's what Jessilynn initially thought. It turned out not to be true. Near the wolf-men encampment there was a deep crack in the side of the cliff, forming a thin cave. Not more than a few feet in it turned completely dark, lacking torch or fire. It was into that darkness the female took her, shoving her to the ground. Even with her age she still had impressive strength.

"Your bow," she said. "Hand it to me."

Jessilynn hesitated. So far they'd yet to take it from her, and it remained slung across her back along with her quiver of arrows. She debated drawing one. Surely she could kill an old wolf. But what would she do after? She thought of the creatures as they'd gathered below Dieredon, waiting for him to fall. She thought of the way they'd torn into the butchered cattle, or even other members of their own race. The fear paralyzed her.

"The bow. Hand it to me. Now."

She did as she was told, giving over the quiver as well. The female held them to her chest, nodding.

"My name is Silver-Ear," she said. "Though I let you live, I am not your friend. Remain here. If you leave the cave, you will die."

With that she left Jessilynn to the darkness. She sat on her rear, arms curled across her knees, and shivered. What did the beasts plan to do to her? Was there something worse than being eaten alive? The other boys at the Citadel had often joked of the crude things wolf-men did, always to innocent maidens of course, but she'd never taken them seriously. It'd been easy to dismiss back then, but now she was so afraid it made every single outlandish story contain grains of truth. They'd rape her. They'd mutilate her. They'd feast on her flesh, then let her recover so they might eat again and again, until she was nothing but a sobbing stump. They'd force her to kneel before the moon and renounce Ashhur, lest the pack have their way with her.

*Stop it*, she told herself. *Just stop it.*

Rumors, jokes, stupid things that meant nothing. She knew that. Again she prayed to Ashhur, but in that deep darkness, it seemed he was so far away. Halfway through her first prayer she broke down. What had she been thinking, accepting a role beside Dieredon? He was one of the legendary heroes, and she was just...well...

She was just an exhausted, frightened little girl in a cave surrounded by monsters.

Movement from the cave entrance pulled her attention away from herself. Yellow eyes glinted, and despite her best efforts not to, she let out a gasp. It was the two identical wolf-men. She could tell just from their size. The cave was deep enough that they could stand side by side, and they loomed before her, peering down like she were an alien thing.

The one with the white around his eyes kneeled lower, then began to ask questions.

"What do you know of the towers beyond the river?" he asked.

Jessilynn felt a momentary panic as she struggled to understand what he asked of. The Wall of Towers, she realized. It did little to calm her panic.

"Nothing," she said, forcing herself not to stammer. "I've never been there."

"What of the boats, the patrols?"

Her silence was answer enough.

"The lands beyond the river, they have great armies. How many wear metal armor like you?"

Why did they think she knew these things? She thought to guess, but decided otherwise. She would not lie to them, no matter the convenience.

"I don't know," she said. The look the two wolf-men gave her was chilling, and it was clear their patience was nearing an end.

"Your armor. You are a paladin, yes?"

Jessilynn nodded, then realized the creatures might not fully understand such human gestures.

"Yes," she said. "I am."

"Where is the one they call Jerico? Does he still live?"

She did her best to hide her surprise. They knew of Jerico? Earlier they'd mentioned someone like her humiliating their father. Their father...

She let out a gasp, realizing exactly who it was that stood before her. One of her favorite stories at the Citadel had been Jerico telling of how he and Darius withstood an onslaught of wolf-men crossing the river to attack the small village of Durham. They'd been led by a vicious wolf-man named Redclaw. In the stories Jerico never told of what happened to the beast. Now, it seemed she knew. The hatred in their eyes grew all the more frightening.

"Jerico lives," she said. "At the Citadel to the south, training more like me."

"How many of your kind wait for us when we cross?"

Waiting? They had a few boats patrolling the Rigon, barely covering a few dozen miles of land. Ever since the Citadel fell, they'd relied on the elves to fill in the gaps, but with the orcs' conquering of the east, even that had ceased.

"There's no one waiting," she said. "I promise, no one else knows of...of...all this."

Other than Dieredon, of course, but she didn't need to say that. They'd all seen him escape on Sonowin's back.

"You lie," the wolf with the white around his eyes said. His lips pulled back in a growl, exposing enormous yellow teeth.

"No," she insisted, fear clutching her throat. "No, please, I don't!"

"Then what good are you to us? You know nothing of man, nothing of his armies, nothing of what awaits us."

His claws were reaching for her when Silver-Ear called for him to stop.

"Hold your temper, Moonslayer," the female said from the slender cave entrance. The pair turned, and the white-eyed one sniffed her way.

"It is no temper, shaman," he said. "I only seek a meal. This human is worth nothing to us."

"You are wrong," Silver-Ear said, shuffling closer. "She is everything. The other races lose their patience, and worse, their trust."

"What do we need of their trust?" asked the other. "I am Manfeaster, son of Redclaw. Let them fear me instead. We have already slaughtered many to cow their spirits. Should the goblins or birds grumble, we will remind them of their fear."

"You keep them here with fear, but even fear will not be enough when we cross the river into the land beyond. We must have something to make them listen, something to make them trust you long enough for us to secure a strip of land."

"And that is her?" Moonslayer asked, gesturing to Jessilynn. "What does this runt know to help us? She is but a child, and lacks wisdom because of it."

It was so terrible sitting there, listening to them describe her in such a way. These were the beasts they'd been taught about in the Citadel, led to believe they were just vicious, brutal eating machines. To be thought of as lesser by these creatures, as lacking any wisdom, was humiliating.

"She bears the weapons and armor of a man," Silver-Ear said. "It does not matter if she is a child, for just as our own cubs still bear teeth, so too does she threaten us if we are not careful."

"All the more reason to slash her throat," Manfeaster argued.

Silver-Ear came up behind them, and at her beckoning Moonslayer stepped back, giving her room to kneel. Jessilynn curled her knees to her chest, watching, curious what the milky-eyed female wanted of her. What was it about her that the shaman felt was so important?

"Twice we have crossed the river in my lifetime," Silver-Ear said. "Twice we were defeated by men with glowing weapons and silver armor. Your *father* was defeated. Those creatures you've cowed out there know this, and stay only because of fear. But if you can make them believe you, if you can make them accept you as kings…"

Silver-Ear rubbed a claw down the side of Jessilynn's face. She flinched, but the shaman's touch was strangely gentle.

"We hold one so similar to who defeated us before," Silver-Ear said. "And you think she is nothing?"

She stood, turned to face the two.

"Humiliate her," she said. "Enslave her. Parade her before all the races, and let them know we will not be stopped. And her use does not stop there."

Jessilynn's heart was in her throat when the female turned her cold eyes on her.

"You will deny nothing that we say," she said. "Only nod and accept my words. Do you understand me, human? If you do not, then your mutilated body will serve our purpose just as well."

Whatever defiant part of her that existed before that moment felt miniscule in the darkness, stared down by strange, bestial eyes.

"I'll say nothing," she said.

"Good."

Silver-Ear turned to the others.

"I will begin," she said. "I trust you two to continue when I stop."

"One wonders who the pack leader really is," Moonslayer said, his voice carrying a hint of a growl.

"I swore a promise to your father," Silver-Ear said. "Do as I say, lest you insult his memory by preventing me from fulfilling his dying wish."

She walked to the entrance of the cave, glanced back.

"The time is upon us," she said. "Everything we've prepared for, it happens now. Bring her. And bring her bloodied."

The two wolf-men turned to her. She felt the impulse to sob, but she fought it down. She would not weep before these monsters. Moonslayer lifted a hand, and there was undeniable cruelty in his eyes.

"Bloodied?" he said. "If the shaman insists."

With shocking speed he slashed across her face. She felt the claws tearing into her cheek, ripping flesh. The impact sent her slamming to the stone, flooding the darkness with a sudden swirl of stars and light. She felt blood dripping down her neck as well as her throat, and reflexively she coughed. Her left hand brushed her cheek, felt the flesh hanging like ribbons. Tears from the pain rolled down her face as Manfeaster grabbed her neck and lifted her off the ground.

"Come, brother," he said, carrying her as if she and her armor weighed nothing. "Let us show the rabble our prize."

Once outside the cave, Manfeaster slung her over his shoulder like she was one of the cattle they'd brought in the night before. Amid her delirium she saw the entrance to her cave, saw her bow and arrows lying against the stone beside it. She felt a desire to grab it, not to kill others, but to send an arrow through her lower jaw and into her skull. This was torment. This was the Abyss. Sinful or not, she couldn't help it, not when she thought of what her face must look like. Not while it throbbed with unbearable pain, dripping blood across the fur of her tormenter.

Wolf-men gathered around them as Silver-Ear and the two brothers led the way toward the center of the ravine. They parted easily enough, only a few nipping back. All eyes were on her, and she closed her own so she would not have to see them. She was only a curiosity, not a threat. On and on they walked, until she was violently thrown to the ground. The force of her head striking the dirt jarred her eyes open, and she let out a cry. Moonslayer put his foot on her chest, holding her down.

"Stay put," he told her.

Jessilynn nodded, glancing around. They were in the center of the ravine, in a place sectioned off from the other camps. Every race had a place to be represented, she saw, from the goat-men to the bird-men to the diminutive goblins. In the very middle of it all stood the two-wolf men, with Silver-Ear nearby. The creatures howled and cursed one another, but when Silver-Ear threw her head back and howled, they quieted enough so they might hear her words.

"All you monsters of the Wedge," she said, turning so she might address the races. "You know why you are here. You know of the land beyond the rivers, rich with game, with green grass and clear water. It will be ours, as it was in the days of old. And it will happen, because for the first time in an age we will be united. We will be free. We will serve kings!"

"Kings of the Vile!" roared the wolf-men, and scattered among the other races were a few who took up a similar cry.

"In times past we failed, broken and alone," Silver-Ear continued. "Our greatest could not succeed, for our enemies were strong. But behold now their strongest."

The female was at Jessilynn's side instantly, grabbing her arm and yanking her up so they might see her armor.

"This," said Silver-Ear, "this *weakling* is all that remains of they who once defeated Redclaw. Where once they sent mighty warriors, now they send whimpering girls. Where once they wielded swords and shields of light, now only a flimsy stick of wood. Look at her. All of you, look upon the greatest mankind may throw against us! Our age has come, the age of our kings!"

Louder now the wolf-men howled, and their excitement seemed to be infectious. Jessilynn clenched her jaw, determined to stay silent. The shaman's words insulted her, but there was nothing she could do about it. The idea of her being weaker, inferior, burned deep in her belly, playing on fears she'd carried since those earliest nights listening to Jerico's stories.

"But that is not all," Silver-Ear continued. "This human, this girl, knows everything. She knows of the boats. She knows of the towers. She knows where the armies move against us, and what evil magic they will try to use to keep us imprisoned in this wretched land. This broken thing will tell us everything. By the words of a single human, we will crush *all* humans!"

She turned to the two brothers, nodding slightly so they might know she was finished. Moonslayer stepped forward, beginning his speech with an ear-splitting howl that seemed to go on forever.

"We have no reason to be afraid!" he cried. "We have no reason to kill one another. The strong must eat the weak, but none here are weak. It is the humans who are weak. Their flesh, their hands, their will…it is weak, and we will crush it. Together, we will forge a kingdom of the Vile, and we will be your kings."

Manfeaster jumped in, his timing flawless.

"We do not ask you to kneel," he shouted to the other races. "We do not ask you to serve. We only ask you follow us, listen to us, so that you may join us in this conquest. Let us together crush the humans, and go to a land so fertile, so grand, that our kind will never go hungry again!"

"We are the sons of Redclaw," Moonslayer roared. "Not just us, but all of us, and together we will finish what he began!"

Jessilynn was too tired, too delirious from the pain and blood loss, to take in the cacophony that followed. She'd listened best she could, her horror slowly fading into the background of her mind. It was all too much. The way the creatures looked at her, the goat-men with their long faces, the goblins with their strange, unblinking gaze, it was as if she were some entity from another world. Perhaps she was. All of them stared with a hunger, a sense of greed that she no longer wished to see.

"Your patience wears thin," Manfeaster told the throng. "So know that the time to act is now. This pathetic human is the sign. Tomorrow, we march for the river! Tomorrow, let every human heart tremble with fear!"

This, more than anything, whipped them into a frenzy. The goat-men brayed, the hyena-men yipped, goblins laughed and clapped, and the bird-men squawked. Over it all howled the wolf-men, loudest and greatest of them all.

"To your feet," Silver-Ear said as the two kings began howling to continue the excitement. "Before one loses control and tries to eat."

The shaman's hand took her own, and as if she were a child she was led back to the cave. Once inside she collapsed to the cold ground. The bleeding of the wounds on her face had begun to slow, but still the pain remained. Silver-Ear stared at her, then let out a soft grunt. Tied to her fur were thin strips of dried leather, holding small pouches made from skin. From within a pouch Silver-Ear pulled out a collection of leaves.

"Chew this," she said, offering them to her. Jessilynn put the leaves into her mouth, then carefully bit down. The gashes in her face made any movement agony. The leaves were soft, yet when she chewed they were horribly bitter. Her eyes watered and her chest heaved.

"Do not vomit," the female said. "Chew, but do not swallow."

Jessilynn did so, striking the ground several times with her fist to help her concentrate. At last the shaman reached out her paw.

"Spit."

She gladly did so. Silver-Ear took the disgusting mush, narrowed her eyes at it, and then grunted again.

"Lie on your back."

Jessilynn slowly settled down, the ground feeling somehow comfortable despite its hardness. More than anything she wanted to sleep. A dim hope in her still clung to the idea that when she awoke in the morning everyone would be gone, and instead

Dieredon would be there, cooking her breakfast. She closed her eyes, slowed her breathing.

Silver-Ear pressed the wet glob against her cheek. It was like salt poured into her open wounds, and Jessilynn let out a scream. The female easily held her down, growling at her.

"Stay still," she snarled.

Jessilynn did so, even as the tears ran down the sides of her face. More of the substance pressed against her cheek. She gritted her teeth, choking down sobs. It burned like fire, but after a moment's time, the sensation finally started to relent.

"Sleep here," Silver-Ear said. "I will bring you food in the morning. Remember, step outside this cave, and I promise you nothing but death."

With that, she was gone. Jessilynn breathed in, breathed out, as the din of roars and growls echoed inside the confines of the cave. Twenty thousand creatures, all ready to feed. They'd march west soon, crossing the Rigon and into the lands beyond. How many innocents would die? She couldn't begin to guess, but the truth of it made her ache. And who would stand against them? Would Jerico be there? No, he was south in the Citadel, oblivious to the threat. Darius? Dead. The other heroes of old? All dead, all gone. The Wall of Towers was all that was left, and Jerico had made it clear what state they'd been in for years. She doubted things had improved since the Gods' War. The towers had fallen before, retaken only with Darius's help. But now?

Now the only paladin to stand against them was her, and she lay marred, broken, and weaponless. Worst of all, she couldn't help but think it her fault. It didn't make sense. It didn't have to. Lost in her fear and pain, it seemed so blatantly obvious. Her pride, perhaps. Her desire to be better than others.

*I'm sorry,* she prayed as she waited for exhaustion to claim her. *I'm sorry, Ashhur. Whatever I did to deserve this, I'm so, so sorry.*

The only answer she received was blessed, dreamless sleep.

## 20

They alternated turns summoning the shadow portals to take them south. Through it all Qurrah remained silent, his nerves never calming despite the fact they crept closer to Ker's border each passing moment. What did a border matter to men with wings?

"An acceptable loss," he murmured as they camped that night. "Acceptable. Ashhur help us all."

Tessanna glanced at him, and he saw the question in her eyes. He shook his head, still not wanting to talk about it. More than anything he felt such an immense betrayal at the words he had heard. When he'd expected death, when he'd deserved it, they'd denied it to him. They'd declared him forgiven. Ever since then, he'd felt changed. He'd tried, in his own meager way, to better understand the mercy and grace Ashhur's priests had preached. Oh, he often felt he failed to live up to it, but the concept had been there, giving him hope, giving him a glimpse of a future where he could sleep without the weight of a thousand corpses on his conscience. More than anything, he carried hope that it would not be Karak's arms he went to upon his death. He would not spend eternity in a darkness lit only by Velixar's glowing red eyes.

And now, when he sought only to help, only to repair, he instead found the angels ready to give him the death they'd declared him free of all those years ago.

"We're not going to be safe," Tessanna said, absently tossing kindling onto their fire. "Azariah knows where we live."

"You think they will come hunting for us?"

Tess shrugged.

"I don't know. You won't tell me everything, so I must guess. But something's wrong, I know that. Mordeina should have felt peaceful, but instead it felt…"

She shook her head, struggling for the right words.

"Like everyone was holding their breath," Qurrah said.

"Yes, like that. Like everyone must keep one eye on the sky."

Qurrah thought of the paladins who'd fought in Ashhur's name, now secluded in their Citadel. What would Jerico think if he walked through those streets? What would he have said if he'd stood there in the middle of the angels' council and saw them nodding as simple farmers asked for the death of their fellow man?

"If they come for us, you're right," he said. "Our home isn't safe."

"Then where is?"

Qurrah remembered King Bram's words when they'd last spoken at the bridge, when Antonil's army had come marching.

"We first refused to stand by Bram's side and condemn the angels," he said. "I think I might be changing my mind..."

◈

Qurrah had never been to the city of Angkar, and now that he had, he wasn't impressed. Its walls were tall, but Veldaren's had been taller, and Mordeina had multiple walls built close together to form brutal killing lanes. There were no special defenses, no significant battlements. No, the only thing that impressed Qurrah about the seaport was that it had escaped the Gods' War so thoroughly unscathed. When other countries and cities had fallen, it had thrived, which spoke to the careful manipulation of its ruler, King Bram Henley.

"The walls will mean nothing to men with wings," Tessanna said, taking in the city beside him from the worn road leading to the main gates.

"It's not the walls," Qurrah said. "It's who owns them. If we're under Bram's protection, and angels come for us, it'd mean war. Harruq won't let that happen."

"What if he doesn't have a choice?"

Qurrah shook his head.

"Then all the more reason for us to be careful."

She fell silent as they walked down the road, as if deep in thought. Qurrah held her hand, squeezed it tight.

"Must we kill them?" she suddenly asked.

"Who? The angels?"

She nodded. Qurrah sighed.

"I fear we might."

"I don't want to kill them. I'm scared to."

He frowned at his lover.

"Scared? Why?"

She shook her head, and with the way she regressed into herself he knew he would receive no answer. So instead he lifted her hand to his lips and kissed her fingers.

The most immediate thing they noticed when stepping through the walls was the smell. It was of salt, sea, and fish, damp wood and overgrown moss. It was vibrant, if a bit overwhelming. Tessanna seemed to love it, though, inhaling deep and smiling. It was good to see, and Qurrah grinned despite the stench.

"It's alive here," she said. "So unlike Mordeina."

Qurrah shrugged.

"Mordeina smelled better."

She winked at him, but did not counter. The traffic was light, and merchants called to them from both sides of the road. Qurrah meant to ignore them, but Tessanna drifted away. She looked over the food and trinkets, saying nothing, only drinking it all in with her eyes. Like a child, thought Qurrah. Despite his impatience, he let her go from booth to booth. A darkness had settled over her the past few months, he knew that. What he didn't know was why, so anything that chased it away, anything that brought out the joy he knew was buried deep within her, was something he would encourage.

At last she returned to Qurrah, a guilty expression on her face.

"I was bad," she said. "The man gave me a shrimp because I was pretty."

"Hardly that bad," Qurrah said, taking her hand so they might resume walking toward Bram's castle.

"I might have leaned forward before asking for a taste. Very far forward."

Qurrah rolled his eyes.

"You're insufferable."

"You suffer well enough."

"You say as you lean forward."

He laughed, and she squeezed his hand

The castle had three tall towers rising from the corners of its walls. Two of them were plain enough, though the third easily stood out from the others. From what Qurrah had learned of the city when first moving into the west years ago, that tower was known as the Eye. Its door was a deep crimson, oversized and bolted shut with a blatantly exaggerated lock. Above the door were ten skulls carved out of stone, leering down as if mocking anyone who might seek to enter. All three towers had guards stationed outside, plus the main castle gate. Figuring the direct approach to be the best, Qurrah walked up to the guards at the gate and bowed low in respect.

"I've come to speak with your king," he said. "My name is Qurrah Tun."

"Sure you are," said one of the two, snickering at him. "And I'm a bloody angel."

The guard looked to his comrade, as if to share a laugh, then saw the wide-eyed look he was getting. When he turned back to Qurrah, his mouth dropped open a little.

"You mean, he…he's…"

"I *am* Qurrah," he said. "Now either sprout wings, or find your king."

"Begging your pardon," said the other. "But he's in the Eye. We're never to disturb him when he's in the Eye."

Qurrah sighed, and without waiting for their permission he began walking alongside the castle wall toward the great red doors of the Eye. The guards hesitated, then rushed after him. Tessanna remained at his side, and she giggled.

"You scare people so easily," she said.

"One of the few benefits of our reputation, I guess."

"I just think it's your glare."

"We can't let you go in," the guard said, moving as if to cut in front of them yet still too frightened to do so. So instead he kept stepping in and out of their way, as bothersome as a fly.

"I'm not going in," Qurrah said. "Calm yourself."

This had the opposite effect.

"Then what are you going to do?"

Qurrah stared up at the Eye, noticing its various windows, all of them constructed of stained and colored glass to hide whatever happened within. Still, the glass would be thin enough for them to hear. Putting magic into his voice, he cried out, his words like that of a bellowing giant.

"King Bram, Qurrah Tun requests your presence!"

The two guards who'd been stationed before the Eye drew their weapons as the two from before clutched their ears and winced. Tessanna, meanwhile, just laughed.

"First Mordeina, now here," she said. "I think guards everywhere will soon hate us."

"Drop your weapons!" the first guard shouted to the others. "King Bram named him friend at the Bloodbrick!"

They looked far from convinced, but thankfully the great red doors cracked open, and out stepped the king himself. Qurrah let out a sigh of relief. How nice to be his brother, who was cheered as a hero everywhere he went. Qurrah doubted Harruq had to endure terrified guards every time he tried to visit someone.

"I expected your return months later," Bram said. "Did you change your mind about traveling to Mordeina?"

"Sparrows dream of traveling as fast as us," Tessanna said, and she curtseyed to the king. "But we did indeed change our minds."

Bram's eyes sparkled for a moment, no doubt hoping he interpreted Tess's speech correctly. Qurrah took her hand, then gestured to the tower.

"We would like a word with you," he said. "In private."

"Come inside the Eye," Bram said. "I assure you, there is no more private place in all of Dezrel."

Mildly curious about the interior of the over-exaggerated tower, Qurrah nodded his head, then followed Bram through the doors. Directly before them was a single staircase, looping upward through the low ceiling. They climbed the stairs, emerging onto the lone floor of the entire tower. This ceiling stretched high above them, and decorating the massive wall space were hundreds of paintings. They showed men fighting angels, demons, trolls, orcs, and even a few creatures Qurrah had never seen put to drawing. In every image, Qurrah realized it was men who fought them, never the monsters against one another. Torches burned at regular intervals, which, combined with the various stained glass windows, ensured each painting was given visibility. In the center of the room was a large wooden table, the wood well-aged. Carved in perfect detail atop it was a map of the world of Dezrel.

"Forgive the theatrical nature of the place," Bram said as he took a seat before the enormous table. "But the walls are sheer inside and out, which leaves no place for spies. No ears at these walls, not even those of an angel, so speak your mind."

Tessanna wandered over to the table, admiring the map. Her fingers drifted over a representation of the Elethan Mountains, her fingertips brushing their pointed tops painted a snowy white.

"They don't need to hear us," Tessanna said absently. "Just find us."

"I'm not sure I understand," Bram said.

Qurrah took a seat beside his wife. The chair felt slightly oversized, leaving him feeling like a dwarf. He frowned but ignored it.

"You were right about Mordan," he said. "Things there are foul, and over the few days we spent in Mordeina, they turned all the fouler."

"How so?" Bram asked.

"Assassins made an attempt on my brother's family, well-paid assassins that even after death I could learn nothing from. As for the angels…"

Qurrah sighed, not wanting to get into it but knowing he had no choice. Before he could, Tessanna interrupted.

"This map isn't right anymore," she said, staring keenly at the northwestern corner.

"My dear, this map is older than my father's father, but I assure you we've kept its borders and representations very precise over the years," Bram said.

"It's still wrong."

She slid around the side, then placed her hand atop of the carved city of Mordeina. Her eyes flared wide, and after a few words of magic, her hand began to glow. Bram tensed but remained seated. Qurrah watched, merely curious. He sensed no real anger from Tessanna, just a vague unease. When the spell enacted, he understand why. Rising from the wood was a small city glowing entirely out of light. It hovered above Mordeina, a shimmering replication of the golden city of Avlimar. Its light shone across the entirety of the west, casting long shadows.

"Forgive me," Bram said. "It does appear my map was incomplete."

"Without Avlimar, it never will be," Tessanna said. "You can't forget it's there. You can't remove it. The angels are coming, and they will not care that you are a king."

Bram snapped to attention.

"Coming here? Why?" He stared at the two of them, and it seemed his mood improved despite his breathless words. "They're coming for you, aren't they?"

"I don't know," Qurrah said, slumping in his chair and rubbing his forehead. "But I fear they will. The people of the north are demanding retribution, wanting nothing to do with penance and forgiveness for murderers and thieves. And in Mordan, there's no better known murderer than I. You promised us protection if we needed it, and now we are here for just that. Will you give us shelter?"

"You'd have me spill blood to protect you?" Bram asked.

"If it must come to that," Qurrah said.

The king stood, walked around the table so he might put a hand on Qurrah's shoulder.

"You are a citizen of my nation," he said. "I care not where you were born, but from now on, your roots are here. Your home is here. And I promise you, from the highest noble to the lowliest serf, no man of my kingdom will be subjected to the angels' judgment. Not during my reign."

From below they heard the heavy rumbling of the door opening, following by it shutting. The three turned to see an older knight come noisily up the stairs. Without saying a word he grabbed a pitcher from a side table, filled a tall cup, and then plopped into a chair beside Qurrah. The half-orc recognized him but could not quite place the face.

"No word yet from the east, your grace," the newcomer said. "I've kept our soldiers on alert just in case, since there's no telling when Antonil will be making his way back to our borders. For all we know, the first orc army he meets will whip his behind and send him crawling back to us. Might not have more than a day or two's notice if we're to meet him at Ashhur's Bridge."

Bram chuckled, gestured to the man as he guzzled down his drink.

"Qurrah, Tessanna, meet my most trusted knight, Sir Ian Millar."

"Charmed," Ian said, tipping his cup.

"I hope this man won't be the one put in charge of protecting us," Qurrah said, offering a wry smile. "Otherwise I might try to steal away his cup so there's a chance of him remaining sober."

"Just try it, half-orc," Ian said. "We'll see just how much your reputation's been inflated."

"That's enough of that," Bram said. "Ian, these two will be our guests for the next few weeks. They suspect angels might be coming for them, and this is something that must not be allowed."

"Is that so?" Ian said, raising an eyebrow. "How politely are we to tell the angels to piss off? With flowery words, or with lowborn gestures and swears?"

"With a sword," Bram said, darkening Ian's mood. He finished off his cup, then set it down atop the representation of Veldaren.

"Aye," he said. "I can do that. If you two would follow me, I'll show you to your rooms. Other than Bram's own quarters, there's no safer place in this castle."

"Will there be windows?" Tessanna asked as they stood.

Ian paused, scratched at his face.

"Hrm. Perhaps I need to rethink just where the safest place is…"

⸎

The safest place was far from what Qurrah expected, but he could not deny the logic. The accommodations, however, could have been better.

"Now I know a dungeon's not the finest smelling of places," Ian said as servants rushed all around him. "But there's no windows and only one entrance, which we'll have guarded at all times."

"Tales of your king's generosity will spread for miles," Qurrah said as he watched two servants haul in a feathered mattress. They'd swept and cleaned the cell best they could,

# The Prison of Angels

though nothing would ever remove the lingering, dingy feel of the place. Their only light was from a small torch on the opposite side of the hallway. Still, the sheets and bed were soft, and both Qurrah and Tess had stayed in far worse conditions.

"It should," Ian said. "Given all he's risking for you two. To be honest, I'm not sure you're worth it."

"Risk?" Qurrah asked. "He risks the lives of a few guards. Surely any king can risk that."

"Qurrah," Tessanna said, touching his arm.

Ian glanced at the servants, then snapped his fingers. They hustled out, the room mostly furnished. The two nearby cells had also been emptied and cleaned, the prisoners moved deeper into the dungeon, behind one of the many doors that helped separate the various blocks.

"Your girl gets it," Ian said once the servants were gone. He leaned against the bars and crossed his arms. "Have you thought about what will happen if angels do come demanding you, and we refuse?"

"They'll either leave, or you'll kill them," Qurrah said, as if it were obvious.

"True," Ian said. "But think long term for a moment. Just try."

"It'll be war," Tessanna said quietly. "Terrible, brutal war."

"A war I don't see us winning," Ian said. "At least, not as we are. Perhaps if you two lived up to your various legends we might stand a chance. But we'd be going up against the might of the angels, plus Mordeina's far larger army. You were at the Bloodbrick. You saw their show of might."

"Might currently spent fighting orcs," Qurrah argued.

"Aye," Ian said. "And just imagine how quickly they'd turn back around if they heard rumors of war. You two coming here puts us all in danger. I'm not one to complain. My life is on the line pretty much every day I put on this armor. But if you're going to stay here, if you're going to let my men die to protect you from some winged maniacs, all I'm asking for is a little appreciation."

Qurrah bowed his head.

"My apologies," he said. "I should better control my tongue. I am thankful for all you do, and pray that our time here in this dungeon will be long and uneventful."

Ian nodded his head, then pushed off from the bars.

"Much better." He tossed them an iron ring. "Here's the keys to the cell, just in case you need to lock yourselves in. Angels might be strong, but I doubt they'll be breaking open bars with their bare hands. Try to stay in here as much as you can, but you're free to walk around the city at your leisure. Servants will come to see if you need anything—food, drink, whatever. Other than that, enjoy your stay. I've got some patrols to schedule."

He left, the heavy door to the dungeon slamming shut with a bang. Qurrah stood in the center of their cell, feeling as if his feet were bolted in place.

"War," he said softly as Tessanna flung herself onto the bed. "Is that really what we create by coming here?"

"Don't blame yourself," Tessanna said, stretching out on her back. "If it wasn't us, it'd be someone else. You heard Bram. He won't let a single man or woman be judged, and over the past years I'm sure many who were spared the angels' wrath have crossed the Corinth into Ker's lands."

"Pale comfort," Qurrah muttered.

"But comfort nonetheless."

He joined her on the bed, and Tessanna curled her body into his, her face pressed against his chest and her eyes closed. Slowly he brushed her long hair, his mind far away.

"Tess," he whispered. "Can you sense the angels?"

After a long pause, she nodded.

"They're not like men," she said. "They burn in my mind if I let it wander."

Qurrah knew he should ask, but he was frightened to. Taking a deep breath, he let it out, then asked anyway.

"Do you sense angels coming toward us?"

Another long pause.

"Yes."

"How many?"

She curled tighter against him, kissed his neck.

"Enough," she whispered.

## 21

Tessanna watched her lover sleep and wished she could do the same. He lay half dressed, the result of their lovemaking. Despite all that had happened, he looked peaceful. For that, she was jealous.

In her mind, the voices whispered.

*You turned against me. You betrayed me for a god that will never love you, never forgive you. His angels come, and they carry not a crown in their hands but a sword. You ran from me, and you now run from them. Who is left, Qurrah? Who is left?*

Tessanna balled her fists, clenching her jaw so tightly it bared her teeth.

"You're a dead god," she whispered. "Your priests are scattered, your paladins in hiding. All faith in you is broken."

She never expected an answer, but it seemed Karak's dim voice heard. She felt unseen eyes turn to her, felt her presence finally acknowledged. It sent a chill down her spine, she who had long existed under the watchful eyes of the goddess.

*So too were Ashhur's followers broken, in a time not so distant. The world changes, daughter of balance. You above all should understand it can change again.*

The presence vanished, the oppressive weight on her chest lifting, only to be replaced by another presence that burned in her mind like fireflies.

The angels had arrived.

The sound of shouting awoke Qurrah from his slumber. His eyes snapped open, his mind immediately alert. Grabbing his clothes, he began to dress. When he saw Tessanna sitting at the foot of the bed, already awake, he was hardly surprised. No doubt she'd sensed the angels' presence long before they actually arrived.

"Have they landed yet?" he asked her.

"I don't know."

Her voice was calm, emotionless, but there were tears running down her face. Feeling strangely guilty for them, he kissed both her cheeks, then held her close.

"Together we can withstand anything," he told her. "Anything."

She smiled up at him, and he pulled her to her feet.

"Where are we going?" she asked.

Qurrah shook his head.

"I won't cower in here while others die for me. If there's to be a fight, then I will be a part of it."

He wrapped his whip around his arm, its tightening weight a comfort to him. Done, he stepped out from the cell and climbed the stairs leading to the dungeon's exit. To his surprise, he found it locked from the outside. He beat his fist against it, calling out to the guards on the other side.

"Let us out!"

"Forgive me," a man shouted. "I have orders not to."

Qurrah groaned.

"That stupid bastard."

"It seems he knows you better than you thought," Tessanna said, and a smile flickered briefly on her face.

Before Qurrah could ponder ways of smashing the door open, a voice rang out. Despite the thick walls of the dungeon he heard it clear as day, leaving him certain that it was some sort of clerical or divine magic.

"Qurrah Tun!" cried an instantly familiar voice. "Our council has convened. We have capitulated to man's law, recognizing mankind's authority to rule themselves as Ashhur has granted. Come forth, and accept your fate with dignity and grace."

"Dignity," Qurrah snorted. "What a damn fool."

His bluster was fake, and it was obvious Tess knew it as well. That voice, that powerful, intimidating voice, only belonged to one angel: Judarius, the most dangerous of all when it came to combat.

Qurrah pressed his ear to the door, for he heard a faint shouting in response, that of Sir Ian.

"Get your bloody-ass wings off our land, you pompous piece of duck shit. You're not welcome here. Qurrah's staying, you're leaving. That clear?"

There was a long pause.

"This is your last chance," Judarius shouted. "Qurrah, I beg of you, come forth. No man must die needlessly this night. Will you let others suffer and bleed for naught?"

*War*, Qurrah thought. *This moment will spark war. I can stop it. I can be the hero my brother has always been.*

He almost did just that, but something stopped him. The thought of kneeling before the angels and presenting his neck filled him with sickness. That wasn't a noble sacrifice. That was just death. Pointless, meaningless death. Worse, it felt like spitting in the eye of Ashhur for all he'd been given. He couldn't do that. He wouldn't.

"Open this door," Qurrah told the guard on the other side.

"I'm under orders to…"

"Open it, or I destroy it."

The door opened, and Qurrah stepped out, Tessanna at his side.

Stretching out before them was a great courtyard, the dungeon located just within the castle's outer walls. Filling the courtyard were over two hundred soldiers, with even more rushing in from the city. Hovering in the air, their bodies clad in shining golden armor, were over thirty angels. Their swords and spears were drawn, tips glistening, looking hungry in the night sky. In the center of the angels' formation flew Judarius, his enormous mace hanging loose in his right hand. With their departure from the dungeon, the angels' attention turned his way. He felt dozens of eyes upon him, and it made his skin crawl. Still he stepped forward, refusing to be cowed.

"Here I am," Qurrah said.

"Get back inside!" Sir Ian shouted. Qurrah ignored him.

"I'm here," he said instead. "Right here. But I don't accept your judgment. I don't accept your execution. You aren't on the side of righteousness, Judarius. None of you are. Fly away. Fly now. It's *your* souls these deaths will weigh upon, not mine."

Judarius's body dipped up and down as his wings beat the air. He stared at Qurrah, and behind those gold-green eyes a battle raged.

"So be it," the angel said, and with those soft words, the courtyard erupted in chaos. Five of the angels dove for Qurrah, with the rest attempting to cover either side of their flank, preventing the soldiers from closing in behind the assault. Feeling his whip tighten hungrily, Qurrah summoned his magic, a grim smile on his face. This was what he was best at. Not hiding. Not politics. An enemy was before him, seeking to challenge his strength. Life or death, it was now in his hands, hands which burned with purple fire as he raised them to the heavens. Violet orbs shot out, two dozen of them swarming with flames. The five angels banked and curved, avoiding death. One failed, his wing clipped by an orb. It burst in a great explosion, flames bathing over his body and sending him crashing to the ground.

The rest were almost there, and Qurrah dove to avoid their slashes. Tessanna, however, appeared to have no intention of hiding. Taking in a deep breath, she let loose with a shriek so loud it seemed the very air roiled with it.

"FLEE!"

It hit the angels like a physical force, two slamming into the ground, the other two banking upward, far away from them. Qurrah lashed a grounded angel with his whip, charring black his golden breastplate. The angel endured, and he blocked the second lash with his vambrace. Sword drawn, he rushed forward. Another lash wrapped around the angel's foot, trying to trip him up, but a flutter of his wings kept him steady. Sword lunging for Qurrah's chest, it seemed nothing would stop him.

So Qurrah clapped his hands, not bothering to. His body became shadow for the briefest of moments, just long enough for the angel to pass straight through him. The being spun about, reacting well to the ploy, but Tessanna was the faster. She leapt forward, her hand touching the feathers of his wings. She said nothing, only smiled as fire spread across white feathers. The look upon her face was chilling, even to Qurrah, as a horrible scream escaped the angel's throat. The angel slashed at Tessanna, a valiant last attempt as his body burned. Tessanna ducked underneath the sword, stepped closer, and pushed against him. His armor cracked, blasted as if struck by a great maul. The angel flew back, landed with a crash, and lay still.

"Stand firm!" he heard Sir Ian screaming above the din. "Stand firm, hold your lines!"

The angels had switched tactics, looping up and around to make simultaneous passes from opposite directions. As Qurrah watched, a dozen angels slashed through the gathered soldiers, their weapons easily puncturing their armor. Before the men could strike back the angels were already lifting into the air, propelled upward by a simple twist of their wings. Tens of men lay dead from the pass, and tens more died as the angels repeated the maneuver. Soldiers continued to flood in from the outer city, but it seemed they were dying as quickly as they came.

"We have to stop them," Qurrah said.

"You can," Judarius said, landing on the ground before him with a *thud*. His enormous mace left a small crater in the stone. "Surrender, now. No more must die."

"Can you handle him?" Tessanna asked, her eyes still locked on the combat beyond.

"I can try," Qurrah said.

Tessanna kissed his cheek, then rushed around Judarius, to where the greater battle raged. Judarius met his eyes, and his gaze was clearly pained.

"We mustn't do this," Judarius said. "Angels and men are dying."

"By your orders."

The angel shook his head.

"I won't debate this with you. Your magic is powerful, Qurrah, but against me you are nothing. Spare the lives of others."

Qurrah laughed, living shadows gathering in the palms of his hands.

"The only life you can spare is your own," he said. "My brother defeated you once. Do not think me incapable of the same."

The corner of Judarius's face twitched, as if holding back a smile. He opened his mouth to speak, but then rushed forward instead. The sudden action nearly ended the fight before it began. Qurrah slammed his wrists together, desperately pouring his power into a physical shield of swirling darkness. The mace smashed into it, showering the two with yellow sparks. Qurrah braced himself, felt the impact all the way down to his knees. Teeth clenched, he let his full strength roll out of him. He was not a weakling. He was not some inferior power compared to Harruq. He'd broken the prophet. Compared to Velixar, Judarius was just a bigger, beefier version of his brother.

The mace slashed again, and Qurrah blocked it as before. This time the impact was not so severe, the half-orc's feet firmly planted, his spell strong enough to send the mace flying backward. Qurrah took advantage of the temporary reprieve, dashing toward one of the dead angels. He had only a moment's breath of time, but it was enough to close the distance. Sliding to his feet, he slammed his fists against the body, flooding it with power. Bones tore from the flesh, snapping free of the ligaments and cartilage holding them, and they hovered in the air. Like a tornado they swirled around him, each one shimmering violet. Judarius swung, but when his mace connected with one, it was as if he struck a wall of stone. The shockwave rolled over them both.

Qurrah smirked.

"A big man with a club," he said. "Is that all you are?"

Touching the corpse again, this time he ignited the blood. With a sweeping motion he pulled massive amounts of it into the air, flinging it at Judarius like a wave. The blood caught fire, lighting up the night. Judarius moved faster than anticipated, though, avoiding the attack. Sizzling, the blood splashed across the ground, charring everything it touched. Before Qurrah could strike again, Judarius began to dodge. He didn't quite fly, but he used his wings to keep himself in perpetual motion, swirling around Qurrah with incredible speed. Twice Qurrah flung bolts of darkness, but his aim was never accurate enough.

"You're wrong," Judarius said, continuing his maneuvers. "I am no man."

His mace struck again, the entire angel's might behind it. The bone shield cracked and broke, turning the various pieces into powder and flinging Qurrah through the air. He bit his tongue as he jostled and bounced after landing, seemingly taking forever to come to a halt. Judarius flew closer, lifting the mace again.

"No," said the angel. "I'm something better."

"Then prove it."

Down came the mace and up came Qurrah's hands. More of his magical power poured out, slowly draining his reserve. His mind had begun its familiar ache and he found it increasingly difficult to concentrate. The shield surrounded him, protected him, but this time the shadows cracked like thawing ice. He screamed, demanded himself to be stronger. Judarius pressed down on him with incredible strength. Did the war god ever possess such might?

The shield shattered, and the resulting shockwave sent him to the ground, gasping for air. His ears rang, his vision blurred. Coughing, he glanced up at the rest of the conflict. The angels continued to circle, but their attacks had grown less frequent. Every time they tried to assault, Tessanna was there, flooding the sky with fire and lightning.

"You fight valiantly," Judarius said, his footfalls heavy. "But this is at an end. On your knees, so you may die with dignity. If your soul is pure, you have nothing to fear. Ashhur will still take you into his arms."

Qurrah rolled onto his back, laughing. Blood filled his mouth, staining his teeth.

"You truly believe this, don't you?" he asked. "You actually think you're doing his will?"

Judarius lifted his mace.

"I pray you know peace," he said.

Before he could slam it down, Qurrah hooked his fingers into twisting shapes, enacting a spell. He became shadow, but instead of having the weapon pass through him, he passed through the very ground. Below him was the sprawling dungeon, and with a cry he landed hard onto the floor of a cell. For a moment he felt afraid to look, for if he'd rematerialized in the wrong place, such as between two walls, there'd be nothing he could do. But he felt no pain, and it seemed a bit of luck was with him. When he'd cast the spell, he'd fully expected to end up with prison bars piercing parts of his body.

Groaning, he pushed himself to his feet. He was in the empty section near the entrance, though when he tried the door he found it locked. Taking out the key Ian had given him, he tested it on the lock. Sure enough it opened, the skeleton key usable on all cells within that section.

"What now?" Qurrah wondered aloud. He looked to the entrance of the dungeon, curious how long it'd take Judarius to figure out where he was. It turned out not long at all. The hinges twisted, the center of the iron door bowing inward. Two more hits and it blasted open. Judarius stood in the jagged breach, mace held in both hands. He looked annoyed.

"You would be a coward?" Judarius asked, folding his wings inward so he might descend the stairs into the underground dungeon. "The life you have, the very breath you take, was a gift from Ashhur through Azariah's hands. For even one of your crimes you should have been hanged, yet we showed mercy. But the world is not ready for this mercy, Qurrah. The world doesn't know how to live without abusing everything, even things most pure. Your death is only a small step toward a greater peace on Dezrel. Can you not accept this, and accept the returning of your gift?"

"Seems to belittle the gift if you ask me," Qurrah said.

Judarius sighed as he passed by the cells, the sides of his wings brushing against the bars.

"If only Azariah were here. He would make you understand. He would know how to explain it for one as wise as you. But me, well, I command armies. I crush my enemies. This is your last chance, Qurrah, your last chance to do something good."

Qurrah knew there was nowhere else to go, so he stood firm, preparing one last desperate gamble. Because of the bars, Judarius could not dodge or maneuver. Hands together, Qurrah pulled at the well of his energy, sapping every last bit of it. It had been so long since he'd fought and he felt himself tiring prematurely, failing to live up to what he knew he could be. He prayed that what he did next would be enough. It had to be. A beam of pure darkness shot from his palms, the very center of it swirling with stars and moons and things for which Qurrah had no name.

Judarius saw the attack and braced, the thick head to his mace in the way. The two connected, and the angel let out a cry. The muscles in his legs tightened, and he pushed forward step by agonizing step. The magic hit the mace and splintered, unable to continue on against the eternity-forged weapon. Still Qurrah poured his power outward, continuing the spell, challenging Judarius to withstand. Step after step, each one a trial.

But withstand he did. His mace slammed into Qurrah's gut. He let out a whimper, collapsing onto his back. Judarius put a foot atop his chest, holding him in place with such weight that he struggled to breathe. The mace lifted in the air.

"So selfish," said the angel. "That's all you've ever been."

"*Judarius!*"

The angel flinched, and Qurrah twisted so he might see what was happening. There in the entrance of the dungeon stood Ahaesarus, his sword in hand.

"Let him go," he said. "There's been enough death this night."

"The council—"

"Will convene again," Ahaesarus said, taking another step. "Release him."

Slowly the mace lowered, and Judarius cast a look to Qurrah that he could not interpret.

"If you insist," Judarius said. He removed his foot, and the half-orc gasped in air. Ahaesarus stepped into the cell Qurrah had opened so Judarius might pass, then approached. Qurrah slumped on his knees, still struggling to recover.

"Qurrah," the angel started to say.

"Get out," Qurrah said, his voice raspy. "I don't want to hear a word."

Ahaesarus stared at him with genuine sadness in his eyes.

"I will honor your request," he said. And then he turned, exiting the dungeon. Qurrah rubbed his raw throat with a shivering hand and wondered. What madness was going on in Avlimar?

Slowly he made his way to the dungeon entrance, stumbled up the stairs, and exited through the broken door. Before him, the courtyard was a horrific sight. Over a hundred men lay dead, their bodies pierced by spears and cut open by frighteningly sharp swords. Scattered among them were the corpses of angels, a third of those that had come to claim him. Ian's soldiers gathered at the gates of the castle, where King Bram had emerged after the battle halted. So far it seemed no one spoke to the other, the two sides just remaining in place.

"King of Ker!" Ahaesarus shouted, flying to join his fellow angels. "What was done here was our own fault, not of Mordan and her rulers. I ask that you forgive the rashness that led to such deaths, and know that we will do all we can to make this right."

"My men are dead," Bram shouted back. "Attacked in the night so you could capture a man under my protection. How do you make that right?"

Ahaesarus paused.

"I do not know," he said. "But we will find a way. Let there be no need for war. No army will march your way, and no angel will disrespect your borders again."

Bram hardly looked convinced, but he said nothing. Without any fanfare, the angels turned and rose into the air, their wings sending them far into the distance within moments. Qurrah let out a sigh, and he leaned against the door frame of the dungeon. Closing his eyes, he waited for the pounding behind his eyes to cease. But it seemed silence would not be his. All around he heard shouting, men hustling about. Bram spoke to him not long after, having walked his way.

"I knew they would come for you eventually," he said. "Don't worry. Our army is already prepared to march. Should Mordan's army declare war…"

"My brother would never do such a thing," he said. In the distance, he caught sight of Tessanna through the chaos, and it made him strangely nervous.

"Leave us," he said, not caring that he gave an order to a king. Bram took a step back, seeming surprised by the anger in his voice.

"Careful, half-orc," Bram said, but he turned to the rest of his men and shouted the order. "To the barracks! I want us ready to march by sunrise if need be! Grieve now, prepare now. We'll bury the dead come the morning light."

The king glanced his way, but Qurrah ignored him. Instead he weaved through the bloody fallout of the battle, stepping over the dead so he might reach his lover. Tessanna sat on her knees, the body of an angel straddled across her lap. Her fingers stroked his face as if he were her own child. Long black hair cascaded down her shoulders, settling over his body like a shroud. The ache in her eyes was almost painful for Qurrah to witness. For a long while he said nothing, just watched the soldiers hurry to and fro, until at last the courtyard was empty but for them and the dead.

"Tess?" he said, breaking the silence.

"They're beautiful," she said, trembling fingers brushing the angel's cheek. "So beautiful."

"We had no choice."

She looked up, tears in her eyes.

"You think I don't know that?" she asked. "They're lost, they're broken, yet they're still divine. They're a glorious light, and it's blinding us all."

Qurrah knelt beside her, offering her his hand. She ignored it.

"What's wrong?" he asked her. "What bothers you so?"

Tessanna let her hair hide her face. Her voice dropped down to a whisper.

"I should have let them kill us," she said. "I know that now. The world would be better for it."

Frustration bubbled up in Qurrah's chest.

"No," he said. "No, you shouldn't have. I'd give my life for something good, Tess. My belief in Ashhur, it's tentative, it's fragile, but I still feel something there, something worthwhile. But this? No. I'd die for Harruq. I'd die for his family, and I'd die for you. I gave my life at that bridge, for men who rightfully wished for me to suffer. But I will not die for *nothing*. That's all this would be. That's what these angels' brought with their blades. Nothing. And that's why they're wrong."

He offered her a hand, but still she refused.

"You don't understand," Tessanna said. "What am I, Qurrah? What was I born for? I and my mirror, we were both born for balance. Mira killed an ancient demon. She fought against us, and died distracting Thulos, saving hundreds of lives. She was my mirror, my opposite in everything. She was light. She was good. Me?"

She laughed. Qurrah touched her shoulder, and she yanked it violently away.

"I'm a danger," she said. "To you. To me. To the entire damn world."

"You're not," Qurrah insisted, trying to keep calm. What was happening to her? Why was the madness rising so quickly in her eyes? She'd been better over the past few years…hadn't she?

"How can you know?"

"Because your power has faded, Tess. You played your role in the Gods' War. This is what Celestia wanted."

"Is it?" Tessanna asked, and she laughed again. The sound of it sent a chill crawling up Qurrah's spine. She was breaking before him, he realized, and he felt helpless to stop it. Tessanna let the angel slip from her arms, and slowly she stood.

"Do you know what I felt when I killed Ashhur's angels?" she asked.

"What?" he dared ask.

In answer she lifted her arms. A wind blew, swirling in from nowhere. The darkness in her eyes grew, pushing away any hint of whiteness. Her head tilted to one side, and when she spoke, her voice was filled with torment.

"Power."

From her back grew enormous ethereal wings, the feathers made of shadow and dust. They stretched further and further, greater than he'd ever seen before. A dress of pure darkness formed about her, clothing her as if she were a queen from a plane far beyond their own. The wind howled, swirling around her, teasing her hair, flapping her dress. Within its fabric he saw stars dance. Slowly her wings lifted her into the air. Qurrah stood before her, feeling so small, so confused. Deep down, he knew he was losing her, and nothing else mattered compared to that.

"Tess!" he screamed, trying to gain her attention. She looked down at him, but it was as if she didn't know who he was.

"I can see it," she told him. "I can see the golden star breaking. I can feel the world groaning, taste the rivers of blood on my tongue. And I can stop it."

"No!" Qurrah screamed. "This isn't you. This isn't who you are! You're not a puppet. You're not their slave!"

"With a thought," Tessanna said, her voice deep yet strangely hollow. "I sense it, Qurrah, that city of gold and pearl. Everything to follow, I can crush right now. The seed must be ripped from the soil. The world must be spared from what comes next."

"No, damn it!"

Qurrah rushed her, demanding her presence, refusing to wilt before the tremendous power he sensed building within his love.

"Remember who you are!" he screamed up at her. "You don't have to do this. You aren't evil. You aren't the destroyer. Let it go, Tess. Let it go!"

She continued staring north, seeing things that were far beyond his sight. Her outstretched hand trembled, and the ground trembled with it. Tears ran down her face, and her lower lip quivered. The empty look on her face then changed, replaced with terrible sorrow.

"I can stop it," she said, her voice more her own. "Please, Qurrah, let me stop it. Let me destroy while I still can. Mother wants me to bring back the darkness."

"Never again," Qurrah said, feeling his heart pounding in his ribcage. "Let it all go."

Her arms curled around her chest, and she bent over as if she'd been stabbed in the belly. Her wings fluttered, flared out wide, and then exploded in a frantic eruption of fading feathers. A scream tore from Tessanna's very soul, and she arched her back, her head snapping violently from side to side. The dress of stars and darkness vanished, replaced by her own. And then she fell.

Qurrah caught her in his arms, collapsing onto his rear beneath her weight. Cradling her, he cried, rocking back and forth as he clutched his beloved to his chest. Time resumed, as if the whole world had paused to witness their spectacle.

"No more," he whispered. "No more. We won't play their games."

Tessanna's eyes fluttered open. When she looked up at him he saw love in them, and he nearly broke down again.

"I'm sorry," she said, pressing her face against his robe. "I'm so sorry."

She cried, and he held her, and all alone they endured.

## 22

By day the orcs lurked in the distance, baiting them, daring them to separate their numbers. By night came the raids, never at the same time, and never from the same direction. It was enough to drive Tarlak mad.

"We'll never make it to Angelport," he said as he stood in the center of their enormous camp beneath the blackened sky. "By Ashhur, I don't even think we'll make it halfway."

Sergan stood beside him, shaking his head as a cry of alarm came from the south, the third in the past hour.

"I'd celebrate just making it another day," he said as they ran toward the call. Tarlak knew it'd be over before he got there. It almost always was. They arrived amid the confusion, with dozens of soldiers readying swords and shields. All around were their tents, gaping holes in the tops, many with spears still jutting from the fabric. Despite the commotion, no combat took place, the orcs having already fled.

It took little time to find out what happened. Orcs had taken out the guards with arrows, then a large group had rushed the camp, throwing spears from a distance before retreating. All in all they'd lost only seven men, but that wasn't the raid's purpose. The men were afraid to sleep, constantly roused by their hit and runs. By day they marched in a desperate attempt to reach Angelport, and by night they suffered the raids.

Tarlak looked to Antonil's large tent in the distance, feeling like there were stones in his gut.

"We won't make it," the wizard whispered as a fourth alarm sounded from the north. "You damn fool."

The following morning, Tarlak sat before his tent, legs crossed beneath him, and ate his meager gruel. Normally he'd have whipped himself up something more appetizing via magical means, but his supply of topaz was low, and worse, he didn't want to feast so fine in front of all the other exhausted men. It'd been one thing on their march out, well-supplied and in good spirits.

Now, though...now he ate the mush and wondered how long it'd take before he opened himself a portal and fled west.

Despite his odd garb and reputation as a wizard, Tarlak tended to be on the popular side, but not that morning. No one wanted jokes. No one wanted anecdotes and stories of faraway places. So used to his newfound privacy, Tarlak was surprised when Sergan plopped down before him, his own bowl of food in hand.

"At last," he said. "I thought I'd never get to eat."

"You here for company?" Tarlak asked, raising an eyebrow.

"Here hoping no one thinks to look for me next to the oddball wizard."

Tarlak shrugged.

"Fair enough. I can cast an illusion spell over you if you'd like, turn you into a buxom lady. Should buy you at least an hour."

Sergan said something indecipherable with his full mouth. Tarlak assumed it was a colorful way of saying no.

"Suit yourself," he said, leaning his chin on his hand and looking to their destination. In the far distance was a set of hills, and once they crossed over them it was nothing but flat grasslands until they reached Angelport. Hunting would go down, hurting the army's already dwindling supplies. Tarlak tried to think of an upside, got nothing. So he set his bowl aside and watched Sergan eat.

"We need to change his mind," he said.

"Good luck," Sergan said, wiping at his beard. "I've never seen him like this. Even when we were fleeing the war demons he was never this determined."

"What set him off?"

Sergan wolfed down another spoonful of gruel.

"I don't like to say things I don't know for certain, especially about my king. But if you were to press me, I'd say pride. All those years ago, we were running for our lives, doing everything we could to hold together and protect our people. But now he's a king. He's got a legacy, he's got tens of thousands of soldiers. Lords have been hanging all over him, and his reputation in Mordeina is in the shitter. He wants this, he *needs* this. To go back home unable to capture Veldaren a second time..."

Another spoonful.

"I think he'd stomach this gruel better than he would that bad a failure."

*Of course it's pride*, thought Tarlak as he let out a sigh. Pride, the one thing that couldn't be reasoned or bargained with. He looked to the hills, trying to convince himself that Angelport really wasn't that far away. A faint speck made him frown. He cast a spell to improve his eyes, making them sharper than an eagle's. What he saw made him curse well enough to impress a veteran like Sergan.

"What is it?" he asked.

Tarlak enhanced the spell, and only the sheer audacity of the attack kept him from panicking. In fact, it left him vaguely amused.

"Get the men ready for battle, now," he said. "I'll keep us alive until then."

"Keep us alive? What in Karak's hairy codpiece do you mean…"

And then the first dozen stones catapulted into the air from the far hillside. While Sergan swore up a storm, Tarlak summoned his magic, his mind racing for a solution. A magical shield would endure too much strain against so many, especially with both the weight of the stones and the enormous space he'd have to cover. Shattering each individually would take too much time. Wind would do nothing. That left him one option: smacking them right back.

"Out of the way!" he shouted, and ripped chunks of the ground around him. Hoping he didn't accidentally fling one of the soldiers with them, he hurled the pieces into the air, doing his best to track the downward velocity of the enemy projectiles. One after another he threw them, the mid-air collisions shattering rock and dirt across the hillside, with much of it raining down upon the army. Still, far better they be pieces of broken stone than ones the size of a tent. Of the twelve, he stopped ten, and he did his best to ignore the casualties the remaining two caused as they crashed through their ranks with unrelenting speed.

Like bees with their hive struck, the army rushed to prepare, scurrying about grabbing shields and swords. Meanwhile, rows of orcs scurried over the hills. Tarlak stopped estimating after the second thousand. More and more rushed over, and with a ferocious cry they charged, the hill increasing the speed of their assault. Tarlak wanted to give them an old-fashioned wizardly greeting, preferably with fire, but couldn't as twelve more stones shot over the hill, the catapults just barely visible even with his enhanced eyesight.

"One caterpillar, two caterpillar, three caterpillar, four," Tarlak said as he flung more chunks of earth. "Come on, you can do better than that!"

The exclamation was to himself as he watched three make it past his defenses. The orcs slammed into the hastily prepared line, numbering at least five thousand, and Tarlak watched another volley of twelve boulders soar into the air. His mind focused, he hurled more chunks of earth, the area around him looking like a great carved groove. All twelve he shoved aside, killing their momentum or shattering them entirely. He let out a cry, wishing he could see the faces of the orcs as they watched their ambush falter.

And then another twenty catapults rolled over the hillside on creaking wooden wheels.

Tarlak scratched at his goatee.

"Shit."

Over thirty stones hurled into the air, and Tarlak found himself glad that they couldn't see *his* face. His arms were a blur, curling and throwing, the movements helping to focus his mind. Giving up on using real earth, he started hurling great balls of ice from his palms. Conjuring matter out of nothing was a greater tax on his strength, but he couldn't afford to delay. In a great barrage they flew every which way, some missing, some connecting. Ice shards fell upon the army as the stones slammed through tents and snapped bones, bouncing and rolling as to make a mockery of Antonil's growing lines of soldiers.

"Get up the damn hill!" Tarlak screamed, using magic to increase the volume of his voice. Antonil's soldiers were swarming toward the front, and despite the casualties and lack of preparation, they still outnumbered the orcs nearly five to one. They surged ahead, trying to push through to the hill beyond, where they could attack the catapults. Tarlak let out a whoop, then took in a deep breath as another volley unleashed. Whoever commanded the orcs, Tarlak knew the man had them working double-time loading and releasing those enormous stones.

As boulders and rocks fell from the sky, he wished he could see himself from afar. It had to be impressive. He laughed as the stones shattered, laughed as he felt himself slowing with every spell, the catapulted stones landing all around him, only a few missing due to so many men packed into such a small area.

*That's enough,* Tarlak thought as Antonil's army gave chase up the hill, nearing the halfway mark. In the short reprieve between attacks he cast a spell, gathering power above the hillcrest. Great blasts of lightning tore through the orcs working there, splintering three of the catapults. Tarlak let out a gasp afterward, and deep in his forehead he felt a throbbing.

"Could really use you here, Harruq," Tarlak said, thinking of the last time they'd had to deal with orc catapults. With a wind spell he'd sent Harruq and Haern over a great chasm, letting the two expert fighters slaughter the defenseless orcs. What he'd give to have either of them with him now.

More heavy stones. Tarlak tried to predict which were the most accurate, and therefore do the most damage. Flexing his fingers, he gripped the stones in his mind and crushed them to powder. It was a far slower process, but a more certain way to counter. He was only able to stop six that time, the rest crashing down all throughout the emptying camp.

Tarlak watched the fight, hoping Antonil's men would reach the catapults before another volley. That hope died when the orcs in flight suddenly turned and charged. Joining them were several thousand more that appeared over the hill, obviously kept in reserve for such an occasion. As Tarlak's eyes widened he saw groups of a thousand coming around the far left and right flanks, the orcs running as fast as their bulky legs could carry them. The distance was such that it'd take a couple minutes to reach the fight, but they'd slam into both sides of the vanguard, which was currently lacking even the slightest defensive formations. Meanwhile, orcs continued to swarm over the hillside, using their weight and the height of the hill to fling themselves into the human lines.

Trapped in the middle of all those orcs, there was little Antonil could do, and nowhere for his men to go. Another volley of catapults released, and it took immense willpower for Tarlak to continue his defense. A flawlessly executed ambush, and even though he guessed Antonil to have twice the number of men compared to the orcs, they'd still take devastating casualties. What had happened? Who in the world was this orcish commander?

Tarlak let the next volley hit, knowing those deaths wouldn't matter if the greater bulk of their forces upon the hills were destroyed. Opening a portal, he stepped through and appeared at the base of the hill, where the soldiers were still trying to force their way up.

"Left and right flanks!" Tarlak screamed, pointing toward the distant orc forces. "We need lines, shields at the front. Move!"

He heard commanders relaying his orders, and he turned his attention away from them to the fight up top. The last volley of stones had smashed through the remnants of their camp, taking few casualties with so many making their way to the hill. Praying the next volley was as foolishly aimed, he summoned the last of his magic. Fire burst around his hands, and with a dark grin he began to hurl balls of flame toward the orcs along the top of the hill. Over a dozen slammed into the hillside before detonating. The fire spread in all directions, leaving enormous gaps in the orc assault. The men, once they reached the crest, found their enemy thinned and without reinforcements, and with such an advantage they quickly chopped them down.

When the last of his fireballs burned out, Tarlak fell to one knee and vomited. He glanced to either side, saw the conflict had begun in earnest. The outnumbered orcs fought with ferocity, but Antonil's men were well trained, and despite all that had happened, they still had numbers on their side. Upon the hill, the thousands of men pushed on, with Antonil at their forefront, his golden armor shining. Antonil wished him the best of luck.

With his enhanced eyes, he scanned the hill, searching for the commander. As another volley released, he caught sight of a man in red armor, with black wings curled around his sides. Tarlak's blood ran cold.

A war demon, leading an orc army?

The catapults had not pulled back as far, and the stones rained down upon the hill. Their speed was less, but it didn't matter, not with such weight. Tarlak clenched a fist, trying to force out one more spell. At the nearest projectile he hurled a bolt of red lightning that struck the boulder's center. Instead of halting it, it exploded into heavy chunks which rained down upon the men.

Tarlak caught sight of one such piece heading toward him. He raised his hands, summoning a shield to protect himself, only to find his well of magic empty. The rock continued unslowed past his hands, striking him across the head. His body spun, the world shifting at sickening speed.

His body struck ground. All around him he saw feet rushing ahead, continuing to join the fight.

Then darkness.

## 23

They propped Jessilynn by the exit of the ravine so all would see her as they marched. Jessilynn endured it best she could, her mind clouded by whatever herbs the shaman had placed upon her wounded face. Two wolf-men guarded her, with explicit orders to kill her should anyone attempt a rescue.

"I hope your elf friend is wise enough to stay away," Silver-Ear had said after relaying the instructions to the brutes.

Jessilynn said nothing, only nodded. Occasionally she looked to the sky, hoping to see Sonowin's great wings, but they were never there. More and more she grew convinced that Dieredon had abandoned her so he might fly west to warn the people of Mordan. And while she knew it was the right thing to do, the course of action that'd save the most lives, it did nothing to remove her feeling of abandonment as she stood there, her arms tied with primitive ropes to a wooden stake. The creatures snarled at her, lapped their tongues and gnashed their teeth. Her eyes closed, she pretended not to hear them, not to be afraid.

Once the ravine was empty, and the various races had exited, Silver-Ear returned for her, along with an escort of wolves.

"Come," the female said, taking her wrist. "Moonslayer would have words with you."

They left the ravine, Jessilynn half-walking, half-dragged across the yellow grass. Up ahead she saw the great mass of bodies that was the combined army, but they did not go to them. Instead they slowed, coming upon a small fire. Moonslayer sat waiting, hunched over the fire with the bones of his meal at his feet. Several wolf-men were with him, taller than the others, stronger. His most faithful and trusted, she decided, as Moonslayer stood upon her arrival. Manfeaster was not with him, but she could only assume he was farther ahead, leading the army in his brother's absence.

"On your knees," Silver-Ear said, shoving her to the ground. Jessilynn let out a small cry and remained where she'd fallen. Without saying a word, Moonslayer turned around, grabbing something that had been hidden behind him. He tossed it her way, where it landed with a loud clang. Jessilynn frowned, not understanding what was expected of her. The object was an enormous shield, the front bearing the crest of the army of Mordan.

"What of it?" she finally asked.

"Pick it up," the wolf-man said.

If it was a trap, it was a strange one. Slowly getting to her feet, she walked over to the shield, feeling the eyes of the monsters upon her. The metal was cool to the touch, and heavier than what she could use with any sort of proficiently. She lifted it before her, settling into a basic stance. Apparently whatever she'd done was wrong, for Moonslayer lashed it out of her grip with a swipe. She flinched, expecting an attack, but instead he went back to where he'd been sitting and this time retrieved a sword. He tossed it at her feet.

"Pick it up."

She lifted the sword, careful to keep the tip pointed downward to show she had no crazy ideas. There were a dozen wolf-men surrounding her, and it'd take more than a rusted blade to slice and dice herself free. Again she was judged poorly, the blade knocked out of her hands. The enormous wolf-man lunged forward, wrapping his paw around her neck and lifting her up.

"You said you were a paladin," he growled. "You lied."

The glow, she realized. They were looking for a glow, something to match the stories of Darius and Jerico. Trying not to panic, she fought for breath through his grip.

"I am," she insisted. "I can prove it."

Moonslayer dropped her. His back curled so he might stare at her eye to eye.

"How?" he asked.

"My bow," she said. "I need my bow."

"I left it at the cave," Silver-Ear said, having been standing nearby, watching the events.

A quick snap from Moonslayer sent one of the wolves racing back toward the ravine. Jessilynn sat on her knees, focusing on breathing in and out. She didn't know why he wanted proof of her being a paladin, nor did she care. All that mattered was finding a way to survive, and keeping her eyes open for a chance to escape. She could do that. No matter the humiliations, they would not break her.

Silver-Ear beckoned Moonslayer over, and she whispered something in her soft, gravelly voice. Whatever it was, the wolf-man wanted no part of it, and he pushed her aside. Jessilynn looked away, unable to explain why she felt she might earn their wrath if they caught her watching.

"Human," Moonslayer said, walking over to her. From her knees she looked up at the beast. "There are those who doubt you are what I say you are. This must be settled. You will have your bow, and you will prove that you are a paladin."

He leaned closer, so that she might smell the blood on his teeth.

"But if you are lying…"

"I'm not," she said. A thought came to her, and she couldn't stop herself from saying, "Lying's not my style."

Moonslayer ruffled his nose at her but said nothing. Pacing, he waited until the wolf-man with her bow returned. The creature dumped it unceremoniously before her, scattering arrows out of the quiver. When she held the bow she saw the string had been cut. Shaking her head in annoyance, she reached for the quiver, earning herself a growl from those gathered around her.

"The string," she said, trying to explain. "It's broken, but I have a spare."

With that she continued what she was doing, removing the old drawstring and then pulling out a new one from a long pouch on the side of the quiver. Looping the bottom on, she stood, braced it with her legs, and then hooked the other side. That done, she stared Moonslayer in the eyes.

"The arrows will have the glow," she said. Moonslayer flattened his ears and nodded, urging her on.

Jessilynn bent down and picked up an arrow. This was it, she thought. She could fire an arrow into the air, the glow alerting Dieredon to her presence. Perhaps he could assault the crowd before they realized what was going on. The idea vanished as quickly as it came. There was no way Dieredon had somehow lost track of her. If he was nearby, then he already knew. That was just how he was. On the other hand, if he wasn't near…

She looked to Moonslayer, who watched her closely. Moonslayer and Manfeaster were the two responsible for the entire army, the fearsome leaders that kept the rest in check. It was fear that prevented total anarchy and breakdown, fear that would not last if the wolf-men squabbled over leadership. How much might she disrupt their plans if she took him down? She'd be forfeiting her life, but how many lives might she save in doing so? This was what she'd sworn to do, to give her life so others may go on.

The arrow touched the string. Moonslayer was to her left, and before her were two wolf-men, who stepped aside to give her an empty space to shoot through. Her heart hammered in her chest. She refused to look at Moonslayer, to even let him guess at her thinking. Up went her bow, and she tightened her grip. When she pulled back the string, the arrowhead lit up, the metal pulsing softly with a blue glow that was far fainter than she preferred. The wolf-men around her saw it, and several let out soft growls.

Now, she thought. Now was the time. Turn and fire, send the wolf-man leader to his grave. Save hundreds, maybe thousands.

She released the arrow.

It sailed through the gap, slicing through the night before striking ground. With a loud crack it hit, shattering rock. Jessilynn let out the breath she'd been holding, the weight of her inaction bringing her to tears.

No, she couldn't do it. She was a coward. If Jerico saw her then, she could only imagine the disappointment in his eyes.

"It is not the same as the stories," Moonslayer said as he took the bow from Jessilynn's hands.

"It is enough," Silver-Ear insisted. "Let them all see it. She is still a champion of mankind, no matter how weak she appears."

Moonslayer stood, studying her with those intelligent eyes of his.

"Very well," he said. "I will find Manfeaster. If you want a demonstration, shaman, then you shall have one."

He handed the bow and quiver off to another, then lifted Jessilynn into the air, draping her over his shoulders. One giant paw held her feet, the other arms. The position jammed her armor

## The Prison of Angels

into her stomach, but she kept the discomfort to herself. For some reason she knew if she mentioned it, the wolf-man would only make it worse. She felt like a child as he carried her, racing along the ground with his tongue hanging out one side of his mouth. The rest of the wolf-men followed, leaving Silver-Ear to lag behind.

After an hour of running, Jessilynn felt she could take no more. She'd had nothing to eat in the past twelve hours, so when she vomited it was just air and bile. Whenever she gagged, Moonslayer pulled her further past his neck so she would not stain his fur. On and on they ran into the west, each jostling step bringing pain to her spine.

At last they came upon the new encampment of the creatures. It was spread out along the flatlands, each race gathered separate from the others. In the center of the army they left a gap, just like they had in the ravine. It was there Moonslayer ran, dropping her on the ground and assigning two of his wolf-men to guard her. Jessilynn remained still, eyes closed, and it was not long before she drifted away into sleep.

Consciousness returned with a claw stabbing into the side of her arm. She cried out, and when she opened her eyes she found Moonslayer standing over her.

"The tribes are gathered," he said. "On your feet."

She slowly stood, her head pounding furiously. All around the creatures massed, come to watch whatever demonstration Moonslayer had planned. From what she could tell, she'd slept for at least an hour, maybe two. It wouldn't be long before the sun began to rise. The giant wolf-man paced before them all, letting them see him, letting them witness his size and power. And then he began his speech.

"I told you this human is a warrior of her kind, the best they might raise against us," Moonslayer yelled. "Yet I hear you speak when my back is turned. You call me a liar. You say she is no paladin. You say you have fought humans bigger, stronger, more dangerous than this little whelp. Then let me show you how wrong you are."

Her guess at Manfeaster's location had been wrong after all. From the west he came running at full speed, as if his return just happened to coincide with his brother's speech. Instead of running on all fours, he ran on two, for carried on his back was a human child. Jessilynn choked down a cry seeing him. The child looked hardly more than seven years old, his clothes torn and his body splashed with blood. Along with Manfeaster came several more wolf-men, and they too carried men and women on their shoulders. Most appeared dead but for two, the child Manfeaster carried and a middle-aged man.

The bodies were dumped just outside the ring, but the two living were set down not far from Jessilynn. The boy looked around with white-shocked eyes, too frightened to cry. The man fell to his knees and grabbed the boy, holding him against his chest as he kept his head down and his eyes closed. His father, thought Jessilynn, seeing their hair was the same color. Who were the rest of the bodies? Were they his family, his friends?

"We have crossed the river!" Manfeaster roared. "We have tasted the flesh of humans. No boats stop us. No armies meet us to fight. They are weak, and we are strong."

Moonslayer walked over and handed Jessilynn her bow.

"Show them," he said to her. "Let them see what you are."

With a dawning horror she realized what he wanted. The father and child? That would be how she proved her abilities as a paladin of Ashhur?

"No," she said. "No, I can't. I can't do this."

"You will," Moonslayer growled.

The rest of the vile creatures hooted and howled, driven wild by the scent of fresh human blood. The wolf-men stood guard over the bodies, the feast not yet ready to begin. It was to be entertainment first. Caught in a nightmare, Jessilynn drew an arrow. She nocked it, then stared at the father and son. They were both terrified and crying. She didn't blame them. All around were monsters.

"I can't," she whispered, suddenly loosening her grip. To murder one of them, just to spare her own life? Had she lost her mind?

"Is that so?" Moonslayer asked. He shot a look to Manfeaster, who nodded, understanding the unspoken message.

In a single smooth motion, Manfeaster took the boy from the father's arms, flipped him into the air, and then smashed him headfirst into the rocky ground.

"No!" cried Jessilynn, her scream echoing along with that of the father.

Two of the creatures beat down the man when he tried to rush Manfeaster, their claws ripping into his flesh until he crumpled to his knees. Moonslayer leaned closer, his words rumbling in Jessilynn's ears.

"Show them," he whispered. "Show them, or we eat the next alive."

It was all too much. Legs shaking, she looked upon the grieving father. His body was covered with gashes, and blood mixed with his tears and snot. Only the wolf-men holding him kept him away from the body of his son. Jessilynn thought of him lying on his back, screaming while the wolves and the birds tore into his flesh, feasting. Her arms shook, and a shudder convulsed through her.

As the vile creatures howled, she pulled back her arrow. What she did…was it murder? No matter what she chose, the man would suffer, the man would die. This was compassion, wasn't it? Was it mercy? Or was it cowardice, a way to escape the guilt of watching such a horrific sight? Her eyes flicked to the boy's corpse. Already one of the wolf-men was licking the blood off him.

*I can't do this*, thought Jessilynn. *Please, Ashhur, forgive me. Take him home.*

She let loose her arrow.

It smashed into the man, blasting him out of the wolf-men's arms and flinging him back several feet. His chest caved in, and blood shot from his mouth. The image burned into Jessilynn's mind, yet no matter how badly she wished to close her eyes to shut it all out, she could not. The corpse rolled along the ground, expending the last of its momentum. All around her the monsters cheered, thrilled with the sight and in awe of the demonstrated power.

"Did I not say she was their champion?" Moonslayer roared. "Yet she is nothing to us. She is our toy, our slave, our meal.

Man's time is at an end. All of us, we will have a land of our own, and we will take it by force!"

"Onward to the river!" Manfeaster cried, joining his brother. "It is near. Can you not taste your freedom? Come now, and taste it in the blood of the humans!"

The feast began, and still Jessilynn could not force herself to look away. Her mind felt frozen, her emotions in shock. Tears ran down her face, yet she was unaware she was crying. A warm hand touched her shoulder, and she shivered.

"Come," Silver-Ear said, gently taking the bow. "You will sleep at my side this night, but first we have many miles to walk."

Jessilynn had no heart to respond, no words to say. She followed the shaman into the night, and though she was surrounded, she'd never felt so alone in all her life. Tearful eyes looking up at the stars, she wanted to scream at Ashhur, demand he answer for such abandonment.

It was then she saw Sonowin's wings, the winged horse like a distant bird flying through the night. Dieredon sat atop her, just a dark speck. Still watching, still waiting for a chance to rescue her. Jessilynn wept, unable to cope with such a mixture of relief and torment, knowing she'd not been abandoned.

Knowing there was nothing he could do to save her.

※

"We should prepare our army," said one of Harruq's advisors as he sat on Antonil's throne, hunched over and thoroughly miserable.

"What army?" he asked. "You mean the one that left with the king?"

"There are more soldiers in Mordan than just them," said Sir Wess, captain of the guard in Mordeina and the man left in charge of keeping the peace during their king's absence. The surly man spoke slowly, as if he thought Harruq a child. "Most lords kept retainers, especially the northern lords. Retaking a distant land is one thing, but this is Ker. This is our doorstep, and we cannot risk them retaliating while we're unprepared."

Harruq looked to the queen, who sat quietly beside him. Her hands were folded in her lap, and she shook her head when he caught her gaze.

"No," Harruq said. "We're not going to make this worse. I've already sent a messenger to apologize. If Bram's got any shred of sense in him, he'll accept it, and we'll all pretend like this never happened."

"But you don't know what has happened," said another of the advisors. "None of us do. Would it not be wiser to prepare?"

Before Harruq could answer, the doors slammed open, and in walked Ahaesarus in all his regal splendor. He pointed at Harruq.

"Come with me," he said.

Harruq lifted an eyebrow.

"Uh...care to say please?"

Ahaesarus stared at him, then let out a sigh.

"Please," he said. "I've called another gathering of the angels, and I would like you to bear witness."

Harruq shot a look to Susan, unsure of what to do.

"We need to know what happened," she said. "Go with him. I'm sure you'll be safe."

*Probably*, Harruq thought as he stood. But he was taking his swords with him just in case. He wanted to ask outright about the incident in the south, but Ahaesarus didn't appear to be in the talkative mood.

"If you need anything, Susan will handle it," Harruq told his advisors, pushing through them. "As for me, I'll be with tall and handsome."

Ahaesarus led the way, out into the open courtyard, and then turned.

"Your hands," he said. "We fly to Avlimar."

"I want to know one thing before I go," Harruq said, now that they were relatively alone. "Is my brother all right?"

Ahaesarus hesitated, then nodded.

"He battled Judarius for some length, but is otherwise unharmed, as is his wife. Now will you come with me?"

"Of course," Harruq said, offering his hands. "Just don't drop me, please. It'd be a poor ending to an already awful day."

Ahaesarus grabbed him by the wrist, beat his wings, and into the air they soared. The land was a steadily shrinking blur beneath them as they approached the floating city. Harruq closed his eyes, knowing it helped with the vertigo. While he didn't normally consider himself afraid of heights, he decided he could always make an exception when he was so high up that the castle looked like one of Aubrienna's toys.

He opened his eyes when they set down on one of the many outer ledges of Avlimar. It was immediately apparent something was afoot, given the thousands of angels circling about the city. Harruq wondered what it meant. Qurrah was alive, but that didn't necessarily mean he was free. For a terrified moment he thought he was being brought to witness his own brother's execution. His hand drifted to his swords, and he tried not to show his sudden nervousness.

"So when do I hear exactly what happened in Ker?" he asked as nonchalantly as he could, which wasn't very nonchalant at all.

"I stopped the attempt to punish your brother before Judarius could finish the execution," Ahaesarus said. "King Bram's soldiers fought to protect him, and both men and angels died in the conflict."

"And so what is it we go to now?" Harruq asked as they walked down the pristine, golden streets.

"The forum."

The half-orc couldn't remember when he'd seen Ahaesarus so cranky. No, not that, he decided as the angel led him along. He wasn't cranky, and he wasn't being short-tempered...he was nervous. That realization made Harruq's own nerves fray. What could someone as powerful and influential as Ahaesarus be nervous about? Was there something he wasn't telling him? Just what did he plan on doing in this council? Sadly, he knew he'd get none of those answers, so he kept his mouth shut and his eyes and ears open.

The forum turned out to be an enormous oval building, open at the top and built with a multitude of rows steadily rising higher and higher, each seat facing a central point. There were no doors, for the angels all flew in from the sky to take their place. Ahaesarus helped Harruq over the wall, but instead of finding him a seat he kept the half-orc beside him on the smooth marble flooring of the forum. Looking about, seeing the thousands of angels watching, Harruq got an inkling as to why Ahaesarus was nervous. More surprising, though, was that Harruq was not the only non-angel to be there. On the other side of the dais stood Lord Maryll, his arms crossed over his chest. He looked unbothered by the numbers, and seeing Harruq, he only offered a polite nod.

"Harruq," Ahaesarus said, the two of them alone in the center. He kept his voice a whisper, for it seemed even the slightest noise carried far. "When my angels flew about the nation to perform their new orders, you told me to do something. You told me it wasn't right, and that I should know it. For that, I want to thank you. No matter what any priest, any scribe, and any king might say, I know in my heart that what you said was just. What I do now, I do because of you."

With that he turned, spreading his arms and wings wide so he might address the gathered thousands. Harruq stepped aside to give him room, feeling awkward standing there with nothing to do. He almost joined Kevin just so he wouldn't have to be alone, but quickly rejected that terrible idea. Better awkward and alone than near that pompous jackass.

"Before I begin, let us pray for wisdom, guidance, and mercy from our beloved Lord," Ahaesarus said, and a heavy silence fell over the forum, so quiet that Harruq could hear every cough, every shift and rustle of feathers. A moment later, in eerie unison, the angels looked up, and Ahaesarus spoke his prepared words. Harruq listened, daring to hope something might be salvaged from the disaster down south.

"Angels of Ashhur," Ahaesarus began. "Mere days ago we met to discuss our future in the land of Dezrel. We heard the thoughts of men, their ideas of justice. Mercy and forgiveness could still be for the soul, but the body must still be punished. And so we made our decision, and with heavy hearts carried that decision out."

The angel shook his head, and he took a deep breath.

"I am here to tell you all that I am revoking that decision. We will not carry out justice in such a manner, not anymore."

The following outburst was immediate and deafening. Harruq winced at the noise. Ahaesarus slammed his hands together, demanding attention, and it was granted.

"We will not be their executioners!" he cried to them. "We will not be their murderers! From here on out, we will judge as we have, determining their innocence or guilt. But then we shall turn them over to the humans, to let them see fit the punishment for their crime. We will not spare the guilty, but neither shall we execute them. We will wash our hands of all of it, and let mankind decide the fate of those who would harm one another, steal from one another, and let darkness overcome their hearts instead of grace and love."

"We had a vote," a voice cried out above the rest. Harruq spotted the source, and was not surprised to see it was Azariah. The priest stood, gesturing to the rest of those gathered in the forum.

"Do our thoughts no longer matter?" he asked. "Will you stand against the majority?"

"I will do more than stand against it," Ahaesarus replied. "I will deny it to its very core. This is not what Ashhur brought us here for. This is not how we win over their hearts. Let no one fear the sight of an angel. If you think otherwise, so be it, but my word stands."

"*Your* word?" Judarius asked, emerging from the crowd to stand before Ahaesarus. Harruq noticed he carried his mace, one of the few there who wielded a weapon. "And what of *our* words? What of our vote? Do you deny our say in such a matter? What if we are unwilling to let such things be?"

Ahaesarus stood to his full height. A hard edge entered his voice, and his message was chilling.

"Let any who would slay a human come forth now, and challenge my role as leader of our kind. Come forth, any of you. Show me how great your desire for blood truly is."

A taut silence stretched over the thousands, and Harruq saw them glancing at one another. Judarius in particular looked ready to speak, staring eye to eye with the larger Ahaesarus. And then he turned away, spread his wings, and flew out of the forum.

"As I thought," Ahaesarus said. "All of you, we are to represent the glory of Ashhur and perform his will. This is the best way I know how. Now go. There will be no debate, and I have nothing else to say."

More rumbling, more discontent. The angels flew away in a great rustle of feathers and noise. Harruq looked across the marble and saw Kevin watching them fly away with a contemplative look on his face. Would this placate the man? Or would such capitulation only provoke him further? An angel came over, took him by the arms, and then they were gone.

Harruq waited, feeling more and more self-conscious as the forum grew steadily quieter. A few flew over to Ahaesarus to assure him of their support, but they were not many. At last they were alone, just Harruq and Ahaesarus. The angel approached, and he looked like he carried a heavy burden on his shoulders.

"Do you see why I wanted you here?" he asked.

"Not quite," Harruq said, shaking his head.

"I wanted you to see this. I wanted you to know the changes we make, changes you must help enforce. We need more judges. We need clearer laws. I want you to tell us what to do with the guilty, and what to do with the repentant. In this, I hope we might better meet the desires of the people compared to the senseless violence we so recently spread throughout the night."

"I'll see what I can do," Harruq said, immediately thinking it was something Susan would be far better suited for. More than ever he was glad she'd stayed behind after Antonil's departure. "Though I wouldn't expect any miracles."

"I never do," Ahaesarus said. "But that doesn't mean I won't pray they happen. Do you think our actions will provoke a war?"

Harruq crossed his arms and frowned.

"I don't know," he said. "If one happens, I'm determined to make sure it doesn't start on our end. I've given up predicting King Henley. If he wants a war, then we'll have a war, but until he marches into our lands I'm going to do my best to prevent any further provocation."

Ahaesarus reached for Harruq for the return flight. Before he could, Harruq looked away, feeling embarrassed.

"You saved my brother's life," he said. "Thank you."

"And I think you might save the souls of my angels," Ahaesarus said. "In that, Harruq, I think I owe you far more than you owe me."

Harruq laughed.

"Well, in that case, remind me to call you on that sometime. Maybe you can listen to a few hundred petitioners. That might even things up a bit."

Ahaesarus grinned as they soared into the air.
"Did you not just say to never expect any miracles?"

## 24

Loreina Henley sat on her throne, her husband's seat empty beside her. In her lap was a letter, and though she'd read it three times already, she read it a fourth. It didn't seem it could be true, yet the haggard man before her, plus the wax seal of King Antonil, both insisted it was.

"How far behind you are they?" she asked the messenger.

"We're marching at the fastest pace we can manage with such little food," the man said. His clothes were stained with sweat, and he looked like he hadn't slept in days. "I'd say two weeks at most, your grace."

Loreina nodded.

"My servants will find you a room and prepare you a bath," she told him. "I'm sure you're hungry, and if you'd like to eat before resting, tell them."

"Thank you, your grace," he said, bowing low. Servants came, having heard her orders, and ushered the messenger out of the hall. Loreina sat there, tapping the letter against her leg. She read it a fifth time, still unable to contain her excitement.

*To friend and king,*

*The orcs number far beyond what I ever dreamed in my darkest of nightmares. The east crawls with their kind, though that is not the real danger. Someone leads them, someone wise, someone they fear. My men whisper it a demon who survived the Gods' War. I do not know, but only tell you so you might understand the danger you face on your eastern border. My army is crushed, my supplies ruined. We were ambushed on the way to Angelport, left with retreat as our only option. We come to you now, humbly and afraid, asking for aid and shelter when we reach your lands. My men are already starving, yet we face days of marching until we reach safety.*

*Whatever aid you offer, I will pay back tenfold. And please, prepare your men. An army of orcs is growing, and I fear their leader will not be satisfied with just the ruins of the east.*

*Your friend,*
*King Antonil Copernus.*

There was nothing particularly shocking about the letter. They'd long known an orc commander had risen among them, though the idea of it being a war demon was unsettling. And that Antonil had been defeated was no surprise, given his failure years ago in attempting to complete the same fool's errand. But knowing they were out of provisions, exhausted, begging for aid? Now *that* was something she could use. It was an opportunity her husband musn't squander.

"Turn away any petitioners," she said to her guards as she stood. "I fear I will have far too busy of a day for any more."

Bram was overseeing his army, as he had ever since the angels attacked in the night. Loreina had watched the battle from the window of her room, and still she had nightmares about it. The way the angels had dashed through their soldiers, slaughtering them as if they were children fighting against men...

She shook her head to clear away such thoughts. Fear was unbecoming of her. Lifting her skirt ever so slightly so she might increase her pace, she stepped out into the courtyard. Despite the hard work of many servants, there were still signs of battle everywhere. It seemed until the next year, when the grass regrew in spring, there would be the red blood staining the green. As for the cobblestones pathways, well, it'd taken three days of scrubbing to make them their original gray, and even then she saw missed spots here and there. Bram had told her the final tally. A hundred and twenty-nine men dead, and in return, they'd killed a paltry eleven angels.

Fear was unbecoming of her, and such failure was unbecoming of their soldiers. And so the men drilled, and plotted, and worked out ways to kill men who flew through the air on pearly wings. As she left the courtyard and entered the training grounds surrounding the barracks, the men halted what they were doing so they might pay their respects. Loreina smiled at them, knowing such small gestures did wonders for morale. In the middle of all the chaos was her husband, arguing with Sir Ian.

"I'm telling you, archers aren't effective against the angels," Ian insisted. "Either they dodge them on the way down or outrace them on the way up. It's only if we can get them on the *ground* that they'd take the significant casualties necessary to justify the extra training."

"Not if the volley is large enough that..."

Bram stopped, noticing her presence. Loreina dipped her head in respect, then kissed her husband's lips.

"A letter," she said, handing it to him as she pulled away.

"From who?" he asked. His eyes lit up as he saw the name at the bottom. "Oh really?"

Loreina waited as he read it, and was not surprised to see him immediately go over it a second time.

"How long ago did you receive this?" he asked, suddenly looking up.

"A few minutes ago. A messenger came riding in from the east, and our bridge guards escorted him here as fast as they could."

Bram nodded, and his face hardened into a frown that she knew meant he was deep in thought.

"If we might speak alone?" she asked Ian, who promptly bowed.

"Of course," he said. "Milord, fetch me if you need me."

With Ian gone, they were alone despite the hundreds of men milling about, clanging swords. Their words would go unheard in such a din. Loreina slid beside her husband, wrapping her arms around his waist.

"This is it," she said. "This is everything we've waited for."

Disturbed, he looked her way, his frown deepening.

"How so?"

"Their numbers are weakened, and they are in no shape to fight. Meet them at the bridge. Show them you will not be taken advantage of."

Bram glared, and he guided her toward the exit of the barracks. It seemed even with all the noise he would not speak of such things in public.

"Are you mad?" he asked as they stepped out. "You saw what thirty angels did to our forces. That was within our own castle, with Qurrah's lover to aid us. Thousands fly above the skies of Mordan. Even if we crush Antonil, war will still come to our nation, and against that might we'll be trampled."

"When did I speak of war?" Loreina asked, letting a hard edge into her voice. Her husband should trust her better than that, and it annoyed her when he would not fully think her ideas through. "When did I speak of crushing that fool of a king? I only ask that you exercise the rights you possess."

Bram shook his head.

"What you're asking is dangerous, Loreina. If Ahaesarus meant what he said, we still might escape open warfare. I once thought we would stand a better chance, but that was before seeing what they could do. Their weapons make our chainmail look like butter."

"Don't you think I know that?" she said. "I watched from my window as our men, good men with families, bled out and died because those fanatics were determined to get what they wanted. They came at night, without warning, into our very capital. What happens when they come for you? Or for me?"

She saw the anger in his eyes and knew she had him.

"All I ask is that you be the king I know you are," she whispered, softly kissing him from his neck to his ear. "All I ask is that you let me sleep knowing I am safe. Can you do that?"

He nodded.

"We'll have little time if we want to meet them at Ashhur's Bridge," he said. "Forgive me. I must give out the order."

She smiled and let him go.

"Of course," she said.

He hurried back into the barracks, and her heart swelled with pride. This was it. This was the first step toward their freedom.

Trying not to look in any particular hurry, she walked back to the castle. When her servants went to follow, she dismissed them, claiming she had a headache and desired solitude. It was only a half-lie. She climbed the winding stairs to the upper floors, then smiled at the man guarding her room. Slipping inside, she twisted the lock, then rushed to her private chest of things. Amid the various junk was a single scrap of paper, hardly larger than her palm. It was faded brown, and looked as if it'd been forgotten at the bottom of the chest for decades.

The Prison of Angels

Taking the scrap, she went to her husband's desk and opened his inkwell. Taking a quill, she wrote two simple words in its center. That done, she put the quill and ink away, then walked over to their window. She pushed it open, felt the breeze blow against her. Her heart aflutter, she lifted the paper to her lips then slowly breathed across it.

Immediately the paper snapped to life, folding over and over on itself, reshaping, becoming something else. Throwing it out the window, Loreina smiled as the paper bird took flight, rising higher and higher into the air, the words *Antonil approaches* safely folded into its very center. Loreina watched until it was gone, her hands clasped before her chest and her eyes alight.

❧

King Antonil parted the rough fabric with his hands and looked inside.

"How does he fare?"

Tarlak lay on a pile of blankets, in one of the few wagons they'd manage to salvage after the ambush at Kinamn. His hat was beside him, exposing the wicked bruise just above his temple. A bit of his hair was missing, shaved off by the elderly surgeon overseeing him.

"He fares fine," Tarlak said, lazily lifting an arm in greeting. "I dare say I'm sick to death of this bumpy wagon. I think walking would be better for my health, and my sanity."

"You have my pity," said Antonil.

"Thank you," Tarlak replied.

"I meant the surgeon."

"He sleeps more than he complains," the surgeon said. "Though the herbal milk I give him is probably to blame. The infection is gone, praise Ashhur for that. In a week, maybe two, he'll be back to his old flamboyant self."

"Nonsense," Tarlak said. "I'm my flamboyant self right now. See this smile? That's the smile of a happy man."

"The smile of a drugged man," Antonil said, chuckling. "Cut down on the herbs. I think it's time he regained a bit of his lucidity."

"I might have to take some myself then," said the surgeon. "You cannot imagine what this man is like when ill. I've known children who handled toothaches better."

"We'll be at Ashhur's Bridge within the hour," Antonil said as Tarlak stuck his tongue out at the surgeon. "Soon we'll all get the rest we need, and even better, the food our bellies have been grumbling for. Will that make up for the wizard?"

"It'll do."

Antonil patted Tarlak on the leg.

"Get better," he said. "Oh, and try not to be too annoying."

"No promises," came slurred speech from the wagon as Antonil hopped back down. His smile, while natural in there with Tarlak, soon became forced as he wandered through the rest of his army. Of his thirty thousand, only five remained, and very few of them walked with their heads held high. Their faces were sunken and thin, crying out for sleep and food. Antonil wished he could give it to them, and he thanked Ashhur they had finally made it to Ker.

The loss of so many made him sick to the stomach whenever he thought about it. He'd been at the front, trying to reach the catapults shattering their ranks. When they finally broke through the orc line, their commander had issued a retreat. From atop the hill, Antonil watched the orcs pull away, and he denied his men a chance to chase after. There was no point. He guessed the orcs had two thousand left, maybe three. Perhaps they would have overrun them, but he didn't want to risk it, not with a broken army. They'd left the dead where they were upon the hillside, gathered up every shred of supplies into their few remaining wagons, and then traveled west. From then on, the orcs had left them alone, as if knowing they'd accomplished what they needed to keep their land safe.

Retaking Veldaren was now but a dream. Antonil did his best to accept it, to push that sting aside while there was nothing he could do about it. Securing aid from King Bram was all that mattered now. Whatever promises he had to make, he'd make, and whatever humiliation he must endure, he'd endure. If he had to kiss Bram's ass cheeks he'd do it, so long as it got food in his soldiers' bellies.

At the head of the army were their few horses, and Antonil mounted one. Despite everything, he had to appear lordly, especially before a fellow king.

"Are we ready?" he asked Sergan, who had been waiting for him.

"We've given out the last of our water," he said. "Our food will last maybe three more days, but I kept it rationed. No sense being wasteful until we know how badly Bram's going to gouge us for his aid."

"You're a good man, Sergan," Antonil said. "What would I do without you?"

"Go hungry and thirsty, I'd say," Sergan said with a tired smile. "At your word, we'll march."

"Consider that word given. Let's go home."

The army moved out, and it didn't take long before they caught sight of civilization. The smoke of campfires drifted lazily into the air from the direction of the bridge. At first Antonil was heartened by the sight, but then, as the river neared, he felt worry growing in his empty stomach. The number of fires, the amount of smoke, was far beyond any normal garrison. They'd received no response from the messenger he'd sent out, but that wasn't surprising. His orders had been to forgo sleep and rest as much as possible on the way to Angkar. Most likely he was recovering from the trip, hopefully in far nicer conditions than Antonil and his marching army found themselves in.

"That's a lot of smoke," Sergan said as he sidled alongside Antonil, showing he'd noticed the same.

"If Bram's there, it'd make sense for him to have an escort."

Sergan shrugged and stared at the sky.

"Big escort then."

Despite their apprehension, there wasn't much else for them to do but continue on. When the bridge came in sight, the army gathered there did little to improve their mood. Just as when they entered Ker through the Bloodbrick, Bram had gathered his ten thousand men and set up camp before the bridge. Antonil was too exhausted to feel anything more than mild irritation.

*Must we go through this again?* he wondered, thinking of the tireless back and forth squabbling, the vague threats and posturing. Of course he would. These were his men. They'd risked their lives for him, for a land many had never been to before, and most likely would never see again in their lifetimes.

"Keep the men calm," Antonil said, glancing back at the rest of his army. "I don't want anyone trying to rush across. Bram will want some sort of payment, I'm sure of it, and I want to know what that payment is before we cross."

"Yes, milord."

His five thousand slowed, then came to a shuffling stop before the entrance to the bridge. Antonil rode ahead, not bothering with an escort. He saw Bram dismounting from his own horse and walking out to meet him.

"Friend!" Antonil cried, widening his smile. "It is good to see you."

Bram stopped just outside the bridge, and he slowly shook his head.

"I dare not say the same," he called out. "What is it you come here for?"

Antonil hid his frown as he gestured to his army.

"Did I not say as much in my letter?" he asked. "My men are hungry and thirsty. An orc army ambushed us, their numbers greater than we ever thought possible. I...we...all of us require aid as we travel toward Mordan, and I will gladly pay you back a hundred times if need be."

Bram stared at him, and the lingering silence made Antonil unconsciously reach for his sword. What was it that the man so clearly debated?

"No," he said, his sudden words slicing through the silence. "You will not be entering my lands."

Antonil stood frozen, with only years of training keeping his voice calm despite his inner furor.

"What do you mean?" he asked.

"When you last came here, you mocked my right to enforce my borders," he said, shaking his head. "In doing so you mocked the right of my sovereignty. You scorned the power of my crown. The nation of Ker is not your servant, nor your slave, nor your child. If you would return to your home, then go another way."

"Another way?" Antonil said. "There is no other way. Please, Bram, let me make up for my pride, but do not punish these men."

# The Prison of Angels

"This has nothing to do with your pride. Your angels flew into my lands under cover of night. They killed my guards, all so they might capture a man under my protection."

The words hit Antonil like a sledge.

"What are you talking about?" he asked.

"Ask them, should they come for you," Bram said. "But I was promised freedom from your angels' tyranny, and I was not given it. I warned you, yet you would not listen. Already your angels kill my men, and now you would have me feed an army allied with such beasts. No, Antonil, I will not let you through. If this is the only way for you to understand the dangers you court with Avlimar, then do this I must."

Briefly Antonil pondered an attack, but he was outnumbered, and when previously crossing the bridge he'd seen firsthand the extensive defenses they'd built into it. There would be no forcing his way across, not in the state his men were in.

"Please," he said, his voice softer. "Bram, don't do this. Don't punish my men like this. They'll starve."

Bram crossed his arms and looked away.

"I am not without mercy," he said. "I'll send across some wagons containing food, and there is plenty of water to boil from the river. It will tide you over for a time, perhaps long enough for you to think on your many errors. Oh, and Antonil, don't try to have anyone swim across. I assure you, we'll be watching."

Bram turned, cloak flailing behind him as he crossed the bridge. Antonil heard the first of many fearful cries filter through his army, yet there was nothing he could do. He clutched his sword tighter, teeth clenched, and cursed Bram in every way possible.

---

"So what are our options?" Sergan asked as they settled down for the night around a small campfire. The two were separate from the rest of the army, the other generals scattered throughout to ensure order. Antonil wanted to be alone with his friend, to speak his mind without fear of panic or scorn.

"I'm not sure what other choice we have," he said. "It seems Bram is determined to humiliate us, but I don't think it extends beyond that."

"You don't know that," Sergan said. "What was that nonsense about the angels?"

Antonil shook his head.

"Supposedly some of them attacked Bram's castle. I don't know any more than that. If it is true, then I don't blame Bram for his fury. Such an action breaks every promise I've ever made him since the Gods' War."

"Anger or not, the man's still acting like a bastard," Sergan said. "We can't just sit here, can we? The food he gave us will tide us over for a week, but no longer than that. If we don't do anything we'll be at his mercy, holding out our hands like lowly beggars."

"Which is what he wants," Antonil said, poking his fire with a stick. "He wants his power over us acknowledged. No one in Mordan will expect our return so early. He'll keep us here, helpless, frustrated, and then make some sort of outrageous demand I'll have no choice but to agree to."

"We still might have a shot at crossing farther upstream," Sergan said. "You have friends at the Citadel, and I know they have their boats."

"We don't have the food to travel that far north. Besides, the Citadel houses thirty people, maybe forty. They won't have enough supplies to feed five thousand."

Sergan grunted, accepting the rejection.

"Well, what about the wizard? Perhaps he can do something, get a few of us across the river with an ice bridge or something."

"Tarlak's too weak for that," Antonil said, shaking his head. Still, something about what he'd said sparked an idea in his mind, and he looked around, feeling a sudden surge of excitement.

"A map," he said. "Where is my map?"

"What for?"

Antonil ignored him, instead hurrying into his tent and throwing open his strongbox. He came back out, unrolling the paper and laying it out on the seat he'd been sitting in.

"Wizards," Antonil said. "I completely forgot about the wizards."

Sergan leaned over to look at what Antonil pointed to. There, halfway between Ashhur's Bridge and the Citadel, were the twin towers of the Council of Mages. Sergan saw it and immediately paled.

"Forgive me, my liege, but you're insane."

"Why? With that many wizards, surely they would know a way to supply us, and they have a bridge spanning both sides."

"But…but they're wizards. And more importantly, they're reclusive, unpredictable wizards that hate being bothered by anyone, kings or not."

Antonil stared at the two little towers, one marked with red chalk, the other coal.

"That's where we're going," he said. "I know it's a risk, but we can't stay here. I refuse to let Bram lord over us in such a way."

"We'll be traveling through his lands without permission if we cross this way," Sergan said.

"At this point, I don't care. Most of that land is full of farms and wilderness. We'll beat him to the Bloodbrick before he finds out, and whatever token force he might have there won't be able to stop us."

Sergan scratched at his chin, and finally he let out a sigh.

"If you think it'll work, then that's what we'll do," he said. "Though let me say now that I don't like it. Never trust a wizard. That's wisdom to live by."

"Do you think Tarlak would agree?" Antonil asked.

Sergan let out a sharp laugh.

"You kidding me, your highness? He's the one I heard it from first."

Antonil smiled, finally feeling his mood lifting. He had a plan, a course of action. Regardless of the risk, at least he wouldn't be helpless before Bram's army.

"Get some sleep," he said, rolling up his map. "We have a long march. We'll head southeast, make Bram think we're hoping one of the fishing villages along the coast of the delta survived, and then curl north and cross Karak's Bridge once we're out of sight."

"So let's say this works," Sergan said. "We sneak across the river through the help of our mysterious wizardy pals, race through the wilderness, and then cross the Bloodbrick back into Mordan. What then?"

Antonil paused before the entrance to his tent. He didn't want to lie to his dear friend, and so he didn't.

"Then we return to Mordeina," he said. "And once we've gathered another army, we'll see just how well Bram is capable of defending the borders he's so proud to protect. The man spat in the faces of our men this day. I have watched nations fall, angels appear, and gods die. Did he think this would be what broke me? No. Bram should have known better. Much better."

He entered his tent, put aside his sword, and slept.

## 25

The army of wolf-men slept not far from the Gihon River, waiting for the right moment to strike. The night before, Moonslayer and Manfeaster had bid farewell to the other various races, sending them either farther north or south, depending on where he wanted them strike. Jessilynn had listened as they gave them their orders, chilled by their cold, brutal efficiency.

"Let no boat pass you by," Moonslayer had shouted. "Leave the towers blinded and alone. One by one, they will fall. On the night of the full moon, make your attack. Let none survive. Eat well, my fellow creatures of the Wedge. Feast, and enjoy your freedom!"

The towers were the only line of defense against the Wedge, their boat patrols designed to keep any of the beasts from crossing. But Jessilynn knew they were few and undermanned. Could they handle an army consisting of even *one* of the races, let alone their combined might? *Of course not*, thought Jessilynn as Silver-Ear dragged her to where she would sleep for the night. The towers would fall, and beyond them were miles upon miles of farmland and simple villages. How many would die before anyone even knew the severity of the threat?

Yes, she thought. Moonslayer was right. The beasts would feast well.

"I have no chain to tie you," Silver-Ear said. "But if you move from my side, you will suffer whatever fate you earn."

They walked to the center of the camp, surrounded by several thousand of the beasts. Jessilynn felt their eyes upon her, their noses sniffing the scents she left behind. She nodded at Silver-Ear to show she understood. Not long after, the camp settled down to sleep. Wide-eyed and awake, Jessilynn lay upon the grass and watched the sun rise.

When Sonowin appeared, flying in from the west, she dared hope. Lying perfectly still, she watched as the winged horse circled above. She wished she could somehow communicate with Dieredon, but there was no way. In the very heart of the camp, the slightest noise would be detected by the wolf-men's sharp ears.

Dieredon had Sonowin fly far to the east, then south, and then finally loop around north. Jessilynn was confused at first by what he was doing, but she eventually put it together. The rest of the creatures, the goat-men, the bird-men…they were all gone. He had to realize what it meant. She watched the sky, waiting, wondering what he would do. He had to have seen her there in her armor, like a strange metal flea among the sea of fur.

The elf flew lower, dipped around, and then flew even lower. Jessilynn slowly reached up a hand, trying to wave at him, to let him know she was willing for him to make any attempt to save her, no matter how desperate. Even that small movement made the chain of her armor rattle. Not loudly, and she could barely hear it herself, but Silver-Ear's hand lashed out, old claws curling around her arm. The female leered at her with milky eyes.

"On your knees," she said. "Push your face to the dirt."

Jessilynn did as she was told, folding herself into the demeaning position. Silver-Ear stood above her, and her claws traced along the flesh of her neck. She shivered, wondering if this would be the end.

"I see him," the shaman said. "Your friend is skilled, but is he wise? Let us see how brave he is, and how much your life might mean to him."

She didn't know what to say. Silver-Ear leaned in close, her nose bumping against her cheek.

"I want your face in the dirt until the sun sets," she said. "Should I see your eyes on the sky for even a moment, I will rip out your throat myself. I am old. Do not think I require the sleep of a young pup."

Jessilynn closed her eyes, shifting her shoulders in an attempt to find a more comfortable position. Within moments her back started aching, and she thought of the long day ahead. Steeling herself, she shifted again, trying to slow her breathing, trying to remain calm. She heard Silver-Ear rustle beside her, settling in. Jessilynn dared not look to see if she remained awake.

Time passed, slow and dreadful. Her back tightened, and she moved her legs as often as she could. At last, sheer exhaustion won over, and she slept.

"Wake, girl," said a rough voice, punctuated by an upward blow to her stomach. Jessilynn let out a scream and rolled onto her back. Looking up, she found several wolf-men standing over her, Moonslayer among them. He grabbed her arm, yanking her to her feet.

"The night is young," he said to her. "Why do you sleep?"

It was mockery, and he flung her onto her rear. Her stomach twisted, and she yearned for something to eat or drink. She curled her knees beneath her, wondering what it was they wanted now.

"Stand," Moonslayer said. "Stand, or die where you sit."

She obeyed, trying to interpret the look he gave her. There was something in his eyes, something frightening. As she crossed her arms before her, one of the wolf-men tossed her bow at her feet, along with her quiver of arrows. She made no move for them.

"My army attacks," Moonslayer said. "The weaker creatures are committed. I have no need of you anymore, human."

"It is a waste of time," Manfeaster said, joining them from beyond the camp. All around the wolf-men were in a stir, wrestling with one another, preparing for the upcoming battle. "I say we eat her now, let the blood of a paladin mark our victory."

"We will," Moonslayer said to his brother. His eyes turned back to her. "But first we have a hunt."

He gestured to the bow.

"Take it," he said. "Run. Flee west, or north, or wherever you think you might hide. My wolves are anxious for the battle, but the moon has not yet risen. You will entertain us until then."

"You risk lives needlessly," Manfeaster said.

"And any who would die at her hand would die anyway. Besides, her teacher defeated our father. Her kind has stopped us for centuries before. Let our pack tear her apart and prove we will be beaten no longer."

Jessilynn watched the brothers stare at each other. It was Manfeaster who relented, flattening his ears and turning away.

"Enjoy the hunt," he said to the others.

Moonslayer gestured to the bow.

"Take it," he said. "Run."

She scooped the quiver up, slung it over her shoulder, and then did the same with her bow. She looked at the wolves, hardly believing it came to this. All along she'd desired escape, but now they would let her go freely?

*No, not freely*, she thought as she saw the hunger in the eyes of the wolf-men around her.

"You should have listened to your brother," she said to Moonslayer as she took a step backward.

The enormous wolf-man bared his teeth.

"We shall see."

His howl pierced the night as she turned to run toward the river. Behind her she heard Moonslayer howling, his deep voice slowly growing fainter by the minute.

"A hunt!" he cried. "A hunt, a hunt, gather for a hunt! The heart of a paladin is our prey!"

They would find her, she knew. As she ran she looked to the sky, daring to hope. She scanned the stars, the miniscule clouds. She stared so long she stumbled from not watching where she ran. As she hit the ground she banged her knee on a rock, sending a spike of pain shooting up her leg. Struggling to a stand, she bit down her cry. With her hope turning to dread, she looked to the sky again.

Dieredon was nowhere in sight.

On and on she ran, cramps tightening her sides. She'd been starved, and given little water to drink. Already her head grew light from the exertion, but there was nothing she could do but press on. On a whim she changed the angle of her path though she knew it wouldn't matter. The wolf-men were excellent trackers, and out there in the wild her scent would stand out like a fire in the darkness. As the land passed her by, she wondered how much time they would give her.

A few minutes later she heard her answer in the communal cry of dozens of wolf-men. The sound was her death knell, yet on she ran. When she saw the Gihon floating softly before her, she let out a cry of her own. Her armor...she couldn't swim with her armor on! Frantically she yanked off the heavier parts weighted down with chain, flinging them to the ground. When she was down to just her leather under padding she slung her bow and quiver over her shoulder and then rushed into the water. The cold was shocking. Much as she dreaded it, she plunged her head beneath the surface and began to swim.

Upon reaching the other side, Jessilynn pulled herself from the river, gasping for air. Tears ran down her face as she tried and failed to crawl beyond the shoreline. Her feet remained in the water, her hair a wet rope looped around her neck. It wasn't far enough. It'd never be far enough. The wolf-men hunted her, and their noses would not be fooled by something as simple as a river. Within the hour, perhaps even the minute, they would find her. And this time they would not let her live. Moonslayer had made that quite clear.

"Please Ashhur," she begged. "Please, I can't do this. I can't, I'm not like them. Help me, god. Help me!"

She shrieked it out until she lost breath, her mouth locked open from her crying. She'd seen what the wolf-men did to their prey, the way they tore into flesh with their claws and ripped muscle from bone with their teeth. Would she die quickly, or would they torment her? Panic twisted in her gut, stabbing her like a rusted knife. It seemed so cruel. Dieredon no doubt flew overhead, still looking to rescue her as she assumed he had been trying to do all along. Yet now she was free and unable to signal him in the night. If only he'd been watching when they released her. If only Sonowin could stay aloft longer. If only she'd never agreed to go with the elf in the first place.

The frustration gave her the strength to stand, and with eyes wide she ran, her back to the river. Hardly ten feet out her bare foot struck something hard, and down she went. The sudden jolt made her bite her tongue. Warm blood filled her mouth, and it took all her composure to keep from breaking down a second time. Turning to spit, she saw what had tripped her. It took a moment for her mind to register what it was, for it made no sense.

There, in the middle of some random forest beside the Gihon, was a greatsword nearly as tall as her. The hilt was black, finely carved, and when her fingers touched the metal it was surprisingly warm.

"I see you found my sword."

Jessilynn started, spinning around on her rear and bracing herself with her arms. Before her stood an imposing man, his blonde hair long, his eyes a startling shade of blue. His armor, though, she recognized his armor. It matched what they wore at the Citadel. From the metal a faint hue pulsed with his movements. Too tired to understand, too tired to flee, Jessilynn dared feel a glimmer of hope.

"Who are you?" she asked, afraid of the answer.

"I'm not sure you've heard of me," said the man. "My name is Darius, and I think I'm a bit before your time."

Her mouth fell open. Was she dreaming? Was she dead?

"Jerico," she stammered. "Jerico told us about you."

"Did he now?"

"He said you were one of the most faithful paladins he'd ever met. He's often used you as an example in our lessons."

Darius smiled as if he were amused.

"I guess I shouldn't say I'm surprised. I hope his lessons are better than they used to be in Durham. A fine man, but a dreadfully boring speaker."

The man walked over to her side and knelt. Jessilynn flinched despite herself. What was he? A ghost? An angel? A lost spirit come to haunt the place he died?

"Do not be afraid," he said. "I'm here only because you need me."

"You'll help me?" she asked. "The wolf-men, they'll be here any minute. You could kill them, you could…"

She stopped as he shook his head, interrupting her.

"Not in that way, Jessilynn. My days of fighting are done."

He picked up his sword. Immediately the blade vanished into pure white light, not a hint of steel remaining beneath the brightness. Darius stared at it, still smiling.

"What is truly troubling you?" he asked. "You've always been brave. I don't need much help to see that. Why are you so afraid to stand against the enemies chasing you?"

She looked away as she thought. She wanted to give a true answer, not some weak, flippant excuse. Whatever was happening now, it was something special, and she wouldn't spoil it with a pathetic lie.

"Because I can't be like you," she said, finally meeting his gaze.

"Like me?" he asked. "No, dying pretty quickly makes you like me."

"That's not what I mean! You, Jerico, Lathaar…you were heroes. Nothing was stronger than you. You didn't run away. You didn't kill others just to spare yourself. Every time I try to be like you, to be strong like you, I… I can't do it. I'm nothing compared to you, and I never will be."

Darius sat down before her and laid his sword of light across his lap.

"I once murdered an innocent family to prove my loyalty to Karak," he said, his voice softer, quieter. "I once stood by and watched an entire village burn, and I did nothing to stop it. How you see us, the way you embrace these stories…that's not us. We bled like you. We cried like you. Most of all, we failed just like you. We begged and pleaded for our god to save us, to protect us, as we faced enemies we never thought we'd defeat. We were far from perfect, can you not see that?"

She sniffled, then wiped her face with her sleeve.

"Then how did you do it?" she asked. "Jerico once faced an entire army of demons and didn't falter. How could he do that if he wasn't better? If his faith wasn't stronger?"

Darius reached out a hand and gently pushed wet strands of hair from her face.

"The only thing that made us special was that despite our terror, despite our fear, despite our doubts and sorrow, we fought anyway. Even when we thought it hopeless. Even when we knew it would cost us our lives. That's all you can do, Jessilynn. With every breath we try to make this world a better place, hoping in the vain that someday, in some beautiful future, our acts of faith and goodness will overshadow those who know only how to destroy."

Gently he leaned forward and kissed her forehead.

"You're not abandoned. Not forgotten. Not unloved. Never forget that, and never believe otherwise."

Jessilynn broke down at his words, crying not out of sorrow, but from joy. The whole time she'd been dragged about the Wedge as a puppet for the wolf-men, she thought it had been her fault. She'd thought her faith too weak, her cowardice too great for her to deserve her god's love. To know otherwise, to know every stupid failure had done nothing to ruin that love…

She looked up at Darius and laughed despite herself.

"Can I hug you?" she asked, still wiping away tears.

Darius grinned.

"Why not."

She lurched to her feet and wrapped her arms around his waist. Touching him set her nerves alight, as if she hugged a bolt of lightning. Quickly she let go, stepped back, and blushed a fierce red. Darius shot her a wink, dropped his sword to the dirt, and faced the north.

"Wait," she said as he began to walk away.

"Yes?" he asked, turning back.

"Why…why are you still here? Shouldn't you be with Ashhur and his angels?"

Darius shrugged as if it were no big thing.

"I'm still waiting for someone," he said. "Isn't it obvious?"

"Who?"

He smiled.

"Jerico. Tell that bastard to hurry up and die. There's this spot by a lake I want to show him."

A wolf howled, and instinctively she looked to the river. When she turned back, Darius was gone, and the sword had lost its glow. The night returned to darkness, lit only by the stars dotting the clear sky.

It was like stepping out of a dream. Jessilynn stood perfectly still, yet to catch her breath. When another howl came from the river, answered by several others in the hunting party, she closed her eyes.

"I'm sorry if this is stupid," she prayed. "But I'm not running."

She grabbed Darius's sword and hurried to the Gihon. At its edge she jammed the blade downward, surprised by how easily it slid into the dirt. Once certain it was secure, she pulled her quiver of arrows off her shoulder and looped it around the handle of Darius's sword. When she stepped forward, it put her arrows within easy reach of her hand. Her fingers rustling through the feathers, she counted them.

## The Prison of Angels

Nine arrows, nine wolf-men to put down. Grabbing one, she readied her bow, took a deep breath, and gazed beyond the river to the Vile Wedge. In the shadows she saw the yellow glint of hungry eyes. Those she dared not count. Closer and closer they ran, their outlines visible in the moonlight. In a single smooth motion she pulled back her first arrow, saw the blue-white hue surround the arrowhead. It was still weak, but it was there.

*Let the arrow do its work*, she thought, remembering Dieredon's words. *Just let it fly.*

As the first wolf-man reached the river, she did just that. The arrow streaked through the night like a flash of thunder, blasting into the creature's muscled chest. With a whimper it fell. Without thinking, without hesitating, she drew another arrow and sighted anew. More wolf-men were at the river's edge, and one by one she shot them dead. They were many, and soon they splashed through the Gihon, swimming toward her while snarling with bared teeth.

She shot an arrow through the closest wolf's mouth, dropping the creature into the water. Two more tried to swim beneath the surface, but when they came up gasping for air she loosed her arrows.

Six. Seven.

Still the bodies surged into the river. Still she held firm, grabbing for arrows and relying on instinct. They were reaching the other side now, the upper halves of their bodies emerging from the water dripping wet. They raked the air, they howled, but her arrows flew true. The shine on their arrowheads grew brighter and brighter, and when they struck the wolf-men it was like they were hit with a battering ram.

Ten. Eleven.

Her mind dared not think, she dared not look, as her routine continued. One after another she fired, her arrows gleams of deadly light, and after each one she'd feel soft feathers touch her fingers when she reached for just one more.

Fourteen. Fifteen.

Hairy bodies floated downstream, and from the other side roared several wolf-men that had come running at the tail end. She shot one dead, her arrow connecting with its jaw and hitting with such impact it tore off its head. Others dove in the water, howling, biting.

Seventeen. Eighteen.

Some tried to flee, but they died like the others. They'd have hunted her, and once they killed her they'd have continued on. Beyond the river were hundreds of farms, homes, innocents who would have felt the hatred of their claws. She wouldn't let them. She couldn't.

The monsters were all but dead. One last wolf-man emerged from the river, teeth bared with fury. She recognized his size, recognized the white circles about those hungry yellow eyes. Moonslayer was so strong, so fast, and it seemed even the river would not slow him as he rushed toward her. It'd take more than one arrow, she thought. Surely even she could not take him down with a single shot. Jessilynn looked down to her quiver, trance breaking, and she saw it empty. For the briefest moment she felt panic as she turned to face one of the Kings of the Vile.

Moonslayer's muscles were taut, his legs curling in for a leap. Refusing to give in, refusing to let him win, she felt her instincts take over once more. Empty handed she reached for her string and began to pull it back.

Tears filled her eyes. She didn't understand. How? How was it even possible?

Nocked in her bowstring shimmered an arrow of the purest light. She felt its feathers against her skin, impossibly soft. The head was slender, sharp. The wolf-man howled, lunged. The arrow flew, exploding with radiance. She heard bones crack as the creature's momentum reversed with jarring speed. Into the river landed the corpse, vanishing beneath the dark waters.

In the sudden calm she stood holding her bow. And then she laughed. A grin spread across her face, huge and dumb, and she felt helpless to stop it. Taking her bow, she grabbed the string, aimed to the sky, and released anew. Arrow after shimmering arrow sailed high, continuing on as if they would escape the very world itself.

"I'm here!" she cried out to the stars. "I'm alive!"

After only a few minutes, and three more arrows, she saw the dark shape slicing through the blanket of stars, heard the heavy beating of Sonowin's wings.

## 26

"I still don't like it," Tarlak said as the towers loomed ever closer. His head was heavily bandaged, and he looked unsteady atop his horse.

"We're far past doing things we don't like," Antonil said, riding beside the wizard as the remnants of his army made their way north along the river. "Twice now I must return to Mordeina with my head hung low and my tail between my legs. And what will any say if I try for a third campaign? If thirty thousand is not enough, then what?"

"Perhaps we should give the land up for lost?" Tarlak suggested after a moment's hesitation. He winced as if expecting an outburst, and Antonil understood why. The words stung, but there was too much wisdom, too much truth in the simple statement.

"I'd prefer it if you were wrong more often, wizard," he said.

"Me too, honestly."

They turned their attention to the towers. There were two of them, each standing on opposite sides of the Rigon River. The one on the western side had its bricks painted a sheer black, making it seem as if it were built out of obsidian. The eastern side was built like the other, tall and cylindrical, except with its stones colored a deep red that invoked a sense of blood and danger. Spanning the river, held up by what Antonil assumed to be magic, was a lengthy stone bridge connecting the tops of the two towers, its bricks a mixture of red and black.

"Is there any significance to the color?" Antonil asked, hoping that learning more would put his mind at ease about the strange structures. The more unknown something was, the easier to fear it.

"The black is the Master's Tower," Tarlak said. He closed his eyes and held the side of his face for a moment, grimacing as if against a wave of pain. "These are the men and women who rule the roost. Their numbers vary, but it's never more than twenty. As for the red, that's where the apprentices go to learn. Anyone can apply, if they're insane enough. Few are accepted, and even fewer actually survive the process."

"Is learning magic that dangerous?"

Tarlak chuckled.

"To graduate, you have to beat one of the mages on the Council in a duel. If there is an available seat on the Council, the duel is merely one of skill, not to the death. If the Council's full, well..." The wizard shrugged. "There's really only one way to open up a seat."

A shadow had passed over Tarlak's face as he spoke, and Antonil sensed there was far more the man was hiding. He felt bad to be so inquisitive, what with Tarlak in such poor shape, but his curiosity was stronger.

"Were you ever an apprentice there?" he asked.

"I was supposed to be," Tarlak said. His speech was slow, as if he were deeply tired. "My father paid a lot of coin to have a man named Madral prepare me, teach me some rudimentary spells to help ensure my success as an apprentice. But Madral...there was a reason he was considered a renegade among the Council. He worshipped Karak in secret, and helped topple the Citadel back in the day. Given how my father was a priest of Ashhur, you can imagine how well we got along once I discovered that fact. I was barely sixteen when I confronted him. The way he looked at me, as if I were less than a flea in his eyes...I don't know how, but I killed him. I'm not sure I've ever been more frightened."

Antonil gave him a moment of silence, instead staring at the nearing towers as he thought. Well, that explained the moment of darkness in Tarlak's routinely cheery attitude.

"You could have joined the Council, couldn't you?" he said. "Isn't that how the rules worked?"

Tarlak nodded.

"Yes, I could have, but I refused. The Council guards magic so jealously, and my time with Madral did much to scar my opinion on such matters. That, and I'd have faced waves of challenges from the apprentices, some twice my age. I couldn't do it. So I took what money I had left and worked to create my little band of mercenaries. The rest, you could say, is infamy."

Antonil elbowed the wizard in the side, doing his best to smile.

"I'd say it turned out all right," he said. "Sure, there's been some tough times, but you're friends with a king now. And some claim you helped save the world. That must count for something."

For a moment he got nothing, but then Tarlak laughed.

"Don't think for a second you're getting out of your debt with a few sunny words," he said. "And I'm running up interest, too. Saving the world doesn't come cheap, and neither will healing this head wound."

They rode for a while in silence. Antonil felt better seeing Tarlak's spirits rise. Perhaps if they could not cross the river, they could still send out hunters, maybe spear some fish as a way of sustaining things until the Tarlak was well enough to create a way to cross the river on his own. When the towers were only two hundred yards away, Antonil raised his hand and ordered his army to slow.

"I don't want them to think we come with threats," he said. "Do you think you'd have more luck requesting passage across the river than me?"

"Pretty as I am?" Tarlak asked, gesturing to his bandage. "No, I don't. They've tried to kill me twice, Antonil. Like I said, they guard magic pretty closely."

"So you're saying I should keep you hidden in the back?"

"I'm saying they will either let us pass, or they won't. There's no way of telling, not with them. They're recluses for a reason, and the Gods' War didn't help matters any."

Antonil muttered a curse against all spellcasters under his breath, then ordered his army to halt. Despite the worry in his gut, he rode ahead, determined to show the Council he was neither afraid, nor attempting to intimidate them. All they wanted was to cross a bridge so they could return home. Why did it have to be so bloody complicated?

"Just speak," Tarlak shouted from behind. "They'll hear you, I promise."

Antonil swallowed, chose his words carefully, then shouted up to the red tower that rose so high above him.

"Wizards of the Council, I am King Antonil Copernus of Mordan. My army has suffered many casualties, and our stores of food dwindle. I ask that we may cross the Rigon by way of your bridge, and receive any supplies you'd be willing to give us. I promise all kindness will be repaid, and any price within reason will be met twice over."

With that, he waited. His horse shifted uneasily beneath him, as if smelling the approach of a distant storm. Patting her neck, Antonil once more called out to the towers.

"What say you?"

Strangely, it seemed his horse's instincts were correct. The sky above, which had been white with clouds, suddenly darkened. Antonil kept his horse still as he heard worried cries from his army behind him. It was just intimidation, he told himself. The mages wanted to show they were in control. To confirm this, he glanced back at Tarlak. When their eyes met, he saw the wizard's concern, and rocks twisted in his gut.

All along the face of both towers various stones shifted, opening to create dozens of windows. Antonil felt his heart jump. At last he would receive his answer.

And he did, in the barrage of a dozen balls of fire, each larger than the size of a house.

His jaw fell open, panic freezing him in place. No, he thought. It couldn't be. Why? What had they done? Looking back, he saw the fire slamming into his troops, detonating in great explosions that sent bodies flying. Lightning struck from the sky, its thunder rolling over them like mocking laughter. Soldiers fled in all directions, and following them came the fire and lightning, now coupled with lances of ice and massive boulders, all from those open windows.

So far untouched, Antonil broke free of his terror and kicked the sides of his horse. Turning about, he raced toward the dying remnants of his army, seeking one man in particular. Tarlak Eschaton stood on the ground, having abandoned his horse. Silver light shone around his hands as he tried to summon his magic.

"Can you protect us?" Antonil shouted.

"I can't," Tarlak screamed. "Damn it, Antonil, I can't stop them all!"

Several of the incoming spells shattered, but they were too few. Antonil watched, his throat constricting as he listened to the screams.

"Stop it!" the king screamed to the towers. "Stop it, are you mad?"

Lightning struck. Blinded, Antonil was thrown from his mount. He landed hard on his head. Gasping for air, his vision swirling with color, he saw faint images of his men, those he had promised to lead to victory, to safety, and watched them die amid a horrible mixture of fire, lightning, and ice. Their bodies burned, their bodies bled. So horrible, so futile, and why? What had he done?

The barrage lessened, nearly all of his army broken. Antonil staggered to his feet, found Tarlak on his knees still trying to cast a spell.

"I can protect us," the wizard was mumbling. "I fought gods. I can protect us, I can protect…"

From the windows of the tower shot three balls of flame, their centers a deep blue, their outer ring a brilliant orange. All three were aimed their way. Tarlak grabbed Antonil's hand, and accompanying a scream of pain a translucent shield formed before the two. The first fireball exploded. The heat washed over them, rolling about as if they were in the center of furnace, yet they were not yet burned. The second hit, Tarlak screamed, and the fire passed.

Before the third reached them, Antonil pulled his shield off his back. Despite the burns on his face, despite the blood dripping from his mouth and nose, Tarlak was still trying to protect them. Knowing it hopeless, Antonil shoved him to the grass, dove atop him, and raised his shield. Tarlak continued to mumble, and strangely he heard Aurelia's name.

"I'm sorry," Antonil whispered, thinking of his kingdom, his wife, his child. All of it lost, all of it in peril.

"Protect them, Harruq."

The fire washed over him, burning away flesh and melting his armor, consuming the life that was his and ending his short, bittersweet reign.

From high atop the Master's Tower, the Lord of the Council watched as the last of the army was buried in a wave of magical attacks. Satisfied, he turned to the lady at his right.

"Inform the capitol," he said to her before descending the stairs that led up to the roof. "If Kevin wants the throne, it's his to take."

"Of course," said the silver-haired lady. From the pocket of her dress she pulled out a scrap of paper. With a soft breath she blew across it. The paper folded in on itself, over and over, until it had taken the shape of a dove. Its wings flapped with the speed of a hummingbird, and then into the sky it shot, racing north at speeds only angels could hope to match.

---

Kevin stepped into Susan's room, and she spun about, ready to berate him.

"Are the guards outside daft?" she asked. "You might have caught me in a state of undress."

She meant it as playful banter, but the seriousness of his look stopped her. He held a piece of paper out to her as he approached.

"Your guards are dead," he said.

Susan's mouth fell open, and she took a step back toward her bed.

"What?" she asked.

In answer he gave her the paper. She took it, unfolding the delicate material to reveal a simple message.

*Antonil is dead.*

She looked up, saw the hope in her brother's eyes.

"What is this?" she asked. "What does this mean?"

"It means my men have already cleared the city walls, and they'll be here in moments. Where is the half-orc?"

Susan's mouth suddenly felt dry. This was it. This was everything she'd feared of her brother, reaching fruition at last. She'd always told herself it'd never come this far. Apparently, she'd told herself a lie.

"He's with Aurelia, in their room," she said, still in a daze. "Will you kill them?"

Kevin put his hands on her shoulders, his hard gaze staring down at her. It made her feel small. It always did.

"Harruq was named steward by your husband. If I do nothing, that brute will rule, not you, not your child. By the time Gregory comes of age, do you think he'll even have a throne to inherit? Harruq is the angels' puppet. You know this. You've seen it."

"Don't do this," Susan whispered. "Please, you don't need to do this. At least let their little girl live."

Kevin swallowed.

"This is an ugly business," he said. "I'm not sure if she can be spared. No one must know what takes place here. We can still save our land, my dear sister. It will just take a little sacrifice. Can you do that for me? Can you be strong like I need you to be?"

Susan tried to push him away, but he held onto her, his grip on her arms tightening.

"You bastard," she said. "You'll kill us all, won't you? My baby boy, even him, you sick—"

He slapped her across the face, silencing her. A hard shove knocked her to the ground. Shaking his head, he pulled out a small length of rope that had been looped about his belt.

"I do what must be done," he said. "Something you'd never understand."

She wanted to laugh at him. What must be done? She'd married a stranger so their household could prosper in the chaos following the war. Just a man of common blood, a man who loved his lost homeland more than her. She'd sat in the shadow of a half-blood hero, named steward because she was seen as too vulnerable to be declared ruler herself. For family, for friends, she understood enduring such things. But this wasn't for family. It wasn't for country. She saw greed in her brother's eyes, a lust for power she should have quashed years ago.

"You won't kill them," she said, giving him her hardest glare. "Harruq's stronger than any man you have, and the elf's magic is unstoppable. They'll escape, and when they do they'll tell the whole world of your betrayal."

Kevin smiled that confident smile of his as he forced her to her knees, wrapping his rope around her wrists.

"My dear sister, trust me," he said as men in strange clothes and gray masks entered the room behind him. "I've taken care of that."

## 27

"What do you think?" Harruq asked as he held up two different shirts, one crimson and shiny, the other a deep, subdued green. "Which will look better on me at the ball tonight? I want tough but smart. Think we can do that with these frilly outfits? You know, Haern always managed to…"

He stopped, mouth hanging open, as Aurelia suddenly collapsed, falling off the bed and onto her knees, her hands clutching the sides of her head.

"Aurry?" he asked, rushing to her side. She let out a gasp as he put his arms around her, holding her against him.

"Stop it!" she screamed, her eyes rolling back into her head. "Stop it, you're burning him!"

And then, just like that, it ceased. Her body crumpled and he held her, stroking her hair, completely baffled and terrified because of it. For a long while she trembled in his arms, crying softly. It was only when she finally sat up, sniffling and wiping at her eyes, that he was convinced she'd regained her senses.

"Tarlak," she said. "That was Tarlak. He's dead, Harruq. Antonil as well. They're all dead."

He opened his mouth, closed it. Her words were a knife to his heart.

"No," he blubbered. "No, that's not right. You…what you saw was a dream, a vision, maybe you…"

"Stop it," she said. "I know what that was. He was trying to warn us about something. All I saw was fire. I felt it, Harruq. Antonil dove atop him to save him, but they both burned."

"Warn us?" Harruq asked. He was still trying to wrap his head around the idea of such good friends dying in so terrible a way. "Warn us about what?"

She rose unsteadily to her feet.

"The king is dead," she said. "I don't know if he knew I heard, but Antonil's last words were him begging you to protect his family. Think, Harruq. Gregory's now the heir. Who benefits most? Who's now in the most danger?"

Before she'd even finished her sentence Harruq was belting his swords to his waist, not even bothering with his armor.

"Where's Gregory?" he asked as he cinched the belt tight, then looped the extra leather beyond the buckle into a knot. When finished, he tossed Aurelia her staff from a corner of the room.

"He and Aubrienna are with their tutor," she said as she caught it.

"Good, they're together. That'll save us time. Once we get them we'll gather some guards, keep everyone on alert. There's not going to be any sort of coup today, I promise."

They left his room and hurried down the hall.

"Stay calm," Aurelia said, pulling on him to slow him down. "There's no way anyone can know about it yet."

"You know about it," Harruq countered.

They reached the stairwell and climbed to the upper floor of the castle. Down the hall stood four soldiers holding short swords. Harruq nodded at them, then barged through the door they guarded. Gregory and Aubrienna sat at small desks, scraps of paper before them. Hovering over them was an older man with white hair, the tutor brought in to teach the children their letters. Gregory was fairly young for it, but Aubrienna had taken to writing. Both their hands were smeared with ink, and at his noisy entrance they jumped.

"Lessons are over," Harruq said to the tutor. "Go on home."

The old man bowed, clearly confused but not pressing for a reason. He said goodbye to the children, then left. With him gone Harruq checked every part of the room, even what seemed like empty spaces. Haern had taught him how well the best of the best could hide in plain sight. Once certain the room was secure, he flung the bolt on the door in place, locking them inside.

"Keep playing," Aurelia told Aubrienna when she asked what was going on. Beside her Gregory had fallen silent, watching with his ink-covered hands in his lap, staining his outfit black.

"We've got some time to think," Harruq said, feeling infinitely better now that he was with his daughter. "Now that Antonil is…"

He paused, glancing at Gregory.

"...not around," he continued, "that means Gregory's king, right?"

"They won't let a child rule at such a young age," Aurelia said.

"Then it'll be Susan. We need to get her to safety. She'll be next in line to rule."

Aurelia gave him a look, and he realized he was still missing something.

"What?" he asked.

"A steward is appointed to rule when a child cannot," she explained. "And in this case, the king's last act was to appoint such a steward. Susan won't rule, Harruq. You will."

Harruq's emotions felt too raw to act appropriately, so he just acted like himself.

"Shit." He punched the wall, ignoring how much the stone hurt his hand. "Shit, shit, shit!"

He caught both children watching him, and he felt his neck flush.

"Sorry," he muttered. "Ignore daddy's mouth."

"Susan's life might still be in danger," Aurelia said, keeping her voice subdued in hopes Aubrienna and Gregory would not pay attention. "If anyone wants to usurp the throne, she'll still need to be eliminated."

Harruq nodded, trying to think. He'd accepted his position thinking it'd only be temporary. In a year at most Antonil was supposed to return, having conquered the scattered orc armies. But now...Gregory wasn't even four. How long until the boy was considered a man by law? He didn't know, but he severely wished he did. Eight years? Ten? He thought of the years passing, the weight of everything on his shoulders, and felt panic rising in his chest.

"I can't do this," he said. "I can't. I can't keep going, I can't rule for that long even with Susan's help. She'll have to do it. She *has* to." He walked over to the window, gesturing out to the city stretching out before them, a great expanse of homes and shops. "I can't rule all that! I can't..."

He stopped, leaning farther out the window and squinting.

"Aurry, get over here," he said. When she did, he pointed to the street. "What is that?"

She joined him, and with her sharper eyes she spotted men marching up the road toward the front of the castle. He estimated at least four hundred, maybe five. They waved no banners to show their allegiance, but their tunics looked familiar. He couldn't place it, but Aurelia could.

"Kevin," she said. "Those are Kevin Maryll's men."

The two shared a look. There was no valid reason for Kevin to be marching so many men into the castle. No reason but one. As they watched, craning their necks down and to the right so they might see, they noticed Kevin walked ahead of the throng, talking with the castle guards. As the doors opened to let him in, he stabbed one of the guards, then rushed inside. His soldiers followed, using their very bodies to prevent its closure. Harruq swore as he jerked his head back inside the room.

"Time to go," Harruq said. "Make us a portal and take us somewhere far, far away."

"What of Susan?" Aurelia asked as she began the motions with her hands.

"I'll come back for her once you three are safe."

Her look said she wasn't happy with the idea of him remaining behind, but she focused on casting her spell. Harruq waited, expecting the familiar blue line to rip open before him, tearing into reality and creating a gateway to somewhere well-known to his wife. But instead nothing happened. He blinked, glanced around thinking he'd missed something.

"What's wrong?" he asked.

Aurelia frowned, and her brow furrowed as she concentrated harder.

"Something is...strange," she said. Again she tried casting the spell, and again nothing happened. Harruq watched, his anxiety increasing tenfold.

"I think I know what's going on," she said after a third time yielded similar results. To test, she went to the window. Ice surrounded her hand, forming into a thin lance that she hurled out the window toward the courtyard. Barely an inch beyond the window ledge the ice dissolved away as if it had never been. Harruq grimaced, confused but knowing that whatever it meant, it wasn't good.

"The entire castle is surrounded by some sort of invisible…wall," she explained. "No magical spell can make it through without disappating. Worse, it's disrupting any sort of translocational magic. I've tried opening portals, even to somewhere inside the castle, but they won't take. I can't get us out, Harruq."

He could only follow half of what she said, but he understood the deeper meaning behind it.

"Kevin's ready for us," Harruq said. "He knew you would be with me."

The two shared a glance, each thinking the same thing. If Kevin was ready for them, if he'd gone through all the trouble to trap them there, then he wanted them for a reason. Most likely, he wanted them dead.

"He seeks the throne for himself," Aurelia said. "We're just obstacles in his way."

"We're more than obstacles."

Harruq opened the door, to where the four guards waited. All four looked nervous.

"Steward," one said. "We thought to interrupt, but weren't sure."

He didn't need to ask about what. From the floor below they could hear the faint sounds of steel hitting steel. Kevin's men were swarming the castle, killing all of the guards.

"We've been betrayed," Harruq said. "All of you, get in here. Guard the little prince with your lives."

Despite their apparent nervousness, the men saluted and hurried inside. Harruq glanced up and down the hall, his mind racing.

"We can't hold them off forever," Aurelia said, coming up behind him. Aubrienna clutched her mother's hand, her eyes wide with fear at the sudden commotion.

"Sure we can," Harruq said. "But we don't need to. There's a scepter back in our room. If I can get to it, we can summon a whole army of angels to protect us."

"What about Susan?"

Harruq looked back into the room. He couldn't get the scepter and Susan, at least not both at the same time. Aurelia could go, but that left the children with only four guards to hold off Kevin's men until one of them returned.

"There's nothing we can do," he said. "We'll just have to hope she lives. Stay here. I don't care if they brought a thousand men. You're strong enough to stop them."

He kissed her, then bent down to wrap Aubrienna in a hug.

"You stay safe," he said to her, kissing her cheek. Standing, he drew his swords and went over the layout of the castle in his mind. No matter which way he went, he'd need to go down the stairs to the lower floor. Presumably the floor was already lost, the guards within overrun. If only he could get down there without need of the stairs, bypassing the bulk of the forces...

He looked to Aurelia.

"The outside of the castle's been blocked," he said. "But not inside, right?"

His wife gave him a confused look, then understood.

"I won't be able to get you back up," she said.

"Leave that part to me."

Aurelia went to nearest door, pushing it open. Inside were simple beds, clean and unused for some time. Gathering her energy, Aurelia unleashed it in a focused point, blasting a hole in the stone floor just large enough for Harruq to hop through. Peering down, he found another room, this one far fancier, reserved for visiting lords and ladies. Beside the bed lay a heavy gentlemen, blood pooling around his throat. Harruq shook his head, then turned back to his wife.

"Love you," he said before hopping down. He landed atop the bed, rolled off, and then drew his swords.

"Should have put my armor on after all," he muttered as he slid to the door, which was slightly ajar. Glancing out, he saw soldiers rushing down the hall, their tabards bearing the Maryll family crest. All wore heavy chain mail for protection. Harruq winced again.

"Really, *really* should have put on my armor."

When he decided the hall was as empty as it would get, he burst out, then spun in an attempt to orientate himself. To his left were over fifty men filtering into the stairwell leading up. On his right were only a few, and they froze at his sudden appearance.

Harruq barreled down the hall toward them, relying on surprise to take them out quickly. The first tried to stab him but woefully underestimated Harruq's speed. Without slowing, Harruq slashed his throat and sidestepped his collapsing body, swatting aside the second's hesitant defense before shoving his swords into the man's stomach. The chainmail resisted, but the magic in Harruq's swords was strong, and they pushed through to pierce flesh.

With a roar, Harruq yanked them out, kicked away the body, and slammed both blades down against the paltry attempt to block by a third soldier. The steel shattered, Harruq's ancient blades flaring red as they continued on, chopping through either side of the man's shoulders to crush in his collarbones. Using the swords to maneuver the corpse, he flung it behind him, into the path of the soldiers breaking off from the stairwell.

The way was clear, and he ran like mad toward his room. From all sides he heard scattered combat, and he tried not to think on how many died. Would Kevin execute the servants, too? The cooks, the cleaners, the errand boys, all to hide his crime? He prayed not, but the screams he heard said otherwise.

A glance behind him showed at least fifteen men in chase. The breath in his lungs felt like fire, and again Harruq chastised himself for growing so lazy. Orcish heritage might have granted him extra muscles and stamina most men could only dream of, but it meant little when he spent two thirds his day in a chair, chugging down wine to keep himself from going out of his mind. The stone walls were a blur as he ran. He turned a corner, slamming into a group of four soldiers.

"Coming through," Harruq muttered, his momentum continuing through the jumble of arms and legs. Two the men managed to stay on their feet, and they swung weakly at him. Easily dodging their surprised flailing, Harruq hamstrung one, shifted a step to his right, and stabbed Salvation straight through the man's throat. He left them there, racing along before the rest of those chasing him could catch up.

His room was just up ahead. He stared at the door with his eyes wide. Getting back to Aurelia might be impossible now, but if he could barricade himself in his room and summon the angels, they could turn the tide, saving them from Kevin's madness. All he needed was the scepter in his closet. Without slowing, he blasted through the door with his shoulder, catching it with his left hand upon entering so he could immediately fling it shut behind him.

Jamming in the lock, he had to hope it held as he dashed for the closet. Pulling out the scepter, he clutched to it like the desperate prayer it was. At the window to their room he pointed the crystal outward and spoke the command word. Light built up around it, forming into a pillar. When it shot out, that pillar halted mere feet beyond the window. Harruq blinked at it, remembered the protection Aurelia had said had been cast around the castle.

"Well," he said, the door shaking behind him as something heavy slammed into it. "That's not good."

Shrugging his shoulders, he spoke the command word again, and then with all his strength he hurled the scepter out the window. It curled end over end through the air, and once beyond the barrier, the pillar of light whipped around as if held by a wild, drunk angel. Preparing his swords, he turned to the door and braced himself to fight whoever might break through.

The lock shattered, despite no pressure exerted on the door at the time. Before Harruq could even realize what was going on, he felt a sharp pain in his stomach. Letting out a cry, he stumbled to his knees as lightning surged through his insides, dissipating into the wall behind him. The force of the attack knocked him backward, and he cracked his head against the stone wall. Vision swimming, he stared as two men with masks leisurely stepped into his room.

"Not…" Harruq said as the men raised their hands, unleashing more of their power. "Not…fair…"

Darkness came for him, and all he could think was that surely things were supposed to have gone differently.

◈

Aurelia watched until Harruq was gone from sight, then returned to the makeshift classroom. Inside were the four soldiers, waiting with drawn swords and doing their best to hide their anxiety.

"Get away from the door," Aurelia said to them. They obeyed, shuffling awkwardly to the far side. Once sure the two children were safely behind her, she put her hands together, focusing a spell.

"Now open it," she said.

They did. Ice stretched from her fingers, growing, spreading out from one side of the doorway to the other, sealing them in with a wall of ice.

"That should slow them for a while," she said.

"More than that," said one of the soldiers. "They'd need a ram to break through ice that thick."

She smiled at him, a young man with barely any stubble on his face.

"Perhaps," she said. "I hope you're right, but I fear Kevin prepared for my tricks."

From the outside they heard muffled noises, undecipherable arguments and shouting. Through the blue of the ice Aurelia could make out dark shapes of men on the other side. Telling herself to remain calm, she took Aubrienna's hand and led her and Gregory to a corner. She overturned two desks and set them inside.

"Stay in here," she said, kissing both.

"Are they bad men?" Aubrienna asked her.

"Yes, very bad men."

"Will you stop the bad men?"

She ran a hand through her daughter's beautiful brown hair.

"You bet mommy will," she said.

She touched the stone bricks that made up the floor, and they clung to her like honey. Lifting it upward, she formed a wall, overlapping the desks. Higher and higher she pulled the malleable stone, creating a dome that sealed away the children. At the very top she left a hole so light and air might still enter. From within she heard sniffling, but both children remained brave. Proud of them, Aurelia turned, eyes focused on the ice barrier blocking the doorway.

"I don't know how Kevin's planned to kill me,' she told the guards. "But the ice will let him know where I am soon enough. Please understand what I ask of you. If any of you refuse, I will let the ice remain, and we'll wait for the trap to unfold to its fullest. Otherwise, I plan on taking down as many of that bastard's men as I can before he knows what's hit him."

She met their eyes, saw their apprehension had disappeared, leaving behind only bravery and determination.

"I'm not one for hiding," said the youngest of them.

"We'll be outnumbered," said another.

"That's what I'm here for," Aurelia said. "Draw your swords."

Electricity encircled her hands as they readied themselves. With a thunderous roar she unleashed her fury upon the ice. The lightning blasted it outward, showering the stunned soldiers with painful shards. The spell continued on, finding plenty of bodies for its ravenous power. Kevin's soldiers screamed as the lightning swirled through them, frying lungs and knocking dozens to the ground.

Among the smoking ruin of the dead, the rest of the soldiers gathered themselves, raised their shields, and charged.

"Stay clear of the doorway!" Aurelia shouted to the four. "Take out those who make it through!"

They listened, and even if she hadn't said so they most likely would have figured it out anyway. From her hands tore another blast of magic, this time of fire. The inferno bathed over the men struggling to enter the room, turning their shields to ash, their armor to liquid. With barely a moment to breathe, she unleashed a second burst of fire, refusing to relent. She'd seen their numbers when they entered the castle. Each one she killed was one less to threaten her family. One less to keep Harruq from safety.

The four with her looked on, awe and wonder etched across their faces. Only a rare few made it through such overwhelming destruction, and they were easily dispatched by the guards. Aurelia collapsed to one knee after the last spurt of fire, ignoring the momentary dizziness. Blood had begun to pound through her veins, and despite the strain she suddenly felt shockingly alive. It was more than she could say for the fools allied with Kevin Maryll, somehow convinced they could defeat a sorceress like her. So far the last barrage seemed to have cowed them, for they did not try to enter, and they stayed far from door's edges.

"It's only five of us," she shouted to them, a dark grin on her face. "Is this all you can do?"

## The Prison of Angels

She stood, her fingers dancing. Before the others could stop her she rushed out into the hall, twirling on her feet. Her first spell unleashed great flashes of light from her palms, blinding any unfortunate enough to be watching when it went off. All around her, Aurelia saw soldiers gathering, at least a hundred on either side. She felt a thrill surge through her, pride in the danger she represented. Gregory was under her protection, nearly half of Kevin's forces coming to take him, but they could not surpass her. They couldn't even begin to understand the raw power they faced.

Arms spread wide, she unleashed that power. From either hand arced lightning, bouncing from man to man, igniting their nerves, burning the flesh beneath their armor. Letting out a scream, Aurelia poured more strength into the spell. The lightning focused, became a beam that blasted through her enemies, punching holes in their armor and ripping men in twain. It continued down either side of the hall, the power of its shockwave knocking to the ground even those who the beam had missed.

And then the spell passed, and she stood alone before the survivors. Blowing them a kiss, she stumbled back into the room, collapsing in the arms of one of the soldiers.

"Buy me time," she said, pushing herself off him.

The four stood side by side, swords ready. It seemed even they were afraid of the carnage she'd unleashed. It almost made her laugh. If only they'd seen her in Woodhaven, dueling the prophet. Now *that* had been a fight.

She stepped back, already feeling better. It felt like forever since she'd been forced to battle in such a way, pushed to her very limits to protect the lives of those she loved. She wouldn't say she missed it, but she couldn't deny the thrill it gave her. The four guards tensed, but it seemed like the remaining soldiers had no desire to challenge her…though she wasn't certain just how many soldiers she'd even left out there to fight.

Just when she was thinking things might be easier than she hoped, she saw a small, painfully familiar sphere roll to a stop just before the soldiers' feet.

"Get back!" she screamed, knowing it was already too late. Her magic useless, she could do nothing as a man and women wearing matching red and gray outfits vaulted into the room, twisting and turning to avoid the guard's useless defenses. Their twin daggers lashed out, finding openings in their armor. Desperate, Aurelia ripped a chunk out of the wall and hurled it with her mind, the momentum continuing on despite coming into range of the voidsphere. One of the soldiers had his throat slit, and as he fell the stone slammed into him, knocking him into the hallway. The assassin before him tumbled aside at the last moment, avoiding the hit. Aurelia held in a swear as she readied her staff.

With the guards dead, the two assassins rolled a second voidsphere toward her, chasing after it with frightening speed. Aurelia twirled her staff, reminding herself that Harruq was faster. She'd fought him before, which meant she'd faced the deadliest there could be. With her elven grace she shifted and spun, her body like water as she avoiding a combination of thrusts and slashes. Her staff continued spinning, knocking aside the attacks she could not avoid. The exhaustion, the pressure of such intense focus, wore on Aurelia quickly, and it took all her willpower to fight down the panic she felt rising in her. There was no way she could win. Retreating with each step, she would soon have nowhere to go, no way to fight back. With such proximity to the voidsphere, she felt naked, deprived. Twice she tried to shift the fight toward it, so she could smash it with her staff, but the assassins seemed to be aware of her ploy.

At last she couldn't keep up the necessary speed. She shifted her body left when it should have gone right, and with a cry she felt the tip of a dagger pierce her shoulder. A heel connected with her midsection, and then an elbow struck her across the face. When she fell to her knees, fists rained down upon her, knocking her to the ground and stealing the breath from her lungs. Fighting back tears, she pushed herself off the floor, only to be beaten again.

Defeated, she lay there, struggling for air. The stone cold against her cheek, she stared at the entrance to the room as one of the assassins sat atop her, binding her wrists together. Mere feet in front of her lay the voidsphere, glowing its soft, mocking rainbow of colors. As if from another world she heard Aubrienna and Gregory crying, and the helplessness, the inability to go to them, gave her far more pain than the bleeding wound in her shoulder.

Through her tears she watched Lord Kevin Maryll stride into the room, dragging the queen along by the arm.

"Even knowing you'd be difficult, you still surprise me with your tenacity," Kevin said, shaking his head and smiling at her.

The female assassin grabbed her by the hair and yanked her head up. As she let out a cry, the assassin scooped up the voidsphere and jammed it into her mouth. Her slender fingers pushed, overriding her gag reflex to shove the object farther down her throat. Her body heaved, followed by an unstoppable coughing fit as the assassin pulled away her fingers, but there was little Aurelia could do as she swallowed the voidsphere, bringing its accursed denial of magic down into her very stomach.

"Harruq will kill you," Aurelia said as her face was shoved back to the floor.

"Will he now?"

Kevin moved aside, his grin spreading. Behind him were two more of his strange assassins. Into the room they stepped, and with a heave they dumped before her the unconscious body of her husband.

## 28

The first thing Harruq realized when he came to was that for some reason he was still alive. The second was a distant sound, like a wailing, that he couldn't place. The third was that his chest hurt worse than any sword wound he'd ever suffered before. When he opened his mouth to cry out, he felt something hard strike him across the face.

"Stop your screaming," he heard a voice say from the darkness. Harruq didn't recognize it, but he knew it was the voice of someone he hated. Forcing his eyes wider, the darkness became a blur of gray, followed by color. Realizing where he was, and what was going on, the world suddenly came into focus with shocking clarity and speed.

Kevin Maryll stood before him, holding a sword in his hand. With his other hand he held his sister, whose wrists were roped together before her. All around Harruq were the strange assassins with the gray masks over their faces. More stunning to Harruq, besides being alive, was that he was unbound in any way. His temper flaring, he moved to attack Kevin, assassins be damned, but Kevin took a step back and pointed to the side.

"Now, now," he said. "Wouldn't want to do something we'd regret."

Harruq hesitated just long enough to glance in the direction Kevin pointed. His heart froze when he saw Aurelia being held by one of the assassins. Her arms were behind her back, and the woman holding her kept a dagger pressed against his wife's throat. Behind the gray mask the assassin's eyes glinted, as if hoping he would make a move. He wondered why Aurelia made no attempt to free herself with a spell. Even with a dagger at her throat and rope around her wrists, he still trusted her to be resourceful enough to escape. Did one of them hold a voidsphere? That had to be it, despite the fact he didn't see one anywhere.

"Fair enough," Harruq said, remaining put. He felt his insides churn, the pain in his chest flaring up again, but he forced himself to ignore it. "I'm here, we're all here. We can talk, right?"

"Yes, we can," Kevin said. He shoved the door shut behind him, leaving him alone with his four assassins. "This is private, but you can trust my friends here to keep their mouths shut. As for you, Harruq, I'd ask you to keep quiet as well, difficult as it may be. For once, I need you to listen."

Harruq nodded. He glanced around, trying to find his daughter, and he spotted a strange stone dome in the far corner of the room. Muffled crying came from within. As if following his gaze, Kevin let go of Susan and approached the magical creation.

"Clever, if a bit crude," Kevin said, looking it over. "A good maul should break through in time. Your daughter is in there, isn't she, Harruq?"

"Leave her out of this," Harruq said.

"I will, if you do as I say. This is a historic day, a chance for humanity to save itself from its captors. But you'll need to do something for me, you half-blood freak."

Harruq shot a glance at his wife. Her eyes were glassed over, but when she met his gaze, he saw the helpless fury in them.

"What is that?" Harruq asked.

Kevin put his back to the stone dome and gestured to Susan.

"I need you to kill my sister."

Susan flinched as if she'd been slapped, but she stood tall, glaring at her brother silently.

"Excuse me?" Harruq asked.

"You know you cannot leave this room alive," Kevin said, stalking closer. "Antonil named you steward, and your false rule cannot be allowed to go on. But your wife, though, your daughter…they can live. Do as I say, and I'll only exile them. They can go live in the forests with the elves, or the Wedge with the dogs for all I care. All you have to do is one simple little task."

Harruq looked to Susan, trying to read her. She softly shook her head.

"This doesn't make sense," Harruq said. "The angels won't let you…"

"Won't *let* me?" Kevin interrupted. He shot forward, lashing out. His knuckles slammed against Harruq's mouth, and it took all his self-control to not respond. "Won't let me? That we require their permission for *anything* is proof enough I do what must be done. Don't you get it, Harruq? You put so much faith in them, even when I warned you not to. Those angels will not be able to lay a hand on me. By the time they get here, the castle will be mine, with the crown upon my head. And I'll offer to go before the entire kingdom, bearing witness that it was you, the lowborn half-orc, that killed my sister. And do you know what those angels will say then? They'll tell all the world that I speak the truth."

"The angels will know," Aurelia said, wincing as the assassin holding her pressed the dagger tighter against her throat. "They're not fools. They'll figure out what you've done."

"It doesn't matter," Kevin said, shaking his head. "I've spent years telling the people of Mordan that a time would come when the angels would make a play for power. Years and years, insisting the angels would usurp our lords and kings. This city is a hair's breadth away from riot, as is this entire nation. What do you think would happen if I, the rightful heir to the throne after Gregory and Susan's death, were suddenly overthrown by our guardian angels? Can you imagine it, the glorious rebellion rising up against them? Even if they kill me, I'll be a martyr for all mankind. We must be made free. We must escape the reach of their wings."

Kevin gestured to his sister.

"Do it," he said. "Do it, or watch your wife and daughter die."

It all felt like a bad dream, one Harruq had no way to wake up from. Slowly he walked over to Susan, putting a hand on her face. She leaned against his touch, her eyes meeting his.

"My life is forfeit," she whispered to him. "So do what you think is right. I won't condemn you for that."

Two of the assassins stood guard over Kevin. A third hovered by the door, holding Harruq's two swords. The fourth kept hold of Aurelia, ensuring his wife made no move to escape. Harruq faced them all, took in a deep breath.

"I'll do it," he said.

Kevin smiled, then reached out a hand toward the assassin by the door. Instead of handing over one of his swords, the assassin gave Kevin his dagger.

"I'm not a fool," he said, tossing the dagger at Harruq's feet. "The last thing I'm giving you are the swords you killed a god with."

Harruq grunted, and carefully he bent down and picked the dagger up by the handle. He didn't want to make any sudden movements, for the one holding Aurelia looked ready to draw blood at a moment's notice. The dagger felt tiny in his beefy hands. Turning to Susan, he slowly reached out, grabbing the ropes around her wrists and tugging them free.

"She dies with dignity," Harruq said, glaring at Kevin before he might protest. "You owe your sister that, at least."

The lord waved a hand to show he accepted. Harruq turned back to Susan, stepped closer.

"Do you trust me?" he asked her.

She nodded.

"Good."

He lifted the dagger, pulled it back to thrust…and then turned and hurled it into the face of the assassin holding Aurelia. It punched through the cloth, burying into an eye. Flinging Susan to the ground, Harruq lunged for the assassin holding his swords. His foe dropped them. With one hand the assassin drew his remaining dagger, with the other he reached outward. Lighting circled around his palm, then streaked toward Harruq's chest. But this time he was ready, and with a scream he crossed his arms and pushed onward, denying the magic, denying the pain.

Dipping his body as if to grab for his swords, he instead flung himself forward. His body smashed into the assassin's, and together they collided with the door. The hinges shook but held. The same could not be said for the bones in the assassin's chest as Harruq's fists slammed into them. A vicious elbow dislocated the vertebrae in his neck, and down he dropped. Harruq turned, surveying the battle in an instant with training long since beaten into him by Haern.

Aurelia's hands were still bound behind her, but instead of trying to free herself, she'd run forward, ramming her stomach into the desk Aubrienna had been drawing upon. The impact bent her over, and she vomited all across the ink scribblings. One of the remaining two assassins rushed toward her, and Harruq panicked, knowing he could not reach her in time. Her back was turned, she couldn't escape…

But Susan was free, and as Harruq scooped up his swords she dove between Aurelia and the assassin. She had no defense, no weapon, just her body. With brutal efficiency the assassin thrust his dagger into her throat, twisted it, and then flung her aside.

"You bastard!" Harruq screamed, legs pumping. Aurelia rolled off the desk, and then Harruq was there, his swords blocking the downward thrust of the assassin. Their blades connected, but Harruq's body felt more alive than it had in ages. Compared to Thulos, the man's speed was nothing, his skill substandard, and with a single looping cut he batted aside the assassin's defenses and then stabbed his swords deep into his chest. Roaring out his fury, he kicked the body back and then settled into a defensive stance over his wife.

"Stay back!" Kevin screamed as the lone assassin rushed to the stone dome. Fire circled around the man's hand, just over the hole at the top. "Stay back, or they die!"

Harruq froze, horrified by the thought of his beloved Aubby burning to death. Kevin saw that hesitation, and the victory was clear in his eyes.

It died the moment Aurelia flung a lance of ice across the room, its sharp point ripping through the last assassin's chest, spilling innards across the floor.

Kevin lifted his sword in defense. Harruq stalked closer, and if not for the death around him he might have laughed. Aurelia gave him no chance to show the man how outclassed he was. Ice shot from her fingers, several bursts that wrapped around his wrists and ankles, pinning him to the wall. In vain he struggled against them, his sword clattering harmlessly to the floor.

"That's it," Kevin said, face turning red from his struggling. "Bring the angels. Have them hold me trial. You want to see riots? You want to see who the people truly believe in all this?"

"Not you," Harruq said. "Not anymore."

With one single swing he let out all his fury, all his exhaustion and sorrow. Condemnation cut clean through his neck, severing Kevin's head. It hit the ground with a sickening *plop*. Growling like an animal, Harruq picked it up by the hair and then flung it out the window.

"Fucking lunatic," he said, shaking his head.

He heard Aurelia let out a cry, and he turned. She'd rushed to the dome, and with a wave of her hand moved aside the rock.

Tears ran down her face as the two children flung themselves against her, holding on with desperate strength while they cried. Harruq wanted to relax, wanted to go to them, but they weren't safe just yet. He checked the door, ensuring it was locked, then wondered when the remaining soldiers might come looking for Kevin. No doubt he'd wanted Susan's death to come about in private, where no one could contradict him to the angels. Perhaps that might buy them time...

"Harruq?" said a voice. The half-orc turned, unsure where it'd come from. He saw Ahaesarus leaning into the window, one foot on the ledge, his wings flapping to keep him balanced. He was too big to fit inside, but he could see within.

"I saw the scepter," the angel said as Harruq approached. "The doors are locked, and they would not allow me entrance."

"You're about five minutes too late," Harruq said. "Kevin's dead. His men attacked the castle, hoping to usurp the throne."

A shadow spread across the angel's face as he listened.

"Are you safe where you are?"

Harruq glanced about, shrugged.

"Safe as anywhere in this castle."

"Good." Ahaesarus pushed off from the ledge.

"Where are you going?"

The angel leader drew his sword.

"To get more of my kind," he said.

With that, Ahaesarus flew away. Staggering toward Aurelia, Harruq passed Susan's body. He leaned down once, put a hand on her face so he might close her eyes.

"I'm so sorry," he whispered. "Thank you for trusting me. I'm sorry I didn't do better. I should have. I..."

He let it go, instead went to his wife. He fell to his knees beside her, wrapping her in his arms.

"I thought we'd lose her," Aurelia said, glancing over at him. Tears ran down her face, but she'd composed herself well enough.

"Never," Harruq said, kissing her forehead before taking Aubrienna into his arms, where she curled up against his chest.

"Never again."

## 29

Daniel stood in the top floor of the Blood Tower, feeling very old. It'd been eleven years since Sir Robert had died and control of the Wall of Towers passed over to him. Staring out the window at the river beyond, he wished anyone else had taken his place in the aftermath of the Gods' War. Someone younger, someone with energy. Because as he watched in vain for another boat to return, knowing it would not, he felt too damn tired to do anything about it.

"This is your fault, Antonil," he muttered as he turned away. "For once, couldn't you have looked to this country's defense instead of your old home's?"

For years he'd requested more soldiers, and for years he'd been denied. At first it was because everyone was needed to help rebuild the land. Then came the first failed campaign to retake the east, followed by the even larger second. And through it all, good men, men he needed to man the boats and patrol the wildlands of the Vile Wedge, were instead sent to die in a foreign land. Whenever someone would whisper the title The Missing King, Daniel had always made sure his ears were deaf to it. The last thing he wanted was to punish one of his few men for saying something he actually agreed with.

Daniel descended the steps of the tower and stepped out into the bright light of the full moon. His two hundred men were out and about, as per his orders. Something was amiss. He felt it in his gut, and so he'd kept them awake, not even bothering to assign shifts. The signs were too similar to before, made all the more frightening by their suddenness.

"Has Johnson returned?" Daniel asked as he approached the docks. Several men were gathered there, and they all shook their heads.

"Not yet," said one of the men. Daniel was hardly surprised, but he tried not to let his frustration show.

"Keep looking," he said. He spun, making his way to the wall that surrounded the tower before dipping into the shallower portions of the river. He climbed the steps, then looked out across the Gihon. Patrols walked past, and he squinted against the light of their torches. Two days ago it had started. There'd been no warning. No casualties, no reports of deaths like when the wolf-men first started preying on the people of Durham, marking their eventual assault. No, one night his boats simply had not returned. He sent out two more, one north, one south. The one north had been a patrol, the one south to check with Tower Red to see if they had encountered anything unusual.

The northern boat never returned, and so far they'd yet to receive word from the south. Glancing at the full moon, he felt the pale orb put fear into his blood. Something was definitely wrong, and no matter what it might be, he didn't have the manpower to fight it. An hour before he'd sent out a rider to the Castle of the Yellow Rose to plead for aid from Lord Hemman. Beyond that, there was little he could do but wait and pray.

"Sir!" one of the patrolmen shouted, rushing alongside the wall and waving his arms to get his attention.

"Yes?" Daniel asked, turning.

"A boat at the docks!"

Daniel felt his tension easing. Perhaps it wasn't as dire as he thought.

"Is it Johnson, or someone from Red?"

"I don't know," said the soldier. "I just saw it from the wall."

Daniel climbed down the steps to the ground, and he saw many other soldiers hurrying toward the docks as well. He couldn't blame them, a bunch of nervous men stuck armed and ready with nothing to do but wait. The crowd parted easily enough, and when Daniel caught sight of the boat his hopes were dashed. The man from Tower Red looked pale, and he saluted Daniel upon his arrival.

"Sir," the man said. "I...forgive me. I don't know how to say it. Tower Red is gone."

"Gone?" Daniel asked, feeling ice thickening around his spine.

"The goat-men," he said. "They rushed us from the Wedge, thousands of them. I managed to escape during the attack. I was ordered to, I swear. I ain't no coward. But they smashed down the doors of the tower like they were nothing, and against that many, we couldn't…we…"

Daniel grabbed his shoulders and shook him to force him to calm.

"Deep breaths, soldier," he said. "Tell me again, how many?"

"At least two thousand," the man said. "Please, we have to get help. We have to go back there. They might still…"

From beyond the river came a single, high-pitched shriek. Following it were thousands more, a sound so painful that Daniel clutched his hands to his head, his fingers jammed into his ears. He knew that sound, though never in such terrifying volume.

"To your places!" he screamed, hoping they heard his voice above the noise. "Man the walls, and form ranks along the river!"

He drew his own sword and rushed to the nearest staircase leading up to the wall. Before he even reached the top he saw the swarm growing on the opposite side of the river. Bird-men, a veritable legion, flapping their wings and shrieking like the wild things they were. Their feet were long, their claws sharp, and the river was a paltry defense against them.

"Everyone along the river," he shouted, realizing the bird-men intended no delay, no siege to prevent flight. The water roiled as the creatures dove into it, using their wide, flightless wings to push them forward. When he was back on solid ground, Daniel grabbed the nearest man and yanked him close.

"Get to the stable," he shouted into the man's face, determined to be heard over the chaos.

"Sir?" he asked. His eyes were wide, but he appeared to be in control of himself.

"Take the fastest horse and ride to the Yellow Rose! They have to know. This isn't just a single pack."

"Then what do I tell him it is?"

Daniel glanced at the river, where the first of the bird-men were being hacked to death by his soldiers as they attempted to scramble out of the water.

"Tell them it's an army," he said. "The whole damn Vile Wedge has come for blood. Now go!"

He shoved the man back, then rushed to the river. They had just enough men to form a single line along the shore. With the water slowing the beasts, the advantage was theirs, at least for a short while. Daniel thrust his sword, letting a bird-man impale itself on the blade while its enormous beak snapped futilely at his neck. He twisted the handle before kicking the creature off, then he swung again and again, batting at a second bird-man that flapped free of the river with an awkward gait. His sword easily crushed its thin bones.

All around him men screamed as beaks snapped down on their arms and long raptor claws raked against their exposed flesh. *Two hundred against thousands*, thought Daniel as he continued to hack and slash. But what more could they do, other than buy time for his rider? Daniel thought of the people beyond, the farmlands that waited like ripened berries for the beasts to pluck. Two towers falling in the same night? What did it mean?

"Fall back!" he screamed. Bodies of the dead floated all throughout the river, obstacles against the remaining forces, but too many bird-men were making it clear of the water. "Fall back to the tower!"

Daniel led the way, his old legs pumping as hard as they could. Others passed him by, younger and faster than he. From behind he heard screams, wet snapping sounds, and overwhelming it all was that continuous, mind-numbing shriek. Into the tower he ran. Several soldiers stood at the door, watching. The moment the last man entered they slammed it shut, flinging the heavy bolts in place. Immediately the door shook as bodies smashed into the other side. Digging soon followed, sharp claws scratching grooves into the thick wood.

"Find anything you can to block the door with," Daniel ordered before climbing the stairs. His bones ached, but he ignored the pain easily enough, for even on good days his body gave him trouble. To the very top of the tower he climbed, opening a hatch in the ceiling. He grabbed a wrapped package from his closet, then up he went, climbing onto the small flat space. Other than a few stacked stones there was nothing to keep him from falling, and on his knees he overlooked the surrounding area. The full moon kept the land lit, and he directed his gaze to the river.

The bird-men continued swimming across. At least three thousand, he guessed, as the creatures swarmed throughout the inner compound, looking like a horde of vermin from that height. A few failed to climb the sides of the stone, the rest taking turns scratching at the door. Daniel shook his head, knowing it would not take long before the door fell.

Goat-men. Bird-men. Daniel's gut told him the wolf-men were a part of it as well. A coordinated attack. He shivered to think of who could ally the beasts together. It was their constant squabbling that had kept their numbers in check for all these years, their inherent hatred of each other that had protected the people on the other side of the river from any real danger. But somehow that was gone.

"Ashhur help us all," he said.

He unwrapped the package. The gold of the scepter shone in the moonlight. Daniel lifted it above him and spoke the command word. The blue pillar shot into the sky, the beacon visible for miles upon miles. He stared at it, daring to have hope. Twice more he activated it, and each time he noticed the bird-men below staring up as if mesmerized. He wondered what the creatures' pathetic brains thought of the light. Perhaps they knew what it meant. After all, they'd coordinated an assault on multiple towers. Despite his years, not to mention his experience, he still hadn't given enough credit to the beasts.

"Where are you?" Daniel muttered, staring at the sky. He'd never called for the angels before, but this seemed as perfect a time as any. At least he might inform them of the attack, ensuring that the riders he sent to Lord Hemman didn't have their warnings go unheeded. The minutes passed, interminable due to the constant squawking and screeching.

At last he saw white wings. They were almost above him by the time he spotted them, for they came from the east. Daniel raised his arms, waving, but something was wrong. The wings were even larger than he expected, and as the creature dipped, he realized it wasn't an angel at all, but a winged horse. Two people rode atop it, their bodies just faint silhouettes. Slowly he lowered his hands, and he felt his innards tighten. Silent, he watched as the horse circled twice, then continued west.

From the horse shot a blinding object. An arrow, Daniel realized, as it smashed into one of the bird-men. It was only one, and then they were gone, flying toward the Castle of the Yellow Rose. The acknowledgement made Daniel feel better, but only by a miniscule amount. At least someone else, one of the elven Ekreissar, apparently, would help spread the tale. Perhaps an army might be raised in time. Perhaps thousands of lives might be spared.

From below he heard the shattering of wood, and he glanced down to see the tower doors had broken. His men fought bravely, using the cramped space of the doorway to their advantage, but defeat was inevitable. He had barely fifty men left. Against three thousand, what could they do?

One last time he used the scepter, calling Ashhur's name so the light would pierce the night. As it faded, and the starlight replaced it, he let out a sigh. Wherever the angels were, it wasn't where they were needed. From his limp hand he let the scepter drop. Down the side of the tower it fell, smashing as it hit ground. A puff of blue smoke rose from the pieces, drifting away to nothingness as the bird-men swarmed through the gateway, killing their way ever higher.

At last he heard movement from the hatch, which he'd left open. Drawing his sword, he turned. A single creature came climbing upward, its wings making it difficult for the thing to get a grip on the rungs. Daniel shoved his sword down its throat, then kicked in its beak. It fell, the noise alerting the rest to his presence. The monsters scrambled upward, biting at his thrusts, using their impressive strength to hurl themselves at the hatch, ignoring the ladder altogether. Daniel laughed as he fought, thinking he might be able to kill them off one at a time, brawling as the hours passed and he whittled the thousands down at the ridiculously slow pace.

That thought didn't last long. One of the bird-men's beaks locked tight when he stabbed it straight through its throat and into the back of the brain. It fell, hurdling backward so violently that it yanked the sword from Daniel's hand. Weaponless, he backed toward the edge of the tower, preparing himself. He would not be their food. A single step and off he'd go, falling, the ground to be his killer instead of the freakish leftovers of a long-forgotten war.

The first bird-man made it to the top of tower, but it did not find the easy prey it expected. A heavy gust of air blew Daniel away from the ledge, and then a man came falling from the sky, a long blade in hand. The man, an elf, stabbed the creature through the eye upon landing, then kicked it down to join the rest of the bodies in Daniel's room.

"That damn girl is going to be the death of me," the elf said, glancing over his shoulder as he settled into a stance before the hatch. "Consider yourself fortunate for the eagerness of youth."

Behind him, Daniel heard the winged horse let out a neigh, and when he turned he saw the creature hovering just beyond the ledge. A young woman sat atop it, reaching for him.

"Take my hand!" she shouted, and before he lost his nerve he did just that. His step was not far enough, and as she yanked he fell with his stomach bent over the horse's back. That appeared good enough, and into the air they shot, leaving the elf behind.

"Don't take us far!" the girl shouted as Daniel hung on for dear life.

"What?" he shouted back.

"Not you!"

Less than a quarter-mile beyond the tower was a stretch of forest, and the horse landed at its edge. Daniel slipped off, thrilled to be on solid ground. Barely slowing, the pair hooked around and swooped back toward the tower. Daniel watched while on his knees, trying to regain his breath. He felt overwhelmed, pulled back from certain death to a sudden reprieve. At the same time he knew his men were gone, his tower overrun. He didn't know how to feel, other than sick and exhausted. Even from the forest he could hear the sounds of the bird-men, and it filled him with shivers.

Moments later he saw the horse, and he was glad to see both had survived. They landed with a burst of wind, both the elf and the girl hopping off.

"Are you all right?" she asked him.

"I am, thanks to you," he said.

"This isn't good," said the elf, a frown locked across his features. "Sonowin cannot carry the three of us."

"Then we run," the girl offered.

"Indeed." The elf turned to him. "Except for you. Get back on. Sonowin will take you to safety, if you guide her."

"No," Daniel said. "I won't be a burden like that."

"You're not," said the elf. "I need you to raise an army, and send out warnings to all the nearby villages. At least three towers have fallen from what we've seen. It won't be long before the rest are gone, and the entire North is being overrun."

Reluctantly, Daniel climbed back atop the horse, wishing there was at least a saddle. The creature swung her head side to side, neighing loudly.

"Head southwest," he told her. "Can you understand southwest?"

The horse bobbed her head, snorting. Her wings flared wide, and he guessed the intelligent creature did. He looked down at his rescuers. They each stood tall, with long bows in hand.

"What will you two do?" he asked.

"Don't worry," the elf said. "Sonowin will come find us. And until then, well…"

He glanced to the girl. Her face was haggard and scarred, and despite looking like she'd endured a nightmare, she smiled.

"Until then, we go hunting," she said, lifting her bow.

Sonowin's wings beat harder, and away into the air they went. Daniel watched the two vanish into the forest before turning his attention to where they flew. Leaning closer so the horse could hear his words and see his actions, he pointed in the direction where he thought the nearby castle waited.

"Fly on," he said, and the horse obeyed.

Daniel settled back in, his arms wrapped around the creature's neck to keep him secure. Still exhausted, he said a prayer for his dead men, as well as his saviors. It made him sad when he realized he'd never even asked them their names. Perhaps, he thought, if the world was kind, he'd get another chance.

The old soldier shook his head. A kind world. What an insane thought.

Onward they flew, as far behind him the bird-men emptied out from the walls of Blood Tower and continued on, heading for where the farms and villages slumbered.

## 30

Ezekai circled, staring down at the town of Norstrom as the wind blew through his hair. He should land. He knew he should land. Though no scepter had called for his aid, his fine eyes could clearly see the mob gathering below in the square. That they did not call him was unsurprising. Whenever he talked with the rest of his kind, they said the same. The use of the scepters was dwindling, and exclusively for those in need of healing. Ever since that one night they'd given the humans the justice they desired, things had changed. Deep down, Ezekai knew it'd never be the same. He saw the way the people looked at him. There was fear now, just fear. No love to match the love in his own eyes. That Ahaesarus had repealed the decision, and revoked their right as executioners of the guilty, seemed not to matter.

Still, the mob below was growing, and he could not ignore what was happening. Ezekai dipped his wings, and down to the square he flew, landing with a gust of wind and dust. Over a hundred men and women gathered there, and they begrudgingly made room for his landing. To call the reception cold did not give the icy feeling justice. Quickly he took in his surroundings. In the center, still being built, was another pole. The nearby rope showed its eventual purpose. In the arms of two men knelt a woman, her face beaten and her clothes torn.

"What is going on here?" Ezekai asked, trying his hardest to keep his temper in check.

"None of your concern, angel," said the same man that had denied him before, back when they'd hung Saul.

"And who are you, to challenge me?"

"Name's David," he said. "And we don't want your justice. We're capable of doing that ourselves. Bella here's guilty as sin, and we all know it."

The crowd gave its enthusiastic support to the statement. The bound woman, however, did her best to rise to her feet, though the two men prevented her from going to him.

"Please," she yelled to Ezekai. "Please, help me!"

"For what crime do you capture and beat this woman?" Ezekai asked.

"Bella poisoned my little girl!" another woman yelled.

She spoke neither truth nor lie, only an accusation she firmly believed. There'd be nothing useful from her, but Ezekai prodded anyway.

"Poisoned? Why?"

"Jealous," David said. "We all know it, too. Jealous of Mary's girl. Bella has no girl of her own, and she's whored herself about this village trying to get one."

Bella opened her mouth to speak, but one of the men holding her wrapped his arm about her head, shoving his forearm against her mouth to muffle her words. The crowd took up shouting, demanding her life, demanding she hang. Others called out for her to suffer, and the feeling of loathing and hatred made Ezekai physically ill. His wings shook behind him, tiny vibrations he could not stop.

"Let her speak," he said, hoping to at least make things right. "Let me hear her words and judge the truth of the matter."

"We don't need your truth," David said. "We've got people who saw her doing it."

"That's right," another man said, stepping forward. "I saw her putting shit into the girl's cup."

"Me too," said a third, a heavyset man with a beard. "I asked her what, but she said she didn't do nothing, but I know what I saw."

Ezekai's eyes widened, and he felt pain in his chest. They were lying. Both men, lying about what they saw, all to justify the hatred in their heart. What had this woman done? Was it because she was a whore? Or did the love for Mary's daughter demand a scapegoat for them, someone to blame?

The man gagging Bella yelled and pulled back his arm. Blood was smeared across the woman's face from biting him.

"I didn't do it!" she shrieked at the top of her lungs. "They're liars, all of them, I didn't do it!"

Her words struck him like a sledge. She spoke truth. Beaten, mocked, hated…and innocent. Yet despite his arrival, men had continued building, frantically setting up the pole with a hook at the top for them to loop the rope about. The other end would be for her neck, to snap her spine and crush her throat.

"She's innocent," Ezekai said, first softly, then louder. "Innocent. Don't you all know what it is you do?"

"Are you calling us liars?" one of the supposed witnesses demanded.

"I am!" Ezekai roared. "I call you fools. I call you bitter and petty. Release that girl, and let those who laid a hand on her in violence step forth."

"You aren't in charge here," David said, and the cries of the crowd affirmed their agreement. "Be gone, angel. We know why the babe died, and we know who did it. Fly away."

Just a babe, then, not even a child. Fury continued to grow in his breast. Was it an illness? Was it something he could have prevented if only they had swallowed their pride and used their scepter to summon him? How many would die because of their hatred and mistrust?

"Stop it," Ezekai said as a third man wrapped the end of a rope around Bella's neck. "I said stop it now. I will not watch an innocent die!"

The crowd yelled louder. The men surrounding Ezekai pulled out whatever weaponry they owned, hatchets and knives and field-worn scythes. They'd been ready for him, the angel realized. They knew he might arrive. For Ashhur's sake, they probably saw him circling above.

"I said stop," Ezekai insisted. "Don't do this. All of you, you're sick, you're caught up in this ugliness, this hatred. I won't allow it. I *can't* allow it!"

They flung the other end of the rope around the hook, grabbed it as it fell back down. Such insolence. Such blatant insult, to continue on before him. His law meant nothing to them, he saw it so clearly now. The men stared, weapons ready, there to defy him in saving an innocent life. Bella continued sobbing, her voice strained by the tightness of the rope.

Slowly Ezekai drew his sword. An emotion bubbled in him, one he couldn't quite place. He looked to these people he loved, these sinful creatures, and realized he didn't love them anymore.

"If this is how it must be," he whispered.

He flapped his wings, lunging forward as three men grabbed the rope in preparation to pull. David was the first to step in his way, but with a single, powerful cut Ezekai sliced his body in twain. A step, a spin, and his sword arced out, cutting down three more men before they could bring their weapons to bear against him. Panicked screams echoed from the crowd. Half the mob turned to flee, the other half rushing the angel. Ezekai cut again and again, keeping them at bay so they could not overwhelm him. Meanwhile the three men pulled on the rope, lifting Bella into the air. She clutched at her neck, gasping silently as her face began to turn red.

"Damn you all!" Ezekai roared, taking to the air. His sword sliced through the rope, and before she could fall he caught her in one arm. When he landed he pulled at the noose around her neck, trying to loosen it so she might breathe. Before he could, he felt something sharp pierce his side, and he let out a cry of pain. Spinning about, he cut the head off the man who'd stabbed him, then tried to turn back to Bella. Men leapt atop him, pulling at the tender bones of his wings, wrapping their arms about his neck. He yelled for them to stop, pleaded as he flung them aside. The rope, it wasn't loose yet, it wasn't...

Another stabbing pain, and he had no choice but to turn. His sword did its work, their pathetic instruments nothing compared to his blade. Still they rushed him, and still he couldn't understand why. Why this anger? Why such hatred and loathing? Even their fear was obvious, yet they wouldn't flee. Like dogs they died, rabid dogs, and he put them down. Words flashed in his mind, thoughts he didn't want to think. Killer. Reaper. Demon. Was it their thoughts or his? Could he even know?

The bodies around him grew in number, until at last none stood to face him, the rest fleeing back to their homes or the fields beyond. Bleeding from a multitude of wounds, Ezekai turned around. He still had healing magic in him, knew there was always hope if the woman lived, but kneeling before Bella he found her an empty shell. Her soul had moved on, and he prayed it went to a far better place than this miserable world.

"Innocent," he whispered, touching her cooling face with his bloodied palm. "An innocent, murdered...and why?"

He stood, flared his wings and lifted his sword as he cast his judging eyes upon the village.

"Why!" he screamed.

He took to the air, flying faster than an arrow. Like a ram he blasted into the nearest home. Sword drawn, he looked upon the family within. People who had shouted out their anger. People who had done nothing to stop the bloodshed. He judged them, as he did to those the next home, and the people who fled down the streets. Looping into the sky, he found those in the fields, those who knelt begging and pleading as if it might mean something anymore. He judged them all, until his armor was soaked with blood and his sword felt heavy with the weight of a hundred souls.

Judged until there were none left to judge.

Outside their village he landed, nearly crashing to the ground in delirium. He crawled to a nearby stone, pulled himself atop it, and sobbed. He slammed his sword into the dirt, he beat his chest, and he let his tears flow. Why had they done it? What monstrosity filled their souls that they would let such a thing happen? He was supposed to protect them. Was that not why Ashhur had sent him to this world? To chase off the demons and safeguard the populace before it was all lost to darkness? But the darkness was already there. It'd already won, long before he and his ilk had arrived. In every heart he'd felt their sin, felt their anger, jealousy, lust, and fear.

He didn't know how long he knelt there. It might have been minutes, might have been hours. Slowly he felt himself returning to some shred of sanity. There, before that forest, he realized that it was quiet. He no longer felt their presence like a thorn in his mind. He no longer heard their cries of anger. There were none left to sin. None left to spit in the face of their god and deny the gifts freely given to them. There was nothing. No weight on his shoulders. Just…emptiness. Absolute, blessed emptiness.

A shadow crossed over Ezekai, marking someone's arrival. He looked up, the blood fresh on him, his actions clearly revealed. The words of the newcomer broke the silence, and they were so sincere, so seductive.

"I understand."

## 31

"I'm sorry for the long flight," Ahaesarus told him, shouting to be heard over the whipping wind.

"My arms hurt," Harruq shouted back. He hung beneath the angel as they flew over the land, his life literally in the angel's hands. Should Ahaesarus let go of his wrists, he'd fall, and no matter how strong he was, Harruq knew he'd splatter upon hitting the ground below.

"It is not far now."

Not far still meant another ten minutes, and Harruq endured best he could. His shoulders ached, feeling like they were about to be yanked from their sockets. To get his mind off the pain he watched the land below, the hills slowly flattening as they traveled farther south. The grass grew taller, wilder, and soon he saw clusters of trees that grew thicker and thicker until they were full-blown forests. Idly he wondered what would happen if he were to be dropped onto those trees. Would the limbs spear him dead, or perhaps the leaves slow his fall?

He really, really didn't want to find out.

"How far again?" he asked.

"You have the patience of a child."

"The temper, too."

Ahaesarus's wings spread wide and tilted downward.

"Then for both our sakes I am glad we are here."

'Here' was a village bordering the northern edge of the forest. Other than being on the smaller side, Harruq could tell little as to why the angel had been so insistent to fly him here. Ahaesarus circled once, then finished their descent. With an unceremonious plop Harruq dropped to the ground, rolled once, then stood. He brushed the dirt from his armor as he glanced around. It was midday, so most of the men were gone, working in the fields, he assumed. Women gave him curious looks from their windows, and Harruq felt thankful none appeared afraid. One or two even waved.

Which, now that he thought of it, was strange. It was the outlying villages that were growing the angriest with the angel's justice, those on Ker's border the most willing to succumb to violence. Yet as Ahaesarus landed beside him, there was only joy on the faces of children that came running to gather at their feet.

"Did you bring us something?" they asked. "Did you?"

Ahaesarus pulled a large bag off his back and opened it. From within he drew two sweet cakes. They were already crumbling from the flight, and he broke them further into pieces. The children scrambled for them until they were gone. Harruq watched, hiding his smile. He still felt uneasy, and that he was confused helped matters none.

"Follow me," Ahaesarus said.

Not far from where they landed was a house larger than the others, attached to a shed almost as large. One of the children beat them to its door, and a moment later a women in her forties stepped out.

"You are late," she said.

"I was burdened," Ahaesarus said, handing over the sack.

"Such excuses," the woman said. She nodded at Harruq. "Do we get to cook him, too?"

Harruq blinked.

"Uh, no?"

"Shame. You're a beefy one." She gave him a wink, then hauled the sack into her house while calling out several names to come help her. Ahaesarus watched her go, then turned to Harruq, who had finally lost patience.

"What's in the bag?" he asked. "Why do they all love you here? Bribing them with gold?"

"Not gold. Flour."

Ahaesarus beckoned for him to follow again, and as they walked to the forest the angel explained.

"We haven't located all of the demons," he said. "Though Dieredon and his Ekreissar killed many, a few escaped and fled here, to this forest. This village used to live on the meat of their hunts, but the demons killed recklessly, far more than they could have eaten. It is as if their rage against the very world made them lose control. The people here were afraid to hunt, for many died trying. Even the animals eventually fled their wrath."

"Are the demons still here?" Harruq asked, his hands reaching for the hilts of his swords. Was that why the angel had brought him, to help hunt down and kill the last of Thulos's kind?

"No," Ahaesarus said as they exited the village. "They left several months ago, to where I do not know. But by then the people here, they were hungry, their forest stripped clean…they were starving when I found them. Such a small village, they did not have a scepter to summon us, and it was only by chance I flew overhead."

Before them was the forest, and Ahaesarus crossed his arms and stared within.

"The last of their hunters are in there," he said. "They are proud, and in vain they search for deer, squirrel, even a game bird. In time such prey will return, now that the demons have fled. But not soon enough."

"The flour," Harruq said, remembering the sack. "You fly all this way just to bring them flour?"

"I do," he said. "Every day for the past month I've made this flight back and forth from Avlimar. In doing so I have learned something, Harruq, something I would pass on to you. You are to be the steward of Mordan for years to come, and I believe this wisdom may benefit you as well as it has me. Even more so, I want you to learn it before it is too late."

The angel folded his wings against his back and sat in the grass. Realizing they weren't going anywhere for a while, Harruq sat opposite him, shifting his swords so their sheaths did not poke into the ground.

"Well?" he asked. He tried to be flippant about it. He'd always felt uncomfortable with these moments, when someone was trying to give him personal advice. But the solemnness in Ahaesarus made his tone feel childish. Crossing his arms, he looked to the side, berating himself so he would listen.

"Ashhur's land fades from my mind with every passing day," Ahaesarus said. He lifted an open hand and stared at it. "I once touched the garment of my god, yet now I cannot remember his face. Held in these fingers, held…yet now I hold a sword. With every breath I take, I become more like the man I was. Being here, in this land, among this pain and despair, it tears at me, tears at every one of my kind. We came from the sky with swords, with spears, our armor shining brighter than the sun itself. But we've erred, Harruq. We've erred, and I fear it runs too deep for us to heal."

The silence lingered.

"How?" the half-orc dared ask.

"Every day, I bring this village food," Ahaesarus said. "And every day, I remember the lives I am to protect. We were never meant to rule, Harruq. Never meant to be law and executioner. We're trying to change the world, but we'll never succeed, not like this. Through law we tried to conform man to Ashhur's grace. What fools we were. We can't make forgiveness law. We can't enforce grace with a sword. This food I bring has done far more good than I have ever brought about with my blade. We weren't meant to be masters of this world. We were meant to be *servants*. It is from the hearts of men, not their courts, that we shall spread our light. Jerico once told me how, before the Citadel fell, he worked the fields with the men in the village he was to preach to. Yet we angels fly above mankind, separate, watchful. I'm afraid, Harruq. I'm so afraid they feel a judging gaze, not a loving one."

"What does that mean?" Harruq asked, trying to wrap his mind around it all. "Will you put aside your sword?"

Ahaesarus shook his head.

"No. Sometimes a servant must protect his master. But things must change, and it will not be easy. In this, I fear I am a minority among my own kind. Who are we, angels of Ashhur, to bow down and wash the feet of sinners? To bleed and sweat beside them? But they have forgotten. We are men, same as you, and each day we must decide to obey our lord lest we fall. Our wings have not freed us of that need."

Harruq stood and put a hand on the Ahaesarus's enormous shoulder.

"We don't deserve a guardian like you," he said.

"Yet he has sent me anyway."

"Which I think was the point. Could you find a greater pair of sinners than my brother and I? Yet side by side you fought with us, many of your kind even dying for us. No wound runs too deep, not for this. We just have some work to do is all."

Ahaesarus smiled at him and he rose to his feet.

"Mordan is blessed to have you as its steward," he said.

"I wouldn't go that far. These aren't happy times, and the days ahead don't look too sunny, either. Now grab my arms and let's go. I have a little brat's coronation to prepare for."

✧

It was another parade, this one far more somber. The whole affair seemed almost sickening to Harruq as he checked over his armor. There'd be no more chants for the Missing King, at least. No young lasses vying for his attention. The celebration was a sham, a forced event.

"Are you certain of Antonil's death?" Ahaesarus asked, standing with him in the castle hallway.

"Little late to change our minds now," Harruq said. "But yeah, I'm certain. Aurelia knew before anyone because of Tarlak's message, and Kevin all but confirmed it with his attack."

The half-orc let out a sigh, staring off into nowhere as he fought back a wave of sadness. Ahaesarus sensed it easily enough and put a large hand on his shoulder.

"Tarlak was a great man," he said. "And even in death he saved lives. I assure you, his entry into Ashhur's golden land was met with much rejoicing."

Harruq forced himself to chuckle.

"Yeah," he said. "Tarlak would have appreciated a lot of fanfare."

Ahaesarus smiled for a time before it faded. It seemed he could not keep his mind on happier matters.

"We must discover how Antonil's army was defeated," the angel said. "That Kevin acted so quickly…it implies he had a hand in what transpired, and knew the same moment Aurelia did. Just as troubling is the magic set in place to interfere with your wife's spellcasting. We've removed the runes, but that still leaves us to discover who made them. There is also the matter of the reports we've received about the North, of a supposed invasion…"

"I know," Harruq said, interrupting him. "But right now, one thing at a time."

A side door opened and Aurelia stepped out. She smiled at them, then moved aside so Gregory could follow. Harruq grunted, surprised at how much taller he looked, somehow regal in his deep reds and silvers, despite his age.

"I've cast a glammer upon him," Aurelia said, looking him over. "It should make him seem a little taller and a little older. Nothing too obvious, of course, but I think it'll help."

Gregory looked terrified, but he stood straight enough. Aurelia took his hand, and he squeezed it tight.

"Let's go," she said. "The city needs to see its steward."

"Enjoy your walk," Ahaesarus said. "I will meet you at the platform."

Guards opened the door, and the three of them stepped out. Immediately those nearby bowed in respect to the little prince Gregory. Harruq watched, trying to decide if it was forced or genuine. In the end, he didn't know. Glancing down, he saw Gregory still holding onto Aurelia's hand.

"Let go," he said, leaning down and whispering to the boy. "You're to be a king. I'm sorry, but no choice here."

Gregory wasn't happy about it, but he let go nonetheless. Through the streets they walked, flanked on either side by soldiers. It felt like forever, but at last they reached the platform at the bottom. Harruq's heart ached, knowing Tarlak would not be waiting there with Antonil and Susan. So many lost. So many. He didn't know if he could endure it anymore. The war was over. The deaths were supposed to stop. That was how it worked, wasn't it?

When they reached the platform, Harruq saw how tall the steps were. There'd be no way for Gregory to climb them with any sort of dignity, so he picked up the child and hefted him straight up onto the platform. After that he followed, taking Aurelia's hand in his. All around were soldiers, and they knelt in respect.

Gregory stood in the center, and as they'd told him repeatedly, he looked to the sky. With that as the signal, the angels flocked down, taking up positions all throughout the city. Their white wings decorated the rooftops, lined the walls, and filled the streets. The entire host of Avlimar was present, there to pay respects to the boy king. Ahaesarus was the only one to actually

# The Prison of Angels

come and greet Gregory. He landed with a heavy gust of wind, then dipped his head.

"Gregory Copernus, consider me honored to be given such a privilege," he said. In his hands he held the crown Harruq had worn. The half-orc would remain steward until Gregory came of age, but still, they needed the ceremony to reinforce Gregory's eventual right to rule to all of Mordan. Harruq watched as Gregory dipped his head, and Ahaesarus set the crown on his head. It was laughably oversized. Ahaesarus lifted it off immediately after, setting it beside Gregory on his seat.

"Thank you," Gregory said. He looked ready to cry, and Harruq couldn't blame him.

"The honor is ours," said the angel.

Harruq was supposed to then address the crowd, but before he could a great rumbling shook the land. Scattered cries marked its continuing, and Harruq felt Aurelia grab his hand in fear. Mouth open, Harruq looked to the sky, and he was not alone. The shock overwhelmed him as the sound rolled over the crowd, a massive explosion nearly deafening to hear.

"Ashhur help us," whispered Ahaesarus.

From the sky the city of Avlimar fell, crumbling to pieces, the gold and silver shattering across the fields beyond Mordeina's walls. Its spires broke, its streets crashing down upon green earth as whatever magic holding the city aloft ceased to be. Panicked angels took flight, soaring toward the ruins as all around men and women watched in awe.

Aurelia squeezed Harruq's hand tight.

"What does it mean?" she asked as Gregory began to cry.

"I don't know," Harruq said while a third rumble, like that of thunder, marked the last of the eternal city's fall.

## Epilogue

The land before the Apprentice Tower was a blackened heap, with nary a blade of grass still green. Through the ash walked Cecil, just one of many sent out into the mess. Carefully he made his way through the melted armor, wincing at the stains the bodies left on his red apprentice's robe. The destruction had been most impressive, with each of the apprentices competing for the most efficient kill. Cecil had smashed four with a boulder he'd flung from the sky, the massive hunk of rock crushing over a dozen more as it rolled along before coming to a halt. Despite what Esmere claimed, he was sure he'd gotten the most of any.

"Please, no," he heard someone say to his left. He glanced over, saw one of the younger apprentices killing a survivor, a soldier tough enough to live despite the burns covering his body. Cecil barely knew the apprentice, and that he had to use a dagger instead of his own magic to enforce the kill showed how new he was to the art.

Cecil found a collection of bodies, and he knelt down beside the more intact ones, listening. Two were silent, but a third still held breath. With careful movements of his fingers he summoned a thin lance of frost, forming it before him from thin air. It shimmered, then pierced the man's throat. Blood flowed, the lance melted instantly, and then the breathing halted. On and on Cecil went, killing whatever survivors he found. There were so many, though, that soon sweat covered his brow. They were but thirty apprentices scouring the corpses of thousands. Even with none able to provide a fight, it was still heavy work.

After half an hour, and with hardly a word spoken between the apprentices, Cecil began making his way back toward the front of the killing field, careful to make sure there were none he missed. If even one man survived, there would be consequences. Despite his many years at the towers, Cecil still felt a shudder run up his spine at the thought. He shoved fire down the throats of a few more bodies just to be sure, even when he heard no breathing.

## The Prison of Angels

Finally deciding he was done, he hurried back toward the tower, and it was then he heard a cough. Stunned, Cecil looked down and to the left. Barely a foot away was the charred corpse of a soldier. His armor was melted, but in it were flecks of gold. The king, Cecil realized. He wondered if there would be any sort of reward for being the one to find the body. But that was for later. There was no way the king had survived, but the way he was laying...

Shoving the corpse off, he found another man hidden beneath. His face and hands were terribly burned, his yellow robes spotted with black from where the fabric had been consumed by fire. Cecil's brow furrowed. The burn marks looked strange, though he couldn't put his finger on why they appeared that way. Was it how uneven they were, perhaps?

Shrugging his shoulders, he opened the palm of his hand. Amazing as it was that the man lived, he was clearly in terrible pain. His breathing came in wheezes, and though he glared at Cecil with bloodshot eyes, he couldn't speak a word. Cecil was clearly doing him a favor. In the palm of his hand appeared a small ball of fire.

Before he could throw it, the burned man lifted his hand, and from his own palm sparked a thin tendril of lightning. It struck Cecil in the arm, igniting his nerves. His fingers twitched, breaking the spell. Temper flaring, he kicked the stupid bastard in the side.

"Some fight left after all?" he asked. The burned man had nothing to say. His body settled back, as if resigned to death. The fire grew in Cecil's palm.

"Wait."

Cecil recognized that voice, and immediately he dismissed his spell, spun around, and fell to his knees. Roand the Flame, Lord of the Council, stood before him with his arms crossed, his gaze locked on the badly burned man. For a long moment his master thought in silence, and Cecil felt the hairs on his neck stand up. Had he somehow made a mistake? The seconds dragged on, until at last Roand spoke.

"Bring him inside."

Without hesitation Cecil rushed to grab the burned man's arm. Three more apprentices quickly joined in, and together the four carried him across the field, through the doors, and into the tower, where behind them the doors eased shut with nary a sound.

# The Prison of Angels

Note from the Author:

I'm having a hard time coming up with what to say here, because I don't want to sound like a gushing fanboy of my own work. But man, it feels so good to have Harruq, Qurrah, and the rest of the gang back. Two years ago (I can't believe it's already been that long) I finished the fifth Half-Orc book, and at the time it was so surreal. I honestly never expected myself to finish the entire storyline I'd set out back then, given how it'd floated around in my head for so many years, existing mostly in scraps of notes and rambling stories I told to my wife during car rides. But even weirder, yet far more satisfying, was starting up this sixth one.

In between then and now, I've worked on many more novels, and hopefully improved my craft. Those of you who have followed along, I'm sure you've caught the cameos I threw in (Darius!) and hopefully you enjoyed them. Speaking of cameos, that was the toughest thing about this novel. Originally I'd thought it'd be difficult to remain faithful to my characters, but they came back like old friends the moment I brought them out. No, tougher was cutting things down to a manageable level. For those wishing Jerico and Lathaar had been around a bit more, or perhaps Deathmask and his Ash Guild, I promise far more in the seventh novel. Between the scenes in Ker, Mordeina, the Wedge, and Antonil's army, I felt like I had enough plates spinning in the air as is.

The other concern I had was even trickier. The fifth book's ending, while admittedly a bit rushed, was still a solid, happy ending. Thulos was dead, Velixar burned to ash, and Karak defeated. Continuing on, and introducing the upheaval with the angels, and the continuing wasteland of the east, risked ruining everything my heroes had fought for. I didn't want to cheapen the sacrifices so many had made, the lives my characters had lost. At the same time, keeping things perfect and happy sort of makes for a boring story. That's the tightrope I'm walking now, and I guess it is up to you, dear reader, to let me know how I'm doing.

I'm moving immediately onto book seven, and while that one won't be the last Half-Orc novel, I do need to go finish the

Watcher's Blade Trilogy before I can continue. Besides not wanting to leave that story unfinished, I also have an issue where Half-Orc #8 will actually have significant spoilers for the ending of WB #2 and #3. Perils of a shared world, I guess.

I hope you all have enjoyed. If you'd like to send me an email, you're more than welcome to. I've gotten better at responding in a timely manner even! Fire one off to ddalglish@yahoo.com. Also check out my Facebook page at www.facebook.com/thehalforcs or my website at http://ddalglish.com to keep up on pretty much any of my updates.

Thanks for your time, and thanks for coming back to my dark, silly little world.

David Dalglish
November 8, 2012

Printed in Great Britain
by Amazon